'Why do you want me as your mistress?' *And why am I even asking?* Verity wondered.

Max blinked. 'Isn't that obvious?'

'No.' She couldn't imagine why he would want her. According to her aunt and cousins she had nothing to recommend her. Oh, she knew why Godfrey wanted her. Because she was defenceless and he was a swaggering bully.

But Max—*Lord Blakehurst*—was not of that ilk. She had not the least idea why a man with a reputation for taking beautiful women as his mistresses would want her.

'Because I desire you, of course…'

Elizabeth Rolls was born in Kent but moved to Melbourne, Australia, at the age of fifteen months. She spent several years in Papua New Guinea as a child, where her father was in charge of the Defence Forces. After teaching music for several years she moved to Sydney to do a Masters in Musicology at the University of New South Wales. Upon completing her thesis, Elizabeth realised that writing was so much fun she wanted to do more. She currently lives in a chaotic household with her husband, two small sons, two dogs and two cats. You can contact the author at the following e-mail address: elizabethrolls@alphalink.com.au

Recent titles by the same author:

THE UNEXPECTED BRIDE
MISTRESS OR MARRIAGE?
THE DUTIFUL RAKE
THE UNRULY CHAPERON
THE CHIVALROUS RAKE

HIS LADY MISTRESS

Elizabeth Rolls

First published in Great Britain 2004
Paperback edition 2005
Harlequin Mills & Boon Limited,
Eton House, 18-24 Paradise Road, Richmond, Surrey TW9 1SR

© Elizabeth Rolls 2004

ISBN 0 263 84351 3

Set in Times Roman 10¼ on 11¼ pt.
04-0105-87578

Printed and bound in Spain
by Litografia Rosés S.A., Barcelona

HIS LADY MISTRESS

Prologue

Autumn 1817

Verity huddled into the murk by the chimney stack, watching through the shifting veil of rain as the two men, little more than dense shadows in the pouring blackness, carried their grisly burden from the cottage to the cart. The horse between the shafts tucked his tail in and stamped restlessly, snorting as the stench of death reached him. The boy at his head murmured in shaking tones and held his lantern higher.

'One, two, three...' A thud followed as the men swung the body on to the back of the cart.

Her heart tightened. *Oh, God! Please be gentle.*

'Right. Got everything, Jake?'

'Aye...oh, hang on, where's the...?' Jake vaulted into the cart and scrabbled around. 'No. Here 'tis, Bill.'

'What?'

'Thought we'd damn near forgot the stake. Won't do to forget that an' all. Rector be really put out, he would.'

A snort greeted this. ''Taint him as has to drive it in. Is it? Well, come on. Best get it over with.'

'Aye. Here, lad, hand over that glim. You get on back to bed. And don't be thinkin' on this. 'Tis a cryin' shame. But there ain't nothin' to do 'cept obey orders.'

Orders. Her gut roiled as the lantern changed hands and the cart lumbered off. Slipping from the shadows, she followed, just close enough not to lose the sickly light in the blinding rain.

At the end of the village street a swift rattle of hooves sent her scurrying for cover in the lych gate of the churchyard. All that she could see of the approaching rider was that he was tall, and wore a heavy cloak. Clenching her teeth against their betraying chatter, Verity strained to hear what the rider said to the men. The words were muffled in the curtain of driving rain, but the deep accents were unfamiliar. It must be the fashionable stranger who had put up at the inn earlier in the day.

She bit back a sob of fury as the horseman rode out at the same slow pace as the cart. It was none of his business! Did he just want a sensational story to tell his friends? Her fists balled in impotent rage. She must not reveal herself. Surely he would not stay long. She could still do what must be done. Blinking rain out of her eyes, she followed the cart and rider out of the village.

The rain swiftly penetrated her threadbare cloak, chilling her to the bone. She shivered uncontrollably, fiercely pretending that it was just the cold, that there was nothing to fear.

Doggedly she repeated the litany over and over in her mind. *There is nothing to fear. No bears or wolves. Ghosts don't exist. There is nothing to fear...*

Except the dark and fear itself. She had never been out this late at all, let alone by herself... *You aren't alone. The cart is ahead...no one else will be out on a night like this anyway...* A shudder racked her at the thought and she forced her mind away...*nothing to fear...* except her own self-loathing.

Finally the cart reached the crossroads. Trembling with exhaustion and cold, Verity shrank into the hedgerow, crouched on the wet turf, scarcely noticing the branches clawing at her and the icy trickle of water down her back. With a shaking hand she pushed back draggled, soaking hair and peered out of her sanctuary. At least the rain had stopped and the clouds were breaking up so that the moon cast a fitful, nightmarish light.

The lantern had been set down and gleamed on the sodden ground. Close by it she could see a dark, gaping shadow.

One of the men leaned over it and swore. 'Bloody 'ell! Damn grave's about half-filled up with water. Gawd! What a miserable business!'

'Never mind that,' answered the other. 'Least we ain't diggin' it right now. Get him in an' be done with it. Quicker the better, I say. Give me a hand here, then.'

Verity watched avidly as the two went to the back of the cart.

'Wait.' The stranger had dismounted. 'One of you hold my horse. I'll lay him in the grave.'

A choked sob tore free. How *dare* he? That she had condemned the poor broken creature in the cart to be flung into his grave by a curious stranger.

'What the hell was that?' muttered one of the men, shifting uneasily.

Verity put the back of her hand against her mouth and bit down hard.

'Nothing,' said the tall stranger. 'Just some beast out hunting.'

'On a night like this?' scoffed the other. 'Nay. 'Tis easy to see you're from Lunnon! Any sensible creature's deep in its hole by now.'

The stranger's tone mocked. 'Very well, then. What shall I say? That some other poor wight who lies here is crying his welcome to the newly damned?'

Horrified gasps filled the air.

'Don't 'ee say it!'

'Whisht now!'

They stood back as the stranger lifted the body from the

cart. Verity could only watch as the tall figure walked easily to the grave with its tragic burden.

Despair flooded her as she braced herself to see the corpse slung carelessly into the mire. Shock lanced the pain as the bearer knelt in the mud and eased the body to its final resting place. A faint splash told her that the deed was done, and far more gently than she had expected. Shaken, she watched as the man straightened and threw something in after the body.

The murmur of his deep voice came to her. 'We commit his body to the ground—'

'Here, now!' a scandalised voice interrupted. 'Can't have that! Rector said so. 'Tis in the prayer book! Them as lays violent hands on theirselves—'

'To hell with what the Rector said!'

The men shrank back before the sudden fury and the stranger continued. 'Earth to earth, ashes to ashes, dust to dust...' The deep voice faded into silence and tears of gratitude mingled with the rain on Verity's cheeks. Whoever he was, little though he knew it, he was her only friend in this nightmare darkness and she would pray for him all the days of her life.

The older of the two men spoke up hesitantly. 'Ye'd best stand back, sir. Unless ye wants to handle this bit too.'

'No, I thank you!' The stranger jerked back, his voice rough. 'Can't you leave the poor devil be, now? Just tell the Rector you did it! This ghost won't trouble you. Let him rest!'

'Nay, sir,' the man averred. 'Rector says as how it's got to be done. You go along now, sir. 'Tis a nasty, but it's got to be.'

A savage oath greeted this and the stranger stepped away.

One of the others knelt over the grave and raised his arm. Numb with horror, Verity saw lamplight slide wetly on steel and heard the first brutal thud as the sledgehammer struck against wood. Again and again the fearful blows landed in a merciless rhythm, ghastly in its very steadiness. Retching, loathing her cowardice, Verity pressed her hands over her ears, but still the sounds penetrated, pounding in her blood as though her own heart was impaled.

Nearly senseless, she sank fully to the ground, uncaring of the bitter cold leaching into her. Even as she realised that they were filling in the grave, the hammering echoed in her soul in pitiless torment.

It remained only to wait until they left so she could make her farewell.

At last they were gone, and Verity, listening to the final, fading splash of hoofbeats, crept stiffly out of the hedge. Cold shuddered through her as she approached the grave. The weather had cleared slightly and moonlight gleamed through a gap in the clouds, lighting her way to the disturbed sods.

With a despairing whimper, she dropped to her knees in the mud, tears pouring unchecked down her cheeks. 'Oh, Papa, forgive me! I didn't understand...Papa...I'm sorry...I never meant this...I love you...'

Still weeping, she reached into her satchel and brought out her offering. Small and pathetic though it was, she could do no more. If she put up a cross, no matter how humble, it would be torn down. Even a bunch of flowers would be removed if anyone saw it.

Furtively she scrabbled in the wet, cold earth, preparing it for her hidden garland. He would forgive her...he must. He had loved her once...

'What the hell do you think you'll find there? A few miserable trinkets, you cur? I heard you behind us, all the way. I went away to flush you out.'

The harsh voice speared her and she cried out in startled terror as a fierce grip took her shoulder and spun her around to fall helpless on the muddy grave.

Savagely the voice continued, 'Didn't they tell you? All a suicide's possessions go to the Crown. You'll find nothing here, boy. Now leave the poor bastard alone before I give you the thrashing you deserve!'

Dazed, Verity stared up at her captor, but the moon had fled and a tall, menacing shadow filled her vision. She tried to speak, but her throat, swollen with crying, seized, and all that came out was a choking sound.

'Go on! Go and rob another grave!'

Her limbs would not move. Helpless, she watched as the shadow leaned down and jerked her to her feet. Both her wrists were imprisoned in a one-handed grip. Another hand flung back her hood just as the fickle moon slid out again. She stared up, but the moon was behind him and his face remained shadowed.

'God in heaven!' The grip on her wrists slackened at once and she staggered, only to find herself held in a far more alarming captivity with the stranger's arm around her waist. 'You're a girl, a *child*! What the devil are you doing out here? Who are you?'

She forced her voice past the choking terror. 'I…I'm Verity. Verity Scott. He…he…' Sobs closed her throat again.

'Verity? Then…you're his daughter.' The harshness vanished, replaced by horror and compassion. 'What were you thinking of? You should never have come here! How old are you, for God's sake?' A shaking hand pushed wet, bedraggled strands of hair back from her face in clumsy tenderness.

'F…fifteen.'

'Fifteen?! Oh, *hell*!'

She had no will to struggle when he pulled her against him and wrapped his arms around her. Despair and exhaustion sapped her strength and she leaned into him gratefully. He had laid her father to rest with all gentleness possible and given him part of the Christian burial. He had tried to stop the brutal laying of any possible ghost. And he had come back to defend the grave. Unlooked-for comfort seeped into her very bones.

Dimly his voice penetrated. The words didn't matter. The voice was sorrow itself, breaking in its own despair. At last the words reached her. 'I must get you back to the village, before you're missed. Come. I'll take you up on my horse.'

He lifted her effortlessly, shocking her out of her daze. Wildly she fought him and landed in an ignominious heap at his feet.

'No! Not yet!' She struggled to her feet and nearly fell again as she slipped in the mire. He caught her and steadied her.

'Miss Scott, Verity—you can do nothing here. Come away. Don't torture yourself. God won't abandon him...' His voice shook and she felt his hands tremble as they grasped her shoulders.

'I...I brought bluebell bulbs,' she whispered, gazing blindly up into the shadowed face. 'They'll remove a cross or...or anything else. The bulbs won't flower till spring. Maybe they won't realise. Then if...if I can come back one day, I'll be able to find him...' Tears choked her and she turned away, searching for the fallen bag of bulbs.

The moon sailed out and she saw the bag by her satchel at the edge of the grave. Shivering, she knelt again and realised that her companion had knelt too.

He held out his hands. 'I'll help you.'

Fresh tears slid down her cheeks as she tipped bulbs into his cupped palms and tried to thank him. No words came and in silence they planted them.

At last they were done and Verity's companion lifted her tenderly to her feet. 'Come now. With those to deck his grave he will be at peace.'

Her hand clung to his. 'Wait,' she begged.

Dragging in a deep breath, she began in a childish treble, 'I will lift up mine eyes unto the hills: from whence cometh my help...' Her voice cracking and breaking, she stumbled through the psalm she had memorised until she came to the final verses and the strangling lump in her heart silenced her. Shuddering, she dragged in a useless breath, and another, only to feel a powerful arm go around her shoulders.

The deep voice continued for her in steadfast accents, 'The Lord shall preserve thee from all evil: yea, it is even he that shall keep thy soul.'

Drawing upon his strength, Verity found her voice again and they finished together, 'The Lord shall preserve thy going out and thy coming in: from this time forward for evermore.'

It was finished. She had done what she set out to do—all she could do—to make amends for her betrayal. There was nothing else she could cling to.

Strong arms held her as she stumbled and then lifted her to lie cradled against a broad chest. Seeming not to feel his burden, her champion strode along the lane, uttering a piercing whistle. A whinny and trotting hooves answered and the horse loomed up before them.

She found herself lifted to the horse's back and held there as her rescuer sprang up behind her and drew her back into his arms. His cloak was flung around her in heavy protective folds and she realised that she had been wrong. She did have something to cling to. She had this stranger, whoever, whatever he was, and she would cherish the thought of him all her days.

'Will you tell me your name?' she whispered.

The arms tightened as the horse broke into a slow trot. 'Max.'

'You knew him, didn't you? How?' She had to find out. She couldn't bear to know nothing of the one person who had comforted her grief in a shattered world.

'He was my commanding officer. My superior in every way. A gallant officer and a gentleman. Remember him that way, Verity. And I will remember him as blessed above all men.'

A sob tore at her. Blessed? How could he say that? She could not even frame the question. The horse came to a halt as the moon flickered out again, gleaming hopefully in puddles and on wet hedges.

A gentle hand lifted her chin and she gazed up, seeing him

clearly for the first time. Weary eyes looked back out of a harsh, angular face, all colour leached in the silver wet moonlight. Even as she gazed, the face twisted in a sad smile. 'You don't believe me, do you, little one?'

Mute, she shook her head.

The smile deepened and he bent to press a light kiss on her brow. 'He died blessed with a child as gallant and loyal as himself. No man could ask for more. He would be proud of you, Verity. As proud as you should be of him.'

The horse moved on slowly and Verity turned and wept unashamedly on Max's chest. *He doesn't understand; doesn't know what I did.* If he knew...

But he didn't know and he held her, rubbing his cheek against her wet hair as the horse picked its way slowly back to the village.

Gradually some of the chill left her. The warmth beneath Max's cloak lulled her, vanquishing the nightmare, and she dozed, only waking fully when they reached the village and Max spoke.

'Who is looking after you? Have you any family?'

She looked about, puzzled. They had pulled up outside the inn. 'Pardon?'

'Who are you staying with? I'll see you to the door.'

'Oh.' She tried to sound indifferent. 'I'm still at the cottage. I...I believe my uncle is coming for me tomorrow.'

A low voice spoke from an upper window. 'That you, sir?'

Max looked up. 'Harding! Good man. Come down, will you, and take the horse.'

'Aye, sir.'

Verity clenched her teeth against a shiver. She could make it back to the cottage alone from here. It was only a step. She made to slip down, but found herself held firmly in place. He leapt off and lifted her down, steadying her as she stumbled on legs stiffened with cold.

'Gently,' he said, supporting her.

The rest of her might be half-frozen, but her heart felt as though someone had lit a fire under it.

A moment later the inn door opened and a small man came out with a lantern.

'Everything all right, sir?' Then, 'Who the devil's *this*?'

The arm around her tightened. 'Harding, this is Miss Scott. Can you rub Jupiter down while I see her home?'

Harding lifted the lantern higher. 'Miss *Scott*?'

She flinched at the light, shrinking closer to Max.

The lantern lowered. 'I'm that sorry, lass. About everything. He was a brave man. You go with the major. God bless you. I'll see you later, sir.'

'Harding?'

'Yessir?'

'Don't wait up.'

'Sir?'

'Don't wait up.'

'Don't…? Oh, aye. No, sir. Goodnight, sir.' He led the horse away.

'I shall be quite safe now,' Verity protested. 'You needn't—'

'Don't waste your breath,' he advised her and swung her up into his arms. 'I'm taking you home and that's all there is to it.'

The easy strength in his arms shocked her into silence until they reached the cottage and he set her down gently. 'Key?' he asked.

A bitter laugh escaped her. 'It's not locked. They didn't leave anything worth stealing.'

He opened the door

The darkness within was total. 'Wait,' she said and made her way carefully to the table, fumbling for the candle and tinderbox she had left there.

Her numb fingers struggled with the flint and steel. Again and again she tried to strike a spark. A small sob of frustration escaped her at her clumsiness. An instant later both flint and steel were taken by gentle, unerring hands and light flared as the spark ignited the rags in the box.

'Sit down,' he said brusquely as he set a chair by the fire and squatted down to touch the candle to the kindling and faggots laid there. Verity obeyed and watched in bemused fascination as he tended the fire and then prowled around the kitchen, looking into every corner. Warmth stole through her, despite the damp clothes.

'Go up and bring some dry clothes down here.'

That jerked her out of her doze. Blinking up at him in the shadowy, dancing light of the fire, she asked sleepily, 'Whatever for?'

His voice was very patient. 'To put on. You need to get dry. Quickly.'

Down here? With him in the kitchen? All of a sudden she was wide awake.

'I'll…I'll change upstairs.' No doubt he was quite harmless, but still…she couldn't possibly change down here, even if he turned his back, blindfolded himself and shut his eyes.

'There's a fire down here,' he growled.

'And so are you,' she countered. 'I'll change in my bedchamber!'

He stared at her. 'For God's sake, girl! You can't possibly imagine that I'd take advantage of you!'

Her cheeks flamed. 'Of course not! It's just that…well, I'd rather change up there.'

A sudden grin lightened his rather harsh features. 'He used to say you were a stubborn little thing. Like your mother, he claimed. Very well, quickly then. I don't want you catching your death of cold.'

Verity fled before he could change his mind.

By the time she slipped into the kitchen, safely clad in her warmest underwear and a thick nightgown, the major appeared to be foraging in the kitchen cupboards. She sat down by the fire to watch.

He seemed quite at home in a kitchen, finding everything with easy competence as though he were used to looking after himself. Finally he came back with the results of his raid. A hunk of cheese, the end of a loaf of bread and two apples on a chipped earthenware plate. 'Is this all?' he asked. 'It's not nearly enough.'

She felt heat mantle her cheeks again. 'I'm sorry. I ate the rest for supper. If I'd known you were coming…' She'd intended this lot for breakfast, but after what he had done, he was welcome to anything she had.

He blinked and put the plate on her lap. 'It's for you! Not me!'

Shaken, she stared at the food. When had anyone last worried about what she ate? She didn't want to look too closely at the answer.

Her stomach protested at the thought of food, but she forced herself to eat, conscious of Max leaning against the chimney the whole time watching her. She found herself much warmer at the end of the scanty repast.

'You need a good night's sleep,' he said abruptly when she had finished eating. 'I've put a brick to warm in the fire. Take it up with you. Do you feel all right? Not cold any more?'

She nodded as she stood up. It wasn't quite a lie. She felt a great deal better than she had a few hours earlier.

'Very well. Off you go.'

'Good…goodnight, Max and…and thank you.' Her voice wobbled hopelessly and she shut her eyes to force back the tears. A powerful arm slipped around her shoulder, pulling her close for a hug. She felt the brief pressure of his lips on her hair and turned in his embrace, hugging him hard.

'I did little enough. Goodnight, sweetheart. Don't forget that brick.' He released her and gave her a little push in the direction of the fire.

As she knelt to wrap the brick in the flannels her competent champion had put ready, she looked up. 'Shall I see you again?'

His mouth tightened. 'Better not, little one. There's nothing I can offer you. I can assure you that your uncle wouldn't approve of me in the least. Go on. Off with you. I'll sit here for a while to warm up, if you don't mind.' He sat down in the chair she had vacated.

'N…no. That's quite all right. But wouldn't you be warmer at the inn?'

He shook his head. 'Not really, no. Goodnight.'

'Goodnight,' she whispered, reluctantly. She backed to the door, unwilling to lose the sight of him before she had to. He glanced up at her and smiled as she reached the door. The smile softened the harsh lines of his face, melting her heart.

Max sat staring into the fire, hating himself. What a hellish mess. He'd been too damned late. If only he'd known earlier the pass Scott had come to—surely he could have done something. His heart ached at the plight of the lonely child upstairs. At least an uncle was coming for her. She had a family to take her in. Although why she had been left here alone passed all understanding.

He grimaced. Given what she had done, it was entirely possible that Miss Verity Scott had remained at the cottage on purpose. Much easier to slip out unnoticed from here.

He glanced around the small room. It might be empty and cheerless, but at least it was clean. No doubt Verity had seen to that. According to the villagers, Scott had became a complete recluse towards the end, refusing to allow anyone else in the cottage, completely in thrall to his opium.

A chill stole through him. No doubt the loss of his arm had been a terrible shock for Scott, but suicide… He grimaced. Probably it hadn't just been the arm. He remembered what he'd been told… *Damn shame, Max. Seems the poor fellow got back after Waterloo to discover his wife had died in childbed. Understand he's been drinking laudanum ever*

*since. Why don't you go down and see if you can help them?
I tried but he wouldn't even open the door. I saw only the
child. She came out and apologised. Said he wasn't well…*

No. It hadn't been his fault… But still, if only Scott hadn't
deflected that bayonet. A clean death on the battlefield for
Max Blakehurst would not have been such a tragedy. If only
he hadn't been swayed by the family insistence that he go to
the embassy in Vienna, he might have heard sooner of Scott's
difficulties, been able to do something. Now all he could do
was mourn.

He couldn't even help the child sleeping upstairs. Her family would look after her now. And the last thing she needed
was to be reminded of this dreadful night. No. She was better
off without him hanging around.

He'd find out where she was going. Perhaps if the family
taking her needed some help he could offer it anonymously,
but otherwise he should stay out of her life.

Verity came downstairs shortly after dawn, wishing she
had defied Max over her supper and left some of it for breakfast. And whatever had she done with her wet clothes the
previous night? Surely she'd simply dropped them on the
floor of her bedchamber, but they certainly weren't there this
morning.

Her stomach rumbled hopefully. She ignored it. She'd have
to set the fire again to dry her clothes when she found them.
There was a little fuel left.

She reached the kitchen and stared. The fire blazed brightly
and her clothes hung over the back of the chair. Nearly dry.

Tears pricking at her eyes, she looked around. On the table
were four eggs, bacon, a fresh loaf of bread, a pat of butter,
some cheese and six apples. And a jug of…she peeped in…
milk. The tears spilt over. Judging by the state of the fire, he
hadn't been gone long. He'd stayed all night, then gone out
to find her breakfast.

He'd even dried her clothes for her. She looked more

closely. The mudstains were nearly gone. He'd sponged them. The grey, bleak dawn brightened suddenly. She had one friend. Even if she never saw him again, somewhere in the world was Max. Someone she could love.

Chapter One

Late summer 1822

'What are you doing here, girl? How dare you waste time reading when Celia's flounce requires mending!'

The girl known as Selina Dering scrambled up and hurriedly put the book away in the bottom half of the battered campaign chest at the foot of her bed.

'I'm sorry, Aunt Faringdon. I…I didn't know that Celia's flounce was torn.'

Lady Faringdon was plainly not minded to accept this excuse. 'How would you know anything if you sneak away to your bedchamber to loll about reading? And no lady sits on her bed like that! She sits properly with ladylike decorum.'

'You and Celia both told me to stay out of the way,' protested Verity. She refrained from pointing out that there was nothing at all in the room save the bed and the campaign chest, its bottom at the foot of the bed and the top acting as a window seat. Certainly nothing upon which anyone could sit with ladylike decorum. Or even reasonable comfort.

'Don't answer back, girl! Do you want another whipping? Go down to Celia now and mend that flounce! Before his lordship and our other guests arrive!'

'Yes, Aunt.'

She spoke to thin air, since Lady Faringdon had already stormed from the room. Arguing was a waste of breath. The mildest protest drew as heavy a retribution as full-scale rebellion. Not even over the hated name *Selina* did she object now.

Resigned, Verity locked the chest with the key she wore on a plaited string around her neck. Giving the chest an affectionate pat, she gathered herself together, picked up her workbasket and left the bleak little room in her aunt's wake. Celia, of course, would be hysterical with fury over the torn flounce, blaming everything and everyone for the catastrophe save her own carelessness.

'Where have you been?' screeched Celia, as Verity entered the elegant bedchamber. 'Just *look* at this! And Lord Blakehurst may arrive at any minute!'

Verity selected the matching cotton and threaded her needle, biting back the urge to point out that Lord Blakehurst would be admitted to the house by the butler and every footman available and would be greeted with all due ceremony by his host and hostess. Furthermore, since he would doubtless repair immediately to his bedchamber to adjust his cravat and swill brandy, he would scarcely notice the absence of his hosts' eldest daughter, with or without a torn flounce. At least that was her considered opinion, based on the observation of other visiting gentlemen. There was no reason to suspect that Earl Blakehurst would differ from the rest in any degree. Except, of course, in being richer.

She knelt down at Celia's hem and began to stitch.

'Hurry *up*!' whined Celia, whirling away to the window and dragging the offending flounce out of Verity's grasp. A ripping sound rewarded this indiscretion.

'Look what you've done!' Celia's shriek of fury outdid her previous efforts. 'Oh, Mama! Look what she's done! She did it on purpose, too!'

Biting back some very unladylike language, Verity turned to see her aunt advancing into the room.

'Ungrateful girl!' cried Lady Faringdon. 'After all we've done for you! The very clothes on your back!'

Verity rather thought the light-devouring black dress she wore was one discarded by the Rectory housekeeper, but she bit her tongue and concentrated grimly on stitching up Celia's flounce as efficiently as possible. With a modicum of luck Lord Blakehurst would marry the girl and prove to be a veritable Bluebeard.

Nothing she heard about Lord Blakehurst in the next twenty-four hours led her to revise her estimate that it would be a match richly deserved by both parties. Lord Blakehurst had arrived late, snubbed at least three people at dinner, whom he plainly considered beneath his exalted touch, and everyone was hanging upon his every utterance.

'Such a personable man!' sighed Celia the following evening as she prepared for bed. 'Terribly rich of course. One can only wonder that he has left it so long to marry! Of course, he came into the title unexpectedly when his brother died three years ago.'

Verity, tidying away her cousin's clothes, thought it entirely possible that no female would have so conceited a man as his lordship must be, only to dismiss the idea. Anyone that rich could be as conceited as he liked and society would still deem him a *personable man*.

'And, of course, he *must* be seeking a bride if he has come here,' continued Celia.

Verity blinked as she put away a chemise. 'Oh?' That leap of logic evaded her. She had yet to learn that a visit to Faringdon Hall was a prerequisite for matrimonially inclined Earls.

'He *never* accepts invitations to house parties, except from his closest friends,' explained Celia, in tones of gracious condescension. Or boasting, more like. Verity shut the drawer with a snap on the chemise. Pity it wasn't Celia in there.

'Conceive for yourself how pleased Mama was when his

lordship indicated that an invitation would be accepted.' Celia preened in the mirror, all golden-haired, blue-eyed conceit. 'Naturally he wishes to court me a little more privately than is possible in London.'

Since when did a house party with over twenty guests afford any privacy for a courtship? Verity swallowed the observation. If it made Celia happy, then who was she to cavil?

'I'm surprised you came up so early, then,' she remarked.

Celia shrugged. 'Oh, Blakehurst disappeared to the billiard room with a few of the other gentlemen. And Mama had to invite that *tedious* Arabella Hollingsworth with her parents, so what was the point? All she does is *brag* about her betrothal to Sir Bartholomew!' Celia pouted. 'So I said I had the headache and came up. Anyway, gentlemen prefer a female to be a little fragile.'

Verity hid a grin. If Celia were as lucky as her erstwhile friend in snaring a husband, namely Lord Blakehurst, then cock-a-hoop wouldn't begin to describe her. No doubt Celia's sudden recognition of Miss Hollingsworth's tediousness had its origins in jealousy. As for fragile—Celia was about as fragile as a viper.

'You may brush my hair now, Selina.' Celia gazed at her reflection in satisfaction, patting a bobbing curl.

Verity reminded herself not to rip the curl out and picked up the silver-backed hairbrush.

'Oh, dear,' said Celia sadly. 'Just look at all those disgusting freckles!'

Staring at her cousin's flawless complexion in the mirror, Verity wondered what maggot had entered her head now.

'I can't see any,' she said unguardedly, 'but the Denmark lotion is there on your dressing table if you need it.'

The reflection smiled spitefully. 'I meant *your* freckles, Selina.'

Verity took a firmer grip on the brush along with her temper and began brushing. Much safer to say it all to her pillow. Unlike Celia, the pillow would not carry tales and earn her further punishment. If nothing else, the Faringdons had taught her the virtue of hiding her feelings under a stolid demeanour.

She shivered. Being Selina made that so much easier. Frighteningly easy. At times it felt as though Verity had retreated into a numbing mist. That one day she might not be able to find the way out again.

Verity wriggled her shoulders pleasurably as the sun poured over them, sinking deep. Not even the basket full of mending daunted her when she had managed to escape from everyone for a couple of hours. No doubt she'd have a few more freckles on her nose to add to the ones Celia had found so disgusting the previous evening. It seemed a small enough price for a morning spent out of doors.

Her mind drifted as her needle flashed over the torn sheet, insensibly soothed by the trickle of the fountain, and the occasional flicker of a goldfish between the lily pads. A contented bee hummed in the lavender behind her. Here she could dream. Pretend that in the house, or somewhere about the estate, was someone who cared for her. She could be Verity, not Selina.

Here in the centre of the maze she was safe for the time being. Except, of course, for her toes. They were in imminent danger of being devoured. She wiggled them gently in the water as she scissored her bare legs and felt the flutter as the startled fish fled.

'Oh, Lord Blakehurst! What a tarradiddle! You are the most *dreadful* creature!'

Celia's most flirtatious simper, followed by a very male rumble, shattered her peace. What on earth was Celia—whom the servants dubbed Mistress Slug-a-bed—doing in the maze at nine o'clock in the morning, let alone with Lord Blakehurst? Not for the first time Verity crashed headfirst into her aunt's towering hypocrisy—only to a man of massive fortune and noble degree would Lady Faringdon have entrusted her virtuous treasure in such a potential den of iniquity as the garden maze. And in any other damsel such behaviour would be condemned as shameless.

Another giggle reminded Verity of the precarious nature of her situation. She surged to her feet, stuffing mending as well as her stockings and slippers into the basket and suppressing a curse as she pricked her finger on the needle. Which path were they on? She had to pick one that wouldn't bring her face to face with Celia and her swain. She shivered. If they caught her here, it would be one more hiding place crossed off her diminishing list.

Frowning, she listened. They weren't far away. She waited, poised for flight. The voices drew nearer. She tensed, then saw a flash of jonquil muslin through a thin patch in the hedge. Realising that she had about five seconds to escape she swept up the basket and fled, bare feet flying across the turf. She reached the opening on the opposite side of the pond and whipped out of sight.

'Whatever was that?'

Celia's surprised question froze Verity. Drat. They'd heard her. She fought to steady her breathing.

'A bird? A rabbit?' suggested Lord Blakehurst. 'Didn't you say your brother would be here?'

Verity just managed to choke back a snort of laughter at the faintly questioning note in his voice, not to mention the suspicion. Heavens! What a slowtop to fall for that trick! That or he didn't know Godfrey very well. Godfrey Faringdon meet his *own* sister in the middle of a maze, in order to play gooseberry? Not this side of Judgement Day. Obviously Lord Blakehurst, petted darling of society, the quarry of every mama with a marriageable daughter, had been neatly cozened.

Unable to resist temptation, she peered around the hedge. If Lord Blakehurst didn't take care, he would find himself leg-shackled to—

Her heart nearly stopped and she jerked herself back, shaking. *It couldn't be. Could it?* Unable to believe what she had seen, she dragged in a deep breath and stole another look. Celia, dressed in her prettiest sprig muslin, with the merest suggestion of dainty ankle below the flounce, was pouting up at...*Max*.

Shock gripped Verity. She couldn't be mistaken. Every feature of that face was etched on her memory. The hard angles, the square jaw. Her heart pounded as she absorbed every detail. Max. Here.

'Perhaps we should go back, Miss Faringdon?'

'Oh, pish!' Celia disposed herself on the seat with a graceful swish of her skirts. 'Why should anyone think anything of it? After all, such good friends as *we* are, Lord Blakehurst...'

Such good friends?

His lordship's voice dripped indifference. 'I'll bid you good morning, Miss Faringdon. Believe me, my friendship with your reputation far outweighs any other consideration!'

Verity nearly choked as Celia's brow knit, trying to work out if this remark added up to a compliment. Even as she watched, his lordship bowed to Celia and made to leave the maze.

Celia leapt to her feet. 'Oh, sir! I must guide you, lest you become confused. Our maze is renowned for all the guests who have become hopelessly lost in it!'

Verity slumped against the hedge. She would have to give them plenty of time before she returned. She listened to the fading voices.

Maybe the maze wasn't such a good place with the house full of visitors. Too easy to become trapped, no matter how well she knew it. She couldn't risk being caught and giving Aunt Faringdon more ammunition.

But Max was here...why? Could he really be courting Celia? Max? Her gentle, tender Max? Did he know *she* was here? *Oh, for goodness sake! Why should he?*

She didn't think she had told him who her uncle was. And apparently Max had left the village very early on the morning

after her father's burial. He would not have seen Lord Faringdon. And what if he found out *she* was here? She bit her
lip. The only way in which he could help her would be to
remove her from the Faringdons' care. And he wouldn't be
able to do that, even if he wanted to. He might force them
to treat her properly while he remained, but after he left—
Despite the warmth of the day a chill stole through her. It
would be worse than ever.

She couldn't understand it. They didn't want her here.
They hated her. Why, then, did Aunt Faringdon refuse to
write her a reference and let her go?

No. She must stay out of his way. Not that he was likely
to recognise her after five years…she'd been a child. A thin,
underdeveloped fifteen seen by a tallow candle. No. He
would never recognise her.

In her dreams Max always knew her instantly, swept her
up on to his horse and took her away. Lord Blakehurst was
another matter entirely. Earls did not sweep indigent females
up on to their precious bloodstock and carry them off to the
obligatory happy ever after. Somehow she had to banish Lord
Blakehurst and think only of Max. Otherwise she had lost
her comforting dream.

The following evening Max, Earl Blakehurst, sighed with
relief as the ladies left the dining room in the wake of Lady
Faringdon. What in Hades had possessed him to accept this
invitation? He hated gatherings like this. A veneer of preten-
sion and affectation on the part of the ladies, concealing a
solid core of hypocrisy. And the gentlemen were not much
better.

Across the table young Godfrey Faringdon's bragging account of some tale involving a lady's companion at another
house party grated on him. He gritted his teeth. In consigning
Colonel Scott's daughter to the care of her loving family, he
had made a serious error of judgement.

'Ah, Blakehurst? You there, old chap?'

He looked across the table to Mr Marlbury.

'You're being chased,' said Marlbury, in a helpful spirit.

Max looked at him blankly. He knew *that*. Celia Faringdon's subtlety at dinner had rivalled her mama's. And as for her little stratagem this morning! He shuddered. That was the stuff of nightmares. Trapped. By a conniving little baggage!

'The brandy!' urged Marlbury.

'Oh.' Max became aware of Thornfield, to his left, attempting to pass him the brandy decanter. 'Sorry, Thornfield.' He poured himself a glass and took a cautious sip. He barely suppressed another shudder. Just as atrocious as the previous night. Lord. The things a man would do in response to a guilty conscience: attending ghastly house parties and drinking appalling brandy to name a couple.

'I say, Blakehurst,' said Thornfield in a low voice, 'Miss Celia seems quite taken with you!' He leered at Max. 'Dare say you've only got to drop your handkerchief.'

Max gulped brandy. One thing he could guarantee: Miss Celia might be taken *with* him, but she would not be taken *by* him. His handkerchief would stay in his pocket. And *he* would stay out of the maze.

'Of course, if that don't appeal,' went on Thornfield, showing remarkable percipience for a man in his inebriated condition, 'you could always amuse yourself with Fanny Moncrieff or Kate Highbury. *They* won't expect marriage.' He attempted a lascivious wink.

Max returned a non-committal reply and reminded himself that he did, after all, bear a certain reputation. But had he realised that Lady Moncrieff and Mrs Highbury were to be present, casting their jaded, world-weary lures in his direction, then he would definitely have reconsidered his strategy in attending.

Oh, the devil! Too late for second thoughts now. He was here and he should have come years ago. Indeed, even being in the house had not yielded results. He had found out nothing, so he would have to ask his host point-blank. And how he was supposed to ask tactfully escaped him.

In the end, he eschewed tact, cornering his host as they left the dining room. 'Faringdon, perhaps I might have a private word with you?'

Lord Faringdon blinked. And then smiled. An oily, triumphant sort of smile that put every nerve on full battle alert. 'Why, of course, Blakehurst. My library is private. This way!' He signalled to his son. 'Godfrey, tell my lady that I am engaged on some urgent business with Blakehurst.'

Max eyed him with extreme disfavour. Good God! The man was fairly rubbing his hands in glee! What the devil did he—? The truth crashed over him. Faringdon thought he was about to make an offer. For Celia. Mentally cursing his own idiocy, Max followed his host to the library.

'More brandy, Blakehurst?'

Max abandoned good manners. 'No. Thank you.'

Faringdon favoured him with a conspiratorial grin and poured a glass anyway, thrusting it at him. 'No, no, Blakehurst. This ain't the same stuff we had in the dining room! Wouldn't waste this on that lot!'

'I've had enough,' Max informed him coldly.

Faringdon stared. 'Had enough? Oh, ah…yes, well.' He took a sip himself. 'To business, then. I take it, you like what you see. She's had only the best, so…'

Max headed him off at once. 'Lord Faringdon, I wonder if you could give me any news of Miss Scott?'

'Miss Scott?' The brandy in Lord Faringdon's glass slopped over.

Max frowned at the reaction. Faringdon's eyes flickered under his hard gaze. Fear.

He pressed on, relentless. 'Yes. I believe her to be a niece of Lady Faringdon and under your care. Her late father was my C.O. and I thought to enquire after her.' He pretended to examine a painting.

'Oh.' Disdain came through clearly. 'I'm afraid she is no longer with us.'

Anger surged through Max and he swung back to stare at Faringdon. Just as he'd feared. Verity Scott had been bundled off God knew where. Somewhere her tragic story could not embarrass the socially ambitious Faringdons. He could see it now—packed off to be a companion to a cantankersome old hag, or immured in some foul girls' school as a drudge. Well, he wouldn't permit it!

He saw with satisfaction that Faringdon had paled and forcibly relaxed his hands. Clenched fists were not the best way to draw information out of a reluctant man. Not discreetly, anyway.

'Perhaps you could give me her direction, Faringdon. I should like to pay my respects.' What had they done to her? Could he help her? Might Lady Arnsworth, his Aunt Almeria, employ her?

Lord Faringdon said quickly, 'I fear you misunderstand me, Blakehurst. When I said that Miss Scott was no longer with us, I meant that she has…that she is…'

Cold horror, laced with shocking pain, shuddered through Max. 'She's dead.' Statement, not question, and something inside him tore apart as Lord Faringdon inclined his head in assent.

'Wh…when?' He could not control the break in his voice. That poor, gallant child. Dead. It lacerated him.

'Oh, quite soon after she came to us, you know.' Lord Faringdon manufactured a sigh. 'All very sad of course, but no doubt for the best. There was nothing much one could do for her after Scott's disgraceful end, you know. Dare say she felt it.'

Max remembered a fifteen-year-old girl crouched, weeping in the mud of her father's grave, planting bluebells, and came close to strangling his host.

'I've little doubt she did.' He hardly recognised his own voice, hoarse and shaking.

Faringdon glanced at him. 'Sure you won't have a drink, Blakehurst? You sound as though something's caught in your throat.'

Something was—bile. A drink wouldn't answer the purpose. He'd be tempted to fling it in Faringdon's face. Somehow he managed to say, 'I take it she's buried in the churchyard, then. I'll pay my respects there.' Bluebells. She'd liked bluebells. He'd beg some bulbs from the gardeners. A queer sound from Lord Faringdon brought him around. His jaw clenched, Max raised his brows questioningly.

Lord Faringdon looked as though he might strangle on his cravat as he tugged at it. 'Ah, well…um…as to that, Blakehurst…no *marked* grave, y'know. Sad, very sad. Weakness in the bloodline, no doubt. Only glad it bypassed my family.'

Max's stomach churned at the import of Faringdon's words. *No marked grave…*

Then she had…the memory of another suicide's grave rose in accusation. He could feel the rain, smell the wet earth… and hear the awful blows… And he saw again a girl's tear-streaked face, heard her breaking voice struggle to finish a psalm, felt the slight, trusting weight in his arms as he attempted to comfort her. Saw dark, shadowed eyes shining in the firelight with tears and gratitude for too little, too late.

Blindly he turned and walked from the room without another word.

Verity slipped away from the kitchens as soon as she had finished helping to count the silver. Swiftly she made her way along the upper corridors towards the back stairs that led up to her chamber.

The sound of footsteps ascending the main stairs hurried her the more. Her aunt had made it quite plain that she was to remain out of sight of the guests. So far she had managed to get through the day without any serious trouble—a run of luck she had no intention of breaking.

Reaching the back stairs, she caught up her skirts and took

the steps two at a time, only to let out a shriek of fright as a shadow detached itself from the wall and grabbed for her. The familiar reek of stale brandy assailed her. 'Let me go, Godfrey!' She hit out at her slightly inebriated cousin and tried to dodge around him, but he caught her easily in the confined space.

'Just a cousinly kiss, then.' He leered at her. At least she assumed he was from the slur in his voice. He usually leered when his mother wasn't looking.

She was trapped between Godfrey above her and the footsteps below in the hall. 'Stop it!' she hissed, clawing at his eyes.

He grabbed her wrists as he jerked his face away and dragged her close. 'Not without my kiss,' he muttered. Brandy and foul breath surrounded her.

'*No!*' Gagging, she kicked out at him and connected with his shin, stubbing her own toe. It was enough. Godfrey yelled in pain and shoved her away so that she stumbled backwards into the hall with a cry of fright.

Her landing scared her even more. Instead of crashing to the floor, she found herself held safely in a strong grip. A very masculine grip that steadied her on her feet and released her. Dazed, she looked up into a dark, harsh face. Bright topaz eyes burned into her.

'*Oh!*' she gasped. 'What are *you* doing here?'

Dark brows lifted in mute question. 'Have we met?'

Her world tipped upside down as she stared up at the one person she must, above all others, avoid. 'N…no,' she lied. 'You startled me. Thank you, sir. I…I didn't know there was anyone here. I…I slipped.'

'Did you?' The deep voice took on a tone of lazy curiosity. 'And did Faringdon slip, too?'

Verity could not suppress a shudder. Suddenly her elbow was taken in a firm grip.

'You may as well come out, Faringdon,' continued her rescuer. 'Let's be quite sure we all understand each other.'

Godfrey emerged from the stairwell and Verity saw with unchristian pleasure that her wild swipe at his face had drawn blood.

'What's it to do with you?' blustered Godfrey. 'This ain't your house!'

Lord Blakehurst smiled without the least vestige of humour. 'The whims of a guest should always be indulged, Faringdon. It appears the wench is less than willing. You will oblige me by leaving her alone. Is that clear?'

Wench? Verity only just choked back the explosion. Safer if he did think her one of the maids. So she swallowed her fury and lowered her eyes. Probably in this clothing she did look like a servant. She had already decided that it was too dangerous to let him know she was here.

Godfrey smirked. 'Unwilling? Oh, she's always willing enough—'

Blakehurst seemed to swell. 'Go. Before I forget that your father is my host.'

Godfrey backed away. 'Suppose you think you'll get a leg across, eh, Blakehurst?' he jibed, settling his sleeves in an attempt to look unconcerned. Then he lifted his hand to his face and stared at the blood in apparent disbelief. The look he stabbed at Verity swore revenge.

Cold fear dripped down Verity's spine. If this came to her aunt's ears—that she had landed in Lord Blakehurst's arms—her situation would be even worse.

'I suggest that you cease to judge others by your own dubious standards, Faringdon.' His lordship's voice descended to outright menace. 'I have absolutely no need to force my attentions on unwilling maidservants. Now take yourself off!'

Godfrey left, with another vicious look at Verity. Her heart sank. God only knew how he would explain that scratched face to his mother, but Verity didn't doubt that she would figure largely.

Shivering, she turned to go. If Godfrey didn't mention Lord Blakehurst's presence, then she was safe. Relatively.

'A moment.'

Slowly she looked back. Almost against her will, her eyes lifted to his face. All hard planes and angles, it held the promise of strength and purpose. Something inside her exulted, rioted, even as she stood motionless, trapped in his gaze. 'My lord?'

'You puzzle me, girl.'

Swallowing hard, she didn't say anything, just tried to look vaguely subservient as she fought the attraction of those eyes.

'Are you a servant?'

Five years ago, three even, Verity would have denied the suggestion without hesitation. Now...now when she knew how easily she could be kicked out, that there was nowhere else to go, now that she understood exactly what her fate would be if they *did* throw her out, she hesitated.

'You don't talk like it,' he went on.

'Nursery governess,' she muttered. It wasn't quite a lie. She did try to teach the younger girls between paid governesses. The gaps between paid governesses had gradually become longer and longer.

'Oh.' He seemed to accept that. 'I'll mention this to your mistress and—'

'For God's sake, *no!*' Shaking, she forced her voice to calm. 'My—' *She's your mistress, not your aunt* '—Lady Faringdon would blame me, not Godf—not him. I'd be sacked. Please, don't!'

'What is your name?'

It nearly choked her, but somehow she got the hated name out. 'Selina Dering, my lord.' And bobbed a curtsy.

Another voice broke in. 'And what, may I ask, is going on here?'

Chapter Two

Verity wished she could turn to stone at the sound of Aunt Faringdon's voice. Or at least to ice so that she wouldn't feel anything. The soft voice bit deep.

'You, Selina! Take yourself off. Presumptuous girl! Go to your room!'

Lady Faringdon turned to Lord Blakehurst, all honeyed smiles. 'I must beg your pardon, Lord Blakehurst. That sort never know their place. I hope you were not too inconvenienced.' She bore Lord Blakehurst away, casting a look over her shoulder at Verity that promised dire retribution on the morrow.

Verity retreated to the stairs and raced up to her dark, chilly little room. Closing the door behind her, she leaned against it, shaking in the cold blackness. Eyes tight shut, she saw again the face of her rescuer. Familiar eyes stared back haughtily. Eyes that comforted her dreams, that she'd never expected to see again in the waking world. The moonlight had never revealed their colour. Burning amber. He hadn't recognised her.

Don't think of him.

Verity prepared quickly for bed in the dark. Shivering, she lit her tallow candle, took her father's journal from under her pillow and got into bed.

She couldn't hide from the truth.

Lord Blakehurst, Celia's supposed suitor, was *her* Max.

Dazed, she let the book fall open where it would. The start of the Waterloo campaign and her father's first reference to '*...my new Brevet Major, Max B. I shall not call him anything else here. His family name and degree have not the least significance in what lies before us. He is, however, a gallant lad, and one I shall be happy to rely on when we finally face Bonaparte. I have good reports of his intelligence and courage from his previous commanders...*'

That was the first of many references. Apparently Colonel Scott had become very much attached to the younger officer. Almost like a son. She shut her eyes, remembering that tiny, dead baby sharing her mother's grave...no, she mustn't think of it, mustn't remember her father's return the next day...

'I think Mary would approve him and Verity would like him. He has a gentle way with women and children.'

A few of the things William Scott had written about Max's way with women should have brought a blush to his daughter's cheeks, but Verity had come to the conclusion that young men were young men the world over. And apparently all the women Max had *entertained* in Brussels had been more than willing. It did not appear that her father had thought the worse of Max for his youthful sins.

Hungrily she read on through her father's account of the weeks leading up to Waterloo. Max was mentioned regularly. In the five years since she had first read this journal, he had come alive for Verity in a way she could not quite understand. She knew his expertise with horses and his fondness for dogs. She knew he hated tea and how he liked his coffee. She even knew how he liked his eggs and bacon. And that he was perfectly capable of cooking it himself.

Above all his kindness and thought for an orphaned child glowed in her memory...*a gentle way with women and children...*

He was as real and precious to her as life itself. And the

Max she had found in her father's journal reassured her that the man who had planted bluebells on a suicide's grave, guarded her sleep and left her a decent breakfast, was not a figment of her imagination. In the past five years he had been her only friend, his very existence her only comfort as she cried herself to sleep. And now he was here, in the house, supposedly courting her cousin.

Shivering, she replaced the journal and snuffed the candle. She had never thought that he might be of such high degree. She wished she could forget.

An hour later she still lay in the dark, wishing Lord Blakehurst had never come to the house. Then she could at least have held on to her vision of Max. Max who, at least in her dreams, might be able to care for the disgraced daughter of a suicide.

Now the image she had held all these years was overlaid with the disturbing reality. An aristocrat who would never give her a second thought. Bitterly she remembered asking if she would ever see him again.

Better not, little one. I can offer you nothing.

No. Earl Blakehurst could offer nothing to Verity Scott. And, if she possessed the least vestige of common sense, she would stay out of his way.

Extricating himself from Lady Faringdon's effusions, Max made his way to the billiard room where he found the gentlemen, except Godfrey. He only hoped he had convinced Lady Faringdon that his meeting with the unfortunate Selina had been entirely his fault. Somehow he doubted it.

The girl's eyes haunted him. Dark, shadowy grey. Trusting. They struck a strange chord in him. Another girl had looked at him like that. He'd failed to help Verity Scott. He was damned if he'd fail to help this girl. A few quietly voiced threats might do the trick.

At the end of a game he said, 'A word with you, please, Faringdon.'

Faringdon turned slowly, setting his cue down with great care. 'If it's about that business you mentioned earlier…'

Max took a careful breath. 'Not exactly, sir. Merely that you might have a word with your son. I found him forcing his attentions on…one of your maids this evening.'

Faringdon started. 'A…a maid? Which one?'

Remembering Selina's eyes, wide with fear of dismissal, Max said, 'How should I know?

Faringdon shrugged and picked up his cue. 'Oh, well. Just a housemaid. Young men need to have their fun. You know how it is, my lord.' He looked knowingly at Max. 'Just a bit of sport. Dare say the wench was not really unwilling—'

Ice flooded Max's veins. 'I assure you, she was most distressed,' he stated. 'And I would have no hesitation in stating that to anyone who asked me.' For all the use it would be. Faringdon didn't give a damn. He added, 'After all, you wouldn't want anyone asking questions about Miss Scott's tragedy, would you?'

To his utter amazement the other man went absolutely white. 'Well, of course I will have a word to Godfrey, but really, Blakehurst! A maidservant! It's not as though she is anybody important.'

Max walked out without another word before he could ask if Verity Scott had been important—before he could choke Lord Faringdon into a sense of his iniquities.

He went up to his bedchamber, where he found his ex-batman folding shirts.

'What the devil are you doing here?' he growled.

Harding grinned. 'Doing me job, sir. It's better than the servants' hall here. Stuck-up lot, they are. Any luck, sir?'

Max dragged in a breath. Then let it out. Verity Scott's death was too raw a wound. 'No. Goodnight, Harding.'

Harding's brows lifted. 'Goodnight, sir.'

The door shut behind him and Max slumped into a chair.

All he wanted was some peace and quiet in which to think. To accept that he had failed Verity Scott as badly as he had failed her father. He had assumed that all was well, that she was safe with her relatives. He had thought there was nothing he could do.

The silence pounded the same message into his brain over and over. He had assumed wrongly. What the hell had they done to her? An image of Godfrey Faringdon flashed into his thoughts. Had Godfrey bullied her? Persecuted her the way he was apparently persecuting that poor girl, Selina?

Bitterly Max accepted that he would never know. That no one would talk for fear of scandal. And he had no way of finding out where the poor child was buried. He couldn't even do as much for her as she had done for her father.

Shutting his eyes, he saw again the despairing child's face. He'd never even seen her clearly in the firelight. Just the bleak misery and fear in her dark eyes. And the trusting gratitude. He didn't even know what colour they had been.

Enthroned on a canopied sofa in her boudoir the following morning, Lady Faringdon ranted at her errant niece. 'And just what did you intend by insinuating yourself into Lord Blakehurst's presence? You conniving little slut!' Without giving Verity a chance to respond, Lady Faringdon swept on. 'To think that we have given you a home all these years, lent you our countenance! How dare you!'

Verity drew a deep breath, reminding herself not to strike her aunt's countenance. 'You can get rid of me easily enough, Aunt Faringdon. Write me a reference so that I can find a position and I'll be gone.'

'Why, you ungrateful wretch! Do you think—?'

She broke off as the door opened and Godfrey walked in. A night's sleep had not improved the livid scratches, and Verity's satisfaction burned coldly.

'Godfrey! How frightful! Whatever happened?' gasped Lady Faringdon.

He shrugged. 'Nothing much. Just *her*—' he cast Verity a spiteful look '—taking exception to something I asked of her.'

Verity shut her eyes briefly as churning fear replaced satisfaction. She could tell the truth about what Godfrey wanted—and be accused of trying to trap him into marriage. To share that particular trap with Godfrey... Better dead.

Breathing deeply, she sank into herself, away from the stream of invective, away from the hatred, letting it wash over her. She forced her eyes to remain blank, uncaring. It was the only defence she had left. A cloak of meekness over the boiling fury within.

The door opened abruptly to admit Lord Faringdon. His bulging gaze lit on Verity. 'Out,' he snapped.

Only too glad to remove herself, Verity headed for the door. And heard Lord Faringdon ask as she opened it, 'What the devil happened between you and Blakehurst last night, boy?' Shock held her, but she dared not remain. She shut the door with a shaking hand and glanced around the corridor. Empty.

Swiftly she bent to the keyhole. She was used to hearing nothing good of herself, and sometimes knowledge was safety.

'Enough, sirrah! You will leave that chit alone until Blakehurst is out of the house! Do you hear me?'

Godfrey whinged unintelligibly, but Lord Faringdon's response came through loud and clear.

'Because if you don't, I'll cut off your allowance for a year. The last thing we need is—'

Whatever the last thing was, Verity missed it. Hearing footsteps, she straightened and fled. She'd heard enough. For the next few days she was safe. Perhaps that would give her time to think of some escape that had not occurred to her in the last five years. In the meantime, she must stay out of Lord Blakehurst's way.

* * *

Verity folded another sheet and added it to the mended pile. Three to go. A quick glance at the clock confirmed that she had plenty of time. Everyone was still out on their river-boating expedition. She had at least two hours before she need expect them. Plenty of time to finish the mending, slip out into the gardens and still get back before there was any risk of being seen. Aunt Faringdon had made it perfectly plain yesterday morning that if she...*had the impudence to importune any other guests*...she would regret it.

There was nowhere else to go. She couldn't afford to be thrown out. Not unless hell froze over and Aunt Faringdon gave her a reference as a governess or companion.

'Which she won't,' muttered Verity, as she reached for another sheet. 'She may hate me, but she'd hate paying twenty pounds a year for a governess even more.' That was the only explanation she could think of for their refusal to let her go. Without a reference she was helpless.

The door opened abruptly and a tall, familiar figure whipped into the room, shutting the door with a speed only equalled by the silence with which he managed the feat. He spoke not a word, but looked around wildly.

Verity blinked as Lord Blakehurst made for the large cup-board in the corner. The doors stood wide and to her utter amazement he slipped into the corner behind the door. Still without a word.

'Umm...my lord...'

He glared at her from his hiding place. '*Ssshhh!*'

Returning the glare with interest, Verity asked politely, 'And your boots, my lord?'

'My...?' He looked down. 'Oh, damn!' His boots were clearly visible beneath the door. 'Quick. Shove that mending basket in front, girl.'

Verity obliged, wondering what could have sent one of the wealthiest peers in the realm scuttling for cover like a startled coney.

A moment later she had her answer. The door opened and Lady Moncrieff looked in.

'Is his lordship about, wench?'

Verity couldn't help her eyes narrowing slightly. From her position she could see the lordship in question. And the very faint shake of his head.

Blandly she answered in her best servant's voice. 'Oh, no, mum. The master went boatin' wiv all the other quality. Do you need summat mending?'

'Lord Blakehurst, girl!'

Verity gritted her teeth. 'Lord Blakehurst? Up here, mum? What would his lordship want wiv the likes of me?'

The delicately curved lips curled. 'Nothing, I dare say. You've little enough to recommend you!'

The door shut with a snap and Verity muttered one pungent and graphic word more usually associated with the kennels.

'Yes. Quite.'

She spun around and met her unwanted companion's smile as he emerged from behind the door. Heat surged across her cheeks. In her anger she'd forgotten his presence.

'She was wrong, you know,' he added conversationally.

'Wrong?'

'Wrong,' he affirmed. 'You have plenty to recommend you,' he went on. 'Brains for one thing. Your accent was inspired.' The smile in his eyes deepened. 'Thank you,' he added.

She resisted the urge to smile back and said shortly, 'I think you'd better go.' Before her lungs forgot how to function.

His brows rose. 'So soon? But I haven't paid my debt to you.'

Her breath seized. If he stayed…if anyone came in… 'There is no debt. You helped me. Please—you must go! If anyone finds you here…' Her voice dried up at his smile.

'They've all gone boating.'

'And the servants—the *other* servants?' she amended, remembering her role. 'You think they won't tattle?' She grimaced. Most of them were only too pleased to have someone to look down upon. One or two were sorry for her, but the rest took their tone from their mistress.

He grinned at her and pulled out a large handkerchief. And ripped it almost in half. 'Our chaperon. I brought it along for mending.'

She scowled at him. Drat the man! She would be in the most appalling scrape if they were caught and all she wanted to do was smile back!

'No one would ever believe that the high and mighty Lord Blakehurst would be seen dead blowing his nose on a mended handkerchief!' she snapped. And shut her eyes in horror. Was she mad? Meek little Selina wouldn't have said that!

An appreciative chuckle made her eyes snap open.

'Not dead, no,' he admitted with a grin. 'That would be a bit much. But I do have a very saving disposition. Hangover from my army days. Ask my valet. He'll tell you.'

'Please, just go,' she begged.

He stared at her. 'Miss…Miss…Selina, you're not scared of me, are you? You don't imagine for one moment that I have any…' he hesitated '…that I would behave like Godfrey Faringdon towards you?'

Verity gasped. '*You?* Like Godfrey? Oh, no!'

His gaze focused. 'You seem very sure.'

She caught herself up. 'I…I…yes. Nothing about your reputation suggests that you…that you…well, anyway, I *am* sure. But please go!'

'Has that little toad bothered you again?' he asked sharply.

Her stomach lurched. 'No. He hasn't been anywhere near me.' She could not repress a shiver. The moment Lord Blakehurst left Godfrey would be at her again.

'Good.'

Her eyes widened at the harsh note in his voice. 'Why should you care?'

He didn't answer. Instead, he came towards her. She forced

herself to stillness, meeting his suddenly intense gaze unblinking.

Slowly he lifted a hand and brushed the backs of his fingers over her cheek, tracing the line of her jaw, the softness of her throat. Every precept of good sense and modesty shrieked at her to strike his hand away. She remained still, captive to his gentle touch. When had she last been touched gently?

The answer shook her to the core. Nearly five years ago. By Max Blakehurst. Only now his touch made her restless, sent shivers rippling through her. She forced herself to remain still, rigid.

After a moment his hand dropped. He inclined his head. 'Good afternoon, Selina.'

The door shut behind him and slowly Verity lifted her hand to the path his fingers had traced.

Twenty minutes later Max rode out of the stable yard. With Lady Moncrieff stalking him through the house, retreat was the only sane tactic. He had no stomach for her ladyship's plans for their mutual entertainment and having her forever cooing about him had become intolerable.

He pushed his horse harder, seeking forgetfulness in the flying hooves and surging power beneath him.

Several miles later the mare's labouring breath told him it was time to turn for home. He drew the lathered animal to a halt, dismounted and loosened her girth.

'Easy, old girl.' He rubbed the sweaty nose. 'I'll walk for a bit. Give you a breather.' Guilt and self-loathing did not excuse riding his horse into the ground. There was no rush, he could take his time getting back. When he did he'd make his excuses and depart. There was nothing to hold him at Faringdon Hall.

Or was there?

Deep grey eyes swam into focus. Wary, shuttered eyes, fringed with the darkest lashes. Selina…what was her name? Dering. Selina Dering. He came to a dead halt. Why the devil would he consider staying for Selina? As far as he could judge, his warning to Godfrey and Lord Faringdon had taken effect. She had said herself that Godfrey had not been near her. What more could he do for her?

His whole body hardened as he walked on slowly, suggesting all manner of things that they could do for each other. From the moment she had landed in his arms the other night he'd been conscious of the attraction. He wanted her. At first he'd tried to ignore it. Told himself he'd acted in her defence from motives of the most disinterested chivalry. It was only half-true. He wasn't disinterested. On the contrary.

Her very refusal to have anything to do with him piqued his interest. Most girls in her position would be doing their utmost to cast languishing smiles, practically tripping over themselves—literally—to engage his interest. Selina couldn't get rid of him fast enough. He grinned. Not what he usually looked for in a mistress, but for her he'd willingly make an exception. God, she'd be sweet...

No! Be damned if he'd behave as Faringdon had, forcing the girl into submission.

But you wouldn't be. All you have to do is offer. She can refuse.

And she would. Her whole response to him suggested that. Far from trying to catch his attention, she had been practically pushing him out of the door of the sewing room. Hardly encouraging, but at least she had some spirit left. Whatever her background was, she didn't talk or behave like a servant.

He faced another truth. When he left, what was to prevent Godfrey taking up where he had left off? Probably at the most he had won the girl a breathing space. He swore under his breath. All he wanted was to shake the dust of this place from him, but he couldn't. Not until he had made quite sure that Selina was safe.

A heavy weight descended on his shoulder accompanied by a satisfied snort. Adjusting his step to accommodate the mare's head, he cast a sideways glance at her and rubbed the

velvety nose. 'Comfortable? Anything else I can carry
for you?'

She whiffled contentedly.

He shook his head and walked on, remembering the unrid-
able filly he'd bought three years earlier. Mistrustful Fidget,
as likely to bite a man as not, with her head on his shoulder
like an overgrown spaniel.

He'd tamed her. Why not Selina? He had rescued Fidget
from a young idiot who was mistreating her brutally. Was
Selina's situation so very much different? He caught himself
up with a rueful grin. Arrogant coxcomb! Selina was a girl,
a woman. Not a filly.

Fidget had been given no choice in her fate. Selina had
every right to refuse. Fidget had learnt to trust him *after* he
had taken her. Selina would have to learn *before* he took her,
if she learnt at all. If she hadn't been too badly hurt. His
stomach clenched at the thought of what she'd likely been
subjected to.

He'd been invited to stay for a fortnight. He had just over
a sennight left. That long to gain Selina's trust—and affection.

Affection? Where did that notion come from? Since when
had he wanted affection from one of his mistresses? All he
wanted from his mistresses was a couple of months of pure
and simple pleasure. Three at the most. Well, maybe not pure.
Very well, *definitely* not pure. But no more than three months.
Not even from the loveliest of them. So there it was—he
wanted Selina. Right down to her freckles.

And if she didn't want him?

His whole being revolted at the thought. He took a deep
breath. If she didn't, he'd have to devise another way of protecting her. It crept into his mind that Selina would be very
different from his previous mistresses. He had the oddest feeling that he might not want to let her go after three months.

He pushed the thought away. He was being fanciful. Tak-

ing her as his mistress would be the easiest and most satisfactory way of protecting her. That was all.

Hurrying along an upstairs corridor the following morning,
Verity heard a breathless voice protesting.

'No. Please, sir…you mustn't…'

She hesitated for a moment. She should be helping Celia
get ready for the riding party… A sob of fright came, followed by a crash and a wail of despair. Anger burned away
her hard-won caution. Hitching up her skirts, she broke into
a run. Rounding the corner she found one of the younger
maids, Sukey, crouched weeping over a tray of broken porcelain. Desperate fingers clawed uselessly at the shattered ruins.

Godfrey stood there, an amused smile on his face. 'Next
time you'll know better than to refuse, won't you?'

Verity felt sick. This would see Sukey dismissed. She
turned on the man responsible like a tiger. 'Leave her alone!
Haven't you done enough? Just go away!'

She hurried to the distraught maid and bent down to help
her, picking up the pieces. Godfrey loomed over both of
them. Furious, Verity surged to her feet, a jagged shard of
porcelain in her hand.

'Were you looking for this? Go away!'

He leapt back, swearing.

'What is…my *Sèvres*!'

Verity barely bit back a curse as she looked up to find
Lady Faringdon, her face mottled with fury, staring down at
the ruined tea service.

She turned on the maid. 'Out! Go and pack. I expect you
out within—'

'It wasn't Sukey's fault!'

That halted Lady Faringdon's tirade. Her eyes bored into
Verity.

Meeting her gaze unflinchingly, Verity lied shamelessly.
The truth wouldn't help. 'I was in a hurry. I bumped Sukey

over as I came around the corner. It wasn't her fault.' *Keep it simple. No explanations. Hopefully she won't remember you were supposed to be going to Celia's room—in the opposite direction.*

She held her breath.

So, from his vantage point just inside his bedchamber, did Max. Obviously Godfrey didn't confine his harassment to Selina. He opened the door a little more.

Lady Faringdon had her back to him, but she looked as though a poker had been stitched into her gown. He focused on Selina, standing between her mistress and the weeping maid. Her face was blank, expressionless, the eyes downcast.

Silence held for a moment. He could see the fierce tension in Selina's body as she waited for the inevitable. Any moment now she'd be dismissed. She'd saved the maid at the cost of her own position. Savagely he reminded himself that it didn't matter, that he'd look after her even if she didn't know it.

Then a blur of movement and a ringing slap. Selina stood unflinching as her cheek flamed scarlet from the blow.

He didn't even realise he had moved. 'Good morning, Lady Faringdon. A little domestic disaster?' He avoided Selina's eyes. If he saw that mark on her cheek he might just strangle his hostess.

Lady Faringdon blanched, her hand going to her mouth. 'Oh!'

Max waited. If she struck Selina again...

'Why, Lord Blakehurst! I do hope we didn't disturb you.' With a suppressed snarl she turned on Selina. 'Insolent hussy! I'll deal with you later.'

Then she snapped at the maid. 'Clean that up and get back to your duties, girl. Godfrey—our guests are waiting to go riding. You should be down already.' Her smile became gracious. 'And you, Lord Blakehurst? Are you not going?'

He lied without hesitation. 'That was my intention, but I

have a letter to write. I'll follow later.' Returning to his room, he listened as steps retreated along the corridor. He'd thought to join the riding party. Not now. He had something else to do.

Chapter Three

He found her in the schoolroom. At first she didn't realise the door had opened and he watched her. Tidying up with a swift, calculated efficiency. Picking up paper, emptying inkwells, shelving books. Apart from the red mark on her cheek, she looked tired. Faint smudges showed like bruises beneath her eyes.

Anger coalesced deep inside. 'Are you all right?' He couldn't keep the fury from his voice. That someone had hit her, hurt her in any way—he swallowed his rage and strode into the room.

'Oh!' Books cascaded from her arms. 'Oh, damn!' She bent down to pick them up.

'Here, let me help you.' He bent down. 'What's this? Miss Mangnell? And good lord—*The Mirror of Graces*? How to be a proper young lady?' He wrinkled his nose. 'My Aunt Almeria swears by this one.'

'Then I'm glad I don't know her,' muttered Selina.

Max gave a snort of laughter. 'So am I.'

She flushed. 'I beg your pardon. I should not have said that.' Wary grey eyes glanced up at him. 'What are you doing here anyway?'

The red mark on her cheek cried out. Biting off a curse,

he reached out and touched it gently. 'I came to see if you were all right. Does that hurt?'

She flinched and he dropped his hand. 'It won't happen again,' he said quietly

She didn't meet his eyes and bent to pick up a book from the floor. 'You can't know that.' Her fingers whitened on the book.

'Yes, I can,' he said. He'd never raised his hand to a woman. And he didn't see himself starting with this waif. 'Why did you do it, Selina? No doubt she will dismiss you later when she has had time to find another governess. Why not tell her the truth?'

'You think she would have believed me?' Careful fingers began to smooth the pages of the abused book. 'Even if she had, she would have assumed Sukey asked for it. That she attracted Godf— Mr Faringdon's attention on purpose. She would have been dismissed all the quicker.'

He couldn't deny the truth of that. But still...his conscience informed him that he was a complete and utter knave to make his dis-honourable offer when she was desperate. He swore mentally. What else could he do? Leave her to be flung out? To starve? Or worse?

His conscience, which had never taken much interest in his dealings with the fair sex, pointed out that what he was about to propose definitely came under the heading of *Worse*. Worse than death, in fact. *The devil it does! I'm not planning to rape her!*

He planned to seduce Selina. Gently. And make sure she had everything she could possibly desire. His blood burned at the idea of teaching her a few things he doubted she had the least idea of desiring. How could she after Godfrey? Best to lead up to it gradually.

'Selina—where will you go?'

Puzzled grey eyes met his. 'Go? What are you talking about, my lord?'

Patiently he said, 'When your mistress dismisses you. She

is unlikely to give you much of a reference. Do you have somewhere to go?'

'Somewhere to go?' He saw her swallow convulsively.

'Yes. I—'

'She won't dismiss me.'

Max, cut off before he'd fairly started, blinked. 'Pardon me?'

'She won't dismiss me.'

Unable to believe that she could mean it, Max pressed on. 'Selina—don't be foolish. Have you thought of another position? Another… type of position.' His cravat was about to strangle him, and the puzzled look she gave him made it worse. Damn! Why was offering a *carte blanche* suddenly so hellishly difficult?!

'No. I have no references. But she won't dismiss me.'

He stifled a crack of laughter. References? He'd never asked for references. All the references he required were flitting around the room before him, tidying away quills, books and a battered globe. Abandoning that tack, he asked gently, 'Sweetheart, what do you want?'

She turned, eyes wide. 'Why did you call me that?'

He didn't know. He'd never called any woman *sweetheart*. But it felt right. It fitted. 'What do you want?' he repeated, sticking to the point. Seeing the puzzled frown deepen, he added, 'Generally, from…from life.' Where in Hades had that come from? He *knew* what women wanted. Pretty, fashionable clothes, jewels, a carriage, masculine attention, all the usu—

'A family.'

'A…*what*?'

She flushed and turned away. 'You needn't mock. I know it's impossible. But you asked.' The break in her voice rocked his world on its axis.

He said carefully, 'You want children?' His mistresses had, one and all, taken whatever precautions could be taken against that catastrophe. A mistress who wanted a child? Deep within something tightened.

She didn't answer, but started dusting. He frowned. That was something she wouldn't need to do again.

'Selina?'

At last she replied. 'That would be nice too. But what I meant was that it would be…I'd like…to belong. To be part of people's lives. Not to be always apart.'

Max's world gave another wobble. 'You have no family? Not even someone to write to?'

'There is no one I can call my kin.' Her voice hardened. 'No one to give a present to. Which is just as well, since I have nothing to give.'

His heart ached for her, even as he realised the advantage it gave him. No family. No one to be horrified and ashamed at the step she was about to take. No one who would refuse to acknowledge her ever again. He ignored his conscience, which suggested it made her even more vulnerable. She would be his. Safe. He moved towards her, removing the duster from her hand and dropping it.

Awareness leapt within Verity at his nearness, at the brush of long fingers over hers. Then her hand was caught in a gentle, inescapable grip, his thumb stroking sensuously over her roughened skin. Everything within her contracted, shivered in expectation. What on earth was he about? She looked up at him, shocked. A mistake.

'Nothing?' His smile deepened and, with it, the flare of something hungry in his eyes. Something warm that melted her, bone deep.

Uncertainly she shook her head. 'I have nothing,' she repeated.

'You have something I want.'

His voice was a deep caress and she realised that he had drawn even closer, that his body brushed against her, that the sharp, tangy odour of his cologne surrounded her, wreathing through the beeswax.

'Would you consider another sort of position, Selina?' he asked quietly.

What? Her mind wouldn't focus, could only absorb the nearness of him, the longing to lean against him. She shook her head to clear it enough to focus on his suggestion of a new position. The Faringdons would not permit it, but she could not tell him that. She dared say nothing that might give him a clue to her identity. 'Without a reference…I have nothing to live on while I find another place.' It was true enough, just not all of the truth. A curl fell into her eyes, tickling, and she pushed it behind her ear. It escaped immediately. Impatiently she lifted her hand again. Then froze.

His hand lifted to her face, pushing the errant curl away from her eye. He didn't bother to tuck it away, but threaded his fingers into her hair in a shockingly intimate gesture. She could feel his thumb circling slowly at her temple, then drifting lower to caress her cheek, her jaw, her throat.

Heat bloomed, and a strange ache invaded her breasts, her belly. A tightening that pulsed to the beat of her heart, suddenly pounding. She could only stare up at him, eyes wide. Her whole body quivered with anticipation, lost in a dreamlike daze. 'My lord?' Her breath shortened. 'I…I don't understand…'

'Then I shall have to explain,' he murmured.

Her breath jerked in. Never before had a man's voice stabbed into her like that. But then again, never before had a man spoken to her as his arms stole about her and his lips brushed her ear. Pleasure rippled through her even as understanding coiled painfully inside. She knew now what he wanted.

A light touch grazed her throat, drifted along her jaw.

Breathless, she looked up, shivers racing through her, and met a penetrating amber gaze only inches away. She felt caged by his warmth, his strength, by the scent of shaving soap and the spicy masculine smell that underlay it. Her hand rose uncertainly, drawn by the faint shadowed roughness of his jaw, her fingers itched to stroke it, test its texture.

She mustn't. She understood now what he wanted. She should draw back, but his eyes and touch held her trapped. Gently. Safe, but suddenly vulnerable. To her own desire. Her breath shivered out and she realised that she had been holding it, that her heart's pounding had nothing to do with terror. And that he was even closer. He leaned forward, his breath a tender caress on her lips. Every precept—of modesty, decorum, every scrap of good sense—screamed a warning. *Run!*

She lifted her face and felt the warm, gentle touch of his lips. Oh, the joy of being touched and held tenderly. With... affection? Featherlight, his mouth brushed across hers in the briefest of kisses. Delight shot through her. His warmth enfolded her. Her lips parted on a soundless sigh and for an instant the kiss deepened, possessing her completely, then it was over almost before she could believe it had happened. With a final, lingering caress at the corner of her mouth, he drew back, releasing her.

Her eyes fluttered open. She hadn't even realised they were shut. He was still close, close enough that she could see his pulse beating in his throat.

His voice came, calm and soft. 'Perhaps that will make things clearer.'

She could only nod, certain that without breath her voice would not function. And then she wondered why she had nodded as though things were clearer. She was more confused than ever. How he could speak so *indifferently* was beyond her comprehension. He had kissed her until her head spun. Grimly she reminded herself of Lady Moncrieff. *He's used to beautiful women. Women who know how to...to please a man. Whatever that means. Why would his head spin? Why would he even kiss her? He couldn't want her. Could he?*

'Well, Selina? Do you understand now?'

Only too well. Braced against the gentleness in his voice,

she turned to go. Oh, yes. She understood well enough. But Max would never try to force her consent.

His hand shot out and caught her wrist.

Shock, as much as his grip, held her motionless. Fear stirred and knotted. She ignored it and fought to infuse her voice with icy indifference. 'Sir?'

'A moment, Selina.'

It was not a request. The grip on her wrist sent the knot of fear twisting through her stomach. *Oh, no. Surely not him too.* Could she have been mistaken in him? Tension singing through her, she faced him, trying to force her breathing to steady.

His intent gaze rested on her face, then dropped to her captive wrist. 'I beg your pardon,' he said. His hand fell from her and she felt bereft, as though part of her had torn itself away.

Resisting the urge to hold the wrist to her cheek, she waited, some of her fear allayed.

'Not all positions require references, Selina. And I can assure you I would be a gentler lover than Godfrey Faringdon has been.'

Tension gripped her again. Carefully, slowly, she stepped back, holding his gaze with hers, certain that any moment he would grab her, drag her into his arms. Men didn't really ask. Men took.

'I…I should not be here, my lord. Please excuse me.' She backed away, her gaze never leaving his face, the bright topaz eyes watching her like a big cat, until she reached the door. Then she fled.

Max swore. She had refused him. Without hesitation. And her life here was hell. She was treated like a slave. How could enduring that be preferable to a discreet and well-paid liaison with himself? She didn't dislike him. She had responded to his kiss. She couldn't possibly have thought he would offer marriage. So why the devil wouldn't she even consider being his mistress? Obviously her birth was respectable. She didn't speak like a servant. Perhaps his offer had shocked her.

After what Godfrey had doubtless done to her? He stalked to the door. Surely she didn't think he'd ever force her? Had he frightened her with that brief kiss? Had she realised the fierce depth of his desire for her? He'd had to control every muscle in his body not to ravish her, plunder the soft mouth. She was sweetness incarnate. It had taken every ounce of willpower to draw back, when all he had wanted... He swore again. She'd only had to glance down and what he wanted would have been all too obvious.

It was still making its painful presence felt ten minutes later when he reached the billiard room. Picking up a cue, he considered his next move. *His next move?* On the rare occasions a woman refused him, he accepted her reply and dropped the pursuit. In fact he usually realised before ever broaching the subject. He sent a red ball crashing into a pocket. Why couldn't he accept Selina's refusal? He shook his head. When had he ever wanted a woman so much that his body continued to ache after she had refused him and gone?

Perhaps she needed time to think it over. She hadn't exactly refused. He ran over her reply. *I should not be here, my lord. Please excuse me.* Perhaps she needed some reassurance that he wouldn't leave her penniless at the end of their liaison. Maybe he hadn't made that clear.

He thought back. And closed his eyes in disbelief at his own stupidity. Apart from telling her that he'd be gentler than Godfrey, he'd offered her nothing. Nothing beyond a casual tumble. No wonder she'd refused. All he had to do was find her and explain...explain what?

He didn't know himself what he wanted. Only that Selina was very different. That in taking her under his protection, he would be doing just that. Protecting her.

*   *   *

Verity lay in bed, shivering. The warmth of the day lingered, but she couldn't stop shaking. Her memory refused to listen to wisdom, continuing to dwell on the tender strength of his hands, the gentle pressure of his kiss. That was bad enough, but for her body to join in the treacherous assault shocked her. What sort of wanton creature ached and trembled at the mere memory of a kiss that had lasted about three seconds?

It would have to last a lifetime. She didn't dare see him again. Grimly she admitted that it was not that she did not trust him. Rather, she could not trust herself. Her whole being cried out to let him hold her, touch her.

Stop it! He wants a great deal more than just to hold you. He wants exactly what Godfrey wants. Nothing else. A gentle, persuasive voice murmured, *Would it be so bad to be his mistress? He would be kind to you...you'd be free. You could purchase an annuity. They'd never dare to take you back after that...even if you are a minor.*

No! She wouldn't, she couldn't. She mustn't. Things weren't so bad that she needed to sell herself into whoredom. Besides, perhaps he didn't want her as his mistress. Chances were she had completely misunderstood him and that he simply wanted to bed her while he was here. That was much more likely. Even if he did want more... She shied away from the thought, shocked at her own weakness.

A little voice asked, *How much longer can you hold Godfrey off? Wouldn't it be better—*

No! If only she could think of some way to leave when she came of age. Just over a year. She shut her eyes in despair at the bitter reality. She had nothing—no money, no other connections. She would be no safer if she did leave.

A soft tap on the door shocked her bolt upright. Who would bother knocking? Certainly not Godfrey...

'Selina? Are you awake?' The deep voice went straight through her like a spear. What could *he* possibly want?

Exactly what he wanted this afternoon.

'Y…yes.'

'May I come in?'

How can I stop you?

'By saying *no*,' came the quiet response. Dismayed, she realised that she had spoken aloud. And that even if she let him in, she was safe enough. He had knocked, requesting her permission to enter. *He has a gentle way with women and children…*

'Come in.' She felt as though those two simple words had brought her to the edge of a precipice, to hang trembling over the unknown.

Clutching her blanket to her, she watched, wary, as the door opened and he came in. His lamp cast a mellow flickering glow so that she saw his face shadowed, as she had remembered it for five long years. In that light she could almost forget that he was Blakehurst. She could almost pretend that this was one of her dreams in which, miraculously, Max had come to take her away. Almost.

He dwarfed her tiny room, needing to bend his head to avoid cracking his six foot plus height on a beam. 'May I sit down?'

'If you can find something to sit on,' she said, deliberately unwelcoming. To her complete consternation he sat on the campaign chest. He appeared to be holding himself stiffly. She wondered if he were uncomfortable. Then she saw the flash of his eyes in the lamplight and had the impression of something held tightly leashed, something dangerously hot.

'I imagine you know why I have come,' he said in a quiet voice strangely at odds with the burning look in his eyes.

Burning? She gave herself a mental shake. She must be imagining things. It was just the reflected lamplight.

'I came to make quite sure you understood what I offered you this morning. I want more than a casual tumble. I would take you as my mistress, Selina. If you still refuse, then so be it, but I thought you might find my protection more acceptable than Faringdon's persecution.'

A gentle way with women… 'Why?'

She thought he blinked. 'Why? Because I'm *asking* you, Selina. Not forcing you. If you become my mistress, it must be willingly.'

'No. I meant, why do you want me as your mistress?' *And why am I even asking?*

He definitely blinked. 'Isn't that obvious, Selina?'

'No.' She couldn't imagine why he would want her. According to her aunt and cousins she had nothing to recommend her. Oh, she knew why Godfrey wanted her. Because she was defenceless and he was a swaggering bully, not far removed from the loutish schoolboy who had once drowned a kitten in front of his terrified little cousin, merely because he knew she was fond of it.

But Max—*Lord Blakehurst*—was not of that ilk. She had not the least idea why a man with a reputation for taking beautiful women as his mistresses would want her.

'Because I desire you of course.' The sudden huskiness in his voice shocked her. 'Because I want to take you in my arms and kiss you and every one of those damn freckles. Because I want to see your eyes go black with desire when I make love to you. Because I want to hear you beg me to take you. And I want to hear you cry out in pleasure when I do.'

As if he couldn't help himself, he reached for her and she jerked back against the wall. Instantly his arms fell to his sides. She heard the rasp of his breath, saw the sudden flattening of his mouth.

'I'm s-sorry,' she whispered. 'I didn't mean to make you angry. You startled me.'

Silence hung darkly between them.

'I'm not angry,' he said at last. 'Well, yes, I am. But with myself for frightening you. The truth is, Selina, that I want you. I wanted you the minute I laid eyes on you. Or, to be accurate, the minute I felt you in my arms.

'Think about it,' he went on. 'Even if you are not dismissed, there is still Faringdon. He may leave you alone while I am here, but what do you think will happen when I leave? At least if you come with me you will be treated well, you will have clothes, jewels and money. A house to live in. After we part you will have a generous sum of money settled on you.'

Any single element of what he offered would be a great deal more than she had now. It would have been tempting…if she had wanted any of it. It was what he didn't mention that tempted her—that briefly there would be someone who cared a little. Someone who would treat her tenderly. Someone *she* could care for. *After we part*… Inevitably there would be a parting. Even now her heart ached in the expectation of pain. Would it be worse to have the joy and lose it, or never have it at all?

He said he wanted to make love to her. Godfrey had told her what he wanted of her in explicitly crude detail that left her shuddering. The word *love* hadn't entered into it. Max's hot words left a burning ache in her breasts, a shimmering glow throughout her entire body that she knew would burst into flame if he so much as touched her. That was why she had jerked back. Max held a far more dangerous power over her than Godfrey Faringdon because she wanted him, despite her mind screaming that she was insane even considering such a step, that she would be ruined, lost forever, should she take it.

It was far too dangerous to accept. If he ever found out who she was… She did not think she could bear the disgust and horror in his eyes. For the drudge, Selina, to accept his offer was unexceptionable. For Miss Verity Scott to become his mistress… She could protect herself against the Faringdons' scorn. She didn't love them, never had, but Max…he would hate her if he ever discovered the truth.

'Selina?' The very softness of his voice caressed her. 'I'm sorry. I didn't mean to frighten you. But believe me, what

we could have together would be very different from what
Faringdon has forced on you.'

She believed him, and did not bother to correct his assumption that Godfrey had already stripped her of her innocence. In a way he had. As had all the Faringdons. She had
very few illusions left as to how the world viewed a girl in
her situation. A drudge. A source of unpaid labour and a
convenient victim for bullying. He had offered her escape.
Not love.

She had to refuse him. But her whole being cried out in
protest at being denied the tenderness he offered. Surely she
could have just one last, tiny taste of heaven, one small joy
to cherish in the years ahead?

'I must refuse you, my lord,' she said quietly, praying that
the lump in her throat wouldn't choke her.

'Must you?'

She could only nod.

'Very well.'

He rose from the chest and picked up his lantern and she
realised that he was leaving. That if she didn't speak now he
would be gone. With all her dreams.

'But, if you do not mind, my lord…I…I should like to kiss
you again.'

He turned very slowly. 'Why? If you do not wish—'

She interrupted. 'I cannot be your mistress, my lord, but it
is not because you frightened me, or that I do not trust you.'

His mouth twisted ruefully. 'If you will offer to kiss me
after what I said to you earlier, then your trust is self-evident.
Are you sure, Selina? Be warned: I have every intention of
using this kiss to change your mind. It will start with a kiss,
but if you want it to stop there, you are the one who will
have to say so.'

She swallowed. He had warned her, that was fair. The risk
was hers, to take or reject. She took it. Trembling, she held
out her hand.

His smile deepened and he came to her.

This time he sat beside her, his weight tipping her towards him, and she realised just how much bigger he was. In the enveloping shadows his large frame loomed over her, the faint scent of cologne teased her senses, wafting over her. She felt his hands on her shoulders, urging her towards him, drawing her with shattering care into his embrace.

Her breathing hitched, drawing the scent, the essence of him, deeper. His large, warm hand slid under her chin, tipping her face up. Delicately he touched her, tracing her cheekbones, her nose, the line of her brows. And where his fingers caressed, his lips followed, tasting, teasing until her breath shivered and broke in pleasure.

Those tantalising fingers found her jaw, stroked and circled while his thumb brushed her mouth, following the curve of her lips. She could feel his breath, hot and urgent at her ear and turned her head, shyly seeking him. She felt him smile as his mouth closed over hers, felt his arms tighten as she melted against him. Instinctively her arms slid around him as she wriggled closer, pressing herself into the heat of his body.

The blanket she had clutched around her fell away, forgotten in the wonder of his mouth moving on hers and his gentle hands holding her close. Hands that explored and shaped her, telling her that she was lovely, that he desired her. Hands that banished the old world and replaced it with a spinning glory of passion.

Clumsily, she opened her mouth a little and returned his kiss, only to feel a possessive hand slip between them and cover one breast as his tongue traced her lips. A shocked gasp ripped from her at the glittering sensation taking her by storm. He took instant advantage. His mouth twisted against hers, opening her more fully and his tongue penetrated deeply in intimate possession. Her mind whirled. Her body melted to warm, flowing honey, drained of all strength.

Slowly, repeatedly, he claimed her mouth until some last vestige of common sense warned her, *If you don't stop him now, you won't be able to. You won't even want to.*

It took every ounce of willpower, but somehow she pushed on his shoulders, pulling her mouth free. She could feel the hard tension in his body, the tightening of his arms as, for an instant, he possessed her mouth fiercely, demanding her surrender. Then he released her and stood, his breathing audible.

'My offer stands. You have only to come to me.'

He was gone, his footsteps fading down the stairs, leaving Verity staring into the dark. Her taste of heaven had been a terrible mistake. His kiss had not given comfort. Instead her whole body sang and throbbed with a burning need that she scarcely understood. Instead of comfort, she had unleashed an appalling temptation.

Chapter Four

Three days later Max left the breakfast parlour in a thoroughly disgusted frame of mind. Lord, what on earth possessed him to remain at this house party? If he had to endure much more inane conversation and blatant toadying, he was likely to brain someone. Probably that simpering chit, Celia. Thank God the wench was too self-indulgent to appear for breakfast. No doubt she sipped weak tea off a tray in her bedchamber and made some housemaid's life a living hell.

Like Selina. He gritted his teeth. He'd not seen her since the night he went to her bedchamber. Plainly she meant her refusal and had taken pains to avoid him. He should forget her, return to town. But the thought of that cur, Godfrey, forcing himself on the girl... Max found his shoulders growing tense and his fists clenching. So he'd put off his departure time and again, telling himself that while he remained she was safe and hoping to see her so that he could ask again, persuade her with a few more gentle kisses. His body ached at the memory of her mouth opening shyly under his, the small, shocked gasp as he tasted her deeply and caressed the tender breasts pressing against him...

He was just as shabby as Mr Faringdon, his conscience informed him. *Why shabby?* he argued. *If Faringdon's been forcing himself on her and she has nowhere to go, then she might have welcomed the opportunity.*

You lousy bastard! his better self protested. *What choice has she got?*

Oh, rubbish! After all, she'd be far better off, and it's not as though I'd leave her destitute afterwards. In fact, I could set her up with an annuity. A little something in the three percents to make her independent. She can always say no. It's not as though I'd force her.

She did *say no.* His conscience pointed that out with unwonted zeal. It also reminded him of another girl he'd failed to save. Unlike Verity Scott, Selina had had her chance and refused it. There was nothing to hold him here. He'd leave tomorrow. In fact, he'd find Faringdon right now and tell him before going riding.

The day passed wearily for Verity with no prospect of rest until evening. She could only thank God for the house party. At least her tasks were still limited to those away from the family and their guests. And maybe tonight she could hide on her stairs again and watch for a glimpse of Max going past on his way to bed.

That was the only time she permitted herself to see him, the only bright spot in a very bleak outlook. And it gave her more pain than pleasure. The temptation to go to him, accept his offer, tore at her.

She shivered. Better that she told him who she was. He'd never take her then. The temptation would be gone. She didn't dare. He'd try to force the Faringdons to treat her better. But what could he really do? She was under twenty-one, a pauper, wholly at the command of her legal guardians. He was Blakehurst, society's darling. The night they had met he had said it was better they did not meet again, that he could offer her nothing.

She had seen him. That was better than nothing. And if he

found out the truth she'd be worse off than ever. Aunt Faringdon would see to that.

During the afternoon she was sent to Celia's bedchamber to do the mending. At least it meant she could sit down. She curled into a tight little ball, shivering despite the warmth of the day, as she stitched at the gown Celia had torn the night before. She wouldn't mind the mending and other tasks if her aunt and cousins would just treat her like a member of the family, if they had not stolen every vestige of dignity from her, down to her very name.

Did Verity Scott even exist any more? Or had she died years ago and been replaced by the silent, unassuming Selina? She was nineteen, for heaven's sake, nearly twenty. She'd had more courage at fifteen. Desperately Verity tried to remember the child who had crept out in a blinding downpour to try and give her father's burial some honour.

Would she dare to do it now? Shame and self-loathing lashed at her. How could she have become so subservient? Grimly, she tied off her thread and snipped it. She had stood up for Sukey. What if she stood up for herself? Now? What if she refused to be Selina any more?

She rose and took the mended gown to the armoire. She had become Selina in order to survive. So she would have to make a decision. Survival, or self-respect.

The next item in her mending pile was a shirt of Godfrey's. A button had come off. Even after laundering, the shirt still smelt of him, reminding her of what was likely to happen after the conclusion of the house party. Sick fear clenched her stomach. She had thought she had nothing left to lose. Apparently she did: survival, or self-respect. She doubted that she could have both.

Celia came up to change for dinner in a foul temper and Verity learned that Lord Blakehurst had disappeared straight after breakfast and gone riding all day. By himself. Again.

Stepping out of her afternoon gown, Celia sat down at her

dressing table in her chemise and petticoat and said, 'He was at breakfast, they told me, and then he simply vanished. Oh, and Mama is furious.' She turned to Verity with a sneer and said, 'Something to do with you, I believe. You're for it when she comes up. She said you had tried to intrigue Lord Blakehurst.'

Fingers suddenly numb, Verity dropped the slipper she had just picked up. Someone had seen them.

'Imagine,' continued Celia, 'you! Attempting to intrigue a connoisseur like Blakehurst! They say all his mistresses are stunningly beautiful and that he flaunts them all over London. But it is all of a piece, I dare say. Obviously cowardice runs in your family and now you have attempted to become a whore.'

Beyond the churning fear something stirred deep inside Verity. Something that had stayed chained for years.

Celia pouted at her reflection and caught up a handful of hair, twisting it this way and that. 'I think I shall have a new *coiffure* tonight. I'm so bored with my old one. See to it, girl.'

Verity's self-control shattered into a thousand gleaming, deadly fragments and her temper stepped free. 'Certainly, cousin,' she said, sweeping up the sewing scissors on her way to the dressing table. 'How about this?' She snatched up a section of hair and slashed with the scissors. 'And this!' Another bunch of curls joined their fellows on the floor.

Celia's shrieks and screams, as she clutched the shorn patches by her left temple and ear, had their inevitable aftermath.

Verity turned calmly enough as Lady Faringdon rushed in. Her ladyship took one look at the ruin of Celia's hair and rounded on her niece. 'Get out,' she shouted. 'Return to your room. I'll see to you in the morning, after I bid farewell to Lord Blakehurst.'

Verity drew in a horrified breath which her aunt observed. 'Yes, that's right. He's leaving. Did you think that you had caught his attention? No doubt your attempt to insinuate yourself into his notice has disgusted him. Now go!'

Refusing to be cowed, Verity said cheerfully, 'Goodnight, Aunt, Cousin. I dare say one of the maids can brush your hair before bed, now that I've lightened the task for her. Enjoy your evening.'

Tearing herself from her mama's enveloping bosom, Celia leapt at her with a shriek of rage, but Verity stood her ground with a little smile and lifted the scissors again. 'Do you want me to even it up a trifle, Celia?'

Celia shrank back. 'Mama! She threatened me!'

'Yes, well,' said Verity, 'after all, what else could you expect of a coward and a whore?' She dropped the scissors and stalked out, slamming the door.

She barely remembered reaching her chamber. Vaguely she noticed several guests appear from their rooms, excitedly wondering what all the commotion was about. One or two even asked if she knew, but she was too shocked at the enormity of what she had done to respond.

Eventually she lay on her narrow bed, staring into the darkness, trying to hold back despair. There was no time to think of a plan for escape, or try to find a position. She had to leave. At once. She'd burned an entire armada of boats to the waterline.

But, oh! It had been worth it to see the look on Celia's face! Despite her fear, she giggled. And Aunt's face! As though the silent, cowed poor relation had suddenly gone mad.

Enough. Now she had to think what to do. Shivering, she faced the truth. If she remained, she was ruined. After this, her aunt would look the other way while Godfrey debauched her. If she left and sought shelter in the workhouse, it would only be a matter of time before some other man took her.

A whore.

Whichever way she turned, she was trapped. Unless...

unless she accepted Lord Blakehurst's offer. She *couldn't*! She didn't dare…did she? Carefully she thought it over. If she took some precautions, misled him a little about her intentions, he would never realise who she was. If he took her, she would be free. Even if they realised who she had gone to, they wouldn't dare take her back, because to do so they would have to admit who she was. The risk of scandal would be too great.

She would have to remain Selina Dering. With a queer sense of foreboding, she realised that, to all intents and purposes, Verity would cease to exist. There would be only Selina. Max must never know the truth. Any of it.

Straight after dinner Max excused himself, muttered something about an early start and went up to his room. Not even the prospect of finding out what had caused the explosion of feminine hysteria shortly before dinner tempted him to remain for longer than was absolutely required by the dictates of courtesy.

That Celia Faringdon had been at the centre of the outburst was evidenced by the fact that she had not appeared at dinner. Lady Faringdon's explanation of a sensitive and easily castdown temperament, Max translated as *spoiled brat who didn't get her own way over something trivial.*

Once in his room, he rang the bell and when Harding arrived, said, 'We'll leave first thing. Have you packed?'

Harding nodded. 'Aye, sir. Everything's ready. Will there be aught else tonight?'

Max shook his head, and then reconsidered. 'On second thoughts, send up a bottle of brandy, and then get an early night.'

Harding hesitated. 'Brandy, sir? You'll have a devilish head in the morning.'

Earl Blakehurst raised his brows. 'I beg your pardon, Sergeant?'

Holding his ground gallantly, Harding repeated, 'You'll have a devilish head, sir. The brandy's damned awful!'

Max managed a disciplinary sort of stare. 'In which case you have my full permission to say "I told you so" and gloat. Just do it.'

'Yes, sir. One hangover coming up, sir.'

Max's mouth twitched. 'Impudent dog! God knows why I bear with you!'

Harding grinned. 'Probably, sir. Omniscient, isn't He?'

Max burst out laughing and sat down on the bed to pull his shoes off.

'Sir?'

'Mmm?'

'Dessay it's not my place to ask, but did you hear anything about the Colonel's lass?'

The laughter drained away. 'I'm sorry, Harding, I should have told you,' he said quietly. 'She's dead. Faringdon hinted that she took her own life. I was too late. Again.'

Harding blanched. 'Oh, Gawd! I'm that sorry, sir.'

'So am I. Goodnight.'

When the brandy came Max uncorked it and faced his failure. Five years. Why the hell had he left it so long to assure himself of Verity Scott's well being? Not knowing the Faringdons beyond a nodding acquaintance, he'd assumed that they would take care of Verity, that she would be safe with them. Damn it, he'd been *relieved* when he discovered that her relations were wealthy.

Not until Lady Faringdon came to the fore this past spring in launching the fair Celia had he begun to wonder.

His fingers tightened on the wine glass and he took a large swallow, feeling the brandy burn its way down. He had thought that the child was better off not being reminded of that ghastly burial, that he should leave her to recover in the care of her family. He hadn't even worried when they didn't bring her up to London for a Season. After all, launching a girl was an expensive business and Verity, as far as he knew, was destitute. All her father's property had been sequestered. They might have provided for her much less expensively.

But closer acquaintance with Lady Faringdon had all his instincts on point. This was not a woman to whom he would have consigned a dog with a thorn in its paw, let alone the shattered, grieving orphan of a suicide.

He piled up his pillows and, sitting back, linked his arms behind his head to stare up into the shadowed canopy of his bed. Too late. Just as he had been too late for the man who had saved his life at the ultimate cost of his own.

William Scott had deflected the sabre that should have killed or maimed him. It had been William Scott whose wound had festered and turned gangrenous. It had been William Scott whose arm had been amputated in a stinking field hospital after Waterloo. And William Scott who had eventually sunk into despair and destroyed himself.

Bitterly he took another swallow of brandy. He should have visited soon after Verity came to live here. Or written to her. Then she might have known that she had one friend who cared for her and remembered her father with gratitude rather than shame. It might have made the Faringdons look after her.

He shuddered, forcing the ghosts away. He could do nothing for them now. They were both at peace. Tomorrow night he would be back in London. Hopefully his twin, Richard, would have returned to town and he could wash the bitterness of failure from his heart. Better to turn his mind to the living and keep on drinking to banish tonight's ghosts. A hangover in the morning was a fair price for that.

About halfway down the bottle an image of Selina flashed into his mind. She had refused him. Twice. There was nothing more he could do for her. He clenched his fists. No doubt if she had to contend with young Faringdon's attentions whenever the distempered cub chose to grace his ancestral seat, then she had good reason to fear what a man might do to her.

Lord, but she'd be sweet though. Those great dark eyes and dusky curls. Her slender figure would be all delicate curves when she filled out a trifle. She had spirit, too. He grinned, remembering the yell of pain from Faringdon, just before Selina had tumbled out of the stairwell—and the marks on his face. Faringdon had endured any number of witty remarks about wildcats the next morning. And she had defended that maidservant.

All of which would go hard against her when he left. Max lifted the glass to his lips and swore again when he found it empty. He reached for the bottle and carefully poured another tot. And another.

Selina had refused his offer. There was not much he could do for the poor girl, unless... Unless he could persuade his Aunt Almeria, Lady Arnsworth, that she needed a companion. That Miss Selina Dering would fit the bill admirably. He could go up to her room now and suggest it to Selina. Give her his direction in town and some money for the fare. Almeria would have her if he offered to frank, say, her box at the opera.

Contemplating the level in the brandy bottle, he hesitated. Perhaps he ought to leave it until morning. Business matters were best undertaken with a clear head. And he had a horrible feeling that he had reached the limits of his control on his previous visit to her bedchamber. It had been damn near impossible to release her then. Now...his whole body hardened, just thinking about the sweetness of her response, the way her body had melted in his arms. If he went now, he'd probably find himself attempting to seduce her into accepting his original offer.

She refused you.

He was still battling with his conscience when he heard a soft tapping on his door. Frowning, he fished his watch out of his waistcoat pocket and stared at it in disbelief. Who the devil would come visiting past midnight? Mentally he ran over the list of guests, wondering which of the bolder married ladies might have decided to live dangerously.

Lady Moncrieff? Apparently she'd given up, but with him leaving tomorrow, perhaps she thought to try more direct tactics. Or Mrs Highbury? The handsome widow took delight in sailing close to the wind at times. He glared at the closed door. Whichever of the two it chanced to be, he had no interest in their shop worn, calculated charms. She would leave if he didn't answer. Then he would go up and find... The door opened. His jaw dropped in outraged disbelief. By God, he'd give the impudent hussy a set-down! How dare she invade his—?

A small figure in a shabby dress slipped into the room and shut the door carefully.

'*Selina?*' He couldn't quite believe it, even with the sudden, and distracting, pounding of his blood.

'Y...yes, my lord.'

The whisper barely reached him. He got the distinct impression that she was holding herself in the room by sheer force of will.

'What do you want, Selina?' Even as he asked the question he knew that there was only one thing she could have possibly come for. Perhaps her initial refusal had been no more than teasing. Perhaps she had thought to get better terms by holding him off a little and his imminent departure had forced her hand. Triumph and desire in equal parts stormed through him.

His conscience twitched, suggesting that he ought to mention the possibility of becoming his aunt's companion. His eyes roved the shapeless dress, remembering the soft curves it concealed. His conscience didn't stand a chance.

She had come to him of her own free will. She was his. Or she would be very soon. Completely. Was she trembling? In the dying light of the fire and a branch of candles he could not be sure.

Her voice came out strongly enough this time. 'I have a proposition for you, Lord Blakehurst.'

Oh? Hadn't *he* propositioned *her*? She hesitated and he waved for her to continue. 'Go on. I'm listening.'

'If your offer still stands, I should like to be your mistress for three months…'

'Three months?' How the devil did *she* know how long his various affairs usually lasted?

She bit her lip. 'Is…is that too long? I realise you probably don't really want me as a mistress for that long, but I thought you might consent to take me for that time to give me a start. After all, your reputation… I thought you could teach me what I need to know…to attract the right sort of attention. Then some other gentleman might…when you tire of me…' Her voice trailed off.

When he tired of her? Realising that he hadn't had any-thing like enough brandy, Max took another gulp. He'd had no idea his reputation had descended to these levels. An ap-prentice mistress, no less. He tried to ignore the ache in his groin, which urged him to get on with the indentures. Fast. And disabuse her of her ideas about *other gentlemen.*

'I see,' he said. 'It might take a little longer than three months.' A damn sight longer if he had his way. For once in his life, he could not see the end of an affair in its beginning. *Other* gentlemen, indeed!

'It might?'

'Oh, yes,' he said. 'Almost definitely. But, of course, there is one thing that would have to be ascertained before I have my solicitor draw up an agreement between us.' A couple of things, actually, like whether or not she really wanted to take this step. But he wasn't telling her that.

'An agreement?'

'Of course. That's how these things are done.'

'Oh. Is it? What would have to be ascertained first?'

He smiled and set down his glass on the bedside table. 'Whether or not you can please me in bed, my dear.'

Watching her closely, he wondered if she were about to flee. God knew he'd been blunt enough. He could see the tension in her body and longed to ease it, to take her into his arms and kiss all her fears away, but it had to be her choice. Faringdon might have taken her innocence, but he would have no part in forcing her any further down this road if she did not wish it. She had refused him very plainly. Perhaps she had meant it, perhaps not. He had to be quite sure.

'You...you do not really want me, do you?' The question ripped into him and he saw her turn to the door. Belatedly he realised that his attempt to warn her, to ensure she knew exactly what she was doing, had shamed her.

'Selina!'

She stopped and looked back, her cheeks scarlet. 'My lord.'

He fought for the right words. 'It's not that. I want you, but when I asked you before, you refused. I won't force you. You must come to me. Of your own free will.'

She took one step towards the bed and halted again.

'That's it,' he said softly. 'Come to me. I will not touch you until you lie naked beside me in this bed.'

A shudder went through Verity as she heard his invitation and understood what it meant. She would have to strip in front of him. Take all her clothes off and walk naked to his bed. And in doing so she would cross the line from respectability to the *demi-mondaine*. She would be an outcast from decent society.

What will have changed? You are already outcast. You're little better than a servant. Worse, in fact, since you don't get paid.

Still she hesitated. She could feel his eyes on her, knew that the choice, and responsibility, were hers and hers alone. No one would be hurt or injured by her actions except herself. And this way she would wrest back control of her life.

Her hands shaking, she fumbled with the first button of her bodice. Her fingers seemed made of wood. They slipped and fumbled, but at last it was undone. Swallowing, she looked down. There were a lot more buttons. A small sound from the bed caught her attention. Fleetingly she looked up and her fingers froze on the second button. He had stripped off his waistcoat and was engaged in hauling his shirt off over his head.

Verity's mouth dried at the sight of his heavily muscled body. Firelight slid and gleamed on the hard curves. She had never realised that a man's body was so different, so very beautiful. Fascinated, she stared at the broad shoulders, the powerful chest with its dusting of curling hair. That was startling enough, but what really surprised her was the sudden urge she felt to touch him and discover all the textures of that magnificent body.

A soft chuckle shocked her eyes back to his face as she realised she had been mesmerised. Her mouth dried out even further as she met his hot gaze.

'Don't forget your own buttons, my sweet.' His voice was full of heated intent. 'I had no intention of distracting you.'

She couldn't do it. Not with his eyes on hers like that. Temptation and warning in one fierce blaze, they threatened to consume her. She shut her own eyes and forced her fingers to obey her. A second button, then another, and another. Button after button, until the dress hung loosely about her. She stood, uncertain what to do next, agonisingly conscious of the unseen presence on the bed, aware of his gaze still burning into her.

'Push it off your shoulders, let it fall to your waist.'

She wouldn't be naked. Quite. She still had her chemise. And a petticoat. Shivering, she obeyed, feeling her nipples tighten in the sudden chill. The dress fell about her hips, caught by their gentle swell.

'You won't be cold for long,' came a murmur. 'I'll warm you.' It sounded like a promise. A moment's taut silence. Then, 'Now push it off your hips. To the floor.'

The heat in his voice sent tremors rippling through her.

Eyes still tightly closed, she hesitated a moment, then drew a deep breath and obeyed. Never had she been so aware of her underclothes. Her skin shivered into life, conscious of every seam, the position of every carefully sewn patch.

'Untie your petticoat.' Abrupt and harsh, his voice froze her fingers and she struggled with the tie, but at last it was done. Yet she hesitated, clutching it in place. She couldn't quite believe that she had stripped off her dress at a man's command and was about to remove her underwear.

'Let it go.'

She opened her eyes slowly. He had stripped completely and lay propped on one elbow. At least she assumed he had stripped completely. She gulped. He had the bedclothes pulled up to his waist and she couldn't imagine that he had his evening breeches on. His eyes were on her, hot and intent. And there were his breeches on the floor.

Oh, dear God. What had she agreed to?

'Let it go,' he repeated.

You have agreed to be his mistress. In a moment you will lie in that bed with him and become his.

Shaking, she released her grip and felt the petticoat slide down her legs to pool around her feet. Her chemise was next. Taking a deep breath, she reached for the drawstring…

'No. I'll deal with that.'

Swallowing she met his gaze. 'But…'

'Come to me now.'

The space between them gaped. She had no idea how her trembling legs would get her there, but she was certain the gap was not nearly wide enough. Or much too wide. She shut her eyes again. At least she still had her chemise.

Wildly aware of soft carpet cushioning her cold, bare feet, she went to him. One momentous step at a time. Until her thighs hit the bed. A large warm hand touched her, curved over the soft skin of her hip, shaping it, learning it. She stood and shivered under the touch of his caress. Then she felt the hand slide over her bottom, drawing her inexorably closer, until, to avoid falling on to the bed, she knelt on it.

'Open your eyes again, my darling,' he whispered. 'Don't hide from me. Come. Trust me.' His hand continued to stroke, teasing her to life, demanding nothing.

Trust me.

Slowly she opened her eyes and looked into his.

Chapter Five

Max thought he might break apart at what he saw there. Fear and desire warred, but behind them both he saw a blinding trust. Not otherwise would she have made herself so vulnerable, stripping in front of him, obeying his hoarse commands and finally coming to him.

Beautiful women had stripped for him before with an expertise calculated to inflame a man, but nothing had ever stirred his blood so much as seeing those slender, shaking fingers struggling with her buttons. The sight had left him burning, consumed by the urge to get out of the bed, sweep her into his arms and finish the job for her. He hadn't been able to wait for her to get the chemise off.

He lowered his gaze to her mouth. Soft and pink, the underlip was gripped between her teeth to still its trembling. He doubted she even knew she was doing it.

God help him, but she was lovely. The chemise was old and worn, its washing soft fabric clinging lovingly to her delicate curves. Her breasts lifted against the thin material and his blood heated at the sight of the darker, tightened nipples. So sweet. Soon, very soon, he'd have her under him, have that soft flesh in his mouth. Desire became a savage ache in his loins, screaming for release. Unable to help himself, he reached out and cupped the underswell of one breast, passing his thumb over the hardened peak.

He felt her shivering and understood. Fear. Not passion. Not yet. Grimly he reminded himself that she had probably lost her virginity in pain and terrified humiliation. Even if Godfrey *had* forced a *yes* from her, what had happened amounted to rape. The thought sickened him.

His conscience made one last stand. 'Selina, you're sure?'

Huge dark eyes met his. 'I…yes.' Then, a shaken whisper. 'Yes. I want this. I want *you*.'

Max felt every breath shiver through her. She had come to him willingly, trusting him. His own need could wait. It wasn't going anywhere. And it was as nothing beside the need to please her, to give her the tenderness and gentleness she deserved.

'My lord?' Her breath broke on her lips as he continued to stroke and caress her breast. Yearning shimmered through her in response, a rippling tide of need that spread out from his knowing fingers in a wave of aching heat, melting her very bones.

The hand stilled and she shifted, pressing herself against it pleadingly.

'Max,' he corrected her softly. 'Here, in bed, I am Max. Your lover. *My lord* has no place here. Only Max and his sweetheart. Come to me.'

His smile drew her heart from her breast, yet behind the tenderness she could sense something tightly leashed. He had asked for her trust. And he had forced nothing on her. She knew that, if at any moment she had changed her mind, she could have fled. He would not have lifted a finger to stop her. Godfrey, she knew, would have stripped and taken her in the time it would take for her to unbutton her dress.

He sat up and reached for her. Hard arms closed about her, drawing her down against his body in an intimate embrace. She lay half under him, surrounded, caged by his strength. Her vulnerability should have terrified her. Yet now she was here she felt safe, protected. Instinctively she put her arms around him, pressing herself closer and lifting her mouth to his.

He took it gently, completely. His tongue traced her lips in a velvet caress even as she sighed and opened her mouth to him. He deepened the kiss, exploring the sweetness of her mouth, tasting, devouring, even as his loins shifted against her in barely controlled urgency.

Breathing hard, he lifted his mouth from hers and pulled away a little. If he didn't... When had it been like this? So wild with need that he felt as though he were on fire with it. She lay beneath him, soft breasts lifting under the chemise at each breath. Slowly her eyes opened.

'My...Max? Is...is something wrong?'

He stared at her, speechless for a moment. Then shook his head. Nothing had ever been so right. He stroked a vagrant curl back from her temple. 'You're too lovely,' he murmured, kissing her gently, revelling in the hesitant response. 'That's all. Just relax.'

Her hair was still confined in the rigid bun. Desperate to slow himself down, to reassure her, he removed pin after pin, releasing the dusky cloud of curls to fan out over the pillow. Smiling, he drew his fingers through the tumbled silk. Cool fire caressed him. 'Beautiful,' he whispered.

With shaking fingers he released the drawstring of her chemise and pushed it down to expose her breasts. Then he lowered his head and did what he had been fantasising about— drew the velvet soft flesh deep inside his mouth.

He felt the shock jolt through her, heard her startled cry. Shuddering with the need to take her, he forced himself to be gentle, tender, patient. His hands shook uncontrollably as he removed the chemise and explored her trembling body, caressing every curve, waist, hip and sweetly rounded thigh.

Urgency exploded inside her as his hands shaped and learned her. All she could do was hold him to her as he lavished pleasure on her with mouth and hands. His hands.

She couldn't think, couldn't begin to comprehend the power they held as they stroked and caressed.

Gentle, deft fingers trailed fire over her thighs, brushed over the soft curls that shielded her secrets. She gasped at the sensation, fire and need blossoming up from his touch, and felt him smile against her neck. Those wicked fingers returned, probing lightly.

'Soon,' he whispered. 'Soon. Let me touch you.' His hand cupped her and his fingers pressed lower.

Aching, burning with need, she shifted her legs apart slightly. The teasing, searching fingers slid between her thighs, probed further and found soft, wet heat. Lightning lanced through her as he stroked with shattering intimacy. She cried out, twisting against him, frantic for more, hardly knowing what she wanted, only certain that she must have it, or die.

Max did know what she wanted. Dizzy with his own need, he resisted the urge to give in, to roll her beneath him and spread her thighs wide so that he could take her. Now. Groaning, he reached for control. He took her mouth again, drinking her cries as he slid one finger into the entrance of her body.

Sweet honey spilled over his fingers in searing welcome, tearing at his restraint. Again and again he stroked, torturing himself. He could wait no longer. She felt so good, so hotly welcoming.

Releasing her mouth, he said hoarsely, 'You're so sweet, so hot. Open to me.' His hands were on her thighs, urging them apart, even as he rolled on top of her, taking her mouth inexorably.

Shock held her motionless as she felt his weight, his strength, felt the hard, urgent pressure of his hunger against her and understood the fierce promise of his kiss. He stopped instantly and his hands rose to frame her face.

'Sweetheart.' He released her mouth and his lips feathered

over her face. 'It's all right. I'm not going to hurt you. I swear it.' Then, in a hard, strained voice, 'Do you want me to stop?'

He would have stopped. Even now. The knowledge dissolved the last of her fears. 'No. No. Please don't stop,' she whispered.

A little of his weight eased off her and he reached between their bodies again, touching her, teasing her, whispering her sweetness against her lips. She cried out wildly, lifting against him in desperate pleading, all her doubts drowning in the rising wave of passion and in the certainty of his gentleness.

With a groan he positioned himself, took her mouth in ravishing possession and thrust deep into her body.

She lay quite still, clinging to him, dazed at the sudden shocking pain of his penetration, dazed at the feel of him sunk deep inside her, stretching her, impaling her. But even as she choked back a sob, the pain eased. His strength and heat possessed her, protected her, inside and out. A gentle hand framed her face as his mouth plundered hers and the blinding pleasure returned as he slid one hand under her hips to tilt her towards him. She gasped in delight as he sank further into her. Shuddering, he pressed even deeper, claiming her completely. Then he began to move powerfully, rocking rhythmically and her body melted, joy searing the memory of pain.

She was dying, close to exploding. Her body had become some winged creature, still earthbound, struggling for release even as he slowed his rhythm. She wept her protest and felt him groan as he lifted over her to thrust deeper and harder.

He took her to the very edge, where pleasure became an agony of need, where the abyss beckoned in tongues of flame. He held her there mercilessly, until she broke, shattering as her body took flight and soared. And she felt him thrust deeper than ever and fly with her until the fire consumed them both.

Max stared up into the shadowed canopy of the bed, watching the flickering shadows cast by the dying fire. He had never felt anything like this. As though he had just taken vows. As though he had pledged his life to something. God help him, if he weren't such a cynical, experienced rake, he'd swear he was falling in love.

With his mistress? He hadn't known this soul-stealing intimacy existed.

A soft, trusting weight snuggled warmly against his left side. A silken arm lay across his stomach, satin limbs entwined with his and her cheek was pressed to his chest, near where her last sleepy kisses had fallen. His heart shook. She had fallen asleep kissing him. When had that happened before?

He had a guilty feeling that he usually fell asleep first after bedding a woman. Never before had he lain there, holding a girl while she cuddled up to him, pressing clumsy kisses on his chest as she dozed off. He doubted that any of his previous mistresses would have even thought of kissing him as they fell asleep. Come to think of it, he doubted *she* had even thought of it—she'd simply done it, as though she couldn't bear to let him go, as though she couldn't get close enough to him, as though she had to touch him or die.

That had been over an hour ago. His arms tightened protectively. Sleep was impossible. He wanted her again. He'd wanted her almost immediately, but she'd been so sleepy and she'd seemed so dazed by their lovemaking. And now she was sound asleep. In his arms.

It was almost as fierce a pleasure as loving her had been. It burnt deeply into him, because he knew that in snuggling up to him, in kissing and touching him, she hadn't *wanted* him. Not in the usual sense of the word. He knew he'd satisfied her—no man could have felt those shivering pulses and not known it. She had wanted *him*. His warmth, his arms. She had simply wanted to be close to him. No one had ever wanted *him* before. No one had ever trusted him so deeply.

Three months. He smiled to himself. There wasn't a chance

in hell that he'd let her go after three months. Which brought him to the question of where she should live. He kept a small house in London for his mistresses. There he could visit them discreetly. He couldn't imagine Selina there. Not in that house. It seemed…wrong, tawdry. He'd have to think of something else.

A soft sigh breathed against him and the warm weight shifted slightly.

'Max?' The lightest of whispers, as though she feared disturbing him. It was more than enough for Max.

'Yes,' he breathed. And rolled her beneath him again.

Verity had awoken to a sense of safety, of rightness, of warmth and tenderness wrapping her against a hard masculine body. She drew the musky, male scent deep. His name breathed from her, part of her now, and she felt his arms tighten as he answered, taking her beneath him again.

Possessive, urgent hands roamed her body, caressing her to heated life. His mouth took hers even as one powerful thigh eased between hers, opening her. Her body softened instantly, melting in response. She knew a moment's tension as he entered her still-tender body, but then he was deep within and delight claimed her.

Max framed her face with his hands, holding her still for his kiss as he slid into the tight, welcoming heat of her body. He groaned, trying to slow down. He hadn't meant to take her this fast, but he was beyond control. And each movement of his body drew those soft, aching cries of pleasure from her, pleading for more, not less. It had never been like this. He made love to her with a burning intensity that he didn't even begin to understand. How could he? He had never even imagined such a thing.

The fire had died completely when he awoke again, aching with the fierceness of his need. She lay secure in his arms, her breath a softly sighed caress on his skin, silky curls spread across his chest. Her body had moulded to him in total relaxation, every curve fitting against him in heart-shaking intimacy. One leg was curled up, the rounded thigh lying over his.

There was no way in the world he would take her to London. He knew now where he would take her. There was a house on his estate where she could live. It was quite isolated, high on the Downs, but she would not be lonely. He intended being with her frequently. And he would settle the lease of the house on her for her life. Along with an annuity. She would be safe then. He buried his face in her hair, breathing deep the scent of warm, sweet femininity.

Unable to help himself, he stroked the softness of her exposed breast, felt his heart clench as she sighed and shifted in her sleep, nestling closer.

Never had it been like this. Something was very different. And until he worked out exactly what it was, he had no intention of letting her go.

The stirring household jolted Verity fully awake just before dawn. She lay quietly, breathing in the warm, musky scent of her lover. Soon she would have to get up, but not quite yet. The feeling of being so safe, so cared for, was too precious to waste.

Would it always be like that? Her body tingled at the memory of his mouth on her breasts, his tender hands teasing her to life and awareness. The soul-shaking moment when he had possessed her completely, taking her virginity. She would never be able to tell him that. He thought Godfrey had ruined her. Otherwise he might not have been willing to take her. She didn't want him to feel guilty. She knew, to her core, his sense of honour.

She also knew that she ought to feel guilty, terrified of the consequences of her actions. Her choice. Her responsibility. She had come to him and offered herself freely. The world would condemn her without hesitation, but she could not regret it. For five years she had dreamed of him, imagining

impossible happy endings to her nightmare: that he would
come for her one day and ask her to be his. That he would
love her and protect her. Half a dream was better than nothing. He had offered to protect her.

She lay still, enveloped in his warmth, secure in his arms.
Surely it was better to have given herself freely than to have
been forced into submission to Godfrey's lust. A shiver rippled through her at the thought and she felt Max's arms
tighten around her, heard a sleepy grunt.

She had to leave. Quickly. Before a housemaid came in to
do the room. If she delayed any longer, she would be caught
and there would be the very devil to pay.

Max lay dozing in the early morning light, part of him
immeasurably content—and part of him aware that something
was missing. He felt incomplete in some fundamental way.
With a sigh he rolled over and reached for… An empty bed
was all he found. Abruptly he realised what, or rather who,
was missing. Where the devil was she? He fell back with a
groan. This was not his house, of course. The last thing Selina
would want was to be caught in his bed, even if they were
leaving today. Come to think of it, she might not even know
they were leaving. He didn't think he'd mentioned it last
night.

Last night… Linking his arms behind his head, he lay back
and smiled reminiscently. She'd been as sweet and responsive
as he'd imagined. No. She'd been sweeter. He had never
known a woman to respond and give herself with such utter
trust. His whole body hardened at the memory of the tender
body that had lain beneath him: the soft cries of feminine
need aroused and fulfilled that had burnt him to his soul, the
shivering completion that had finally broken his control and
brought him his own release.

He thought he knew now what was different. Women had
always given him pleasure, but never before had he thought
a woman had given herself. Lord, he'd never realised that a

woman *could* give herself so completely. It had never been more than an exchange of pleasure. But now... The sooner he arose and got on the road back to London, the sooner he could have Selina in his bed again.

In his life. He knew now what he wanted. He couldn't marry. His word had been given. But he could still have Selina to care for, a family to protect. She would be *his*. His only. *That* was the difference. She was his. To protect. Care for. *Love?*

He flung back the covers and swung his legs out of bed. Harding would be in soon anyway, so... *What the devil was that?*

The small, dark stain in the centre of the lower sheet lay there accusingly. He sat down on the edge of the bed, staring, shock white hot in every vein. It wasn't true. It *couldn't* be true. The evidence before his eyes assured him that it was. Dazedly he thought back. How the devil could he have missed something like that?

You weren't expecting it. You thought Faringdon had had her. And she certainly didn't say anything.

Ignoring the aching desire in his loins, he relived the moment he had taken her. She'd been so soft and pliant beneath him as he rolled on top of her. Her mouth a sweetness of fire under his as he spread her legs apart. He frowned. Yes, she'd stiffened as she felt him pressing against her. Natural enough if Faringdon had abused her. She had begged him not to stop when he offered. He had teased her a little more with his fingers until she cried out, lifting against him, as urgent as he.

He'd taken her mouth and body in the same searing instant, driving deep. So urgently he hadn't realised her innocence. That cry his kiss had absorbed... He winced. Thinking it a cry of joy, of pleasure, he'd pressed even deeper, claiming everything she had to give. He shuddered at the realisation that it had probably been a cry of pain, that whatever pleasure he had given her later, at that moment, he had hurt her. And he had not stopped to ease her pain. He hadn't even realised.

Why hadn't she told him? He had made it clear enough that he thought Faringdon had stripped her of her innocence. Had she thought he wouldn't touch her if he knew her to be a virgin? He took leave to doubt that he would have been capable of quite that much disinterested chivalry. But at least he could have controlled himself and not taken her more than once. He hoped.

His fists clenched on the tumbled bedding. Why *hadn't* Faringdon taken her? What had held him back? The girl had spirit, yes. She had marked the distempered cub's face the other night, but when all was said and done, she was not very big. And there had been no one to defend her. She could not possibly have held out against Faringdon if he had really decided to force her. Why hadn't he?

Max had no hesitation in dismissing the possibility of disinterested chivalry in the case of Godfrey. His own might be dubious. Godfrey Faringdon probably couldn't even define the phrase. It was in the highest degree unlikely that he would ever have been held to account for the rape of a nursery governess. She would have been just one more ruined girl, turned off without a character.

The faint click of the door opening brought him up short. Prudently he pulled the covers back over himself. And back over that telltale stain.

Harding came in and blinked. Then his eyes took on an obliging glassiness as he studiously avoided looking at the devastation of the bedding, his master's clothes scattered around the floor—and closed his mind to the fact that his aforesaid master had, apparently, slept stark naked.

'Good morning, my lord,' said Harding, as he retrieved my lord's shirt, apparently without noticing it. 'I trust you slept…ah…that is to say, that you had a satisfactory…' His façade cracked slightly. He shut up and folded the shirt instead.

'Thank you, Harding.' Max left it at that. 'Perhaps you might pass me my dressing gown.'

'Certainly, my lord.'

'"Sir" will do,' growled Max. He had been 'Sir' to Harding for too many years to change now.

'Yes, sir,' said Harding. He handed the dressing gown to Max and said, 'I know you wished to leave by eight, sir, but in the light of information come to hand, I've taken the liberty of making that nine. Thinking it would give you a bit more time, sir.'

Max knew his man too well to bother with a reprimand. He merely asked, 'What the devil for?'

'Well, what you said last night, about the Colonel's daughter being dead? She's not.'

'What?'

'That's right, sir,' said Harding. 'Been making my own inquiries, I have. In the servants' hall. Asked about her, you see. Thought it might help. Well, they clammed up, the lot of 'em. Wouldn't say a word about Miss Scott. Except one of the maids, Sukey. And she got a clout on the lug for speaking out of turn. But I managed to get her alone last night after the rest had gone to bed. Wanted to find out what happened to the lass. In the end she told me the truth. Miss Scott's not dead, but they treat her like a dog…'

He continued, but Max didn't hear any more. Knowledge and understanding hit him simultaneously, along with flaring rage. He now knew why Faringdon would have hesitated to force 'Selina' and why she had not told him she was a virgin. He'd taken the bait, hook, line and several pounds' worth of sinker. Caught by the oldest trick known to woman.

His father's voice echoed mercilessly in his mind… *Max, if you must fire a pistol—remember the ball has to go somewhere. The consequences are your responsibility…*

He focused back on what Harding was saying. 'So she's here in the house, sir. Shall I—?'

'Don't worry, Harding,' grated Max. 'I know exactly

where to find Miss Verity Scott. And I suggest you get a message down to the stables for my curricle to be sent around immediately.' He found a purse of money. 'Take this. Book a seat on the mail for yourself. Sorry, Harding, but three's a crowd. I have a great deal to say to Miss Verity Scott!'

Harding gulped audibly as he took the money. 'Yes, sir. Will there be anything else, sir?'

'No.' Max dragged on clothes with scant regard for fashion beyond getting them on right side out. When he got his hands on Miss Verity Scott, he thought he might just wring her neck. After which he'd teach her a salutary lesson on the perils of deception and cheating.

He'd fired a pistol. Now he had to face the consequences of missing his aim.

He stalked into the bleak, shabby little chamber without bothering to knock. 'Good morning, Miss Sc—'

The icy greeting froze on his lips in response to the chill emptiness of the room. Nothing. Nothing and no one. The room was empty of all save the narrow, uninviting little bed and—the irony nearly choked him—a very battered campaign chest. The bottom half sat under the window, the top half at the foot of the bed.

Savagely he stared down at the painted letters on the top. Faded and worn, the name of Scott was yet visible. And it was obvious enough where someone had scratched out the first part of a W to leave a V. Ye gods! He'd sat on the curst thing the other night. And all the while the little wretch must have been weaving her plans.

He swore. Why couldn't she have just *told* him? Trusted him. Surely she must have known he wouldn't refuse to help her? That he would have forced the Faringdons to treat her decently, provide for her properly. Dash it all! He'd have provided for her himself if necessary! But no! Trust had little to do with it. She'd decided to chance a throw for the lot— himself included.

She had known perfectly well that she could trust him. She had known who he was from the start. Perhaps even before she tumbled into his arms the other night. He had to acknowledge that she'd stalked her quarry brilliantly. She'd cast her lure and played the fish with consummate skill. He'd been landed so neatly he hadn't even felt the hook.

A startled gasp brought him around, lifting his gaze from the chest. Even now that he knew the truth, it was impossible not to admire her acting as she stared in apparent horror at the painted accusation. His mouth twisted at the blanched cheeks. Perhaps she was genuinely horrified. She couldn't have meant to spring her trap quite this soon.

Wide grey eyes lifted to his. Pain stabbed at him, swiftly buried in icy rage.

'Good morning. I came up to see if there was anything you wished to take with you.'

Her mouth trembled and he fought down a surge of heat as he remembered that same mouth held captive beneath his, open and vulnerable. Pain flared again. He'd thought what they had found special. Damn it! He'd thought *her* special. That he would be able to... *No!* He wouldn't think of it. All the time it had been no more than a honeyed trap.

'I—'

He cut her off. 'Just the campaign chest, then. I'll ask Harding—you *do* remember Harding?—to bring it with him on the mail. We'd best hurry. Explanations are so awkward, are they not, Miss Scott?'

Miss Scott...

The chilly words lashed her. He knew then. His contempt flayed her. An implacable judge had replaced the tender, impassioned lover. And she had been found wanting.

'You...you don't understand...' She had not lied. Not really. Her name changed nothing. Her situation remained the same whether she was Selina or Verity. Or did it? Who had gone to him? Selina, or Verity?

'Oh, I think I understand well enough. Now, hurry. We must be going.'

The meaning of his words finally sank in. 'Then…you'll still take me?' Was that relief, churning her stomach? Or fear? She would still escape. But her hands shook. Had Selina become his mistress, or Verity? To be his mistress as the anonymous Selina was one thing. To be his mistress as Verity Scott, while he judged her with those cold, lambent eyes, was quite another.

'Oh, yes. I'll take you.' His voice cut like a knife. 'After all, with a little schooling you will warm my bed quite satisfactorily. You're eager enough at least. I'll say that for you.'

She felt cold, clammy with horror at the amused boredom in his voice. She had thought, when he made love to her again, that he wanted her, desired her. Now the truth broke over her in a bitter wave. She hadn't satisfied him. But, now he knew the truth, she had disgusted him with her wanton behaviour.

Never in her life had she thought she would say it, but, 'Can't…can't you forget I'm…I'm…*her* and just…just think of me as…Selina?' She couldn't even say her true name. Not with those eyes scorching into her. Not with haughty disdain curving the mouth that had loved her so tenderly. Not when she remembered the tenderness he had shown Selina. His sweetheart.

A harsh laugh broke from him. 'No doubt your father would prefer that, but I'm afraid it's a little late for self-delusion. Get a cloak on and come with me.'

'No.' The refusal was out before she'd even known it was there. She couldn't go with him. Not now. Not as Verity Scott. Not as his whore. And she sensed that was how he thought of her now. Selina's fall he could understand and sympathise with, but for the gently bred Miss Scott to do what she had done was unforgivable. Selina was no more.

'No? May one ask why not?'

'I...I won't be...' She stopped, a blush mantling her cheeks.

'My whore? You're that already, my dear. Quite willingly. I made sure of that. Now come. I have ordered my carriage and I would like to be in London by nightfall. I have our marriage to arrange.'

Everything went misty, colours swirled together dizzily as she clutched at the doorframe. 'What...what did you say?' It came out as a whisper.

'I wish to be in London by nightfall. It's only seventy miles and—'

'No. The bit about our marriage...' Her voice failed. If anything, the disgust in his eyes deepened.

'Oh, for God's sake! Spare me any more play acting, girl! I had enough of that last night. And very affecting it was. But morning is here now, although I doubt you intended to enlighten me quite this soon. I play by the rules. You will marry me as fast as I can get a special licence and find a parson.'

Chapter Six

'No!' Horror tore the exclamation from Verity. Sick and shaking, she stared up at him as the golden eyes narrowed to blazing slits.

'No?' Velvet soft, his voice seared her. 'You lied to me about your name, you tricked me into taking your virginity... Exactly what did you expect of me when I discovered the truth?

'Let me make my position quite plain, Miss Scott: I had no intention of ever marrying, but then neither did I have the intention of taking the maidenhead of my late commander's only daughter. Or anybody's maidenhead for that matter. My opinion of *you* may leave a great deal to be desired, but I have enough respect for your father's memory to make you my wife rather than my whore.'

His lip curled. 'At any rate, I have enough respect for him to attempt to repair the situation. Whether or not my efforts are successful will rest with you.'

'I don't want to marry you,' she whispered. It was a lie. She did want to marry him. But not like this—with his every look and word branding her a whore, a despicable little bitch who had schemed and plotted to trap a wealthy husband.

He laughed harshly. 'I dare say you don't. Not now that you've realised I am not so easily manipulated and controlled as you might have hoped. You've made my bed. Now you shall lie in it.'

'You don't understand!' she cried. 'I never intended you to even know who I was! I never intended to—'

His harsh expletive shocked her. 'Likewise, rubbish,' he snarled. 'There are two possibilities: either you intended to trap me into marriage, or you intended to be my whore.'

'Stop saying that!' she cried. Bad enough her own conscience screaming at her, but to hear him constantly saying it was like a knife thrust, twisting deeper every time.

'Neither intent is honourable.' His hard voice overrode hers. 'Frankly I'm not sure which disgusts me more, but that changes nothing. You will marry me. And by God, you will learn to conduct yourself as befits a lady and your father's daughter! At least I can do that much for him.'

With a sickening lurch, Verity realised that it didn't matter whether he believed she had intended to trap him or not. Whatever he thought, he still despised her, thought her a disgrace to her name. It was not her *per se* whose good name he wished to protect, but her father's. And, perhaps to a lesser extent, his own.

What had she expected?

His voice shattered her thoughts. 'Don't waste time, Miss Scott. You're coming with me, even if I have to drag you kicking and screaming from the house.'

By the time Max's hard-driven horses reached Highgate Hill late that afternoon and he saw London spread out below, he had long since come to terms with the fact that he had made a complete and utter fool of himself. There was only himself to blame for allowing desire to rule him the previous night. If he had listened to that warning voice telling him to take her to Almeria and find her a respectable position, he wouldn't be in this predicament. He'd taken his pleasure. Now he had to take the consequences. Marriage.

His betrothed sat silently beside him. He had not heard a

word out of her since lunchtime except for *no, thank you* to the sandwiches offered her at the Green Man in Barnet, where they made their last change. He frowned. She should have eaten. She had scarcely touched her lunch and she was quite thin enough already.

She had said nothing when it came on to rain and he wrapped her tattered old cloak more securely about her, simply nodded to acknowledge his action. Apparently she didn't even possess a bonnet. She sat beside him in utter silence with her dark curls becoming more and more untidy.

Didn't most females chatter? Wouldn't any normal woman be trying to placate his fury and twist him around her little finger by now? Not Miss Verity Scott, apparently. *She* was indulging in a fit of the sulks and for the most part appeared to find the scenery on the opposite side of the curricle fascinating.

'Is it very much further, my lord?' The small, tired voice took him by surprise. He glanced at her, but she was staring straight ahead, her face hidden by her untidy hair.

'Oh, you can still speak, can you?' He couldn't help the bite of sarcasm in his voice. Especially since his fingers itched to slide into the tumbling curls and push them back. He remembered how they had felt spilling over his chest. Cool, burning silk. His grip tightened on the reins and his horses steadied at the sudden pressure.

She turned away again. 'I wasn't aware I had anything to say that you were prepared to listen to, my lord. Is it very much further?' The voice sounded odd, slightly strained.

He shrugged. 'An hour or so. Hungry, are you? You should have accepted the sandwiches.'

She said nothing and he told himself that she deserved it. That to extend her fit of temper to refusing food was too ridiculous to deserve any sympathy. His conscience suggested that he was being unpleasantly vindictive, that there was little reason in marrying the chit unless he meant to do better than this.

Curse it! How could he ever have any sort of trust or affection for her when she had trapped him? And as for her ridiculous claim that she now didn't wish to marry him! What nonsense!

A movement beside him caught his attention. Miss Scott appeared to be wiping her eye. Wonderful! Now she was going to cry at him. Cynically he waited to hear the inevitable sob. And waited.

With a curse he pulled up the horses and set the brake. There were a few things that they might as well have clear between them right now. Such as that he would not be manipulated by a few spurious tears. He'd had quite enough of that in his life, thanks very much. Setting his hands to her shoulders, he swung her around to face him. And froze as she jerked her face away. He had seen enough.

Her eyes were red and swollen, her cheeks stained with tears. He could even see the marks where her underlip had been gripped between her teeth. All he had intended to say to her fled in the face of one scorching question: for how long had she sat there beside him, weeping silently? He hadn't even known a woman *could* cry silently. How did she intend to manipulate him if he couldn't hear her?

And she looked exhausted, her face white and the grey eyes wreathed with shadows. Yet she had been sitting spear straight beside him. What to say? Anger at her still gripped him, but he reached out to put his arm around her shoulders, to draw her to him. He couldn't help it. His whole angry, confused being cried out in protest before those shattered, reddened eyes.

She jerked back from him. Again.

Without a word, he released the brake and set the horses in motion. Of all the things he resented about Verity Scott at that moment, the most excoriating was that she had made him feel like the lowest of scoundrels.

Never before had Max driven into London delighted to know that his Aunt Almeria was in residence. Usually it took an outright command on her part to get him over her threshold. On this particular evening he pulled up outside her Grosvenor Square townhouse voluntarily.

Verity didn't move. She had been asleep on his shoulder for the last half-hour. He doubted that she had even realised when she finally sagged against him. And she felt right there. Just as she had the night before when she had lain in his arms...

She deceived you. Trapped you. All that sweetness is no more than honey to bait the victim.

It would only be safe to enjoy the sweetness if he remembered never to trust it again. Remembered that it was all an act; that given a chance, she would manipulate him.

Twenty minutes later he took his leave of his startled aunt and sleepy betrothed. Mounting into the curricle, he acknowledged that he could have handled the situation with more grace. That depositing a sleeping girl on the drawing-room sofa, announcing her as his intended bride and that he would be back with the special licence as soon as possible—and in the meantime would Almeria kindly organise a suitable wardrobe at his expense—might not have been the most tactful way of presenting Verity to his aunt.

He had no time to waste being tactful with Almeria. His marriage was none of her business. His brother, on the other hand, had every right to know before Almeria managed to spread the news all over town, which she would do before midnight even if she had to invite herself out for dinner.

He signalled for the footman to stand away from the horses' heads as an elegantly gowned female figure appeared in the doorway.

'*Max!*' it shrieked.

Pretending not to have heard, Max gave his tired horses the office and set off down the street at a spanking trot. God only knew what Almeria wanted to know, but Max was only too happy to leave it in the hands of the Almighty.

All he wanted was to get home. And forget how Verity had clung to him even as he settled her on the sofa still half-asleep. He bit his lip to think of how exhausted she must have been to sleep on his shoulder like that, insensible to the roar of London's traffic and the jolting of the carriage over the cobbles. Something within him rebelled at the thought of leaving her with Almeria.

He hardened his heart. She had trapped him. And, in doing so, she had put him in the position where he would have to break a promise. Several promises. One to his brother, one to their mother, and one to himself.

His bride would have to learn how to conduct herself with the dignity and discretion expected of a Countess. Almeria was one of the *ton*'s highest sticklers. Who better to teach the new Lady Blakehurst how to go on?

A small, apologetic voice suggested, *Yourself, perhaps?*

His jaw set harder. As far as he could see, there was only one way that he could salvage something of the promises he was about to break. And spending overmuch time with his bride would merely remind him of all he could not have.

Max entered the library and flinched as Richard looked up, patently surprised.

'Well, about time! What on earth did you find to entertain you at the Faringdons for so long? I expected you back days ago.'

Max watched guiltily as Richard levered himself out of the chair and limped over to a side table. Half an hour. Half an hour at birth to make the difference between them. Not if he could help it. 'Something came up,' he said. 'Everything all right here?'

'Why wouldn't it be?' asked Richard, pouring a glass of brandy. 'Are you feeling quite the thing, Max? You look odd. Brandy?'

Max tugged at his cravat, which felt abominably tight.

'Yes. Yes, please.' He went over and took the glass from Richard. 'How's... how's your leg?'

His brother stared. 'My leg?'

'Yes. Your leg. The left one. The one I nearly—'

'What the deuce brought *that* up?' Richard sipped at his brandy. 'It's much the same. *Are* you feeling all right?'

'Fine,' lied Max.

Limping back to the chair, Richard lowered himself into it carefully. 'Well, you don't look it. What's happened to set you all on end? Miss Celia's version of hunt-the-husband give you a bilious attack? Don't tell me you've offered for the chit?'

A perfectly genuine shudder rippled through Max. 'No. It's not as bad as that.' He walked over to the window and stared out into the street. Marriage to Verity would not be anywhere near as depressing as marriage to Celia Faringdon. Or would it? He bethought himself of the decisions he had made regarding his marriage and wondered. Celia would not have presented him with any of the temptation Verity did.

The door opened and Clipstone, the butler, advanced into the room. 'A note from Lady Arnsworth, my lord.'

Richard took the note from Clipstone and held it out to Max as though it might bite. 'How the devil did Almeria know you were back? The woman's a witch. Oh, well, better you than me.' This last held a distinct hint of relief.

'Oh, for God's sake!' burst out Max, swinging away to the window. 'I told her everything she needs to know. What more does she want? Read it, will you?'

Raising his brows, Richard broke the wafer and opened the note. *'The girl is still asleep. What is her name?'*

Max came to a dead halt in his pacing. Damn the chit! Would she never stop wrongfooting him? Making him feel a complete scoundrel?

Muttering, he strode over to Richard, twitched the note out of his hand and stalked to the desk. He dipped Richard's quill in the ink pot and scrawled, *Verity Scott*. Without a word he resealed the note and handed it to Clipstone.

'Very good, my lord.'

The moment the door closed behind the patently agog butler, Richard asked, 'Who the devil is this girl and why is she still asleep?' He took a mouthful of brandy.

'Verity Scott. My bride,' announced Max, ignoring the second part of the question. He didn't want to think about the reasons she had for being totally exhausted.

Richard's face turned purple and a fine mist of brandy sprayed across the desk as he choked on the cognac. A muffled squawk from behind the door suggested that Clipstone's discretion had been soundly defeated by his curiosity.

When Richard could finally speak, he spluttered, 'Why, you double-dealing *bastard*, Max! Why in Hades didn't you tell me?'

Shame lashed Max. 'I'm sorry, Ricky. I…I know after I persuaded you to leave Oxford and come home, but you mustn't think this materially alters your expectations—'

'What the deuce are you talking about?' interrupted Richard, plainly incensed. 'The devil take my so-called expectations! I want to know why my only surviving brother saw fit to marry without even giving me the chance to stand up for him! I *can* stand up, you know, despite this curst leg!'

Despite his anger and frustration, Max grinned. 'Probably because I'm not married yet.'

'Oh.' Richard subsided slightly. 'Well, that's all right then. When's it to be, and who the blazes is Verity Scott? Apart from your *intended* bride, of course.'

'As soon as I can get the licence. And I'll be grateful for your support.'

Richard tossed off the rest of his brandy and poured another. 'Rather sudden, isn't it? Do you want to tell me about it?'

Max sat down in a large leather chair. 'I compromised her. Or rather, to be quite accurate, she trapped me. Which is why

I say that your expectations will remain unaltered…' His voice trailed off. It was entirely possible that Richard's expectations were already sunk. He dismissed the thought. Possible, but improbable. He couldn't be *that* unlucky.

'Trapped you? *You?*' Richard sounded as though he might be trying not to laugh. 'A mere Miss Scott managed to snare the untouchable Blakehurst? After you foiled the machinations of every matchmaking mama between Land's End and John-o'-Groat's?' He grinned. 'Well, at least you can count on your heir having a few brains.'

'Ricky.' Max's deadened voice silenced his brother. 'I'm not joking. As far as I am concerned, you will remain my heir. And I promise you, even if the title goes to…goes elsewhere, the unentailed property will still go to you or your son.'

Richard looked up and met Max's eyes for the first time. 'You're serious. It can't be *that* bad!'

Max faced that penetrating gaze and shrugged his shoulders. 'I'm sorry, Richard. This is the last thing I ever intended. And if it were anybody else's daughter, she could go to the devil with my good will.'

Richard sat down again, stretching his leg out before him. 'I've missed something here. *Who* is Verity Scott?'

Gritting his teeth, Max replied. 'She's the daughter of my late C.O. And she was the reason I went to stay with the Faringdons. You know why I feel responsible. I wanted to see for myself that she was all right.'

'And she trapped you.' Richard sounded as though he had bitten a lemon.

'Yes.'

'And you feel you absolutely have to marry her.' It wasn't a question.

'Yes.'

'Max, has anyone ever told you that your sense of responsibility is blown out of all proportion?' Richard shook his head. 'I don't suppose there's the least use in my offering to marry the blasted wench to oblige you?'

Every muscle in Max's body tightened in a surge of primitive fury at the idea of anyone, anyone at all, even Richard, so much as touching Verity, let alone marrying her. Somehow he choked back the savage response on his lips and shook his head.

'Hmm. Very well, you've said it all,' remarked Richard.

'I didn't say a single bloody word!' grated Max.

'You didn't have to,' said Richard drily. 'But you might like to unclench your fists. Or were you planning to start a mill with me?'

Startled, Max looked down. His fists were clenched so hard the knuckles had whitened. Dragging in a deep breath, he forcibly relaxed them.

'Game of chess, Max?'

He nodded. Anything to distract him from the bitter ashes of his dream. God help him, he had a bride. Not a mistress.

Verity sat up with a jolt of fright, staring into the fire-lit room. Chills rippled through her. The bed felt strange, the shadows flung by the dancing fire confused her. When had her cold, miserable little room sprouted a fireplace? Then she remembered. London. Max had brought her to London. Was this his house? She didn't think so. He had brought her here and left her with…a lady. Very elegant and polite. Aunt… Aunt something he'd called her.

Lying back, Verity closed her eyes. She would worry about her situation in the morning. One thing was certain. She would not be marrying Max…Lord Blakehurst. The drive to London had convinced her of that.

His image burned into her behind her tightly closed eyelids. The gentle dream lover had turned into furious, bitter reality. She didn't blame him in the least. She loathed herself for what she had done. How could she have been so shameless as to go to him and accept his offer? *Selina went to him. Not Verity. Verity died and Selina took her place.*

Verity wished she could believe that. But it wasn't true. For some reason Max had slipped past the guard she had set on herself. *Verity* had gone to him, had consented to be his mistress. Selina was gone and Verity was alive again. And her cowardice had betrayed another man.

'I'm Verity,' she whispered into the darkness. 'I love him and I can't marry him.' He deserved better than a woman who would have consented to be his mistress. Who *had* consented to be his mistress. Who had flung herself at him. He deserved a woman he could care for and respect. A woman who could bring more to her marriage than a ruined name and sordid scandal.

She had offered to be his mistress. She had bargained with him, then lain with him. Shamelessly. She shivered at the memory of his mouth and hands. His searing possession of her body. If only she could stop her memories there, with his tender, passionate lovemaking...but memory was like time, relentless, dragging her with it, until she saw again his disgusted, furious face as he stared down at the campaign chest and felt the knot tighten on his neck.

All his bitter words stabbed into her. *He called you a whore. You disgusted him. And he believes you trapped him on purpose.* She couldn't live with him like that. She couldn't live with herself. In the morning she would have to cry off. If he still wanted her, she would be his mistress. But never his wife.

No doubt Aunt...Aunt whoever-she-was would be only too happy to give her a reference and save her nephew from such a disastrous *mésalliance*.

'Cry off?'

Verity gulped. She had expected Lady Arnsworth to be delighted, but the look of outrage on the lady's face suggested far otherwise.

'*Cry off?* First you entrap my nephew and then you propose to *jilt* him at the altar?' Lady Arnsworth appeared to be choking on the words. Her face had become an alarming mottled purple.

Verity felt the room closing in around her, a gilded, upholstered trap. Explanations were useless and her self-control too shaky to attempt them. Biting her lip, she said, 'He…he does not wish to marry me. I *cannot* marry him. Please…you must send him a message…this must go no further…'

Her ladyship snorted. 'According to Max it has already gone too far.'

Verity felt her face flame and Lady Arnsworth's lip curled scornfully. 'Quite so. Now, enough of this nonsense. You are to be married as soon as possible. By special licence. And the betrothal notice will be in the papers tomorrow.' She paused for effect. 'Unless you desire to make him look a complete fool and scoundrel, you will marry my nephew. *He* at least has some sense of honourable conduct, for which you, Miss Scott, ought to be profoundly grateful.'

'But…but surely the notice could be stopped,' faltered Verity. 'No one need know he applied for a special licence—'

'My dear Miss Scott, Max having informed me that I should see you established in society, naturally I mentioned his betrothal at dinner last night. By now all London will know that he is to marry. Unless you intend jilting him at the altar, you have no choice.'

The room swirled around Verity in a gilded haze as the trap crashed shut. Max's words came back to her in mocking torment: *You have made my bed. Now you must lie in it.*

Gripping the arm of the chair until her fingers ached, Verity wondered which of the pair of them would come to regret the marriage more bitterly. Her husband at least would have the comfort of knowing that he had behaved honourably.

Righteous indignation seeping from every pore as she rose, Lady Arnsworth surveyed her errant houseguest. 'My poor sister must be turning in her grave!' she declared. 'But the person for whom I feel the most pity in this disgraceful affair,' she continued, 'is Richard. And as for Max! With all his experience he should have known better, but it is no more than he deserves, to be trapped by a scheming, little adventuress with fewer morals than he has himself!'

Verity swallowed hard as the door shut with what, in a less well-bred woman, would have been described as a bang. Who Richard might be, she had no idea, nor why he was most to be pitied. Why her deceased mother-in-law would be disturbing the graveyard was self-evident. No mother would desire such a connection for her son.

And if Max...*Lord Blakehurst*...had not the wit, or was too idiotishly chivalrous to see it, then she would have to make him see it. Before they reached the altar rails.

Half an hour later Verity trod up the steps of the Blakehurst mansion in Berkeley Square. Despite the warmth of the day she had kept her hood up, carefully avoiding the gaze of other pedestrians.

But when the door opened to reveal an austere-looking butler, she realised that her problems had just begun. Without a word he began to close the door in her face, far faster than he had opened it.

Quick as thought, Verity put her foot in the door. 'No, please...you don't understand. I must see his lordship. It is a matter of great urgency...please.'

The butler's face would have curdled milk in the cow. 'His lordship,' he informed her, 'does not entertain himself with women of your order here. Or anywhere else for that matter! Take yourself off at once, you brazen hussy!' He tried again to shut the door, stamping on Verity's foot in a most undignified way. She gasped as her slippered foot took the blow, but held her ground.

'Please. I'll wait in the kitchen, but tell him Miss Scott wishes to speak with him. I'm...I'm...' She hesitated. What was she? His mistress? His betrothed? All of the above? 'I'm a guest of Lady Arnsworth.'

The butler eyed her dubiously. 'Ah, would that be Miss *Verity* Scott?'

Heaving a sigh of relief, she nodded.

With all the air of a man damned if he did and damned if he didn't, the butler opened the door enough to admit her. 'If you would please to wait in the hall, I shall ascertain whether or not his lordship is at home.'

'Th...thank you.'

As the butler stalked off, she looked about nervously. The hall was furnished with dainty, fussy elegance. Odd. It didn't seem at all the sort of house she would imagine Max—*Lord Blakehurst*—to have. It reminded her of Lady Arnsworth's house. Then she caught a sight of herself in a mirror hanging over a marble-topped console table and forgot all about the furniture. Except that she felt even more out of place.

No wonder his lordship's butler had assumed her to be a denizen of the stews. Her hair had escaped its pins and to describe her cloak as threadbare would be charitable in the extreme. And it had somehow collected a splash of mud on the hem.

None of the fatly upholstered gilt chairs looked at all the sort of thing she ought to sit on. Verity had the impression that, if she moved towards one with the intent of resting her shabby person, they would all rise up in protest at the indignity.

Swift steps on the parquetry floor drew her attention. Nervously she turned, half-expecting the butler to be returning with a phalanx of footmen to evict her. But it was Max.

'Miss Scott! What the devil are you doing here? Have you *no* discretion? Where is your escort?'

Ignoring the last two questions, since she had no acceptable answers, Verity said, 'I must speak to you, sir. Please. It is very important.'

He ran one hand through his dark hair. 'Very well, then,'

he snapped. 'Come into the library. We may be private there. Clipstone!' He turned to the butler. 'I am not at home to anyone. Do you understand? Not to anyone.'

Verity thought the butler might expire with indignation. 'I hope I know my duty, my lord,' he said stiffly.

'So do I,' rejoined his lordship. 'This way, Miss Scott.'

He ushered her into a large, comfortable library. It was by no means as elegant as the hall, but had all the appearance of a room much lived in. By men. Instead of fussy, gilt chairs, large, inviting leather chairs beckoned by the fireplace. Newspapers covered a writing table and two springer spaniels came bundling forward to greet the guest, one with a well-chewed slipper clutched in its jaws.

Delighted, Verity bent down to pet them and had her face enthusiastically washed, the spaniel with the slipper going so far as to lay it at her feet.

'Down, Taffy! Sit, Gus!' The spaniels took absolutely no notice of this command except to wiggle their tails all the faster.

'It's quite all right, my lord,' Verity assured him, petting the dogs with trembling hands. 'I...I love dogs.' The unaffected delight of their greeting nearly overset her. Dogs didn't care for wealth, or fashion. Or if you had totally disgraced yourself beyond all redemption. They accepted you as you were. Shabby clothes, scandal and all.

'Miss Scott, may I present my brother, Richard Blakehurst?'

Horrified, she tried to straighten up, only to sit down very suddenly as one of the spaniels leapt up at her again. She found herself gazing up at a gentleman who resembled Lord Blakehurst so closely her heart nearly stopped. The eyes were a deeper hazel and the hair not so dark, but the resemblance was staggering. Looking closer, she saw that Richard Blakehurst was thinner and that his face was worn, giving the impression that he was substantially older than his brother. Which was obviously impossible since Max was the Earl.

A strong hand under her elbow helped her to her feet. She didn't bother dusting herself down, but held out her hand to Richard who took it gingerly and bowed infinitesimally.

'Forgive me if I don't kiss your hand, Miss Scott,' he said coldly. 'I fear Taffy and Gus have been before me.'

Verity blushed. Then, as she saw the cool appraisal in his eyes, felt all the blood drain from her face. Plainly he resented his brother's bride.

I had no intention of ever marrying...

She swallowed hard. If he had counted on Max remaining single, then he would naturally dislike the marriage, but the way he looked her up and down...he must know there was something clandestine about the situation. 'I...I am honoured to meet you, sir.' She forced the words out, grateful that her voice didn't wobble too much. This was terrible. She *had* to make his lordship listen!

'Ricky, would you mind leaving us for a few moments? Miss Scott wishes to speak to me privately.' The chill in Lord Blakehurst's voice matched that in his brother's eyes.

'If you think it wise, Max,' said Richard calmly. Verity winced at the implications of that. Clearly he had been told enough to believe that his brother had been trapped.

Her pride stung, she said, 'I am come to put an end to this nonsense about marriage. You need have no fears for your brother or your expectations on my account! And I have no objection if you wish to remain.'

'I, on the other hand, have several!' interposed Lord Blakehurst. '*Au revoir*, brother. And if you wish to do me a favour, take Clipstone with you. Before his ear sticks to the keyhole!'

Richard gave a crack of laughter. His whole face eased as he replied, 'Very well, Max. Good afternoon, Miss Scott.'

The moment the door shut behind him Lord Blakehurst turned on Verity and snapped, 'What the devil did you mean by that?'

Chapter Seven

Verity glared at him, lifting her chin. 'Sir, this farce has gone far enough. I cannot possibly—'

'Why on earth didn't you send for me, if you wished to speak to me?' He spoke straight over her. 'Have you *no* discretion, or conduct? No well-bred young lady pays any call unescorted, let alone on a bachelor household!'

'Good,' retorted Verity. 'If nothing else has worked, perhaps that may serve to convince you that we cannot possibly marry!'

He opened his mouth and shut it again. Stunned amber eyes burned into her and Verity fought to keep her gaze steady. 'My God,' he said softly. 'You really mean it, don't you? Why then?'

It was her turn to flounder. '*Why?* Isn't that obvious, my lord? An earl does not marry his mistress! He does not marry a female whose relatives would prefer she did not exist. And I—'

'No—' he flung up one hand '—you misunderstand me. I meant why did you come to my bed if you did not intend to trap me into offering for you? Surely you must have known what my reaction would be when you told me your real name. You can't have thought I wouldn't remember it!'

This time her eyes fell before his as memories of that night shivered through her body. Heat flooded her cheeks and lower. Her breasts ached at the thought of his mouth and hands.

Forcing her voice to a calm at odds with the tumult of her emotions, she said, 'I never intended you to know my real name. Why would you ever realise? The night we… we…met, after we…after Papa was buried, it was dark. I was little more than a child. Why should you ever recognise me? You *didn't* recognise me. If you hadn't seen the campaign chest…'

'I knew anyway.'

She went cold all over. 'You *knew*?'

'Not at first,' he said quietly. 'Did you ever wonder why I accepted the invitation to that house party? Not my usual milieu, I assure you.'

Mute, she shook her head.

'I wanted to know if *you* were safe. If they were caring for you. When your aunt didn't bring you up to town…'

Hysteria rose in Verity's breast and what he was saying faded. *Aunt Faringdon? Bring her up to town? Was he mad?*

'So I came down to find you. But when I asked your uncle, he said that you had died.'

The cold seeped into Verity's heart. 'He *said* that?' No doubt he had wished it was the truth. And in some ways it had been.

'Are you all right?' The sudden concern in his voice startled her. She stared up at him and nodded automatically. That queer feeling she'd had of ceasing to exist…vanishing into the mist…that no one could see her any more… Suddenly she would have welcomed it, for his bright gaze saw too much. And he was too close. She retreated, but it was too late.

'Come. Sit by the fire. You're shivering.' Strong fingers gripped her arm and she found herself being led towards the fireplace and pushed gently into a chair.

'Umm...it's not lit,' she pointed out, dazed at the sudden pounding of her heart at his touch, the trembling of her hands.

Kneeling by the hearth, he commented, 'I may be an earl now, but I assure you I perfectly recollect how to manage a tinderbox!'

In moments the fire was flickering brightly, doing very little to dispel the icy lump in her heart, the appalling realisation that her uncle had actually denied her very existence. So...how?

'How did you know?'

'My valet,' he said, straightening up. 'He found out from that maid—Sukey?—that you weren't dead. So then I knew who "Selina Dering" really was. Why, Verity, why did you do it? You *can't* have intended to be my mistress. What could you possibly have gained?'

Shock gripped her. All the fear and hurt of the last five years welled up, but she managed to say simply, 'My freedom. When I thought about your offer, I realised that it was my chance to escape—if I did something so shocking that they would never take me back.'

He sat back on his heels, staring, horror in his face. 'For God's sake, girl! The risk you took!'

'What risk?' she asked quietly. 'I had nothing to lose.'

His eyes glinted. 'I beg to differ. You certainly did have something to lose! And *I* took it!'

She shut her eyes, fighting against a pounding tide of desire as her body quivered under the memory of the first instant when he had been deep inside her, part of her. His scorn hurt far more than the loss of her virginity.

When she managed to open her eyes she did not meet his furious gaze. 'It is irrelevant—'

'The hell it is!' he exploded. '*You* may choose to think it—'

'Totally irrelevant,' she insisted, clenching her fists so hard the nails dug into her palms. 'My cousin...' She shuddered at the thought of losing her virginity to Godfrey. Controlling herself, she whispered, 'Rather than have it stripped from me forcibly, I chose to give myself to a man I...trusted.'

Max had to strain to hear those last halting words, but they hit him like a body blow. She had trusted him enough to surrender her body to him—but not enough to tell him who she was. She had used him. 'Why didn't you *tell* me?' he asked, hating the harsh note in his voice, but the strain of not hauling her into his arms and proving how *un*trustworthy he was seemed likely to kill him.

'That I was a...a virgin?'

'That too,' he said grimly. Knowing he had hurt her shamed him. 'Why didn't you just tell me who you were? Ask for my help.'

Her eyes flew wide. 'Why didn't I...? But you would never have taken me as your mistr—'

'No! I damned well wouldn't have!'

'So I couldn't have escaped!'

His conscience mocked. 'You didn't think I'd help you?'

'How?' The simple question floored him. 'I'm under twenty-one. Lord Faringdon is my guardian. I have no money, no other relatives who might take me in. The Faringdons would have left me on the parish, I think, but apparently my grandmother vetoed the idea. Since they count on her leaving a substantial fortune to them, of course they kept me. Since I was saving the wages of at least a governess and one lady's maid, my aunt refused to write me a reference. What could you have done if I had told you who I was? Once you were gone, my situation would have been even worse.'

'And after our *liaison* ended? After I had taught you your trade?' He couldn't keep the bitterness from his voice. God! He'd thought it funny at the time, endearing that she had no idea of her effect on him, that she'd never need another lover.

She flushed. 'I...that *was* a lie. I never intended to become...to take another... I was going to purchase an annuity.'

'A *what*?' His brain grappled with that.

A puzzled frown creased her brow. 'An annuity. You know. Consols, government bonds. You buy them and they pay you three per cent per year.'

Hell! He *knew* what an annuity was! He felt very slightly better. Not much, but a bit. At least she had not really wanted to be anyone's mistress. But the inescapable fact remained: she *was* someone's mistress. His.

'Let me get this straight,' he said harshly. 'All you wanted of me was safety and security? And you don't wish to marry me.'

He thought she hesitated, but then she lifted her chin.

'Yes. I mean, no.'

An awful thought came to him. She didn't want a career as a courtesan—thank God—but neither did she want to marry... He felt sick. Had he...?

'Verity—I know I hurt you. If I'd known—it won't be like that again...' His voice shuddered into silence. It wouldn't be like that at all. He couldn't take the risk of a child. Not if he was married to her.

'It's not that!' she broke in. 'You didn't...it wasn't...I can't marry you. If you want me, I will be your mistress, but...'

'*The hell you will*... What the devil is going on out there?'

An indistinct uproar in the hall resolved itself into a single voice that Max recognised, but couldn't quite identify.

'Out of my way, sirrah! I'll see his lordship and be damned to the lot of you!'

Verity's cheeks turned grey, and her eyes dilated so much they turned black with fear.

Faringdon.

The time to think, to reason with her, had flown. Only action could save her now.

Max gripped Verity's shoulders. 'Listen,' he said. 'There's no time. In the last ditch, do you wish to remain free of your relatives? At any cost?'

She opened her mouth, but nothing came out. The convulsive movement of her throat stabbed at him, but he said harshly, 'Quickly, Verity. Do you trust me?'

She nodded.

'Very well. I'll invite Faringdon in. Follow my lead and don't volunteer anything. Above all, don't contradict anything I say.' He bent over her and caught her chin, forcing it up. 'Remember. Back me up. It's your only chance.' Unable to help himself, he caressed the silky soft skin, lingering on the delicate line of her jaw, the suddenly fluttering pulse in her throat. The fierce surge of desire shocked him.

Grimly he wrenched his fingers back and stood up. 'Whatever I say, Verity.' Then he walked to the door and opened it.

Lord Faringdon stood in the centre of the hall, covered in dust, his face red with fury.

'Do come in, Lord Faringdon. Did I leave something behind? I rather thought I had everything needful.'

Max noted with savage pleasure that his calm voice had an anything-but-calming effect on Faringdon. His hectic flush became purple and his fists clenched.

The moment he crossed the threshold of the library his gaze fell on Verity. His jaw dropped and his eyes bulged as his Adam's apple worked convulsively. Speech exploded from him.

'By God, you carry your little affairs with a high hand, Blakehurst! But you've gone too far this time! Stupid, too. Did you think I wouldn't realise she'd gone with you?'

Max pretended to consider this. 'No. I didn't really think you that lacking in wit. Honesty, yes. I confess that I do have a query there.'

Faringdon swung around. 'What the devil do you mean, sir?'

Anger coursed through Max. 'I asked you, Lord Faringdon, for news of Miss Scott and you informed me that she had died…'

His lordship pounced on that. 'Nothing of the sort! Said

she was no longer with us. You were the one who assumed—'

'An assumption you did nothing to correct and, indeed, fostered!' snapped Max. 'In fact you implied that she had taken her own life!'

'Nothing to do with you!' roared Faringdon. 'She's under my guardianship and—'

'Not now she isn't,' Max informed him. He stepped to Verity's side and picked up her hand, pressing it in warning. 'She's under my protection now.'

Faringdon smiled knowingly and his voice took on an oily tone. 'Of course she is. But do you really want it known that you seduced an innocent girl away from the care of her family? That you had her openly in your house? I think not, Blakehurst. You see, your reputation is well known. Naturally I lied to you. To protect my ward from your, er, *dishonourable* intentions. Of course, if you wished to make me a little payment, a contribution to the care she has received…' He smirked knowingly. 'After all, according to the bed linen, you got your money's worth!'

For a moment Max could not quite believe his ears—that Faringdon would bargain Verity's lost innocence to sell her into whoredom. Right on the heels of a threat to claim he had only been trying to protect her virtue.

Verity's sharply indrawn breath warned Max that she had understood as well and he spoke straight over her. 'I will take leave to inform you that your ward has done me the honour of becoming my wife. The notice will be in the papers shortly. Any further insults and you will meet me!'

'What?' shrieked Faringdon. 'I forbid it! You have no right!'

Max took an even firmer grip on Verity's suddenly trembling hand. Faringdon's reaction stunned him. Surely, surely the man couldn't be this stupid!

'She's under age,' sneered Faringdon, recovering himself somewhat. 'I'll have it set aside. And she's returning with

me at once. I don't know what pack of lies she's told you,
Blakehurst, but—'

Max shrugged. 'You could set it aside, but what reason
would you give? That I'm after her money and took advantage of her? That I am unable to support her in the style to
which she is accustomed?' He snorted. 'You might have me
there. It would certainly never occur to me to treat her the
way you did.'

'Damn it, Blakehurst! You can't just—'

'I can and have.' Max cut him off. 'And you may like to
consider the esteem in which his Grace, the Duke of Wellington, held Colonel Scott. Believe me, if I carry this story
to him, you will be hard pressed to set foot in society again,
Faringdon. The notice will appear in the papers and unless
you wish to ruin yourself you will accept it with a good grace.
Good day, my lord.'

'Not so fast, Blakehurst,' said Faringdon. 'As Miss Scott's
guardian, I demand to hear what she has to say. I find her in
your house and you inform me that you are married, but I've
yet to hear a word out of my niece.' He turned on Verity.

The door flew open and Max swore mentally as Richard
limped in.

'Everything quite well, Blakehurst? Clipstone seemed to
feel my presence desirable.'

Consigning his over-zealous butler to the devil, Max said,
'Lord Faringdon wishes to assure himself that I have not offered his ward marriage with the left hand only. As a witness
to our marriage earlier today, Richard, perhaps you might
care to assure his lordship that *all is as it should be*.'

Richard stared. 'I...I beg your pardon, Max?'

God help us! Max manufactured a world-weary smile and
sigh. 'Yes, I know, Richard. Shocking, is it not, that he feels
compelled to doubt my word, but never mind. You shall set
him right and all shall be forgotten.'

Richard held his gaze straitly. 'Are you sure, Blakehurst?'

Max returned that challenging look. 'Quite sure, Richard.

Calling him out would be the only alternative. So tedious.'
Silently he prayed that Richard would do as he was bid.
Would not baulk at the lie, thinking to avert disaster.

Shrugging, Richard turned to Faringdon. 'I can't think why
you would question Blakehurst's word. The marriage has
taken place. Are you satisfied?'

For an answer Faringdon spun on his heel and strode out,
slamming the door behind him.

Richard exploded. 'You damned—'

Max waved him to silence. Senses straining, he waited...
A reverberating crash informed him that Lord Faringdon had
shut the front door himself. Reluctantly he met Richard's
glare.

'And just what do you intend now?' asked Richard through
gritted teeth.

Max glanced at the clock on the chimney piece. 'Five
o'clock. Ricky, have the travelling carriage brought around
and send Harding to me. You and Almeria will take Verity
straight down to Blakeney. I'll be down as soon as I can get
the licence. You can give the bride away and act as a witness
with Almeria.'

'*What?*'

The cry broke from two shocked throats.

'Ricky!' snapped Max. 'Just go. Now.' He held Richard's
gaze and said, 'There's no help for it. I have to act before
Faringdon realises we lied. I wouldn't abandon a stray dog
to that cur.'

Swearing, Richard turned to Verity. 'Welcome to the family.' And he limped out. At the door he looked back. 'Even
you can't get married that fast! What if Faringdon realises?'

Max shrugged. 'Faringdon's a fool. By the time someone
tells him, with a bit of luck we *will* be married.'

Richard's choice of epithet suggested that Max's idea of
good luck didn't tally with his own.

Verity saw her entire world collapsing around her even
more thoroughly. 'My lord, earls don't—'

'Oh, yes, they do,' he told her. 'Take my word for it.'

* * *

'Wilt thou have this woman to be thy wedded wife...?'

Three days later Verity stood shaking beside Max in the drawing room at Blakeney and listened to the minister's measured tones. This couldn't be happening. She must have been insane to let him sacrifice his freedom for her. He should never have been permitted to do it. At her back she was savagely aware that the bridegroom's aunt and brother agreed wholeheartedly.

'Wilt thou love her, comfort her, honour and keep her, in sickness and in health; and, forsaking all other, keep thee only unto her, so long as ye both shall live?'

'I will.'

Max's calm response jarred on her. He had never intended to marry—

So what will change for him? Nothing. He will be free to pursue whatever mode of life he chooses. The knowledge gave no comfort. Her alternative was to return to Faringdon Hall. A sharply indrawn breath from Max jerked her back.

The minister was staring at her with an expectant look on his face. She looked back blankly.

'*I will!*' Richard muttered behind her.

'I...I will.'

It was little more than a whisper, but it satisfied the minister, for he continued. 'Who giveth this woman to be married to this man?'

Verity stiffened as Richard came forward, possessed himself of her right hand and gave it to the minister. She stiffened still further as the minister placed her hand in Max's. Her mouth dried and a choking lump rose in her throat. How he must hate her! He had not looked at her so much as once, since she had reached the altar.

Max felt the small, shaking hand placed in his and went cold with shock. He had avoided looking at her, but now he did. She looked calm enough, but pale, so pale. And her hand in his felt as though it might shatter with the tension. He could feel the fine trembling. Damn. Was she that frightened of him?

Gently he stroked his thumb over her knuckles and concentrated on repeating his vows. 'I, Maxwell James Blakehurst, take thee, Verity Anne, to my wedded wife...' Another vow. Before God and man. Somehow he would have to try to reconcile it with the other promises he had made. '...to love and to cherish...' he dismissed the frisson of shame. Plenty of people took these vows every day with not the least notion of keeping to all of them '...and thereto I plight thee my troth.'

Could he dishonour himself in that way? A queer thought came to him—could he do that to Verity? Force her into marriage and continue to entertain himself as he pleased?

Verity's husky whisper, repeating her vows, pierced him. No hesitation, just that shattered note in her voice, as though her throat hurt. She hadn't wanted this marriage. She had begged him to release her. He had refused, insisted on marriage. And then Lord Faringdon had arrived, demanding her return. Max didn't doubt that her fear of being forced to return to the Faringdons had broken her resistance to the marriage. It didn't make him feel any better.

'...and thereto I give thee my troth.'

Carefully Max took the glove from her left hand, his heart contracted at the reddened, work-roughened state of her slender fingers, the cracking. Steeling himself, he turned to Richard and found the ring waiting for him. He laid it upon the prayerbook for the minister to bless.

Then he was placing it on Verity's fourth finger. Grimly he saw that there was an especially deep crack at the base of that finger. The ring stuck a little going over her knuckle, then went on with a rush. The only sign she gave that he had hurt her was a sharp little gasp, but it stabbed deep into Max and without thinking he lifted her hand to his lips and gently kissed it.

Startled grey eyes met his.

He forced a smile and repeated after the minister, 'With this ring I thee wed, with my body I thee worship...' Steadily he continued, holding the ring on her finger.

There was no going back now. He listened as the minister concluded, pronouncing them '...man and wife together.'

With aching control he brushed the lightest of kisses over her trembling lips. Verity was his. For better or for worse. All he could do was try to make sure it wasn't worse for her.

By the end of dinner that evening Verity had made several discoveries about dining in polite company. Amongst other things, one must remember to rise at the end of the last course so that the gentlemen might be left to their wine. Neither did one leave one's food on one's plate without even the pretence of eating it. These last two pieces of information were imparted to Verity in the drawing room after the ladies had retired.

'It will require a great deal of application on your part,' intoned Lady Arnsworth, 'if you are to take your place in Society without rendering Max a laughing stock.'

Verity concentrated on not knocking over her teacup, or letting it rattle in its saucer as she set it down. She had no intention of going anywhere near fashionable London.

Lady Arnsworth continued to chart her social course. 'It will be vital that you are seen at all the right places. And with the right people. There is bound to be gossip, but if you behave with decorum, Max's influence should quell the worst.' She fixed Verity with a warning eye. 'We must, however, be realistic. It is in the highest degree unlikely that vouchers can be procured for you.' She sipped her tea, a monument of virtuous resignation.

'Vouchers?' asked Verity.

Lady Arnsworth gave a superior sort of smile. 'For Almack's. Given the likely scandal attending your marriage, it is most unlikely that I will be able to persuade any of the

Patronesses to extend their approval. You may, *perhaps*, be invited to larger gatherings at their homes.'

Several answers suggested themselves to Verity, only to be rejected. Lady Arnsworth was Max's aunt. Rudeness would not be fair to him.

'And there is one other subject upon which I must do my duty,' said Lady Arnsworth.

Already Verity had learnt that when Almeria Arnsworth spoke of duty, then it was bound to be something unpleasant.

'The marriage bed.'

Verity set her cup and saucer down with a rattle like musket fire. 'I...don't think...that is to say, I should not wish you to feel that you must—'

Lady Arnsworth silenced her with a glare. 'Whatever has already taken place, I feel it my duty to apprise you of the very different expectations a gentleman has of his wife, as opposed to his...' she shuddered delicately '...his mistress.'

Verity's face ignited.

'In his wife,' continued Lady Arnsworth, 'a gentleman seeks a mother for his heirs. A gracious hostess. In short, he requires a lady.' Her tone suggested that Max was probably indulging optimism too far if he expected that, but she carried on, regardless.

'In the case of my nephew it would be most unreasonable to expect that he will not continue to seek his amusements elsewhere. Gentlemen such as Blakehurst prefer to take their pleasures *outside* the marriage bed. A lady will not notice these things. Her duty is fulfilled in conceiving heirs. A lady accepts her duty quietly. She understands that any sort of...of wanton response...any display of—' here Lady Arnsworth closed her eyes and breathed deeply '—animal lust, will give her husband an ineradicable disgust of her. For that he seeks the creatures of the bordello. *Not* the sanctity of the marriage bed.'

Max's savage words came back to Verity. *You're eager enough, I'll say that for you.* Pain coiled inside her as understanding came. She had given herself, body, heart and soul—only to disgust him. *You never thought he loved you. You didn't expect that.*

But she had longed for his affection. She thought he had offered that. That in making love to her as he had... *He thought he was taking a mistress. A whore.*

The carpet blurred and a chill stole through her. Dimly she realised that Lady Arnsworth was still speaking. None of it penetrated. Only the dreadful knowledge that she had forever alienated Max. She had hoped that in time he would forgive her for what she had done.

'I hope I have made myself quite clear, Niece.'

Vaguely she realised that a response was necessary.

'Yes. Thank you. Most clear.' She stood up and managed a wobbly smile. 'If you will excuse me, Lady Arnsworth, I shall retire now. It has been such a long day and I am quite weary.'

A cold nod was the only reply.

'Goodnight then, ma'am. And thank you for your advice.' That stung, but after all, no woman liked seeing her family embroiled in a shocking scandal. She rose and headed for the door.

'The bell pull is by the chimney.'

Verity turned and looked. So it was. 'Yes?' Had she forgotten something else? Some appalling shibboleth that would set the household by the ears?

'You should ring for Henty. She will conduct you to your chamber.'

Verity blanched. She had spent the previous two days being shown over the house by the housekeeper, Mrs Henty. The woman's thinned mouth and cold answers had made her opinion of the master's bride unmistakable.

'That's quite all right, ma'am. I dare say she has enough to do without that. She pointed out my chamber yesterday. I'm sure I can find it.' She forced another smile. 'Thank you.' She closed the door behind her carefully and stood breathing deeply. Then she heard voices. Masculine voices. She whirled, every sense alert. Max and Richard coming up to the drawing room. The thought of facing Max, with Lady Arnsworth's summation of a lady's duty an open wound, appalled her. Gathering up her skirts, she fled.

Lady Arnsworth opened fire as Max and Richard walked into the drawing room. 'Your bride declined to keep me company, Max. She has retired for the night. After all my efforts on her behalf! It passes all bounds! Really, Max! Was marriage necessary? It seems to me—'

'Almeria.'

She pursed her lips. 'Yes, Max?'

'Marriage was necessary.'

Her lip curling, Lady Arnsworth snapped, 'Any girl who gets herself into that situation deserves—'

'Enough.' Max spoke far more sharply than he intended, but at least it stopped Almeria's tirade. He felt guilty. Despite the length of table between them at dinner, he was willing to bet that Verity had scarcely eaten a mouthful. The memory of her white face flayed him. Almeria had lost no opportunity to point out her shortcomings, all under the guise of instructing the new Lady Blakehurst. There had been nothing to which he could take exception, but by the time the meal ended Verity had been paler than her simple gown of ivory silk.

A half-drunk cup of tea caught his eye. Damn. She hadn't even finished that.

'Max! A game of euchre?' Richard's patient voice suggested that he had asked at least once already.

Euchre! Refusal was on the tip of his tongue, but he caught sight of Almeria's stiff face. Reluctantly, he agreed. Without a fourth their options were limited and it was vital that Almeria was mollified before returning to London in the morning, otherwise her tongue could do untold damage to the new Lady Blakehurst's reputation.

He'd vowed to protect Verity. He'd deal with her eating habits later.

After several wrong turnings, Verity finally found the right corridor and what she hoped was the right door. She remembered the portrait of a very sour-faced lady hanging beside the door from her tour with the housekeeper. Naturally before her marriage she had slept in one of the guest chambers, not the Countess's chamber.

She opened the door and wondered if she *had* found the right room, or if she had misheard Mrs Henty. This was a sitting room, not a bedchamber. But all the lamps were lit, as if in preparation for someone.

Hesitantly she went in, trying to remember what the woman had said when she pointed the room out. They hadn't gone in. *The mistress's apartments, my lady. His lordship is at the end of the corridor.* Verity had shied away from going in.

Apartments. So this must be the right room. A door stood slightly ajar on the far side. Wondering at the softness of the richly patterned carpet under her slippered feet, Verity went to peep through the other door. Her eyes widened. Surely such a huge and sumptuous bedchamber couldn't be meant for her. Could it?

A very shabby nightgown lying across the neatly turned-down bed, assured her that this was most definitely her chamber. She felt hot with embarrassment that the maid who unpacked should have seen her pathetic night attire. She could just imagine the tittering and whispers in the servants' hall. It would not take long for the truth of her marriage to reach the ears of the servants. Servants always knew everything.

Looking around, she discovered her father's campaign chest in a corner. Its battered, travel-scarred timber looked completely out of place in the elegance of this room. A tear trickled down her cheek and she wiped it away with a shaking hand. Even here in her bedchamber she dared not weep. It was her wedding night. Any moment Max might come through the door connecting their bedchambers—she glanced at the gilt clock on the marble chimney piece—and, then again, he might not.

It wouldn't be Max anyway. Instead of Max, her tender lover and protector, she had Lord Blakehurst—her cold, polite husband. And the thought of sharing a bed with *him* terrified her. She had disgusted him. He thought her little better than a whore. She shuddered. He might not be far wrong, but she could not bear to have him touch her in that way. She had to convince him that he was wrong, that she had not intended to trap him and that, despite appearances, she was not a whore. And how she was to convince *him* of that, when she couldn't convince herself, was beyond her ken.

Hurrying out of her wedding gown, she washed and pulled her nightgown over her head, grateful for its voluminous size and shape. She stared unhappily at the bed. It looked comfortable and cosy with its silk counterpane and rich hangings. And it looked far too large for her.

She could sit by the fireplace, until she felt sleepy. Methodically she moved around the room, turning down the lamps until the room was lit only by her bedside lamp. Settling in the chair, she shivered a little. She had achieved her aim: she was safe. Safe from poverty and bullying. She would doubtless have every material benefit that could be gained from her marriage. Surely she could learn to be happy, to count her blessings?

Safety—wasn't that the main thing? Her gaze travelled around the room again, noting the luxurious furnishings, the richly draped windows and matching bed hangings. Hers now. She looked again. They didn't feel like hers. The elegance of the room mocked her, demanding to know how a little provincial nobody could be worthy of all this. More tears fell.

She wriggled more closely into the security of the chair. Perhaps she should light the fire…

'I trust these apartments are to your liking, madam.'

The deep drawl jerked her out of a doze. Her husband stood in the doorway which presumably led to his own bed-chamber.

Apparently there were worse things than finding your bride tucked up in bed waiting for you. Like seeing her huddled by a fireplace with no fire. He remembered that cold, bleak little room at the Faringdons'.

The fire was set. All she'd had to do was touch a flame to it. Why didn't she? He marched over to the fireplace and bent down. A moment later flames hissed and crackled in the grate. Then he saw what she was wearing. Good God! 'What the devil is that thing?' he growled. He frowned as she tensed and huddled into the chair.

'I was about to go to bed. It's my nightgown.'

Feeling ridiculous, he snapped, 'I can see it's a nightgown. Why didn't Almeria buy some new ones for you while she was spending my money?' The moment the words left his lips he knew he'd said the wrong thing.

The dark eyes narrowed. 'Thank you, my lord. This is perfectly adequate for my needs. After all, nobody will see it.'

His brows lifted. 'Quite.' Then he cursed himself as her cheeks flamed and he remembered his reason for coming to her. Even in that ghastly, all-enveloping abomination, her slender frame looked as though a breath of wind might blow it away.

'Did you ring for some supper? You barely touched your dinner.'

'Yes.'

He'd seldom heard a lie so spontaneous. How he knew it for a lie, he didn't know. He didn't bother arguing. He just stalked to the chimney piece and tugged on the bell pull.

'What are you doing?' she demanded.

'Sending for your supper!' he growled. And wondered at

himself. He'd come prepared to be polite, gentle even. How was it that she tipped him off balance so badly?

She flushed, then paled. 'There is no need to bother your staff, my lord. I…I wasn't hungry anyway.'

'Then you damn well should have been,' he said. 'Sulking won't solve anything.'

'I am *not* sulking!' The fury in her voice shook him, but it was at least better than the utter lifelessness that had gripped her. 'And I'm perfectly capable of deciding when I need to eat!'

'Of course you are,' he said, hanging on to his own temper by a thread. 'So I'll tell whoever comes to send up some apples and bread and cheese that you can eat whenever you decide you want it.' Something simple. He didn't want her to starve, but he was damned if he'd make more work for the staff just because she wouldn't eat her dinner.

Her mouth opened and shut again. 'Apples?' she asked.

He nodded warily. Was she about to rip up at him again?

'And bread and cheese?' All the anger had drained out of her voice, leaving an odd wistful note.

'Er, yes.' Something tore in his chest. Were those tears in her eyes? Before he could be certain she turned away.

'Thank you, my lord. It's…it's very kind of you. It was just that… I'm sorry. I'm sure the dinner was lovely, but all those sauces…and I wasn't really very hungry.'

Kind? Grimly he reminded himself of what her life had been like. He remembered being unable to stomach a large, rich meal himself after years of campaigning in the Peninsula.

'Perhaps you would add to your kindness, my lord.'

He stiffened. Damn. He might have known she would try to twist his momentary lapse to her advantage. What now did she want?

'Possibly,' he temporised.

'I would prefer to request the food myself.'

He frowned, hesitated. Her voice sounded so controlled—expressionless.

'Do I have your word of honour that you will have some food brought up and that you will eat it?'

She nodded, still with her back to him.

'Your word, madam,' he insisted.

Very slowly she turned to face him. 'My word of honour?' The bleakness in her eyes and the taut line of her mouth stabbed at him.

'Yes,' he said. He must ensure she ate something and, deep down, he knew if she gave her word she would keep it.

She held his gaze. 'You have it. For what it's worth to you. Goodnight, my lord.'

'Your servant, madam.' He bowed and left. Closing the connecting door behind him, he leaned against it, wondering... *For what it's worth to you...* What in Hades did she mean by that? That he *couldn't* count on her keeping her word? No. That wasn't it. She had meant something quite different. Did she think *he* would place no value on her word?

The best thing he could do was have a very large brandy and go to bed. Once he got used to the fact that she was asleep in the next room it wouldn't be so bad, and once his body became used to the idea that he would have to maintain complete control of himself in any visit to his wife's bed.

Chapter Eight

Two hours later Max was still awake. Furious with his idiocy, he glared at the connecting door. He had made his decision, dash it all! He was *not* visiting her bed tonight. He'd heard Mrs Henty come up. Twice. Which meant that she'd brought up some food. By now Verity would have eaten it. She'd be sound asleep.

But if she wasn't asleep…if she was waiting for him…had he made it quite clear that he *wouldn't* return that night? Or any other night until he was in control of his passions. The idea that she might be waiting for him…no. He'd have to check.

He opened the door very quietly. If she were already asleep, the last thing he wanted to do was wake her. The fire had died to embers, but the lamp still glowed by the bed. The very large bed that held his wife, sound asleep with one arm curled around the pillow as though she nestled against a lover. Thick, unruly curls fanned over the pillow as once they had fanned across his chest, a temptation of cool, silky fire.

He lurched away from the thought. That way lay madness. He had to retain his self-control, otherwise it would not be safe to share her bed.

She had left the bed hangings open as well as the curtains. The sun would pour through those windows very early. If he closed the bed hangings on that side…she might like fresh air. She certainly wasn't used to a closed canopy. He rarely closed his own hangings.

Treading softly, he went over and looked down at her. Oh, hell! Her eyes were reddened, her pale cheeks tearstained. The pain of knowing she had cried herself to sleep was like a blow over the heart. He gritted his teeth. Tears were easy for a woman. He would not be manipulated by a woman's tears again. Ever. No matter how often she fluttered wet lashes at him.

She didn't flutter them at you. You didn't even hear her. Unlike his mother. Whenever she had cried, the entire household knew about it, let alone his father in the next room.

He stared at her. She claimed she had never intended to trap him, that she had intended to be his mistress. And then buy an annuity. Could she really have thought to carry off the deception? The thought unnerved him. Would he have ever realised the truth, if Harding hadn't found out that Verity Scott was alive?

The remains of her supper sat on the bedside table. Two apple cores and a few crumbs. Damn it. She needed to eat more than apples and bread and cheese to fill out those sweet curves a trifle… He slammed the lid down on that. Thinking about her curves would not help him at all. But she'd be ill if she didn't eat properly. He'd promised—*vowed*, curse it all!—to cherish her. So he should, at the very least, look after her. Letting her starve to death didn't fit in with that at all.

Helplessly his fingers brushed over her damp cheeks. He drew back, shaking. Stifling a curse, he settled the bedclothes around her shoulders, denying temptation, the furious protest of his body that wanted nothing more than to slide into the bed beside her and make love to her, denying his heart that longed to comfort her. At all costs he had to keep his distance from her.

She had nothing to weep for, he told himself harshly. She had what she desired—her safety. Every material advantage.

His conscience nagged. Could he really blame her for wanting safety? She hadn't meant to trap him. Shaken, he realised
that he believed her—that she would never have told him
who she was if he hadn't found out.

If only she hadn't been Verity Scott. A woman whom he
had no choice but to protect with his name. If only she had
been, in truth, Selina. He looked down at her again. Dark
shadows beneath her eyes sent a stab of pain through him.
She must be exhausted. Carefully, he brushed his fingers over
her exposed cheek again. So soft. Silken.

'Sleep well.'

A soft sigh breathed from her as she snuggled against the
pillow and shifted her cheek against his caress. Reluctantly
he withdrew his hand.

Then, very softly, he drew the bed hangings and left.

A shaft of light struck across Verity's eyes. Slowly she
opened them and blinked. Apart from the sunbeam peeping
in, one side of her bed hangings was closed. When had she
done that? Verity snuggled her cheek into soft down, yawn-
ing. She remembered going to bed, but not shutting the hangings. Another memory came to her. A gentle caress and a
velvet dark voice: *Sleep well.* A dream. No more.

She sat up and stretched. She'd made some decisions last
night, about her marriage. She didn't know if she could carry
them out successfully, but she'd have to try. It was the only
way in which she could salvage some of her self-respect.

She would have to make the best of her marriage, show
Max that he could trust her. Somehow she had to convince
her husband that she was not the harlot he thought her. He
had cared for Selina. She was sure of it. Couldn't he learn to
care for Verity? Just a little?

Lady Arnsworth's summation of the duties of a wife
mocked her. She set her chin mulishly. She didn't believe it.
Papa and Mama had loved one another. She *knew* that. And
Papa had been a gentleman, the younger son of a viscount.

He had loved her mother enough to marry her even though his family disowned him for it. And she could remember the physical affection between them. Gentle touches, tenderness that they had never hidden from her.

So she couldn't hide from Max behind the blank mask of indifference with which she had held the Faringdons at bay. She would have to face her responsibilities and learn about running this huge house. She would have to take her meals with him. Make conversation. Try to gain his…his trust…his respect? If she gained that, it was as much as she dared hope for. She had better keep busy. Then she wouldn't have time to dream of how much more she wanted.

There was a light tap on the door.

'Come in.'

The door opened to admit a maid carrying a large and heavily laden tray.

'I didn't ring,' said Verity.

'No, my lady. His lordship gave orders that your breakfast was to be brought up to you.' The girl looked at her curiously. 'Where shall I put the tray, ma'am? Do you want it in bed?'

In bed? Breakfast in bed? She remembered the man who had stayed all night in a cold, cheerless cottage guarding the sleep of an orphan. And had then gone out to find her some breakfast. This was the man she had married. No matter how angry he might be with her, she was safe.

Taking her silence for assent, the maid brought the tray over and placed it carefully on her knees.

Dazed, Verity said, 'Thank you. What is your name?'

'Sarah, ma'am. I'm to wait on you for now.'

'Oh.' Verity smiled. 'Well, that's nice to know.'

'Just till I'm married, ma'am,' said the girl with a curtsy. 'Mrs Henty thought it best. Her ladyship says you'll need a proper dresser in London, so Mrs Henty said I should do it until you can hire one.'

A dresser? One of those horrid, superior creatures, like the one who waited on Aunt Faringdon? Not if she could help it. Lady Arnsworth's assumption that she would go up to London would remain that. An assumption. She could assume until the sky rained potatoes for all Verity cared. And it would thunder to the tune of 'Greensleeves' before the new Lady Blakehurst willingly set foot in fashionable London.

Two weeks later Verity conceded that she wasn't making progress with any of her aims. Despite the fact that Max was excruciatingly polite to her, she doubted that it was due to any increased respect for her. More like respect for himself. She glared at an inoffensive rose as she placed it in a vase and stepped back to view the effect. A few more pink ones, perhaps.

He called her *madam*, or *madam wife*, and treated her with the utmost consideration when she saw him, which was at mealtimes. And Verity had a sneaking suspicion that the only reason she saw him then was that he was determined to fatten her up. Placing more pink roses in the vase, she snorted in a very unladylike manner. No doubt he didn't want anyone thinking he starved her when they went up to London! She had yet to inform him that when he went to London, he would be going alone.

It was bad enough down here. Every time she saw him pain embedded itself a little deeper, cutting at her mercilessly. Max, who had rescued her, been the only one to care for her after Papa's death. Who had actually come to the Faringdons to find her, to make sure she was all right. And she had betrayed him. No matter that she hadn't intended it—he was trapped. And even though she thought he accepted that she had not trapped him intentionally, their marriage remained unconsummated. He made no sign that he wished for her as a *wife*. He never touched her beyond placing her hand on his arm to lead her in for dinner each night.

She bit her lip as she swept up rose leaves from the console table. Judging by the tension in him when he did so, he could scarcely bear to touch her. Lady Arnsworth had been quite correct. He had been happy to take her as his mistress, but he did not want her as his wife. Knowing that her behaviour repulsed him lacerated her. He would be still more disgusted if he realised the shiver of pleasure that pierced her without fail each evening. How could a simple touch overset her so?

Soon he would return to London for the autumn session of Parliament. No doubt he would take advantage of that to seek his amusements outside his empty marriage bed. At least she would not have to see it. She pushed her depressing thoughts away. Right now she had to face Mrs Henty's unrelenting disapproval over the weekly menus. And something was bothering her maid, Sarah. She was sure of it. For the past week or more the girl had looked haunted. This morning her eyes were reddened. Yet she would not confide.

The clock chimed. She cast a glance in the pier glass behind the table and reminded herself that the elegantly gowned creature reflected was not Miss Verity Scott, shabby poor relation, but rather a Countess, Lady Blakehurst, dressed in the first stare of fashion. If she kept on reminding herself, she might even believe it. Better still, Mrs Henty might accept it.

The knock at the door came right on cue as the clock fell silent. Ten o'clock. She took a deep breath. 'Come in.' Not a doubt but that the woman had been waiting outside for the past several minutes putting the finishing touches to her granite-hard expression.

Verity stiffened her spine as Mrs Henty came in, and applied herself to the household matters presented with grim precision to her notice, reminding herself all the while, *You are Lady Blakehurst. The mistress of the house.*

The menus. The linen cupboard. The need to offer assistance to Widow Granger who had lost her only son at sea…

As if that had been a signal Mrs Henty drew herself up. 'I regret, your ladyship, to say that I will be leaving at the quarter day.'

Verity blanched. 'Leaving? Mrs Henty, are you sure that's

necessary?' Much as the woman's attitude annoyed her, she had been there forever and was plainly devoted to the family. She shuddered to imagine Max's reaction when he heard the news. She pressed on. 'You know, I should be loath for any of the older retainers to feel—'

'My decision is made.' Mrs Henty appeared to have turned into solid rock. 'I believe his lordship will provide me with a pension after my years of service?'

Verity stared. 'A…well, yes. Yes, of course he will. If you are quite settled on this, Mrs Henty, I'll mention it to him, but if you…well, if you change your mind, I'm sure he'd be much happier for you to stay on.'

The older woman's jaw hardened. 'Very good of you, madam. I'd take it kindly if you were to tell his lordship.'

Something about her stance alerted Verity. For all her years of service, Mrs Henty didn't want to approach Max herself. Why not?

'And one last thing, madam. About…Sarah.'

Verity paused in the act of shutting her household notebook. 'Sarah? My maid—'

'She's to be dismissed,' Mrs Henty informed her brusquely. 'You'll need to find ano—'

Verity interrupted. 'A moment, Mrs Henty. *I'll* make the decision if any of the maids are to be dismissed, especially the one who waits on me! What is Sarah's offence? Something trivial? Can she be offered another chance?' The thought of kicking even a housemaid out into the world tore at her. Then she remembered something. 'Besides, Sarah is to be married. She told me so at the very start.'

She watched in puzzlement as the woman's mouth twisted. 'Mrs Henty?'

The answer came. Hard and uncompromising. 'Not any more she isn't. And she's breeding.' Her lips set in a thin line and she said no more.

It was quite enough. No normal lady would even consider keeping a maidservant who had fallen from grace in this way.

Verity bit back all the savage things jostling to be said and concentrated on the issue. 'No.'

Mrs Henty's jaw dropped. 'Madam?'

'No. I won't dismiss her.'

'But…she's breeding. She—'

'Made a foolish mistake and ought to spend the rest of her life paying for some man's selfish pleasure?' suggested Verity bitterly. Inside she shuddered. There, but for the grace of God and Max's decency… Poor Sarah. No wonder she looked ill.

'I'll be damned if I cast the first stone! Naturally once she cannot carry out her normal duties we will find other, lighter tasks for her…perhaps the mending, or she can manage the stillroom. That gives us time to think of ways to help her. And when she is brought to bed, we can make sure—'

'You'd do this for her?'

And then Verity noticed. Under the immaculate white apron, Mrs Henty's hands were twisted tightly together. As if in prayer. And her eyes were bright. Too bright. 'Mrs Henty, does your decision to leave have something to do with Sarah's condition?'

The woman's throat worked convulsively. She nodded. Her voice came out as a harsh croak. As if she were about to cry. 'Sarah is my…my niece. My sister's only child. She died when Sarah was three. Childbed. I promised I'd look after Sarah. When she was little I paid for her board in the village. His lordship's mother gave her the place here when she was old enough.' She swallowed hard. 'She's only seventeen, ma'am.'

Verity nodded and patted the sofa beside her. 'Sit down, Mrs Henty. You're obviously upset. Come.'

Stiffly, the older woman sat down on the extreme edge of the sofa. 'Very kind of you, madam.'

'Bother my kindness,' said Verity. 'Tell me about Sarah. Who is the father? Could his lordship do something to…if the man offered marriage and…?'

''Twas Ted Granger, my lady.'

'Ted…? Oh.'

Ted Granger. Widow Granger's lost son. The entire crew had been lost when their vessel grounded on the Goodwin Sands. In a high wind no other ship had been able to get them off. Ship and crew had been swallowed without a trace by the sands.

'She's a good girl!' Mrs Henty burst out and then closed her eyes and gripped her hands more tightly. 'She'd been walking out with him this age past,' she continued in shaking tones. 'They were just about to ask Rector to call the banns. Everyone knew he'd asked her. When he died, she said nothing. Just to leave her be, that she'd be all right. She only told me about…about the baby last night. So I thought if I resigned and took a pension, I could make a home for her and her baby.'

Verity looked at her, really looked at her, and smiled. Instead of seeing a disapproving housekeeper, she saw a woman who cared about her family. Why couldn't this woman have been *her* aunt?

'You'll be a great-aunt. Had you thought of that?'

Mrs Henty blinked. A slow answering smile dawned. 'Not exactly, my lady. A great-aunt…' She dashed away something that sparkled on her cheek. 'I suppose it might be worse.'

'Much worse,' Verity assured her. 'Now, why don't we think hard about ways to help Sarah? There's no need for you to leave unless you really feel it would be best for your family.'

'My…my family…' More tears spilt over.

Verity's eyes stung and her throat closed up. Lucky Sarah to have this stalwart aunt prepared to sacrifice her position and face social ostracism for her sake. She'd be prepared to trade places with Sarah just to know this sort of unswerving love.

After a moment, Mrs Henty sat up and sniffed, wiping her

eyes. 'Well. I dare say that's all settled.' She looked at Verity firmly. 'If your ladyship wouldn't mind a word of advice. Your hair.'

Verity flushed. Her hair was awful. The only way she could manage it was to scrape it back into the most severe bun imaginable. Otherwise it curled around her face in the most annoying way, falling into everything she did. But the bun made her face look so hagged.

'You need to cut it a bit. Just around your face so it can curl. Soften things a bit, that would.'

'Cut it?' Verity stared. Who would do that?

The answer came. 'I could cut it for you, my lady. I was lady's maid to the master's mother until she died. And I'll show Sarah how to dress it better. Lovely hair, it is. So thick and curly.' She nodded in a very decisive sort of way. 'That's settled then. We'll do it tonight.'

With Mrs Henty as an ally Verity's days became far busier and happier. There seemed all manner of things requiring the mistress's personal intervention. Such as the garden.

'A disgrace it is, my lady!' said Mrs Henty roundly. 'The master and Mr Richard spend all their time on the estate and the garden is going to rack and ruin. Barnes is getting on and unless he's pushed he won't do anything beyond the lawns, hedges and trees. Why, you wouldn't believe the trouble I have to go to finding some flowers for your sitting room and the drawing room!'

Verity swallowed. Mrs Henty appeared to think Lady Blakehurst had only to give orders and it would all happen, but how would Max view it? As interference? And that other item of information that Mrs Henty had let drop with seeming casualness... She shied away from that. The garden would be far easier. Surely if Max could see that she was trying to carry out her responsibilities as mistress of his house...if she made it clear that she wished for his guidance...

* * *

She broached the garden over breakfast the following morning.

'My lord, Mrs Henty has brought it to my attention that the gardens need attention.' He looked up with a frown as she sat down with her laden plate. 'Nothing major,' she hurried on, 'but I did just wonder if you had any preferences, plantings you would particularly like… or…or dislike.'

He fixed her with a cool stare. 'The gardens are no concern of mine. Do as you please.' He disappeared behind his newspaper.

Verity gritted her teeth. 'Excellent,' she said sweetly. 'I thought of replacing the knot garden with a fountain court, not as large as Versailles of course, but—'

The newspaper dropped. 'The devil you will!' he said.

She showed him an innocent face. 'Oh, then you do have some interest! And some things you would prefer I didn't do?'

His face slightly red, he said, 'I meant you might do as you pleased within reason! Not turn the place upside down.'

'An upside-down fountain…' mused Verity. 'That *would* be something out of the common way, don't you agree, my lord?'

A strangled sound from the other side of the table caught her attention. 'Can I pour you some more ale? Or are you finding something difficult to swallow?'

Richard looked as shocked as if one of the spaniels had bitten him.

Verity smiled demurely and turned back to her husband. 'There are some things needing attention in the house as well, some rugs that need replacing, pictures that need cleaning, the chandelier in—'

'I beg you will spare me this recital of your household tasks, madam!' snapped Max. 'While I expect my wife to attend to these matters, I do not expect to be wearied with them!'

Verity flinched. She opened her mouth…and shut it again.

She *wouldn't* apologise! Why should she? Then annoyance flared. 'I beg your pardon, my lord, but I am afraid you must be wearied with them for a moment, since I require your advice on one or two matters.'

Max, who had again retired into the *London Gazette*, lowered the paper and stared at her. She met his gaze with outward calm, praying he wouldn't notice her shaking hands. So long since she had stood up to anyone. God only knew what had given her the courage now.

'My advice?' His voice bit into her like a frozen knife. 'My advice is that you concern yourself with keeping the house in good order, rather than wasting my blunt replacing items that may be a little old fashioned, but are still perfectly functional.'

She looked down at the plate of ham and eggs in front of her. And discovered that her appetite had vanished completely. Instead she poured herself a cup of tea, her hands not quite steady handling the massive silver pot.

He spoke again. 'I would remind you that I did not marry out of any particular need for a wife.'

Hurt stabbed deep, but she hung on to her quiet façade. 'Thank you for reminding me,' she said carefully and pushed back her chair. Her plate lay untouched, her cup of tea full. She felt as though she might be sick.

His voice followed her. 'You haven't finished your breakfast. For heaven's sake, Verity, you haven't even touched it! You'll starve!'

She turned and glared at him, infusing her tones with indifference. 'I think, my lord, that at nearly twenty I can judge for myself when I have had enough.'

The door shut quietly behind her, leaving a dazed silence.

Richard broke it. 'You know, Max, one or two of the rugs *are* a trifle worn. And I dare say if you *wanted* to get a better look at any of our forebears, cleaning the portraits would be a perfectly reasonable thing to do.'

More than reasonable, Max acknowledged. Precisely what

she ought to be doing. Going over the house. Setting things to rights. It wasn't as if she had suggested spending vast sums of money as his mother had done on the London house. Had his mother made such a suggestion about a fountain court he'd have known she meant it. At least with Verity he knew she'd been joking, trying to ease the tension between them. She had been trying very hard to do that since their marriage.

I should like to belong again...

Such a simple wish. The one thing he couldn't grant her. He didn't dare let her that close. But he didn't have to hurt her. Did he?

Richard's chuckle gave him further pause. 'Must say she's quick enough. An upside-down fountain! I wish you might have seen your face.'

Max suppressed a savage rejoinder. It would be so damn easy to respond to her overtures of friendliness, to laugh with her, to be friends. His body tightened. He wanted more than that. He wanted to be her lover again.

He looked at Richard, unconcernedly devouring sirloin. His twin. Half an hour between heir and spare. Damned if he'd put that distance between him and his brother.

Leaving the house, Verity walked and ran until she reached the beech woods, ignoring the stitch in her side. *Coward! Can't you do anything but run?* Shivering in the breeze, she forced herself to think again about the tidbit of knowledge Mrs Henty had shared. Max's birthday was next week. Richard's too, of course, since they were twins. Twins. Their obvious friendship and closeness tore at her. What would it be like? To be that close to someone, to know that however much you argued, there was always that tie binding you.

Ties could break. Even ties of blood... Pulling back from that, she remembered once saying to Max that she had no one to give a present to. Well, now she did. But...a birthday. She tensed. And hung on to her common sense. His birthday.

Not hers. Just because she never wanted another birthday didn't mean that other people couldn't enjoy them.

She didn't want to buy anything. She might have plenty of money but, as far as she was concerned, it belonged to Max anyway. The idea of buying him a present out of his own money nearly choked her. She wanted it to be something special, something of *her* and there was only one thing she could think of.

Mentioning her idea to Mrs Henty had earned her an amused smile.

'Oh, aye. He'd like it, right enough. But whether or not you'd get Master Richard to agree! That's another story. Tried to get one done a couple of years back. Master Richard wouldn't have any of it.'

Verity could well believe that. So she'd have to be a little devious and do something she had vowed not to do. Encroach on Richard's space in the library in one last effort to reach Max.

Grimly she focused on the sketch. This should be the last sitting. Richard was ignoring her as usual in favour of whatever he was carving. She could almost believe that she was invisible. She frowned as she tried to capture the twisting fall of a wood shaving. If only this idea had never occurred to her. If only she didn't have this need to reach out to her chilly husband... Her vision blurred and she blinked rapidly. Dratted dust! Or maybe the flowers on the sofa table behind her were making her eyes water.

Just as long as Richard didn't realise that her supposed perspective sketch of the library was a hoax. She risked another glance across at the unconscious subject of her sketch. Asking for his co-operation would have been far simpler, but her courage had failed her in the face of his scornful, assessing gaze when she walked in the first time and met his outraged stare. It wasn't so bad really. He never spoke beyond a brief acknowledgement when she bid him good day, or to call the dogs away from her when they became too demanding of pats and attention.

Flickering a glance at the dogs now snoozing in a patch of sun, she acknowledged that all he wanted was for her to finish as quickly as may be and leave him in peace.

'Tell me, sister—when can I expect to be supplanted by your child?'

Her sketch book crashed to the floor and the dogs looked up, startled. 'I…I… Pardon?' Shock swirled in her brain.

His smile would have flayed an elephant. 'Oh, very good, sister!' And his voice flicked her on the raw. 'Your child. You do understand that I have a vested interest in the issue of your marriage, do you not? That I'd be interested to know when you plan to fulfil your obligations.'

Frowning, Verity worked her way through that as she retrieved her book, trying to understand his meaning, fending off the curious Gus. That Richard was Max's heir presumptive she knew. And if the marriage was childless, then of course Richard would remain his heir. But it sounded as though he thought *she* had some say in it.

Puzzled, she met his eyes. 'I don't quite follow. How is it my fault if—?'

'Good God!' he exploded. 'You trapped my brother into marriage, then refuse him your bed and calmly ask me how it is your fault if he has no heir?'

Heat flamed across Verity's cheeks as his meaning penetrated. That he could even say such things to her shocked her. And the injustice enraged her. *She* had refused her bed to her husband? Had Max told him that?

And the expression on his face. Scornful, mocking.

Her control splintered. 'Let me make something quite clear, *brother*: whatever Blakehurst may choose to believe, this marriage was not of my seeking, but since I was forced into it, I assumed he had every intention of getting an heir. Whatever *his* attitude may be to his vows, I have every intention of keeping to mine! If at any time he wishes to avail himself of his rights...' she paused and bit her lip hard '...then he has only to knock on the door between our rooms. It would be difficult for me to refuse him my bed since he shows no sign of wishing to share it. Until he does, there is little chance of an heir supplanting you. So I suggest you mind your own business!'

She grabbed her sketch book, scattering crayons over the floor with clumsy, shaking hands. She left them, seared by the knowledge that Max had indicated his contempt for her to his brother and blamed her for the state of their marriage. Damn him! Max had refused to heed her misgivings and insisted on the marriage. And now he blamed her!

Later that afternoon she sat curled up on a garden seat near the fishpond, golden warmth pouring down on her shoulders as she sketched. So many years since her mother had taught her... She blinked and wriggled her stiff shoulders. Remembering was too painful, especially the sketch she had done just before her mother's death—the sketch her father had destroyed in his grief.

She changed her position slightly. The sun glaring off the paper was making her eyes water. Focusing on her double subject, she breathed a silent prayer of thanks that they were immobile at last. The three-hour walk she had taken them for after leaving the library had finally exhausted the spaniels and they lay asleep in the sun.

She sketched steadily. If she finished the dogs before they recovered, she could fill in the background at her leisure. As long as she could keep her mind off the reason she was doing this particular sketch. She gritted her teeth. Possibly it would be torn up, or at the very least thrust to the back of a drawer, but it would serve as a sort of unspoken apology to Richard...for what? Using the library in her own home? Obviously her presence had been totally unwelcome since she had found her crayons, neatly boxed and sorted, on her dressing table when she returned from her walk.

Grimly she concentrated; somehow she had to make the dogs look asleep, not dead. Despite herself, she smiled at the way they were curled up together, Gus's nose resting on Taffy's back. A bee hovered over his nose, buzzing loudly. Gus opened one eye, snapped lazily and the bee flew off into a lavender bush.

Her shoulders ached and she wriggled them again.

Slowly, steadily, the sketch progressed and she was able to lose herself in it, forgetting everything. Except for the dull ache in her heart, the ache that whispered she had failed, that Max didn't want her as a wife in any capacity, that he no longer even wanted her as a woman. She thrust the knowledge away. At least she had a home, somewhere she felt safe... She should be counting her blessings. Her neck ached. Unconsciously she reached up and rubbed it, turning her head from side to side to release the sore muscles.

'Madam?'

The quiet, deep voice brought her around with a snap and she gave a cry of shocked pain as every muscle in her neck locked tight. Dizzy, nauseated with the sudden pain, she fought, eyes closed, to control it.

'Verity! Here, let me.' Gentle hands closed on her shoulders, drew her close and eased her forehead against a powerful chest. Careful probing fingers began to rub and soothe the taut muscles of her neck, easing the tightness, relaxing her.

Close. Too close. He was holding her again. Gentle, tender. Memory poured over her in a bittersweet wave, mocking her with the echo of what might have been. If she had not been so foolish, or if he had never found out who she was.

She wriggled, trying to escape, but he held her with effortless strength. 'Please—let me go. There is no need...'

'Shh.' His fingers pressed and kneaded. 'You were rubbing your neck anyway. And you're wound as tight as a watchspring. Just relax. Let me help you. I shouldn't have startled you like that.'

On a silent prayer, she summoned every scrap of control, of diffidence, all the things she didn't possess where he was concerned. Especially in the face of his unexpected concern. No. Not unexpected. Even when he had been most angry with her, he had protected her.

Through the thin muslin gown she felt his soothing fingers shift to her shoulders, rubbing and kneading stiff muscles, easing the tension there. Strong, yet so gentle, they seemed to know every sore spot, every ache—just as they knew her body in other ways. She retreated from the thought, but it was too late. Memory surrounded her, lapping at her, dissolving her defences and washing through her.

She breathed deeply, willing herself to forget. A trace of sandalwood, the musky scent, now slightly sweaty, that was Max himself, and something else—a faint smell of…horse. That was it.

'You've been riding,' she said. And was shocked at the husky tone of her voice. Something had gone vastly wrong with her lungs.

His hands stilled. 'Are you telling me I stink of the stables?'

She shook her head against his chest and shivered at the caress of his waistcoat against her cheek. A snuffle and insistent paw made her look down. The dogs had come to see what madness their humans were at. Gus stood, one paw resting on Max's thigh, the other demanding her attention.

'It's all right, Gus,' she said. 'I'm fine. Down, old chap.'

'Not in his vocabulary, I'm afraid,' said Max, a wry note in his voice. 'The pair of them are atrociously spoiled.' He continued to knead and Verity relaxed further, lassitude enveloping her. She had not realised until now just how tightly she was wound.

Max hadn't realised either. The tension he had found in her shocked him. Like a harpstring, stretched almost to breaking point. Closing his eyes, he acknowledged that it had taken

more than his unexpected appearance to tie her in knots
like that.

And now she lay relaxed, soft and yielding in his arms, as
she had the night he had unwittingly taken her innocence.
Memory was a fire in his blood, the flames licking at the
edges of his self-control. He should release her, step back
from the edge. His decision had been made before the wedding.

She nestled a little closer, her cheek shifting against his
chest. Through his coat, waistcoat and fine linen shirt, the
unconscious caress seared him like a brand.

'I hope your neck feels better now, madam.'

She stared up at him and for a moment he saw the shock
in her face. 'M…Max?' No more than a whisper, shaken,
uncertain. A small hand lifted.

He rose and stepped back, inclining his head politely.

The hand dropped into her lap and she turned away, picking up her crayons.

'Ah, you found your crayons. I asked Mrs Henty to return
them to your room.'

'Oh. Did you? Thank you, my lord. Is there something I
can do for you, or am I in your way here?'

'Not at all,' he said. 'You will disturb no one out here, but
I should point out that this is Richard's home, as well as
mine. He does not appreciate intrusions on his privacy, any
more than I do. Perhaps you might find somewhere else to
sketch other than the library?'

He had spoken gently enough, but the box of crayons
slipped from her hold. Automatically she bent down to pick
it up. What had he said? *Intrusion on his privacy? Richard's
home, as well as mine.* Max and Richard's home. Not hers.
When had she last had a home? Not since…not since her
mother died had she felt that she had a home. A place where
she felt safe and wanted. Loved. A home was more than
safety. To feel at home you had to be wanted. Part of the
family. Not a resented responsibility.

Apparently, instead of attempting to create a marriage she had encroached on Max's privacy. She had forgotten her place, in fact. Pain spread out from deep within her, tearing at her with unsheathed claws. She dragged in a breath, wondering if it would rip her apart, and straightened. Blindly she met his gaze, wondering what to say. Then, 'I was happier as your mistress.'

His jaw dropped. 'I...I beg your pardon?' he asked carefully.

She could practically feel the shock rippling out of him. Turning away, she began repeating her remark. 'I was happier as your—'

'I *heard* what you said!'

A knife, twisting and burning deep within, Verity responded, 'Really? Was that an apology you were offering, then? How very surprising.'

'*Apology?* Why, you little...'

Words apparently failed Max, so Verity took it upon herself to help him out. 'Whore? Bitch?' She kept her back to him, to all intents ordering the crayons in their box. The colours blurred. She blinked hard.

'I had no intention of saying anything of the sort.' Max's voice sounded from much closer.

She whirled, fingers tightening on the box, and saw that he was coming towards her, a strange expression on his face.

'No, my lord? Don't you believe in speaking your mind?' There. She'd said it. Flung down the gauntlet. She only wished it had been the one from the suit of armour in the hall, and that she could have hurled it in his face.

It was possible to control her breathing if she kept it shallow. If she concentrated on every breath, every step, she might manage to escape before the heat behind her eyelids became a scalding torrent. Before she fell apart.

She had tried. And she had failed. Again. Somehow she forced her voice to function. 'I beg your pardon, my lord. Please convey my apologies to your brother and assure him that I won't trouble him again.' Her chin high, she walked past him, teeth clenched, eyes burning with hurt.

It doesn't matter. It mustn't matter.

'What sense was there in being my mistress?' he growled. 'You have what you wanted—safety!'

Fury surged through her and she rounded on him. 'You wanted a mistress. Not a bride. You wanted Selina. Not me. I should have returned to the Faringdons.'

'Verity!'

'Go to the devil, my lord!' Her control cracking, she walked away.

Max stood staring after her, shaken to the core. Had she wanted more than safety? Had she wanted what he had wanted? Whatever that was.

Chapter Nine

Max stalked into breakfast on his birthday, thoroughly out of charity with the world. Apparently he had finally persuaded his wife that their lives should be conducted separately. He hadn't even seen her since their row in the garden. He should be feeling relieved, not worried about whether or not she was eating properly.

'Happy birthday, Max,' offered Richard.

He smiled faintly. 'You too, Ricky. Er…your present wouldn't fit in here. At least she would, but Henny swore that she and the maids would resign in a body, so I left her in the stables.'

'Henny?' asked Richard with a grin.

Max chuckled. 'No, Angelfire's foal. She'll be a beauty. Just up to your weight. Good breeding stock too.'

Richard flushed. 'Damn it, Max! You *can't* give me that filly. With her bloodlines she could be a champion! Another Molly Longlegs. Choose an—'.

'Oh, stubble it, Ricky!' said Max. 'She's yours.'

Richard subsided, still muttering about over generous idiots. Ignoring this, Max picked up one of the parcels beside him on the table.

He cast a guilty glance at the place set for Verity. It would remain empty. But the staff kept setting it for her. The empty chair and pristine silver mocked him. And her words haunted him—*Whore? Bitch?* Would she really have preferred to return to the Faringdons rather than marry him? Damn it! She'd wanted safety and security. Enough to become his mistress. What more did she want now that she had it?

He glanced up and found Richard's gaze on him.

'Not much,' said Richard, flushing.

For a moment his mind blanked. And then he realised that he was still holding the parcel. Unwrapping it, he found a small carving of two spaniels curled up together. He shot a glance at the fireplace where the originals lay in a tangle of paws and drooping ears. He chuckled. Only Richard could have given him this.

All he said was, 'Now I know why you've been leaving such a mess in the library.' No more was necessary. Not with Richard.

Another larger, flat parcel lay beside his place. Frowning, Max picked it up. 'What's this?'

Richard shrugged. 'Open it and find out. It was there when I came in. Almeria, perhaps? She might have sent it via Henny.'

Max dismissed that suggestion with a snort. 'Hardly!' Almeria only noted one's birthday if one chanced within earshot of her discourse on duty and propriety.

He opened the parcel, puzzled. A frame came into view— a picture, then. His breath caught...but how could Richard not have known? Or had he? Yet it seemed so unlike him to consent to such a thing.

Max stared down at the crayon portrait of his brother, caught frowning in concentration over something in his hands. Looking more closely Max could see that he was carving; the artist had even captured the wood shavings curling down in a beam of sunlight. He looked again and smiled. He knew where this had been done. The bay window in the library. The floor there had been littered with shavings recently. He could have been given nothing he would value more dearly. But who had done it? The sketch held him speechless. He could almost feel the sunlight pouring in…

Dismissing speculation, he turned to his brother. 'Thanks, Ricky,' he said simply.

Richard stared. 'What for?'

Max held up the picture. 'This.'

Richard leaned forward over the table. 'Nothing to do with me. What is it?'

Max felt a queer stab of presentiment. 'You must have known. Who did it?' Even as he asked, he remembered the crayons and his whole world tipped over.

Richard rose stiffly and came around the table. 'Who did wha— Good God!' He stared at the sketch in disbelief. 'So *that's* why she kept staring at me! The little—' He bit off whatever he had been going to say and pointed at the bottom right corner.

Max knew who had done it but, even so, steel bands clamped around his heart as he saw what Richard was point- ing at. Entwined initials. A *V* and an *S*.

'You didn't know?' he asked, confused. How the devil had she known about his birthday? And dammit all—she'd signed it with her maiden name! Hurt and shame flooded him.

Richard shook his head. 'No. She *said* she was doing a perspective sketch of the library.' He flushed. 'I…I'm sorry, Max. I wasn't exactly welcoming, you know.' He swallowed. 'In fact, that last time I was damned rude to her.'

Max just nodded. His conscience felt raw. Verity had tried so very hard to breach the wall he'd set between them and he'd rebuffed every shy overture.

He'd been polite, distant, always addressing her formally with the utmost consideration. Even when he snubbed her. But she had kept right on trying. Until that time in the garden when her temper had finally snapped. Swallowing, he faced what he'd done: he'd told her that she was unwelcome in her own home. Verity—who had once told him she wanted to belong again, not to be always apart. He hadn't seen her

since. Literally. She might have ceased to exist for all he
knew. The thought lacerated him. She had wanted to belong.
On any terms. Even as his mistress.

His distance. His sanity. At all costs. Only…he'd never
realised *she* would bear the cost.

Mrs Henty informed him that her ladyship had taken a
picnic and gone for a walk straight after breakfast. That she'd
given orders a few days previously that she would dine in
her rooms until further notice.

He winced at that bit of information. He knew precisely
on which day those orders had been given.

'Thank you, Henny,' he said. 'When her ladyship comes
in, perhaps you might ask her…I mean, tell her…er, suggest
that she might care to dine with Mr Richard and myself tonight.' Good heavens! Could he not even convey a message
to his wife without stumbling over himself?

'Certainly, my lord.'

The stiffness in his housekeeper's voice warned him. He
eyed her carefully. 'Something wrong, Henny?'

Her lips tightened even more. 'Well, it's not my place to
say, Master Max, but…'

Max braced himself. When Henny remembered her place
and called him *Master Max*, squalls lay ahead. He'd been
aware of the friction between Henny and her mistress, but
he'd thought the problem had blown over… Better to let
Verity sort it out on her own terms.

''Twould be better if you asked her ladyship yourself. Told
her last night that she should go down, but she wouldn't take
a bit of notice and she's not eating enough to keep a sparrow
alive. Just picks at her dinner again, she does. Like when she
first arrived. Says she isn't hungry…but if you ask me, she
can't eat when she's upset!'

Max swore and Mrs Henty favoured him with a glare.
'Don't you use that sort of language! Or I won't bother turning the sheep tallow into soap before I wash your mouth out!

Plain it is that her ladyship doesn't feel at home here yet. Maybe she misses her family.'

Max spluttered at the thought of Verity missing the Faringdons and his conscience went straight for the throat. *Are you any better?*

Henny was still speaking. '...and so kind and sweet she was over poor Sarah, well, I didn't know how to thank her.' The old woman dashed a hand across her eyes. 'So understanding. A real lady, she was. Said she wouldn't be the first to cast stones. And telling me that I mustn't leave... Well, after the way I treated her at first, I wouldn't have blamed her if she'd leapt at the chance to be rid of me. But not her. Good-hearted she is, and—'

Max broke in. 'Henny, what the deuce are you talking about? Why were you going to leave? And what's this about Sarah? You mean your niece? Isn't she waiting on Lady Blakehurst?'

Mrs Henty pulled out a handkerchief and blew her nose. 'Yes, sir. So good her ladyship was. I told her I was giving notice and I told her about Sarah, and how she'd have to be dismissed, but her ladyship wouldn't have none of it.'

Max tried to make sense of it. 'Henny, what's this about Sarah? Why did you give notice?'

Her jaw dropped. 'You mean, her ladyship didn't tell you?'

He refrained from telling her that her ladyship's last words to him had been to go to the devil. Instead he shook his head. 'She's told me nothing.'

Mrs Henty swallowed. 'Then... Well, Sarah was walking out. With Ted Granger.'

Max bit his lip. 'Oh, God, no. Was she? I'd no idea. How is she?'

'Breeding,' said Mrs Henty baldly. 'About to have the banns called they were, when he was killed. When she told me...I...I couldn't think what else to do except leave and hope you'd give me a decent pension so I could look after her.' She blew her nose again.

'And?' prompted Max.

Mrs Henty drew a deep breath. 'Her ladyship said to find a decent woman nearby who'd take Sarah as a boarder, with the baby. Maybe a widow with young children so's they could help each other and she'd pay board and a little besides so's Sarah could get ahead. She said she'd do the same even if I gave notice to make a home for Sarah. That it was up to me, but she'd help, whatever we decided.'

'I…see,' said Max. He tried to imagine how any other lady of quality would react to the news that one of her maids was pregnant. Lady Arnsworth, perhaps? Or, his stomach condensed to ice, Lady Faringdon?

Mrs Henty eyed him nervously. 'If your lordship doesn't approve…'

He shook his head. 'Don't be a peagoose, Henny. I…I was just surprised.' *How many ladies of rank would have done that? Most would have flung the girl out penniless. Including Mama.* Not Verity. Having faced that fear herself, she'd never inflict it on another. No. He wasn't really surprised.

'So where is Sarah going?' he asked.

Mrs Henty actually smiled. 'Why, to Martha Granger. Her ladyship arranged it. She took me in the gig to see Martha. And once she got over the shock, Martha couldn't agree fast enough. With the little ones, the offer of Sarah's board was a blessing.' She paused. 'But it's not just that. She said she didn't care if the baby was a…a bastard. 'Twas just bad luck and she'd have something of Ted left to love and a new daughter into the bargain.'

She fixed his lordship with a glare. 'I don't know what her ladyship's family's like, but it's a fine thing when a lady of quality tells an old woman like me that she'd have me as her aunt any day!' She picked up her pile of linen…and waited.

He'd once asked Verity what she wanted—*a family…to belong again*—and he had pushed her away. Told her she had no place here.

The news that she wasn't eating again rocked him to the

core. She had been gaining a little weight, getting some colour in her cheeks. He remembered the journey up to London from Faringdon Hall. She'd barely eaten then. Had she been frightened? Alone with a man who was savagely angry with her? Realising that Henny was still there, he pulled himself together. 'Do you happen to know which way she might have gone, Henny?' he asked.

She smiled. 'She likes the cliffs out over the sands. Likes the view and the birds, I dare say. Shouldn't be hard to find her.'

Max felt every drop of blood congeal as Henny turned to go. Verity…too upset to eat properly, near those damn cliffs. His stomach churned. Six hundred feet high the cliffs were in spots. Fear rose in his throat, acrid and metallic. No. She wouldn't. He didn't believe she would take that way out.

But if she was upset…she might not be as careful as she ought to be. And the cliffs could be unstable. If she were too near the edge…

High on the cliffs, Verity stared out over the Channel. Somewhere in the blue haze lay France. She kept well back from the edge, Mrs Henty's warning fresh in her mind. *You be careful. Tricky the cliffs are. Falling all the time. And the turf is slippery.*

The salt-laden wind buffeted her mercilessly, whipping around her, so that her dress moulded to her. It caught the seabirds and whirled them shrieking aloft. A falcon hovered out from the clifftop, waiting patiently for an unwary pigeon.

She watched it, yearning. If only it were possible to ride the wind, to fly beyond the disaster she had made of everything. Looking back, she could see the foolishness of her decision to deceive Max and become his mistress. If she had realised that he would find out…

And if only she had not been foolish enough to believe that she could regain his trust, that his concern for her was spurred by more than his respect for her father, that some spark of his affection for Selina could be re-ignited for Verity. She should not have married him.

Dreams deceived, phantoms of hope that shimmered into nothing. Leaving only an aching heart with too many bitter secrets entombed. Better to be like the falcon. Alone. Dependent on nothing but the air beneath her wings. At least for the falcon, the air had more substance than her foolish dreams of love.

Yet she had her freedom. Freedom to come and go as she pleased. No one demanded anything of her. Nothing was expected of her. Because nobody cared. Freedom on those terms was as empty as the wind. The beat of hoofs and a yell brought her spinning around.

Mounted on a tall grey, Max was galloping towards her. He pulled up a few yards away and leapt down. 'Verity— come back.' The careful voice had her staring. His face was absolutely white. And he had used her name.

Puzzled, she said, 'I'm not going anywhere. Not really. Just a walk.' She flushed. 'I suppose you think I should have my maid with me!'

He didn't answer directly. 'Please, come away from the cliffs. You—do you know about the cliffs? They can be—'

'Mrs Henty was kind enough to warn me.'

'Oh. Then…then you didn't…'

His voice faltered and shock burst through her as she took in the lathered horse, its sides heaving and realised what he had thought. That she might… Her very soul shuddered at the idea of causing so much grief and pain to another.

'No,' she whispered. 'You can't believe that I would do that to you…that I would…' Her voice failed. Even if Max didn't care for her, he had taken responsibility for her, would blame himself if anything happened to her. She knew to the depths of her soul what that sort of guilt could do.

Holding her gaze, he nodded. 'I…yes. I mean…no. Dammit! I was worried. The cliffs can be rotten in places.' He held out his hand. Eyes wide, she walked to him, avoiding his still outstretched hand. She had stopped dreaming. Surely, soon she would stop hurting?

After a moment he dropped his hand and picked up his reins. 'That sketch...'

She flushed and, turning away, began walking. No doubt it was dreadful, the last thing one should give to a man whose ancestral walls were practically papered with masterpieces, but she didn't need to hear it said. And she didn't need him to see her with tears on her cheeks, even if it was just the wind making her eyes water. Never again would she try to reach out to Max. She had only put the sketch on the breakfast table because she couldn't think what else to do with it.

He caught up with her. 'I didn't realise what you were doing,' he said, his voice stiff. 'If I'd known—'

'I am perfectly aware that you want nothing of me!' she flashed. 'You need not worry. I would not dream of doing it again!'

'I beg your pardon.'

Despite the burning in her eyes, she turned to face him, shaking with rage. 'Just what did you fail to understand this time?'

He reddened. 'That *was* an apology. For what I said the other day. I beg your pardon. Unreservedly. I never meant to imply that you were unwanted. I'm sorry. Will you not forgive me?'

Numbly, she shook her head. 'No. No, it is not necessary. You owe me nothing, least of all an apology for speaking the truth. Good morning, sir. Thank you for your concern, but I would prefer to be alone. You need have no fear that I shall do any harm to myself.'

The hot pricking behind her eyes warned her. Blindly she turned to go. She could eat her lunch in the beech woods. It would be sheltered there, safe, protected. Only something as unfettered as the falcon could live safely out here.

'Verity...'

She kept walking. If only she could have remained Selina.

Max had cared for Selina, enough to call her his sweetheart. Verity was no more than a duty to him.

She came in halfway through the afternoon, damp with a light drizzle, and listened to Mrs Henty's urgings with an aching heart.

'Told me to ask you to come down. Set on it, he was.'

She forced a smile as she untied her damp cloak. 'Thank you, Mrs Henty. I'll remember. Would you send Sarah up to me, please?'

He couldn't have been terribly set on it. He'd said nothing to her out on the cliffs.

Mrs Henty nodded. 'I did tell the master about Sarah. I…I didn't realise you hadn't mentioned it to him yet.'

Verity jerked around from removing her cloak. 'What did he say? Was he angry?' Fear clutched at her. If he tried to stop her helping the girl…she wouldn't stand for it!

Mrs Henty smiled. 'Master Max? No. He didn't mind. He's always been kind and serious-like about his responsibilities.'

Verity turned away to hang her cloak over the back of a chair by the fire. 'Yes. Very kind.' She fought to keep the wobble out of her voice. A man could resent his responsibilities. Deeply. Blinking rapidly, she faced Mrs Henty. 'I won't need Sarah now. I think I might have a nap. Send her up to wake me for dinner.'

A beaming smile chased wrinkles all over the housekeeper's face. 'Yes, my lady. I'll come up with her meself and we'll choose a pretty gown for you!'

Guilt niggled at Verity, but she forced a smile. 'Thank you… Henny.'

Mrs Henty flushed. 'Well, to be sure! You get a good rest, my lady. Get some colour back into those cheeks. You don't want to go showing his lordship a pale face.'

'No,' said Verity. 'I won't.'

* * *

Max stared at Mrs Henty in surprise. 'You thought she *was* coming down?'

Dinner was set out in the small dining salon. Richard leant against the chimney piece, listening, a very faint frown on his face.

Mrs Henty wrung her hands. 'I'm sure she meant to! Told me to wake her in good time. And I helped her change into the prettiest gown. Sky blue with the prettiest pink trim. Lovely she looked! A bit quiet, she was, but there's nothing new in that!'

And now she'd vanished. Max's only comfort was that she was in the house somewhere, avoiding him. He didn't blame her. He'd made it plain that he wished to have as little to do with her as possible and she'd obliged by withdrawing herself. Yet she had still given him the picture of Richard. And she was taking up her duties as mistress of the house, finding out how to go on, carefully taking up the reins of authority when necessary. She had given him exactly what he wanted. Out of sight, out of mind.

The devil she was. He should have thanked her for the sketch out on the cliffs, told her that he would look forward to seeing her at dinner. But he'd been so damn frightened that she might have gone out to the cliffs to... He felt sick just thinking about it. And then he'd let her walk away. She had said that she wanted to be alone.

His conscience piped up on cue: *Perhaps she thought she had no choice?* 'I've given orders for food to be left in her sitting room, my lord,' said Mrs Henty. 'She'll usually eat fruit and cheese. And I said some cold meat. Likely she'll eat it when she comes back. Tired she was after her walk. She slept for a good couple of hours.'

He knew she'd slept. He'd put his head through the connecting door and seen her curled up, fast asleep. She'd looked so pale... His heart clenched. Madness. It was madness to allow himself to care. But if she never knew... Couldn't he look after her without her realising how deeply she affected him? If he simply exerted his authority to make sure she ate properly…made sure she had everything she could possibly desire… A family? To belong?

'Will there be anything else, my lord?' Henny's disapproving voice jolted him back to reality.

'Er, no. Thank you, Henny. I'll find her ladyship myself. Goodnight.'

Mrs Henty didn't deign to an intelligible reply. She snorted and stalked out, her back radiating indignation. The door closed behind her with a decided snap.

'I'd say, *Master Max*,' said Richard, 'that you have been called to account for yourself and found severely lacking in several departments.'

Max grunted.

'Something I should show you, too.'

Max looked up. Richard had picked up a small, framed picture.

'I found this on my desk in the library. God knows how she got them to sit still for long enough.' He walked over and handed it to Max.

With an appalling sense of certainty, Max realised that he knew what it was—the sketch Verity had been working on in the garden. He gazed at it in shamed silence. How many hours' work had the two sketches taken, believing all the time that they would be scorned and yet having nothing else to give?

Richard gave him a searching look. 'Max—has it occurred to you that there might have been some sort of mistake somewhere along the line?'

I'd like…to belong. To be part of people's lives. Not to be always apart.

He had pushed her away. Guilt rose up in a choking wave. 'You'd better start without me. I have to find her.'

Richard's eyes creased in a faint smile. 'I'll have some Madeira while I wait.'

Max opened his mouth to protest and, catching a raised

brow, shut it again. He was halfway to the door when Richard spoke again.

'If you don't mind some advice—take Gus and Taffy with you. One of the reasons that carving looks a bit skewed is that they kept trying to sit on her lap while I was doing it. I can only surmise that she drugged them to get this done!'

Max nodded abruptly and whistled for the dogs.

He ran her to earth in the stillroom.

She didn't look up when he opened the door a crack and peered in. His heart lurched to see her sitting in the glow of an oil lamp, surrounded by shadows, with her head bent, sewing. Lavender bags for her clothes? But the material looked a bit coarse for that. And the pungent smell wasn't right. What then?

He watched her for a moment, the tender, pale curve of her cheek, the slight furrow of concentration in her brow and the steady rhythmic motion of her hands as she worked. Always busy. Every time he saw her, she was doing something. Some small task. Alone. Arranging flowers, sewing, waxing a piece of furniture. And it was never for herself. He realised with a pang that she was used to being busy. Used to having no time for herself. Used to being alone.

Then it came to him—mint. She was using some sort of mint.

Before he could speak, the spaniels, losing patience, shoved past him and charged across the room, hurling themselves at Verity with unfettered delight. Material and herbs scattered as she fended them off.

'How on earth did you two idiots get…oh!' The way she shrank back in her chair was like a slap across the face for Max. Even worse was the immediate recovery. The way she sat straight and faced him. As though she faced a firing squad. With her eyes open.

'My…my lord. Is there something you need?'

He shook his head. 'I came to find you. Dinner is served.'

Moving slowly he came into the room, realising that her eyes never left his face even as she bent to pet the dogs. Like a wild creature, wary, suspicious, she tracked his every move.

'I didn't mean to keep you waiting,' she said quietly. 'I'm not very hungry.'

Something inside him twisted savagely. *Can't eat when she's upset...* He could see she hadn't eaten much recently. She'd begun to fill out, but the fashionable new clothes hung on her again. She needed more than safety.

'I see,' he said. With a faint smile he crouched down and began to pick up the herbs scattered about the floor. The sharp aroma of mint tugged at his memory and his old nanny's voice drifted into his mind. As if it were yesterday he remembered her tucking a sprig of mint into his buttonhole as she imparted a bit of folklore. Without thinking he said, 'In the language of flowers mint stands for virtue.' He heard the implication as the words left his mouth.

Silence burned between them as he sat back on his heels and raised his eyes to her face and saw briefly the pain, doubled and redoubled with each trembling breath. Her hand curved, shaking, over Taffy's head.

Then her face blanked, all expression leached from it as her breathing steadied and her hand resumed its caress. Her voice came, devoid of all feeling even as her eyes were shuttered. 'This, however, is pennyroyal. Its virtue is to repel fleas. For the dogs' beds.' Only the slight tremor in her hand betrayed her as she scratched Taffy's ear, reducing the spaniel to a quivering jelly even as she denied her own pain.

For he *had* hurt her. Again. How long had it taken her to perfect that indifferent mask? How long had it taken her even to realise that she needed one? How old had she been? Fifteen? Sixteen? Unable to help himself, he reached out, laying his hand on hers. The tension in her shocked him. She looked calm, unmoved. But she was taut as a drawn bow.

'I'm sorry,' he said simply. 'I didn't mean to insult you.' Gently he smoothed his thumb over the back of her hand.

The slight roughness drew his attention. Lifting her hand, he looked at it. And realised it was still slightly reddened, chafed from rough work. In a couple of places between the slender fingers he could see where the cracks had begun to heal.

Sharply she tugged at her hand. He held on, ignoring her efforts as well as Taffy's importunate nose. 'Is that still painful?' He stroked one healing crack with a gentle forefinger and felt the fine tremor that took her.

She shook her head. 'No, my lord. Mrs Henty made up some paste of Palermo. And she found some chicken-skin gloves for me to sleep in. My hands are much better.'

'Good.' At least she had found some healing under his roof. But the formality of her response accused him as nothing else could. *My lord.* As though she were beneath his touch. He had done that to her. Taking her other hand, he straightened up slowly, drawing her with him until they stood, hands linked. He looked down at her and found her face raised to his. They stood slightly out of the pool of light. Shadows fell across her face, deepening the dark smudges under her eyes.

Scarcely realising what he was about, his hands slid up her arms, caressing cool silken skin, and on over her throat, where a sudden pulse leapt and skittered under his gentle fingers. To her cheek. Tenderly his thumbs brushed up over the pale cheekbones, as if by doing so he could erase the shadows and coax colour back into them.

'*My lord?*' he asked, continuing to caress her cheek with the backs of his fingers, marvelling at the softness. He'd forgotten how soft and yielding she was. Her breath caught unevenly and then, slowly, one small, hesitant hand lifted to his face. Quivering fingertips traced a wondering path along his jaw, igniting every nerve. He'd forgotten that too…no, that was a lie. He'd *tried* to forget, with a resounding lack of success.

Then, as though she found it nearly impossible, 'M…Max?'

Never before had his name sounded so sweetly on a woman's lips and he bent to kiss it from them.

Verity's senses whirled as she felt the tender pressure of his lips, breathed his musky maleness and tasted his desire as his tongue laved a seductive trail around her lips. For an instant she hesitated, denying the yearning beat of her heart. Madness to surrender, to allow hope to come rushing back with all its doubts and pain. Her body betrayed her, melting in longing as he drew her lower lip between his teeth and bit down with exquisite finesse. A gasp tore from her and instantly his kiss deepened as his tongue slid over hers, stroking, caressing. Possessing.

His arms tightened to steel bands, supporting her as her bones turned to honey and her knees buckled. Her breasts, crushed against his chest, felt swollen, aching with a wildfire need.

He couldn't get enough of her. Of her sweet, yielding mouth, of the soft cry as his hand closed over one ripe breast and he felt the thrust of a hardened nipple stab his palm through her silken bodice. His loins throbbed as he pulled her closer, shifting against her soft belly in an age-old rhythm. But it was more than desire, more than physical need. Something deep within cried out, aching in its very emptiness. Something he dared not look at.

And he wanted her. God, how he wanted her. Never in his life had he been so shatteringly aroused by a simple kiss. Never before had he wanted to…to simply lift a woman onto the nearest table and take her.

Shock hit him like a sledgehammer as he realised that that was precisely what he was about to do: lift his wife on to the stillroom table, push her skirts to her waist and take her. He had already backed her to the table. Somehow he released her mouth and stepped away slightly, gripping her shoulders to disguise the shaking of his hands. The effort of letting go left him feeling bereft, as though part of him had been ripped away.

Breathing raggedly, he forced his voice to function. Forced it to sound calm, in control. 'We'd better go down to dinner. Richard will be waiting for us.'

All that kept Verity on her feet was the edge of the still-room table under her bottom. She registered the support with surprise. How on earth had she got there? She took a careful breath as her shaking fingers found the table edge, and eased herself away from it. Her legs still worked.

Dinner. He did want her to come down. And he had kissed her. Oh, how he had kissed her! Had he forgiven her? Hope blazed brightly as she looked up at him. And dimmed. His face looked set, hard. As though he were angry about something. Cold fear slid through her. Had she disgusted him again? 'Ma—my lord?'

At that his face softened. 'There is no *my lord* here, only Max.' He offered his arm to her.

Her heart leapt in response. 'Max,' she whispered, unable to quench the welling hope slicing through her. Never before had she realised that hope could be a double-edged sword. *Only Max. But not his sweetheart.*

Chapter Ten

Richard smiled as they entered the salon together. 'About time,' he observed. 'Hurry up. The champagne's de-bubbling even as we speak.'

Verity accepted a glass in a complete daze. What had happened? Why the sudden change in the pair of them? Whatever it was, she found herself seated at the table, champagne fizzing gently in a glass and a selection of dishes being offered to her. And, miracle of miracles, her appetite had returned. She listened as Max and Richard chatted about the day's news. Repairs to a cottage on the estate, a tree that needed taking down.

After a while Max turned to her and said, 'You're very quiet. Did your walk tire you?'

'A little, but I slept this afternoon.' She was doing a lot of that recently. So many changes. So much confusion. She often needed a nap after lunch even if she didn't go for a walk.

He went on. 'You asked my advice on some household matters the other morning…'

She flinched, remembering his rebuff. 'I…yes. They weren't very—'

'We've established that an upside-down fountain will not amuse me. What else was on your list?'

Her jaw nearly dropped at the gently teasing note in his

voice. Simple, unalloyed joy shimmered through her, closing her throat. 'Some of the pictures, the portraits on the landing, seem rather grubby. Do you know of someone who could clean them safely? It seems a pity not to see your ancestors—'

A crack of laughter from Richard startled her. 'You wouldn't say that if you'd known any of 'em! Pack of pirates and wreckers, the lot of 'em,' he assured her. 'I'm sorry to disillusion you about our noble heritage, ma'am, but the first Earl made our fortunes wrecking along this coast. Picking over the ruins of ships flung on the Goodwins and elsewhere. Not exactly an edifying character.'

'Oh!' said Verity faintly. *Pirates? Wreckers?* 'Then you would prefer them left as they are, my lord?'

Max appeared to be trying not to laugh. 'Richard exaggerates,' he said. 'Only the first Earl was quite such a villain. The rest of us have been perfectly, ah, respectable.'

Richard nearly choked. 'Respectable? *Respectable?*'

Max smiled openly. 'Frederick was respectable,' he offered.

Richard snorted. 'And a slow top into the bargain!' he said. He glanced at Verity. 'Our older brother,' he added. 'He died in a hunting accident three years ago.'

She blinked, the strangest sensation washing through her, of being included, being part of something. Part of their teasing banter. Part of their relationship.

'Papa?' suggested Max.

'Obviously,' agreed Richard. 'Mama would never have married him otherwise. But the rest of you...' He winked at Verity. 'Our mother was very respectable.'

Verity paled. Obviously the present Countess was letting down the side a trifle. 'Oh. I...I see.' Her throat contracted.

Max looked up swiftly. 'Mama? Respectable? Lord, yes. Far too respectable to tell her aunt a lie to save a servant from dismissal, let alone shelter a pregnant maid.'

Her jaw dropped. Was he saying he preferred her to his well-bred, well brought-up mother?

Max smiled and reached for her hand. 'She didn't like the first Earl's portrait very much. She wanted to put him in the attic, but our father refused. I've always rather liked him. After all, he did make our fortunes! An inspiring thought.'

'I see,' said Verity, wondering where her breath had gone. How could a gentle handclasp squeeze all the air from her body? Could he see how deeply he affected her? Would it shock him? Desperately she tried to recover. 'Then...then I shall have your disreputable ancestor cleaned up to inspire you.'

'You do that,' said Richard. 'A little inspiration will do him the world of good. Speaking of which, could you not find a subject more inspiring than my poor self for your birthday gift?'

A hot blush mantled her cheeks. 'I know it wasn't very good, but—'

Max's quiet tones cut her off. 'It was exactly right, although I must say Richard got the better bargain with a portrait of the dogs!' His smiled warmed her. 'Thank you.' he continued. 'I meant to say something earlier today and when I came to find you just now, but I...we got...distracted and...' His voice died away and Verity felt hot all over remembering what had distracted them in the stillroom, and saw that queer hardening of his jaw as their eyes met.

He spoke again. 'Which reminds me, you must tell me when your birthday is.'

Her birthday. Her knife and fork clattered on her plate. 'I...no. No. I don't have a birthday.'

The blank astonishment on his face would have been funny if not for the pain cutting at her deep inside. 'Well, of course you do. Everyone has—'

'No!' She struggled to stop her voice wobbling. 'Please. I hate having a fuss made. I would rather...please, Max.'

'But...'

'Verity, I understand your father was Max's Colonel,' said Richard.

Relieved, Verity nodded. Anything was better than explaining to Max why she no longer had a birthday.

'He must have been quite a fellow to keep Max in order. Max always said what a fine officer he was. I'm sorry I never met him. Not to mention thank him for saving Max's life—'

'Stubble it, Ricky.' Max's growl barely penetrated as Verity froze, slowly, from the inside out as the wound deep within cracked wider, leaching cold…guilt…anger…and bitter shame, slicing like a jagged, icy knife.

Her father had saved Max's life. And she had destroyed, then taken, his. Because of her birthday. Somehow she returned an answer—what, she had no idea. It was hard enough holding her voice steady, emotionless, without listening to what she said as well. Embarrassment at her rudeness scorched her cheeks.

Richard continued as though he hadn't noticed. 'And Max always said your father could wipe him off the chessboard. Tell me, did he teach you?'

Shaking inwardly, Verity assented.

'Excellent,' said Richard. 'You can give me a game some time, then.'

'I…I…yes, of…of course.'

Surely she could play chess without remembering her father? Without remembering those dreadful games just after his return, when he was still making an effort to hold himself together, when he could still bear to look at her. Just. Before he would suddenly sweep the pieces from the board and walk away.

She gripped her hands together to still their shaking. Richard was talking cheerfully about chess; gradually her turmoil steadied and she looked up.

Max's bright eyes blazed into her, a frown knotting his brow. His mouth looked set, hard, as though she had angered him again. The icy knife twisted cruelly. If he knew what she had done, anger would become outright loathing. How long could she live with him without confessing the truth? She looked away, her cheeks flooded with shame.

Three hours after retiring Max was still pretending to read in bed. He had stopped trying to remember the title of the book some time earlier. The words danced before his eyes as he finally acknowledged his mistake. He should never have kissed her again. Not in the stillroom and certainly not at her bedchamber door three hours ago. The clock on the chimney piece chimed in unrelenting correction.

All right then! Three and a quarter hours ago! Who was keeping count?

He was. Every aching, yearning minute felt like a life sentence in frustration.

Guilt didn't help. He knew damn well that she had understood and responded to his desire. That she had every reason in the world to be waiting for him to walk through that blasted door and make love to her. At some point he would have to explain to her the truth of their marriage. Not tonight, though. Right now, despite the white-hot desire that held sleep at bay, he wanted to shake her.

Tonight he had finally seen the real Verity. Laughing over nonsense. Actually eating without looking as though every mouthful was an effort. With a pang he realised that he had never before seen her completely happy, without the lurking shadows in her eyes.

All the shadows had rushed back with the mere mention of her father. She was ashamed. Scott had not deserved that. He deserved to be remembered with pride by his daughter, not shame. Somehow he had to help her see that. He'd talk to her tomorrow, make her see, remind her of the sort of man her father had been. Tomorrow.

So what was he doing at the door between their rooms with his hand on the doorknob?

* * *

She sat writing at her father's old campaign chest. He smiled as he remembered the times without number he had reported to Colonel Scott and seen him working at it. A typical officer's chest, it had a drop front in the top section that formed a small desk. Battered, its brass corner mounts dull, the Baltic pine struck an incongruous note in the luxury of the room.

'Verity?'

She spun around in palpable shock and jumped up, dropping her quill. 'My...Max?'

The question in her voice, the yearning softness speared him mercilessly. Along with the suddenly flushed cheeks and trembling mouth. Oh, hell! What now was he to say?

Shaken to his foundations, he blundered in. 'He used to talk about you. Did you know that?'

'I...I beg your pardon?'

He went on relentlessly. Somehow he had to make her see. 'About how pretty you were. How clever. He was so proud of you. He used to read bits of your letters occasionally. He said you were as lovely as your mother. That must have been such a comfort to him after she died. Doesn't he deserve better from you now?'

Verity had turned away, whitefaced. 'What do you mean?'

'You use his campaign chest. Don't you think he deserves a little more than shame from you?'

Slowly she faced him. 'You think I'm ashamed of *him*?' The pain in her voice shivered through him. 'Do you think I would have that chest if I were ashamed of him? It's the only thing of his that's mine. I stole it.'

For the first time he heard bitterness in her voice, poison welling from a wound buried deep.

'Stole it? But surely—'

She broke in. 'When the law says "everything" they mean just that: *everything*.' Understanding raked him and he saw that she was shivering, that her eyes were bright with unshed tears.

In a dead voice, she continued. 'I didn't even know what the law was. If I had...I might have thought to hide things before I ran for help. But I couldn't believe he was dead...' Her ragged breath sliced at him. 'God—what a little fool I was...how could I have *not* believed it... Do you have any idea what it does to a man? He'd put the pistol in his mouth... When they came...they said it was self-murder and they started to take everything...he was wearing Mama's wedding ring.'

'Verity,' he whispered, seeing again the terrified child staring out of her haunted eyes. He knew exactly what a pistol fired into the mouth would do to a man. That she should have seen such a thing... His guts churned, leaving a sour, metallic taste in his mouth. Words strangled in his throat and he reached for her.

She jerked away and his hands dropped to his sides. The deadened voice continued, chilling him to the core. 'I begged them to leave the ring...to let me have it, but they said everything was...was forfeit... everything. So I ran upstairs and stuffed what I could into the chest... his books...his sword...the medals. Then I dragged it into my bedchamber and used the sword to scratch away part of the "W". When they came up...I...I lied, said it was mine. I'd put my own clothes on top...' She shuddered. 'They didn't believe me and they started to drag it out, but the magistrate, Sir John, came. And the Rector. I don't think they believed me either, but they made the men leave me the chest at least and his journal. Everything else went...'

'Oh, God. Verity...' He stopped. Her eyes were blank, seeing only a nightmare past. He had no idea what to say anyway. Had she ever told anyone this before? He tried to imagine her telling the Faringdons. And felt sickened.

'I was so angry,' she whispered. 'Because of what he'd done. And then I hated myself for...for being angry. But all I could think was that he'd finally abandoned me, that he hadn't loved me at all. I wanted to hate him. But it hurt so much. And it was all my fault anyway...because I...' She shuddered. 'I try not to think of him because I feel angry and then...then I hate myself. That's why, when your brother asked...' She shivered and said dully. 'It doesn't matter any more.'

That hit him like a body blow. She sounded as though she no longer cared. Then he reached for her, past her instinctive, defensive recoil, and dragged her into his arms. He meant only to comfort her, to reassure her that she was safe.

He reckoned without the yielding curves of her body, and without the wildfire burning in his veins. The moment he felt her in his arms, her trembling body pressed against him, his resolve incinerated. Need flamed in him and he sought her mouth, taking it in a surge of possession. Only one thought remained, hammering in his brain with every pounding heartbeat: *He must not take her. He could enjoy her, pleasure her, comfort her with his body. But he dare not take his own release in her body.*

Hope, which in three hours had died to an aching ember flared up all around Verity, engulfing the barriers she had so painfully rebuilt. She resisted, tried to control her response. But her arms slid around his waist, her hands felt the heat of hard muscle beneath his nightshirt and the walls cracked around her besieged heart. His mouth whispered over hers, destroying her defences and rebuilding all her dreams. For a moment she continued to resist, trembling behind the crumbling barrier, but it burned around her, leaving her exposed and helpless.

With a soft cry she slipped her arms around his neck and clung, felt him gather her closer, felt his fingers stroking, caressing, searching. All resistance melted as his arms tightened to lift her effortlessly. An instant later she was on the bed, his tender hands stripping her with shocking speed. A part of her mind remembered Lady Arnsworth's warning. She must remain unmoved, silent. Tender hands and kisses trailed down her throat, sparking a riot of rebellion under her skin.

Heat pooled in her belly, between her thighs, moist, trembling heat that ached in its emptiness.

Still. Silent. Virtuous.

His tongue touched one taut nipple, laving it. A gasp escaped her. Her body jerked uncontrollably, pushing her breast upwards to his mouth. With a groan of satisfaction he accepted her gift, taking her flesh deep into the moist heat.

She screamed as he suckled, hard, branding her as his, and all restraint was incinerated as her body melted in surrender. He turned his attention to the other breast, until she was only dimly aware of the cries and sobs rippling from her throat, of his fingers teasing over her belly, over the soft curls at its base. When his hand pushed between her thighs she moved them willingly, eagerly, frantic for his touch.

She twisted against him, fighting to get closer, wild to feel his weight crush her in a prelude to the final possession. His body slid lower and his mouth left her breasts, drifting in heated seduction over the tender curves to her belly where he bit and licked gently.

Even as his tongue circled and probed her navel, his fingers echoed the searching, stabbing action between her thighs until she sobbed, helpless and urgent beneath him. She was barely conscious of her own cries and whimpers as he caressed her. His weight shifted and she instinctively relaxed her thighs, expecting his powerful body to settle between them, expecting the hungry pressure of his need.

She froze in shock as she felt him shift lower yet, felt his shoulders wedge her thighs even wider and felt the first hot touch of his mouth and tongue on the soft skin of her thighs where his fingers had trailed fire. A stunning realisation pierced her—where his fingers had led, his mouth followed...and where he stroked her now... Her breathing shattered as one long finger caressed her deeply...no, surely he didn't mean to...he couldn't...

Struggling for breath, she gasped, 'Max...what are you...ooohhh!' Her protest ended in a strangled gasp as he kissed her with an intimacy that nearly tore her world apart. Winged pleasure speared her body at the hot, silky caresses that consumed her in fire, held her quivering on a rack of incandescent need.

Max clung to self-control as she sobbed and writhed in his grasp, as the sweet essence of her passion wreathed through him. Tenderly, mercilessly, he loved her, in the only way he could permit himself. Glorying in the abandoned innocence of her ecstatic response, he savoured every sob, every whimper.

Slowly he brought her to the edge and held her there until her cries became desperate, almost frightened with the cataract of sensation pouring through her. He could feel her need in the frantic shift of her hips between his hands, in the strength of her fingers clutching his scalp. And in the soft, heated liquid pulse of her body.

Grimly he fought the urge, the savage need to surge up her body and take her, to feel her body shatter in release around him. He couldn't, didn't dare...if she quickened with his seed...

His control cracking, he pushed her over into the abyss and heard the achingly sweet scream of ecstasy as she broke, shimmering and convulsing in his arms. Scarcely daring to breathe, he eased himself back up her body and gathered her into his arms, trying to ignore the violent pain of his own aroused flesh. He ached to roll on top of her and sink into her passion-soft body, driving her to completion again. He mustn't. He didn't even dare show her how to ease his aching need. The edges of his control were smoking.

He should leave. Now. Before he lost control. Before he broke his promise. He dragged in a breath that felt like broken glass and tensed, ready to pull away. She shifted in his arms, nestling against him in soul-shattering trust, snuggling her cheek into the curve of his shoulder, her ragged breath a caress on his heated skin. And something else... He lifted a wondering hand to her cheek. His heart shook in his chest as he felt tears.

Dear God… 'Verity—are you all right? I didn't hurt you?' His voice cracked at the thought. Had he frightened her…or shocked her? She was so damned innocent…she couldn't have been expecting what he had done.

She wriggled closer and he felt her cheek shift against his shoulder. 'No…oh, no. I…oh, Max, please hold me…'

He closed his eyes in despair. That same soul-wrenching intimacy he'd found with her before flooded him. He should leave now. Soft, moist kisses trembled over his collarbone and seared his heart. He couldn't do it. Not yet. Not until she slept. He set his jaw to endure.

She awoke in utter darkness, reaching for him. And found only emptiness. Her mind awash with sleep, she sat up. Had she dreamed… no. Her body melted with remembered ecstasy. She couldn't have dreamed *that*…what he had done to her…how he had loved her. Her mind reeled. She could never have imagined such a thing. But he was gone. Without… Her cheeks mantled with heat in the dark, as she searched for the right words. He hadn't…hadn't taken her.

The last thing she could remember was the hard tension in his body as he held her and tenderly caressed her as she drifted… He'd seemed worried…thinking that he had hurt her and she'd begged him to keep holding her, loving the intimacy, the tenderness of his embrace. Expecting that any moment he would want her. Would seek his own pleasure. She had longed for it, longed to give herself fully.

She must have fallen asleep in his arms. And he had been too considerate to awaken her. She smiled in the darkness, joy humming through her, despite the ache of wishing that he had taken his pleasure deep inside her. He had come to her, had made love to her again in a wild passion of intimacy.

There was nothing to be uneasy about. She couldn't, wouldn't believe that she had disgusted him. Why would he make love to her like *that*, encourage her response, if it disgusted him? She smiled into the darkness and wriggled deeper into the soft feathers of her bed. Tomorrow—no, this morning, she would go down to breakfast.

A week later Max stood staring at the door leading to his wife's bedchamber. A week since he had first gone to her bed. A week passed in a halcyon blaze of sunshine and delight in which Verity had blossomed and changed before his eyes.

He felt as though he were being stretched on the rack, closer and closer to breaking point. And it was his own stupid fault. He had spent his days with her as well as his nights. She had accompanied him for drives asking a hundred questions about the estate, his tenants. He had practically force fed her if he didn't think she'd eaten enough, until she complained that she felt like a goose being fattened for the table.

She was happy. Happy, dammit! And he was lying to her. Oh, not directly. But by all the things he hadn't said. By what he was doing. Every night he went to her bed, blew out the lamps and pleasured her with all the skill and tenderness he could muster, denying himself his own pleasure. Even the pleasure of *seeing* her response to his loving. He didn't dare.

He dare not even allow her to fall asleep in his arms. The temptation to take her burnt at his resolve, searing deeper every night. Any other woman he would have shown how to ease him, how to return the pleasure. With her, he didn't dare.

His candle danced and flickered, casting light as fragile as his own control. It would take the merest whisper to destroy it. One touch was probably all it would take to push him beyond the edges of his control. He should return to his own bed. She was too lovely, too tempting. Each night it became harder and harder to leave her. So far she had said nothing, but last night the wistful note in her voice as she bade him goodnight had left an aching hollow.

Madness. Sheer madness. His hand reached for the handle as he blew out the candle and placed it on the table by the door.

Verity waited, sitting up against her pillows. She must be doing something wrong. Each night he came to her and made love to her in the darkness.

Always in darkness. With a sigh she leaned over and turned down the bedside lamp. Max always did that before he joined her in bed to pleasure her until she cried out and begged for release. A tremor took her body at the thought of the tender intimacy of his hands, the heated, silky caress of his mouth and tongue, loving her until the darkness shattered in fire.

Yet he never took his own pleasure, never possessed her body with his. Every night he left her. And every night she could sense the coiled frustration within him, feel the flickering tension. She must be doing something wrong. But what? Her response? But then why did he do all those things that brought her response welling up? She could only think of one thing.

He had once told her that he knew he had hurt her the night he took her virginity. That it would never be like that for her again. Perhaps he wanted to be quite sure that she wanted him…she blushed…inside her, before he took her again. Perhaps…her blush scorched her cheeks…perhaps she needed to tell him, plainly, that she wanted *him*, before he would possess her fully.

Tonight then. Tonight she would tell him. Tell him she loved him, that she wanted him, longed to have his child. He had been so dear and tender with her over the past week. Somehow all the anger had gone, leaving Max, her lover. He had never spoken of love, but she could not doubt that he cared for her a little at least. That he would be gentle with her love even if he never returned it.

Tonight then would be different. Tonight she would finally become his wife. In truth as well as name.

The door clicked open. Then a soft voice. 'Verity—are you asleep?'

'N...no.'

She heard his footsteps, the whisper as his dressing gown landed on the floor and then felt his hard, warm body beside hers.

Gentle arms drawing her close, lips that traced a possessive, aching trail to her breasts. Hands that knew her, demanded every wild response her body could make and then coaxed more from her. Heated kisses that filled her mouth with the taste of his desire and drifted lower over her quivering body to savour her in the sweetest, most shocking intimacy. Until at the last she cried out, twisting and lifting against his caressing mouth, frantic, burning with the need coiling inside her. A need that burst into incandescent delight, spearing her to the core as she fell, shaking with the force of her release. Held together by the strength of her love.

Holding her gently as she came back to herself, Max fought against his own desire. To possess her completely. To be sheathed to the hilt as she shattered in ecstasy... He should leave. At once.

Her mouth brushed his, soft arms twining around his neck, drawing him closer. 'Please, Max. Stay. Don't leave me.'

Pain burst inside him at the naked plea, at the break in her voice as though she barely had breath. A small trembling hand slid down his body, traced the clenched muscle of his thigh, reached further and found his aching, rigid flesh. Restraint incinerated at the touch of her innocent, questing fingers. Dazed, he realised that he already had her half beneath him, that he had pushed her thighs apart...

'Max? I love you so much. I...I want you...inside me. Please?'

He had one thigh cradled between hers and she arched against him, lifting her leg to wrap it around him. Fire burst as her soft, moist heat caressed him. Once. Just once. Surely just once… He pushed her thighs wide, settling between. He reached one hand between their bodies, caressing her, opening her. She was so soft, moist, welcoming…and his, all his. Once. Just once.

'A baby,' she whispered, her mouth quivering against his as he pressed into her. 'Please, Max.'

His blood hammered violently. She wanted his baby. She would be his in the most elemental way possible, bearing their child. Every muscle hardened as he pushed into the supple body surrendered to him. A *baby*. He froze, as every reason he should *not* be sinking into her soft core reasserted itself. With a savage curse he pulled away, rolling off her to lie shaking with need.

'M…Max?' A small, uncertain hand touched his arm.

'No!' The refusal burst from him as he jerked away from her shaking hand and swung his legs to the floor.

Shocked silence hung in the darkness as he left. The slam of the door shook her heart. Alone in the darkness she faced what she had done.

She had pleaded with him to stay. Tears trickled down her cheek. She had told him that she wanted him inside her. Shame burnt her cheeks. He probably thought her a wanton. Worse, she had told him that she loved him, that she wanted his baby. And he had left. Pain was a barbed hook, tearing inside. She had so little to offer him. And what little she had, he didn't want.

She felt like some small sea creature dragged from its protective shell, naked and vulnerable on the beach. She had dared to dream this last week. A week of glorious days when Max drove with her, showed her his favourite haunts and helped her plan out her ideas for the garden. When he explained how the estate ran and enlisted her help with it. Days when her dream of no longer being apart seemed within her grasp. Days when she dared to dream that he loved her. Her dream had turned out to be just that. A dream, an insubstantial mockery of all she longed for. She had destroyed it by asking too much.

Max stared unseeingly at the estate reports Richard had handed him two hours ago. They made no more sense now than they had then. Where was Verity this morning? Was she about the house, or had she slipped out into the garden? She usually came in to see him after breakfast. He hadn't been at breakfast. He'd eaten some bread and cheese earlier and gone for a walk—to avoid her.

He frowned—the yields for the orchards were up. Hmm. Perhaps he should visit them soon. Verity could come. He'd need to find a horse for her. A dainty little mare. Something gentle… He jerked his mind back to the matter at hand.

Extra profits. That was good. He noted the extra profit on a scrap of paper. A couple of cottages needed repairs before winter gales set in. And what about something extra to help out Martha Granger for a year or so? Of course, she'd have Sarah's board, but a little more wouldn't hurt. Perhaps they could ride by Martha's cottage. How like Verity to think of helping her with a boarder…and her son's child… Oh, hell! How the devil had the chit managed to weave herself into the fabric of his life so effortlessly, until he couldn't imagine life without her? Even now, he found himself wishing she had come in as she often did to ask questions about the estate and add up columns of figures for him.

He knew why she hadn't come in this morning. He groaned and pushed his chair back from the desk. Guilt flayed him. Last night… He should have explained to her…why he would never give her a child… And the thought of her having his child burned to his soul. She had all but begged him.

He took a couple of restless steps. What the hell was he to do? All those years of being the spare. The unspoken differences made between Frederick, the heir, and his younger twin brothers, the spares. The distance it had created between them growing up. And then Freddy had died, leaving Max next in line for the earldom with Richard as the remaining spare. Half an hour between their births. Half an hour to make the difference between heir and spare.

He'd sworn to himself that the difference would never become a reality. He might have been able to deal with that. But the promise to his mother remained... Then he'd had to marry Verity.

At first he'd been so damned angry with her that it had never occurred to him that his desire for her would be so overwhelming. He had intended to stay angry and hold her safely at a distance. He'd intended to take a mistress to deal with his physical needs. She had everything she required—a home, security, plenty of money—but he couldn't be angry with her.

Last night... His body ached at the memory of her shy advances, the uncertain kisses, her trembling hands, her body twisting, pleading for his possession. He'd wanted to sink into her so deeply that they would never be truly apart again, to feel her sweetness become a part of him.

He had to tell her the truth—why he'd never intended to marry and why he could never give her a child. Now, when she cared for him, loved him, trusted him. He swallowed. She had told him she loved him, her breath breaking as she pleaded for him to give her a child, her breath the softest caress on his lips... How the hell was he to tell her that he would never give her a child?

Oh, God! It would have been so much easier if he could have held on to his anger. If she were not so sweet, so damned trusting. If it were only a physical need, not this soul-deep yearning to possess her in every way. Body, mind and soul.

His quill sputtered on the page of figures. He muttered a curse and reached for the pen cutter. Again. This morning he couldn't manage the simplest task, such as trimming his pen, without making a mull of it. All he could think of was Verity.

Coming apart in his arms, pleading with him to take her. Offering her love.

How could he accept that and offer her nothing in return, least of all the child she longed for? His conscience went straight for the throat. *You didn't accept it. You flung it straight back in her face.*

Swearing, he pushed the chair back from his desk. The best thing he could do was go down to the stables, saddle a horse and go for a ride. A damned long one. If the saddle was uncomfortable, he only had himself to thank for it. Besides, the ache in his heart was a damn sight worse.

Chapter Eleven

'Check.'

Richard's mildly triumphant tones penetrated the tired haze enveloping Verity's mind. Blinking, she frowned at the chessboard and forced herself to think. The sun poured down on her shoulders as she belatedly recognised a trap, one that Papa had used. She should have seen it coming.

Just as she should have realised that Max didn't want her. Hindsight was a wonderful thing. Now, seeing where she had ended up, she understood exactly how Richard had led her to *point non plus*, with one move that would hand him her king.

She could now see that Max's avoidance of full intimacy with her had been a warning sign, that her own longing had led her into the trap of hoping—worse, of believing that he cared a little for her. She had told him she loved him. Dear God, how could she have been such a naïve little fool?

'Something bothering you, Verity?'

'No,' she lied. And made her move. The only one left. Straight into the trap.

'Checkmate.'

Her king paid the price for her pre-occupation.

Richard gave her a careful look and began to set out the

pieces again. 'You usually play better than that. Your father's teaching?'

She forced a smile. 'Yes. We played a great deal. How is your leg feeling now?'

'Bloody. It's probably going to rain later. And don't change the subject. You never talk about your father. You clam up whenever he's mentioned. And I'm a nosy, interfering brother-in-law. All I know about your father is that he could wipe Max off the chessboard—no mean feat, I might add—lost his arm saving Max at Waterloo and died two years later.' He frowned. 'Max said he shot himself. I'm sorry, Verity. That must have been hellish for you.'

'Yes.'

Despite the warmth of the sun on the terrace, she shivered uncontrollably. She began to help Richard with the pieces, forcing herself to concentrate on setting them out. She had never dared to ask her father about his arm. He had saved Max. At last she understood why Max had felt responsible, for her father, for her. Her shaking hand knocked Richard's queen over. Dear God. If she'd known, if she'd only known…she would never have risked going to Max.

Richard's hand closed over hers. 'Verity?'

She met his eyes. 'I beg your pardon. That was dreadfully clumsy of me.'

'Your father never told you how he lost his arm, did he?'

'No.' She couldn't keep the pain out of her voice as she tried to draw her hand away.

Richard frowned, but he kept his grip on her hand. 'I'm sorry, Verity. If you didn't realise…'

Suddenly she saw what he was thinking. 'Richard, no. I don't blame Max. How could I?' She shuddered. Remembering some of the things she'd seen as a child, when she and her mother followed the drum. Her hand turned under his and she clasped his fingers. 'It…it could so easily have been the other way round. Would you have blamed my father?'

He shook his head with a rueful smile. 'No. But your situation is different. Losing his arm and then destroying himself because of it.'

'Did Max tell you that?'

He stared. 'Isn't it the truth?'

She hauled in a breath. 'Not quite. There…there were other… other…' She faltered as memory clawed at her. *Other things Max knew nothing about.* Her father's return from Waterloo. Maimed. The day after the funeral for her mother and the tiny, longed-for son. His disbelieving rage. And his despair. Especially when he looked at his daughter…

'Not quite,' she whispered. The headache and nausea she had been ignoring threatened to swamp her. She scrambled to her feet and found the terrace swinging about her giddily. One uncertain step…she grabbed for her chair.

'Verity!' Richard's voice seemed to come from a distance, but strangely he was there, holding her, steadying her against his shoulder. 'Gently now. Are you feeling unwell? Come. Let's get you out of the sun.'

She felt his arm slip around her waist, supporting her. Breathing deeply, she fought the nausea. The terrace steadied. 'I'm…it's all right. Thank you. I just felt dizzy for a moment.' She turned slightly and pushed gently on his chest. 'I'll be all—'

'How very affecting.' The bitter voice cut into her.

Her throat seized as she turned, still in Richard's arms, and saw Max standing at the far end of the terrace. He looked as magnificent as ever, long powerful legs encased in buckskin breeches and top boots, his coat slung carelessly over one arm. She could see that he was hot. His shirt moulded wetly to the broad shoulders.

The brilliant amber eyes blazed into her. He was furious. He strode towards them, his face contemptuous. 'Playing off your tricks on another fool, my lady?'

She flinched as though he had struck her.

Richard's arm tightened. 'For God's sake, Max!' he

snapped. 'Listen to yourself! I may not have quite your reputation to live down to, but at least give me credit for enough
nous to pursue the seduction of your bride somewhere a little
less public!' Fury harsh in his voice, he added, 'That is, if
you can't credit me with the decency not to attempt it in the
first place!'

'No, Ricky. I don't think you would.' A bitter smile
touched his mouth. 'I *know* you wouldn't. But she is another
matter.'

His savage gaze swung back to Verity, spearing her. 'Tell
me, madam wife—did you really think to seduce my brother?
Did you think to persuade him to give you what I would
not?'

She fought the redoubled churning of her stomach, the dizziness as his disgust flayed her. What was he talking about?
What had she done? She dragged in a breath, tried to speak
his name, but only a dry husk came out.

His lip curled. 'Perhaps Drury Lane might be the best
venue for your manifold talents, Lady Blakehurst. They are
quite out of place here. Spare us the impersonation of
wounded innocence. It's worked on me twice. Three times is
once too often.'

Understanding broke over her in icy waves as she realised
what he was thinking. And just how deeply he despised her,
how little he trusted her. Shaking, she pulled away from Richard. She could deny it. Surely he would believe her...or, if
not her, Richard.

He went on, relentlessly tearing her apart. 'You were quite
out in your calculations, madam, if you believed that my
physical pleasure in you would addle my brains. As far as I
am concerned our marriage has been consummated. I can see
little point in any further congress between us.'

Nausea turned her cold, clammy. 'You...you mean...' Her
voice shivered into silence.

'That I shall seek my amusements elsewhere in future.'

Verity took several deep, careful breaths that threatened to rip her apart. *His amusements. Elsewhere.* The truth of the past week seared her with shame. She had thought he cared for her as his wife. Instead he had *sought his amusements* in her bed. He had used her as his whore. Did he hate her that much?

His granite-hard face and clenched fists gave her the answer.

'You don't want children?' The moment the question was out, she regretted it.

He gave a crack of scornful laughter. 'The last thing I require of you, madam, is an heir. Richard will remain my heir. I never intended otherwise.'

The meaning of his cold words slammed into her with brutal force. She had disgusted him so deeply he would rather see the earldom pass laterally to his brother than to an heir of his own body. She had thought that he had come to care for her a little, had comforted herself with the thought that at the very least he would want children, sons certainly. And there might have been a daughter or two. A family she could love. A family who might even love her a little. Now even that dream had been stolen from her. He had never intended to give her a child. Truly now she had nothing left to lose.

He proved her wrong. 'Of course you may think the arrangement a trifle unfair, madam.' Glittering topaz bored into her. 'While I, of course, am free to pursue my amusements as I please, you are not.' He went on. 'Under certain circumstances a gentleman might overlook his wife's infidelity. Take a lover by all means, madam, but rest assured, if you ever cause a public scandal you will regret it.'

'Max! Stop it!' Richard stepped between them. 'Listen to me, you damn fool!'

Fear that they might fall out spurred her. She couldn't bear that. 'No, Richard! Don't interfere.' And then anger, burning away the fear. Every breath tearing deep inside, she faced Max, her chin up. 'No doubt you would divorce me if I refused to abide by this.' She felt as brittle as her voice, as though she might shatter at a touch.

'A little public,' he observed. 'A deed of private separation absolving each of us from any further claim on the other would spare me the trouble and scandal of proving your adultery. The only instance in which I would proceed as far as divorce would be if I found you to be bearing a child.'

She could not speak, shuddering protest strangled in her throat as she willed the tears not to fall. He thought her *that* base. And he was waiting, waiting to hear her response. If she opened her mouth again she would be sick. Every breath hurt a little bit more, like breathing glass, but it was all that kept the nausea at bay.

If she didn't leave now... Very carefully she took a step. Everything seemed distant, misty. Her knees shook, but she was *damned* if she'd cling to the chair for support. Blindly, she turned to go. One step at a time. She could manage one step, and then another...if only the flagstones would stop shifting in that odd way. Stubbornly she forced her eyes to focus, ignoring the pain tearing her apart at each fresh breath. She had set the trap herself. And now it had crashed shut. There was no point in denying it or explaining his error. In the end, he believed it because her behaviour made it credible.

'Verity...' His voice sounded queer, distant.

She kept going. Just one more step...and again...

'Verity!' He caught her wrist. With a broken cry she swung around and jerked herself free.

'Don't *touch* me!'

His touch scalded her. Shamed her. When she thought of how she had behaved, the liberties she had not merely permitted, but enjoyed...begged for... And now she understood. He had never intended to let her bear his child. Instead he had used her.

'Don't ever touch me again,' she whispered. 'You said you would seek your *amusements* elsewhere. I...I would...prefer

that…to being your whore.' Her stomach heaved uncontrollably and she turned frantically for the balustrade. Somehow
she reached it and clutched it, breaking her fingernails as she
was sick into the garden.

For a gut-wrenching moment Max couldn't move as the
enormity of what he had done slammed into him. The betrayal was his. Not hers. 'My God,' he whispered as he went
to her. *What have I done?*

He could do nothing except support her as she retched, an
arm over her shoulders as paroxysm after paroxysm racked
her slight form. He glanced up as Richard came to her other
side and glared at him.

'You bloody idiot, Max! Are you blind? She'd be as likely
to betray you as attempt to fly off Beachy Head!' His lips
thinned. 'She felt faint and I grabbed her! That's all!'

He knew that now. Should have always known it. What in
God's name had possessed him? Had he been so desperate
to ease his nagging conscience? With shaking hands he
stroked her shoulders, holding her steady. He ought to cut his
own tongue out.

Finally it was over. She hung limp and shivering over the
balustrade. He fumbled for a handkerchief and wiped her
mouth clumsily. She struck his hand away with a cry of loathing, put both fists against his chest and shoved with all her
strength. He stepped back and faced her, prepared for blis-
tering rage, hurt, condemnation.

Her face was grey and blank, the eyes shuttered, as if the
cry of pain had never been. 'I beg your pardon, my lord.'

All the breath rushed out of him at the quiet, emotionless
words. 'Verity…' he whispered. Her family had spent five
years trying to break her. He had come very close to suc-
ceeding in as many minutes.

'You have made yourself quite clear, my lord. There…
there is no need to say more.'

'Verity…listen to me. I was wrong…it was a mistake…forgive me.' The waxy pallor of her face appalled him. 'Sweetheart…'

She flinched, shutting her eyes and turning away. Instinctively he reached for her, grasping her shoulders. The shudder that ripped through her tore into him. Sickened, he released her and forced his arms back to his sides. *Don't touch me.* He had all but destroyed her. And right now he was the last person on earth who could help her. Silently he watched as she walked away from him and down the steps into the garden.

'For God's sake, Max! Go after her!'

A discreet cough interrupted them.

Swearing, Max turned to find Harding hovering at the doors into the library. 'Yes, Harding?'

'Beg pardon, sir, but your lawyer, Mr Covell, is here with a colleague.'

Max blinked. 'What? I didn't send for him…Ricky?'

Richard shook his head. 'No. Must be a mistake. I'll see him. You go after Verity.' Max winced at the cold note in his voice.

The man at the doors, Harding, persisted. 'Begging your pardon, Mr Richard, but I understood that Mr Covell had sent for himself, as it were. And he was quite set that he must see his lordship.'

Max exchanged a blank stare with Richard. What the devil should he do? He looked at the slight figure almost running towards the woods. What did she need? Not him. Anything but him. Sickened at his own brutality, he acknowledged that. 'Ricky, I'll see Covell. Would you…' Nearly choking on his shame, he lowered his voice. 'If you can find her, take her up and ring for Henny. I'm not being callous. The last person she wants near her is me.'

Richard's jaw tightened. 'Very well.'

His brain still numb, Max went back into the library and waited. Despite the warmth of the day, he felt chilled to the marrow with fear. The devastation on Verity's face haunted him. His father's quiet voice after Richard's accident—*'If you must fire a pistol…'* He had aimed all too well.

The little framed sketch of Richard sat accusingly on his desk. Entwined initials blurred in front of him. Would he never learn the consequences of rash words? He had caused Richard's accident with that foolish dare. Now his unthinking fury had torn Verity apart.

'My lord?'

He looked up and forced a greeting for the two lawyers. 'Good afternoon, Covell. And, er…?'

Covell flushed. 'My lord, this is my colleague, Mr Wimbourne.'

Max nodded. 'Will you not be seated, gentlemen?' He indicated chairs and sat down behind his desk.

Covell cleared his throat. 'My lord, I realise that this is quite irregular, but when Mr Wimbourne approached me— well, the matter struck me as being so serious that I thought it had better be laid before your lordship immediately.'

Max nodded assent. 'Very well. Go ahead.'

To his surprise Mr Wimbourne spoke up. 'I believe that your lordship married recently?'

Suspicion flared. 'If you are acting for Lord Faringdon—'

He was interrupted. 'Nothing could be further from my intent, but since you mention Lord Faringdon, I must assume that you did indeed marry Miss Verity Scott, daughter of the late Colonel William Scott?'

'Yes.' Seduced her, married her, insulted her. *Broken her heart?* She had said she loved him…

Wimbourne's lips tightened. 'Then she isn't dead.'

'Well, of course she—I beg your pardon?' He leaned forward over the desk and said, very softly, 'Please explain yourself, Mr Wimbourne.'

The little man nodded. 'I had the honour of acting for Miss Scott's late grandmother, Lady Hillsden—were you aware of the connection?'

Max nodded. He'd known that Scott had been a younger son of the previous Viscount Hillsden and that there had been some estrangement over his marriage.

Wimbourne went on. 'Colonel Scott married expressly against his mother's threat of disinheritance. An Irish girl apparently, instead of the heiress she had picked out for him. Her ladyship never forgave him—until she heard about his death.'

He swallowed. 'My lord, please to understand that I have, *had*, been acquainted with her ladyship for a very long time. I think she always expected the Colonel to come back and beg her forgiveness. But he didn't. At the time of Scott's death her estate was left divided equally between her other two eldest grandchildren, Miss Celia and...'

'Mr Godfrey Faringdon,' Max finished. 'Go on.'

Wimbourne inclined his head. 'Lady Hillsden sent for me...' He hesitated. 'She was very much affected by the circumstances of her son's death and wished to alter her will.'

'She did so?'

Wimbourne nodded. 'According to her instructions, I drew up a will, leaving the entire estate to Miss Verity Scott, which she signed. Then, some weeks later, I received a letter from her telling me to change the will back because Miss Scott was dead.'

'*What?*'

'Quite, my lord,' put in Covell. 'This is why I brought Mr Wimbourne down.'

Wimbourne went on. 'She informed me that Lord Faringdon had written to apprise her of Miss Scott's death. He said...er...*implied* that the young lady had been very much overset by her father's death and that she had, well, that she had...'

'Destroyed herself.' Max felt sick. His own cruelty was just the latest in a long line of betrayals.

Wimbourne nodded. 'So I drew up yet another will and—'

'You'd better tell Lady Hillsden that she still has a grand-daughter,' suggested Max.

Wimbourne looked grave. 'You come to the nub of the matter, my lord. Lady Hillsden has just died. We were settling the estate and applying for probate when I saw the notice of your marriage in the papers.'

Max eyed him narrowly. 'Surely it would have been easier for you to keep silent.' And realised that his phrasing had been less than tactful.

Mr Wimbourne's chest swelled. 'Easier legally, I grant you, my lord. But I remember Lady Hillsden's distress when she wrote to me about Miss Scott's supposed death. She blamed herself for not sending for the child, for never trying to heal the breach between herself and her son. It would not be easier for my conscience had I not brought this to your attention.'

'I beg your pardon, Wimbourne,' said Max quietly. 'I did not intend to offend you. What do you suggest I should do? Can the will be overset?'

'Does your lordship need the money?'

He laughed. 'No, Mr Wimbourne, I do not. But like you, I have a marked disinclination to permit Lord Faringdon to get away with his deception. At least I assume that was your motive in laying the facts before me.'

Verity's breaking voice echoed in his heart: *It's mine...all I have of him...I have nothing.*

Could he at least secure her inheritance for her? Settle it on her absolutely, so that she had something that was hers, and hers alone? Independent of his wealth? *And if you do that, what are the odds that she will walk away from you after what you just did to her?*

He shut his eyes against a wave of pain. Verity, given her independence, might leave him. Carefully he rearranged the papers before him. It was his decision. As his wife, Verity had no say in this. He could thank Wimbourne for his integrity and say that he didn't need the money. Legally, if that money came to Verity without being tied up in a trust, it *was* his. He would be within his rights not to pursue the issue or to keep the money. The law said so.

Just as the law said that Celia and Godfrey Faringdon were now entitled to Verity's inheritance. Just as the law on suicide had left Verity destitute, dependent on the whim of her uncle, who had stolen everything from her, including her name. Who would have sold her into prostitution to hide his dishonesty.

'How does one challenge a will, Mr Wimbourne?'

Wimbourne shook his head. 'Oh, dear me, no. The last thing your lordship wants to do is actually *mount* a challenge! We must be more cunning than that, my lord. I understand from Mr Covell that your lordship is a military man? A little strategy is what is required here. Yes, strategy. And a willingness to accept a compromise, perhaps?'

The idea of compromising with the Faringdons nearly choked Max, but if the important thing was to give Verity something of her own, then his curst pride could take a few blows.

'Go ahead, then. Outline your strategy.'

'Does your lordship know anything about the Court of Chancery?'

Max frowned. 'Not much. Except that it keeps the legal profession busy.'

Mr Wimbourne's smile verged on the cynical. 'And wealthy, my lord. You see, once a challenge is mounted the estate is frozen. It cannot be touched except to defray legal costs. Sometimes for years.'

'Years?' asked Max suspiciously.

The smile became beatific. 'Years, my lord. Decades, even. Why, we have one case at the moment that began in 1798. I venture to suggest that your children may not live to see the Jennings case settled.'

'How large is Lady Hillsden's estate?'

Wimbourne shrugged. 'Respectable, but not enough to survive that. About twenty-five-thousand pounds.'

Max swore. 'It's useless then. If I challenge the will, the
entire estate could be eaten in legal fees!'

'Exactly. And Faringdon knows that too. Even if you do
not need the money, *he* does.' Mr Wimbourne's smile took
on an air of cherubic innocence. 'After all, he has two more
daughters to provide for, and his own fortune is respectable
rather than handsome...'

Max's jaw dropped at the full glory of the legal mind.
'Then we... would the word be *threaten*...?'

Wimbourne nodded. 'It would, my lord. You *threaten* to
lodge a suit in Chancery unless Faringdon agrees to settle.
For, say...ten thousand pounds? That leaves fifteen for Miss
Scott—I mean, Lady Blakehurst. And the jewellery of course.
You should insist that Lady Blakehurst take first pick of the
jewellery, since it was originally left to her outright. You are,
of course, being very generous in offering ten thousand—you
could even hint at a civil suit for fraud. And, since Faringdon
was, through his wife, Miss Scott's legal guardian, there are
steps that could be taken there. A guardian is legally obliged
to safeguard his ward's interests.'

Max rose slowly to his feet. He leaned across the desk and
held out his hand. 'Mr Wimbourne, it is a privilege to know
you.'

Mr Wimbourne took the proffered hand and inclined his
head. 'Thank you, my lord. It is all a matter of knowing
precisely *where* to apply pressure'

Max knew exactly where he wanted to apply pressure on
the entire Faringdon family. His fists clenched. Right now
he'd gladly strangle the lot of them with their own purse
strings. After that he'd strangle himself.

Richard listened in disbelief when Max introduced Mr
Wimbourne and explained his presence. 'That rat Faringdon

cheated her? Damn it all, Max! You can't let him get away with it!'

Max favoured him with a glare. 'Despite my best efforts to date, I do possess some degree of sense, Ricky. Of course I'm not going to let him get away with it!' Then he lowered his voice and asked the question clawing at him. 'Where… where is Verity?'

They were about to go in for dinner, Max having insisted that both lawyers should dine with them and stay the night.

'In her rooms,' Richard replied. 'I caught her halfway through the woods. Henny is with her. Are you going to tell her about this?'

Startled, Max thought about it. It hadn't occurred to him *not* to tell her, but maybe…maybe it would be better to keep it to himself. Just until they had some idea of which way the Faringdons would jump.

Finally he shook his head. 'Not yet. I…I don't want her any more upset…' He could imagine how she would feel to know the full extent of the cruel hoax that had been perpetrated upon her. He couldn't bear to see any more pain on her face. He would wait. See if it came to anything. If not, he would hold his silence. He met Richard's puzzled regard.

'Tell me, brother—what do you intend to do with this money? It's not as though you need it. Is it merely revenge?'

'No. I don't need it,' agreed Max. 'I'll settle it on Verity. To be hers absolutely. No matter what.'

'No matter what,' echoed Richard. He frowned. 'Then you have considered the possibility that she might le—'

'Yes,' said Max harshly, forcing the word past the ache in his throat. Hearing his worst fear spoken aloud would make it real, give it life. The very thought numbed his heart.

Gentle tapping pulled Verity out of her doze into full, un-welcome consciousness. She felt heavy, lethargic, the result of a night spent weeping. No doubt Henny had brought break-fast. Her stomach roiled. Eggs…ugh.

'Come in.' She rolled over and looked at the door leading into the sitting room. It remained shut.

A quiet voice behind her said, 'I've brought your breakfast.'

Shocked, she whipped around, clutching the bedclothes to her. He was fully dressed, for which she was profoundly grateful, but... 'Since when does an Earl cart breakfast to his...wife?' She forced her voice to sound normal, indifferent. She even met his eyes, although she had to bite the inside of her cheek to hold back the tears. Why couldn't he just leave her alone? She had made some decisions the previous night and they would be a great deal easier to act on if Max would only stick to his chosen role.

'Since he behaved like a brute and upset her so that she didn't eat her dinner.'

Her eyes widened as he came towards her and her grip tightened on the sheet. Seeing him in here reminded her of all the nights he had come to her and made love...No. He hadn't *made love*. He had *sought his amusements*. She had to remember that. He had used her body. Seduction, not tenderness. She had to remember that too. She reached for the blanket and counterpane as well as the sheet.

Heat burned on her cheeks as her body trembled at the memory of urgent desire and shame, remembering how she had twisted and sobbed, begging for more, telling him that she wanted him inside her... Pain streaked through her as she recalled how he'd rolled away from her. Now she knew why. No wonder he hadn't responded to her declaration of love. What man wanted words of love from a whore?

Tension gripped her as he placed the tray on her knees. 'Th...thank you, my lord.' She looked at the tray. Fruit. Scones. Butter and jam. A pot of tea. No eggs. The churning in her stomach eased slightly. But she couldn't help the shiver of awareness at his proximity.

'Would you like your dressing gown?'

The carefully diffident tones alerted her. She looked up and saw him watching her almost…almost painfully. Without waiting for an answer, he turned away and fetched the dressing gown. She took it with shaking hands and wrapped it around herself.

He sat down on the edge of the bed and she jerked back with a startled gasp.

'Please…'

His voice sounded strained. 'Verity, I'm only going to pour you a cup of tea.'

Confusion held her. Why was he doing this to her? He had made it plain what he thought of her. Did he just feel guilty because he had turned out to be wrong on this particular occasion? The fact remained that he had been able to believe it. Easily. She accepted the cup and discovered that a scone had found its way onto the saucer. Tentatively she took a bite. Her stomach still felt funny, but as she ate the scone it began to settle.

Another scone appeared on the saucer before Max spoke again. 'Verity, I'm…I'm sorry…about yesterday. I…I made a mistake. Can you forgive me?'

She stared blindly at the delicate blue-and-white porcelain, cradling its brittle warmth in her cold hands. *A mistake.* A mistake he could not have made without her help. He accepted that he had been wrong this time, but not trusting her, he would think it again and again.

Without looking at him she nodded. If she met his gaze, she'd break apart. Let him think her indifferent. He had neither believed nor wanted the truth. Her decision was made. All she had to do now was carry it out. He had himself given her the weapon she needed.

It took every scrap of courage to keep her voice light. 'No matter, my lord. At least there is no misunderstanding between us any more. Don't—' her throat seized, but she pressed on '—don't refine on it any further, sir. There is not the least need.'

'I…see.'

Her tea cup rattled as she set it back on the saucer, startled by the harshness of his voice. Proudly she lifted her chin and stiffened her backbone. 'So, my lord, what are your plans for the day?'

For a split second she thought he hesitated, but then he said, 'As a matter of fact, I must go to London for a week or so. Some business that I should attend to personally.'

Dizziness swept through her and with it, nausea as his savage words flayed her again...*I prefer to seek my amusements elsewhere in future.* He was going up to London to do just that. A business matter. Something he paid for. And her duty was to turn a blind eye to such things.

Lady Arnsworth had made that quite plain. *Gentlemen such as Blakehurst prefer to take their pleasures outside the marriage bed. In their wives they require decorum... A lady will not notice these things...* She ought to be grateful that he no longer wished to use her for his pleasures, that she'd had no idea of how to please him.

Drawing on every reserve of strength, she manufactured a bright smile. 'When do we leave, my lord?' London would serve her purpose admirably.

Alone in the library half an hour later, Max sat contemplating the ruin of his marriage. He had disgusted her, probably sickened her. Worse, he had hurt her beyond all forgiveness. She recoiled from his touch, from his very presence. So why in Hades had she elected to come to London? Certainly not for the benefit of Lord Blakehurst's company. He didn't blame her. He didn't much like being in the same room as Lord Blakehurst right now, let alone the same skin.

The best thing he could do for Verity was arrange for her to be introduced to the life that could be hers as Lady Blakehurst. Social, fashionable London. As a Countess, she would be accepted with Almeria's support. The peculiar circumstances of her marriage would be forgotten soon enough.

He forced himself to examine all the possibilities. She

might well take a lover. His throat closed. He would be well served if she did. She had offered herself and her love to him. And he had flung them back in her face, along with her trust.

He knew, with shattering certainty, that he would never be able to bring himself to do as he had threatened and disavow a child. His own blind stupidity and jealousy had created the situation. He would have to live with the outcome and protect her from the consequences. And in the meantime he would have to try to win her back. As his wife.

He groaned. At some point he would have to tell her the truth—why he had never intended to have children. In wedlock, anyway. Oh, hell! It would have been so much easier if she had been Selina, his mistress. He could have had his cake and... An odd thought came to him. He had barely known the supposed Selina Dering. What would have happened when he came to know her? When he discovered the woman he now knew? Would he have felt comfortable about *her* bearing his bastard child? Even if she hadn't turned out to be Verity Scott?

The thought of Verity quickening with his seed left him shaking with sudden passion. His. In every way possible. Nothing less would satisfy him. And as he realised that, the truth hit him like a lightning bolt—he'd have married her the moment he found she was increasing. He'd never wanted a woman as deeply as he wanted her and he'd never wanted to protect a woman before. From everything, even from himself if necessary.

She had loved him. Why else would she have tried so hard to breach the coldness between them? She had loved him. And he had spurned it. She had gifted him with her innocence. And he had treated her like a whore. Finally and worst, she had trusted him. He had taken her trust and trampled it.

There was only one way to regain her trust. He would have to give her his trust. He stared blindly at his entwined fingers. *His* trust. That was the easy bit. There remained the small matters of her innocence and love. In return for those he would have to give himself. And his love.

He faced the truth he hadn't dared to admit. He loved her. And for Verity to accept his love, she would have to trust him enough to risk her heart again. Trust. It all came down to trust.

Chapter Twelve

'Wake up, Verity. We're nearly there.'

The deep, velvet dark voice drifted into Verity's dream of warmth and safety. And affection. It wrapped around her warmly, smelling of leather, sandalwood and something musky and she sighed contentedly and snuggled closer, rubbing her cheek against the strength enfolding her. More sounds penetrated her dream. A rumble of wheels and clattering hooves. Voices and the occasional crack of a whip.

The arms holding her shifted, tightened and the voice whispered, 'Sleep a little longer then.' Followed by gentle pressure on the top of her head and a featherlight touch of lips at her temple.

Max had held her like this once. Tenderly soothing her to sleep after making love, keeping her fear and guilt at bay with his strength and warmth. She had dared to dream that there could be more, that one day he would love her in the way she loved him. She had dared to whisper of love, the dream had felt so real. Even now, she thought, her dream felt real…so real.

The carriage came to a halt and with it, Verity's dream. Abruptly she became conscious that the arms holding her were all too real, that she was snuggled on Max's chest with his cheek resting on her hair. That she was safely wrapped in the thick travelling rug Max had insisted she bring. Every fibre of her, body and soul, ached to stay exactly where she was, for the dream to continue. Every nerve tautened, mustering the will to pull away, back beyond her defences.

He spoke again, in cool, dispassionate tones. 'We've arrived, Verity.' Careful hands lifted her away and set her down on the seat. She shut her eyes briefly, resisting the urge to wriggle back into his arms and beg him to hold her. Never again could she let him close. Being pushed away cut to her very core.

Breathing slowly, Max watched her. She looked deliciously tousled, her curls hopelessly tumbled on her shoulders. Scarcely surprising since he had been unable to resist the temptation of removing her pins and tangling his fingers in the silken, cool tresses.

The need to pull her back into his arms and kiss her senseless hammered in his blood. He mustn't. The sudden tension in her body as she woke seared him. *Don't ever touch me again.* She didn't want him near her, let alone kissing her.

The chaise door opened and the steps were let down. He stepped out and turned, prepared to assist Verity down.

'I can manage for myself, my lord.'

The words cut into his heart. His touch sickened her. Even the simplest gesture of courtesy. Every instinct screamed at him to lift her into his arms, to hold her close. Sharply he turned away and nodded to the waiting footman to assist her.

He watched her precede him into the house, her head high, her back straight. Gone was the gentle, vulnerable girl who had trusted him. Now grey eyes blazed at him like twin swords. He had honed the blades himself.

In the hall he remembered that he had a gift for her. Something he ought to have given her before they were married. 'When you have changed for dinner, my dear, I would be obliged if you would join me in the drawing room.'

His heart ached at the tiredness in her face as she looked at him. 'Of course, my lord.'

* * *

Verity stared at her reflection. Heavens! She was so pale her freckles nearly stood out in relief. She pinched her cheeks. That was worse. Now she looked feverish.

'Will there be anything else, my lady?'

'Hmm?' Verity blinked at the rather prim-looking dresser. Apparently Max had sent a message to Lady Arnsworth telling her to find a suitable maid. Whatever might be permissable in the depths of Kent, a pregnant lady's maid would cause a furore in London. The idea had tempted Verity, but she couldn't possibly use Sarah like that. 'No. Nothing else…ah, Cooper. Thank you. That will be all.'

'My lady's jewellery?' Cooper flushed slightly.

My lady didn't have any, but she simply shook her head and said, 'No, thank you, Cooper. I'll ring for you later.'

Cooper curtsied and went away, leaving Verity frowning at her reflection. The gown was well enough. She found that she loved the slide of silk against her skin. It shivered through her, reminding her of… No! She mustn't think of Max's kisses and tender caresses. They had meant nothing to him. They must mean nothing to her.

Verity fixed the fashionable reflection with a glare to remind her that she had to go down to the drawing room and pretend indifference to her husband. Above all, she had to ignore her body's response every time he touched her. She could not keep pulling away. There would be times when he had to touch her. To lead her into dinner. He might even have to dance with her and she would have to behave as though her bones had not turned to honey and her lungs still functioned.

Painfully she realised that although she might, just might, be able to control her body's response to Max, her heart was another matter entirely. She could not control her heart's response, but she would have to make sure he never saw it.

Verity found her way to the drawing room easily enough, but she hesitated outside the door. On her previous brief visit

to the mansion she had only penetrated as far as the front
hall and library. She had never expected to live here. As she
opened the door, she realised that the last time she had been
in this house she had come to cry off her betrothal.

Max stood staring into the fire, but he glanced up and
smiled as she came in. A brief, constrained smile. 'Tired?'
He looked frowningly at her.

'Oh, no,' she lied. Damn him. She didn't want his consideration, his kindness. Everything would be so much easier if
she could hate him. But she couldn't. And she couldn't let
him close again.

'I have something here for you.' He reached into the
pocket of his coat. 'I'll have the rest of the jewellery taken
to your room, but I wished to give you this now. I should
have done so when we became betrothed, but I...it slipped
my mind.'

He came towards her and she fought to remain unmoved.
Indifferent. Cold. Think of ice or sn—

He took her hand and the ice dissolved in steam. Trembling
at the fire that poured through her, she tried to pull back, to
conceal her yearning, but he held her captive. The ring slid
on to her finger and he released her.

'Oh.' Shock robbed her of speech as she gazed at it. Red
fire winked back at her, dancing and shifting in the lamplight.

'The setting is very old. It's been in the family for gener-
ations.'

'But...no.' She couldn't wear this. A family piece. No.
Trembling, she made to take it off. 'I might lose it, or—'

His fingers closed over hers. 'Leave it there. It is yours.
Absolutely. To lose or keep as you will. Your betrothal ring.'

'What are the stones?'

His mouth twisted. 'Rubies. What else?'

What else indeed. But she was not a virtuous woman. If
she were, she would not be married to him.

Max watched her leave the dining room as the covers were
removed, so he could enjoy his wine in solitary state. He

wanted to go after her, sweep her into his arms and upstairs into his bed. He hadn't realised quite what a strain being with him would put on her, let alone having to touch him. The ring had glowed on her finger in sumptuous mockery all through dinner. She'd been so tense as he put it on her that he'd wondered if she might break.

Rubies. What else? His own words haunted him. Had she thought his choice of ring a subtle insult? That she was *not* beyond the price of rubies? That he believed she could be bought by a gift of jewellery like…like any of his ex-mistresses? He hadn't meant it like that. But if he went to her and tried to explain…

She needed time. Space. If he followed her now, she'd feel hunted. And he wasn't sure enough of his own control. Perhaps it would be better to allow her to go her own way for a while and find her feet in society. Almeria would keep an eye on her. She could not come to any harm under Almeria's legendary shield of propriety.

Verity re-read the note from Lord Selkirk and put it down on her dressing table with a grimace. A third drive with Selkirk in ten days would be just the thing, of course. More than enough to have tongues wagging maliciously. Especially if she danced with him twice tonight. Again. She shivered. Dancing with him was horrible. Something about him felt…slimy. And he didn't bathe properly. Always under the overpowering rosewater lurked the sour reek of stale brandy and stale humanity.

So different from Max… No. She wouldn't think of him. What was the saying? Out of sight, out of mind? At that rate she ought to have practically forgotten his existence. Except for the great ruby that glowed on her left hand.

Almeria had recognised it. *Good God! I hope he warned you how valuable it is! My sister never dared to wear it.*

Verity pushed away the queer thought that Max had trusted

her with part of his family heritage. He had sent the rest of
the jewels to her rooms the following day. Every time she
wore one of the settings it reminded her that he did not trust
her with the one part of his family heritage that she cared
about. He would not permit her to bear his legitimate children. His bastards would have been another matter.

Selkirk. She would have to dance with him tonight. But
she couldn't bear driving with him this morning. The swing
of his phaeton, combined with his smell and perennially wan-
dering hands... Ugh! she couldn't do it. Not even for the
sake of stirring up more gossip.

What else could she do this morning? Shopping? Lady
Arnsworth thought she should do a great deal of that, but it
seemed pointless. Why buy more clothes when one's wardrobe held enough clothes and more hats than one knew what
to do with? Lady Arnsworth apparently failed to see how any
female supplied with a mere week's worth of morning gowns,
afternoon gowns and promenade gowns and *two* weeks'
worth of evening gowns, plus the requisite slippers, gloves
and associated falals, could possibly deem herself adequately
provided for.

'Don't be ridiculous, girl,' she had said. 'Your husband
has given you *carte blanche* to spend what you like. Most
women would give their eye teeth for such *largesse*!'

The term *carte blanche* ripped at Verity's façade. Max
poured out money on her until she was well nigh choking on
it. From all accounts Lord Blakehurst had been renowned for
his generosity towards his mistresses. She didn't want another
penny. Especially since she had donated most of this month's
pin money to an institution for reformed prostitutes.

What else was she supposed to do with it? When she attempted to pay modistes and milliners, she discovered that
Lord Blakehurst had given instructions that the bills be sent
to him! No doubt he was checking to see that his bride created the right impression in fashionable circles.

She stared at her reflection in the mirror. Then she glared.

She was turning into a complete and utter watering pot. The sort of feeble, moaning creature she despised. She had come to London with a plan. And judging by the reactions of all the component parts of society to the scandalous new Lady Blakehurst, she ought not to have the least difficulty in implementing it. She was finished with weeping.

Her reflection glared back, clad in a chemise, petticoat and peignoir. She had yet to decide what she was going to wear. And what she was going to do. She could, of course, simply retire to the drawing room and read. One or two people might call, but she could almost guarantee that otherwise she would spend a peaceful day. Except…something stirred in her mind. Oh, drat! That wretched luncheon that Aunt Almeria wanted her to attend. Followed by an At Home.

Almeria intended to call for her. Verity thought carefully. She could send a note around, saying that she was indisposed. No. Almeria would ignore a note. And she'd walk straight past Clipstone if he tried to deny her.

She could go to the Green Park, a thoroughly rustic, and blessedly unfashionable, destination. The air smelled less like cabbage water there and although the cows might not be the most chatty of companions, they were at least accepting. And they did something useful, which was more than she could say of most of the London ladies she had met.

'A walking dress, please, Cooper,' she told her prim London dresser.

'Yes, my lady. Which one would you like?'

Did it really matter? Apparently it did. Which one had she not worn for several days? 'The blue one with the flounce, please.'

Fifteen minutes later she walked into the drawing room. 'Richard!' She stared in disbelief at her brother-in-law sitting by the window, his bad leg stretched out before him. 'Whatever are you doing here? I thought you hated London.'

He looked up with a smile. 'Good morning, Verity. I wondered when you'd be down. How do you do? Setting London by the ears?'

Forcing a smile, she asked, 'When did you arrive? Does Ma— His lor— Your brother know that you are here?'

He cocked his head on one side. 'I arrived last night. Max asked me to come up. I saw him at breakfast. Didn't he mention it?'

She came further into the room. 'Oh. Well, it's lovely to see you. Are you staying for long?'

'Max didn't say?'

She gave up trying to avoid the subject. 'I saw Ma—your brother very briefly in Bond Street yesterday and, no, he didn't mention it. What are you doing? More carving?'

He nodded and sat back in his chair, picking up a chunk of wood and a small sharp knife. 'It's one of my hobbies,' he said. 'I learnt how after my accident. There was a lot of time on my hands.'

Verity nodded as she sat down at the secretaire and opened it. She could understand that problem. 'How old were you?'

'Twelve. They thought I might not walk again, but Max and I proved them wrong. I probably wouldn't have without his help.'

Shocked, Verity put her pen down and turned to look at him. 'What happened?' Twelve. And he'd thought he might never walk again.

He shrugged. 'I fell off one of our father's hunters. Well, to be accurate, I didn't fall off. That was the problem. He fell on me. I was lucky not to lose the leg.' He smiled at her shocked face. 'Verity, it was a long time ago. And it was entirely my fault. We had been forbidden to ride Papa's hunters ever since Max fell off one.' He grinned. 'We were forbidden before that. All that changed was we got caught. But you know what boys are. Immortal. It can't happen to me. Don't waste any pity on me. I had enough of that from our mother.'

'I'm sorry.' Her voice came out stiffly. 'I didn't mean to give offence.'

'None taken,' he assured her. 'Mama just never let go of the subject, or ceased to blame poor Max. Sometimes I think the idiot wished *he'd* been the one with a smashed leg. I got the sympathy. He got the blame.' He changed the subject. 'Where are the idiots Taff and Gus? Out with my equally idiotic twin?'

'They're not idiots!' said Verity indignantly, ignoring the reference to her husband. 'You like them!'

He smiled. 'Of course I like them. Doesn't detract from the fact that they're idiots. They're both incurably gun shy and they still haven't worked out that slippers are not usually considered suitable as a meal. Are you busy this morning?'

She hesitated. 'Yes. I was just going to send a note around to Lady Arnsworth and then go out.' Her heart ached for someone to talk to. Someone to relax with. But if she stayed and Max came back... Better to leave now. Besides, she didn't want Almeria to call and find her there.

Richard cocked his head to one side. 'No time for a poor cripple?'

'I...I... Oh!' Bursting into laughter, she picked up her pen. 'Richard, that's dreadful! For a moment I thought you meant it!'

'Not so dreadful,' he said comfortably. 'Not if it made you laugh.'

Glancing at the clock, she said, 'I could stay for a little while.'

Max paused outside the drawing room door as he heard a shout of laughter. Good lord. That sounded like Richard. But what was he doing in there and who on earth was with him? It sounded for all the world as though someone had just told him a bawdy after-dinner story. Gus and Taffy leapt at the door, scrabbling furiously.

He opened the door, fully expecting to find one of their

more unregenerate friends with his brother. Richard sat in a chair by the window, and seated on the other side of the embrasure was Verity. But not the same Verity of the past two weeks. His heart leapt to see again the laughing, engaging sprite of that week at Blakeney, before he ruined everything.

Richard was lying back in his chair, nearly weeping with laughter. Wiping his eyes, he gasped, 'Oh, God, Verity! She must have been beside herself! What did she say?'

But Verity did not answer. It was as if by opening the door Max had either broken a spell or cast one. All the laughter and animation died out of her vivid face, leaving her blanched and lifeless the moment she saw him. His heart gave a sickening lurch and the urge to go to her, to sweep her out of the chair and into his arms, ripped through him.

And if he did? Painfully he reminded himself that she could scarcely bear to be in the same room as him. That she loathed the sight of him. And that she had every right to do so.

'Oh, hullo, Max.' Richard's grin drew a reluctant response from him. 'Verity was just telling me that she got so annoyed with the insufferable Celia, that she actually cut a great chunk out of her hair! Get off, dog!' He fended off Gus, who bounded off his lap again with no hint of offence. He leapt up at Verity instead.

Max blinked. Good lord! Was that what all the brouhaha had been over that last night at the Faringdons'?

'You cut off her hair?' he asked, smiling. 'Is that why she didn't appear at dinner that night?'

Verity nodded.

Max held his breath. Would she…?

A brief smile flickered. Directed at Richard. 'I'll leave you now. You'll be wanting to talk. Good morning, my lord.' She walked out and all Max could do was open the door and let her go.

Nothing had changed. Verity still held him at bay, beyond

a wall of ice. Nothing had ever hurt as much. Because he knew now that the laughing girl he had fallen in love with was still there, hiding from him in case he hurt her again.

He turned to his brother and said, 'Wimbourne sent around a note. The meeting with Faringdon is set for this afternoon at Lincoln's Inn.'

If nothing else, at least he could attempt to restore her inheritance.

Verity kept her head high as she left the drawing room; it was definitely time to escape to the Green Park. Lady Arnsworth might think she should spend her time paying calls, but Verity had noticed that unless she paid calls in the company of Lady Arnsworth, people seemed never to be At Home. So many butlers favoured her with an unctuous smile while informing her, *'I regret madam is not At Home'*, that she heard the words in her dreams.

It didn't matter if they despised her. The gossip would reach Max all the faster, which was a good thing. She told herself that all the way up to fetch her pelisse and a book. And back down to the hall.

Just as she opened the front door, a shocked voice spoke from behind her. 'Where the deuce are you off to?'

Mentally arming herself, she turned to face her husband. 'A walk,' she said, 'in the Green Park.' Perhaps he'd think she had an assignation.

He blinked. 'The *Green* Park? Why there? It's not very fashion-able.'

'No,' she agreed. 'It's not, but the cows there are much nicer.' Without waiting for him to work that one out, she slipped through the door and shut it.

Max stared at the closed door for a full minute, unable to believe that she had meant what *he* would have meant by a remark like that. The cows there were much nicer than…what? He grinned. The cows in Hyde Park? The only cows in Hyde Park had reticules and parasols in place of horns and tails. And she *couldn't* have meant that! Could she?

He frowned. She should take her maid, but he hated to force that on her. She couldn't come to any harm in the Green Park. The only dangerous cows in London wouldn't be seen dead in the Green Park.

Walking back into the library, he fended off the spaniels and sat down at the desk to stare uselessly at the sworn copies of all the documents Wimbourne had provided in preparation for their meeting. Visions of shadowed grey eyes haunted him, and a broken voice crying, *Don't touch me!* If he reclaimed her inheritance for her, would he lose her completely? *Could* he lose her any more completely than he had already?

By the time Verity reached the Green Park she knew she must speed up the execution of her plan, before Max's gentleness undermined her resolve. Sitting in the shade of a tree, she considered how to go about it. How did one create a scandal bad enough for one's husband to disown one, without actually…?

She let her book fall and shivered slightly. Of all the men she had met since coming to London, she thought Lord Braybrook might best suit her needs. His reputation was appalling, but when they danced he behaved like a gentleman. Which was more than she could say for some of the men who danced with her. Their hands seemed incapable of remaining where they were meant to be during a waltz.

Braybrook did nothing so vulgar as fondle her during their dances, but she had seen the raised brows and knowing smiles as Braybrook danced with her last night. Lady Arnsworth had waxed lyrical over it in the carriage later. How long would it be before she carried the news to Max?

And how far would *she* have to go to convince Max that Almeria's tales were the truth? An impression was one thing.

All she needed was for Max to *believe* she was having an affair. But what if Braybrook called her bluff?

Her mind sheered away from that and she picked up her book again. She would just have to be careful—'Oof!' Something thumped into her midriff. Dropping the book, she doubled over, gasping for breath.

'Oh, I say! Are you all right, ma'am? George! You great looby! You hit her!'

Another boy ran up to join the freckled urchin bending over her.

'It wasn't my fault! *You* were supposed to be fielding. Why didn't you catch the jolly thing?' Prudently George bent down and retrieved the cricket ball from her lap. 'I'll get this out of your way, shall I?'

With speech still an impossibility, Verity found the laughter bubbling up inside her painful to say the least. Feebly she waved one hand in assent.

'Should you like some lemonade, ma'am?' asked the first boy anxiously. 'We've got plenty. And plum cake and apples.'

From somewhere in the vicinity of her bruised midriff a warm glow spread. 'I'd love some lemonade, if you have enough,' she said smiling. 'And it's Verity, Verity… Blakehurst, not *ma'am*.' Plum cake and apples sounded like a feast after a breakfast of dry toast, which was about all she could stand in the mornings.

Both boys grinned back at her. George spoke up. 'I'm George Cranmore and this is my brother, Ben. I'm awfully sorry I hit you. Are you quite sure you're all right?'

'Perfectly,' said Verity, resisting the urge to rub what would doubtless be an impressive bruise.

'It's a bit of a nuisance, playing with only two,' confided Ben. 'One of us has to bowl and one has to bat, so there's no one to field. And that was a capital stroke of George's. Except for hitting you in the bread basket. Still, I dare say you would rather that than your nose or teeth.'

'Much rather,' agreed Verity with alacrity. Not even Max would believe that Braybrook, or anyone else, was having an affair with a woman minus her front teeth.

'Do stop rattling on, Ben, and fetch the lemonade,' commanded George. 'And bring the lot over here. I'm starving anyway so we may as well have our elevenses now.'

By the time some excellent lemonade had washed down plum cake and apples, which the boys insisted on sharing out scrupulously, Verity knew that their father was a physician with a practice in Harley Street, that they had a little brother and a baby sister and that their mother had chased them out of the house that morning with '…enough food for an army, do have some more cake…' and instructions not to come back until they were either hungry or tired enough to go to bed. 'We kept on waking the baby, you see. Playing cricket in the corridor. And Mama gets very cross about that.'

Charmed by their friendly exuberance, Verity found herself volunteering to field for them. They stared.

George gulped. 'Are you…are you sure? I mean, girls don't usually play cricket…'

'Mama does,' argued Ben. 'Until Baby was coming. Then she said she didn't want any more cricket balls in the tummy. Papa forbade it anyway.' He turned to Verity. 'You aren't having a baby, are you?' His air of innocent concern robbed the question of all possible offence.

His elder brother blushed. 'Stubble it, you little bagpipe! You don't ask ladies questions like *that*!' He turned to Verity. 'I'm awfully sorry. He's only eight, you know. Er…you aren't, are you?'

Gravely, Verity denied it, pushing away the aching sadness that she would never know the joy and pride the unknown Mrs Cranmore must feel.

'Oh, well. I dare say it's all right then,' said George. 'And you can have a turn batting and bowling too, if you care for it.'

* * *

Two hours later Verity took her leave of the Cranmores, promising to come again on the next fine day and to find another dress.

'That one's all very well,' said Ben, frowning at the torn flounce, 'but you'd run better if you didn't trip over your skirts all the time.'

Chapter Thirteen

'They're late,' growled Max, shifting in his seat.

Mr Wimbourne pulled out his own watch and then favoured him with a piercing look. 'My lord, if I might venture upon a word of advice…'

Max sighed. 'I know. Don't give Faringdon cause to think I'm rattled in any way.'

The little lawyer nodded. 'Precisely, my lord. Faringdon has no idea that you will be here. All he knows is that a *caveat* has been entered against the estate. That puts the advantage with you. And while I sympathise with your anger over the way Lady Blakehurst has been treated, it would be as well if you do not allow emotion to cloud your judgement.'

That shot struck home. He had done nothing else since he met Verity.

Richard leaned forward. 'Is Mr Godfrey Faringdon likely to be here as well?'

Wimbourne shrugged. 'No doubt, Mr Blakehurst. He is, after all, a beneficiary of full age. Lord Faringdon attends only as trustee for his daughter.'

A bustle from the outer chamber alerted them.

'Remember, my lord—control yourself,' hissed Wimbourne as he stood up.

'Ah, good afternoon, my lord.' He bowed deeply to Lord

Faringdon. 'Mr Faringdon.' He inclined his head very slightly to Godfrey.

Faringdon didn't bother with any civilities. 'What the devil is this about, Wimbourne? I received a letter telling me a *caveat*—' His eyes bulged as Max turned in his seat and stood up. 'What…what's *he* doing here? I understood this to be a…a private meeting between the interested parties!'

'Quite correct, Faringdon,' said Max, reminding himself not to strangle the bastard. 'I am an interested party. Very interested.'

'Bit late for that, ain't it?' smirked Godfrey.

A hard grip on his arm stopped Max before he had done more than shift his weight. Fury scalded him. Breathing carefully, he glanced at Richard, who had a death grip on his arm. He nodded in acknowledgement and sat back.

Faringdon and Godfrey seated themselves in the chairs Mr Wimbourne placed for them. After a quelling glance at Max, the lawyer had put the chairs at a discreet distance. Far enough, Max noted, for Richard to grab him in time if his control broke again.

'Perhaps you would care to look at these, Lord Faringdon, Mr Faringdon?'

Max knew what the documents were—sworn copies of the original will leaving everything to Verity.

Faringdon tossed his on to the desk after barely glancing at it. 'Means nothing. The will naming my son and daughter as the beneficiaries post-dates this. Lady Hillsden changed her mind.'

Mr Wimbourne's smile reminded Max forcibly of a cat toying with a mouse. 'I beg to differ, my lord. Lady Hillsden's instructions to me were always very clear and she always explained her reasoning. When I drew up her final will, the one naming Mr Faringdon and Miss Faringdon, she told me that she was changing it back because Miss Verity Scott had died.'

Faringdon shifted uneasily. 'You must have misheard... girl's married to Blakehurst.'

Again Mr Wimbourne smiled. 'The instructions were in writing. Perhaps you might care to read her letter...' He passed sworn copies to both Faringdons.

This document was read far more carefully.

At last Godfrey Faringdon broke the shrieking silence. 'Must have been confused. That's what it is. She got confused and made a mista—'

'Hold your tongue, sir!' roared his father.

Godfrey glared. 'Don't see why I should. It's more my business than yours. Old girl got a bit fuddled near the end, and—'

'Made a will while she was not of sound enough mind to do so?' suggested Max innocently.

Godfrey's Adam's apple bobbed wildly as he realised the dangers of unwary speech. 'I...I...she...'

'Much as it pains me to assist your father, Mr Faringdon,' said Max, 'why don't you just hold your tongue?'

'The letter states quite clearly that you, Lord Faringdon, apprised her of Miss Scott's supposed death. That you hinted the girl made away with herself,' said Wimbourne.

'Rubbish!' snapped Faringdon. 'I—'

'Sent her a letter saying exactly that,' cut in Max. 'Perhaps you need to refresh your memory. Show them the copies of that letter, Wimbourne.'

Both Faringdons sat reading, their faces becoming whiter by the second. At last Lord Faringdon looked up and said, 'You can't prove anything. She's dead and buried. No one can say what she would have done...she changed her will more often than her carriage horses, so—'

'There is also the matter of your criminal neglect, Faringdon,' said Max, forcibly sitting back in his seat.

Faringdon's face turned pasty. 'Criminal...' For a moment he looked as though he might faint, then he rallied. 'Poppycock. Utter nonsense…' His protests wilted under the fire of Max's gaze.

'There are laws, Faringdon,' snarled Max. His shoulders tensed with the effort of keeping his voice calm. 'Laws quite clearly delineating the duties of a guardian to his ward. Such as protecting her interests. Such as protecting *her*!'

'Max!' Richard's warning came just in time.

Max clenched his teeth against the urge to choke the life out of both Faringdons.

Mr Wimbourne took over. 'Lord Blakehurst has made a very generous offer. Very generous under the circumstances. He is prepared to settle for fifteen thousand pounds and the jewellery. Leaving ten thousand to be divided between Miss Far—'

'*What?*' shrieked Faringdon over the lawyer. 'Damned if we agree to that! Wouldn't make the offer if he thought it would stand up legally! The money's ours! The courts will—'

Mr Wimbourne continued unperturbed. 'Or mount a suit in Chancery.'

Faringdon wilted. 'Ch…chancery?'

'Precisely, my lord.' Mr Wimbourne shook his head. 'Might take years. Take the Jennings case, for example— 1798 it began. Still running. And like to be after we're all dead and gone. Probably nothing left in the end either.' He shrugged. 'But that's your choice, my lord.'

Faringdon sneaked a look at Max. 'Need the money, do you, Blakehurst? Finding a wife without a dowry a little expensive, are you?'

'You offered me a way out, didn't you, Faringdon?' snarled Max. 'Tell me, when you offered to sell your ward to me as a whore, were you worried that this might come out if we married? If someone who'd been told she was dead saw her name in the papers? So much easier if she became my mistress! Then you could claim that you'd said she was dead to avoid the scandal. Was that it? Did you hope that would save you if your son ruined her? Or did you hope that your treatment of her would one day cause the lie to become truth?' He dragged in a breath. 'No, Faringdon. I don't need the money. But I'll be damned if I let you rob her! Call it revenge, *gentlemen*! You can accept my offer, or I'll challenge the will and see that you get nothing!'

Mr Wimbourne cut in sharply. 'Lord Faringdon, you will naturally wish to take counsel with your lawyers. Shall we meet again? In a fortnight at the same time? That gives you time to seek advice.'

Subsiding into his chair, Max forced himself to remember that backing Faringdon into a corner, where he would fight to the death to save face, would not benefit Verity. And that was what mattered. Giving Verity something that was hers.

Richard spoke up. 'That will be perfectly acceptable, Mr Wimbourne. We will wish you a good day, now. If Lord Faringdon has any query, he may contact you and you may inform us. Under the circumstances, it might be best if the Faringdons refrain from approaching Blakehurst directly. I may have to leave London and there is no saying what might happen if they chanced on him alone!'

Upon returning home and asking for his wife, Max was informed that her ladyship had not yet returned with the dogs.

'Well, that's something,' observed Richard, as Clipstone removed himself from the library. 'At least you know that anyone accosting her will be licked to death!'

'Oh, shut up!' said Max.

Five minutes later the door opened again and Clipstone re-entered. 'Lady Arnsworth wishes to know if you are—'

Lady Arnsworth swept in. 'Really, Max, I must insist that you speak to your wife! If I am to continue her sponsor...'

'Thank you, Clipstone,' snapped Max. He glared at his aunt, who had the grace to fall silent until the door closed. Then she reopened fire.

'To have Clipstone actually deny her to me! Not At Home, indeed!'

'Um, Almeria—'

'It is all of a piece, though—'

'Almeria!'

She glared at him. 'Yes, Max?'

'Verity is not at home.'

The glare intensified. 'I am not a dolt, Blakehurst. Clipstone denied her. I know she is not At Home. I do not demand that you fetch her down. Although I must say—'

'Almeria, she's not merely not At Home, she's out,' said Max, avoiding Richard's wooden face.

'Out?' Lady Arnsworth made the word sound like a bad oyster.

Max nodded.

'But...she can't be! Why, I moved heaven and earth to get her an invitation to Lady Torbury's luncheon! She sent a note to say she was indisposed. And she was to go on to Lady Gwdyr with me afterwards. All the most influential hostesses were there! And in the Park later. Let me tell you, her absence was noted!'

In the face of this appalling programme, Max could fully appreciate Verity's preference for the cows in the Green Park.

Shaking her head at such depravity, Lady Arnsworth continued. 'And her conduct last night! She danced with every gazetted rake in London! Positively encouraged them!'

Max found that he was hanging on to his temper by a thread and took a very deep breath. 'Almeria, surely you could have dropped a word in Verity's ear,' he suggested. 'After all, she has not been to London before. If you don't warn her which gentlemen she ought to refuse a dance, then—'

'Oh, she scarce listens to a word I say!' interrupted Lady Arnsworth. 'I vow, everyone is speculating on it. Especially her flirtation with Braybrook!' She shuddered. 'Why, everybody *knows* his reputation! And *he* wasn't in the Park this afternoon either. *That* was noted too!'

The unsubtle hint stunned Max momentarily. Verity? And Braybrook?

Having hit her stride, Lady Arnsworth charged on. 'And as for—'

Max cut her short. 'I'll speak to Verity, Aunt. No need for you to say any more on this head to her.'

She sniffed. 'Much good it would do! I told her *at length* last night in the carriage how shocked I was, how disgraceful her conduct, but all the girl would do was stare out the window. Even when I warned her about Braybrook's reputation. That he positively specialises in seducing other men's wives! Not a word did she say. Not one word!'

That, reflected Max, with Almeria in full flight, was only too likely. Memory pricked—Verity beside him in his curricle, crying without him even realising it. How much did it hurt to cry silently?

Richard's amused voice broke in. 'Well, give the poor chap his due, Almeria! He hasn't *got* a wife of his own—naturally he has to seduce other men's wives. That's what Max used to do. Stands to reason. Anyway, Braybrook's a friend of Max's. No doubt he's just doing the pretty. No need to fly into the boughs over it.'

Almeria's glare could have shattered glass. 'You may laugh, Richard! I am merely thinking of your poor mama. All her hopes! Destroyed by this disastrous marriage!' She turned on Max. 'For Richard to be supplanted in this way! Good God! From all poor Caroline Faringdon told me, you can have no surety that a child would even be yours!'

'What?' For a moment Max thought the room had sprouted an echo. Then he realised that Richard had started forward as well.

Almeria bridled. 'Well, really, Max. It can come as no surprise to you, after the way you were trapped. Apparently the wretched girl tried to play off her tricks on poor Godfrey, so one can only expect—'

'If I hear that repeated, Almeria, by you or anyone else,

they'll wish they had cut their own tongues out before I've finished with them,' said Max in deadly tones.

'Amen to that!' growled Richard.

'Well!' Her face an unbecoming mottled purple, Almeria stalked to the door. 'I hope I know when my advice is unwelcome!'

Max inclined his head. 'So do I, Almeria. But not as much as I hope you know when to take advice. I shall escort Verity myself this evening. Good day.'

The door shut with a bang.

Unable to remain still, Max paced around the room, swearing.

Perched on the edge of the desk Richard said calmly, 'About time.'

'For what?' snapped Max.

'For you to realise that Verity needs more than the protection of your name.'

Max took a very deep breath. 'Braybrook,' he said carefully. 'Are you suggesting that Verity *is* encouraging his advances?'

Richard frowned. 'Don't start on that again, Max. How the devil would I know? Only arrived last night. If she is, you know who to thank for it. Frankly, I doubt it. But since Braybrook is far too intelligent to maul a lady in public, since his manners are impeccable and he's an all-round decent sort, discounting the fact that he's bedded every bored and disgruntled wife in London, then I think it's possible that Verity might not even realise the danger until the damage is done.'

Max took deep breath. Braybrook? Seduce Verity? He swallowed.

'Damn it, Ricky! Braybrook's a friend of mine!' Wasn't he?

'Max,' said Richard patiently, 'use your brain. The danger is not that Julian *will* seduce Verity. The danger is that the quidnuncs will *say* that he did. With Almeria, I'll wager, at the head of the pack. If that's what she's saying to you, imagine what she's confiding to her bosom bows.'

Almeria's voice echoed through Max's brain: *She danced with every gazetted rake in London.* He didn't believe, couldn't believe, that she would encourage any of them on purpose.

There was only one solution. Richard was right. Forcing Verity to accept the protection of his name had not been enough. It had removed her from her uncle's guardianship, but it would not protect her against what society could do to her if he did not step in and make it plain that she was *fully* under his protection. It remained to be seen how Verity responded to his decision.

He turned to Richard. 'You're right. I'll have to escort her to the evening functions and warn off all the wolves.'

Richard raised a brow. 'Such a hardship. Would I be stepping across the line if I asked why you didn't do that in the first place?'

Max stared into the fire. 'Verity wants nothing to do with me. She cannot even bear to be in the same room. You saw how she fled this morning.'

Richard's mouth twisted. 'Yes. I saw. But…'

'I didn't want to force anything on her,' said Max carefully. 'I thought if I gave her time, a breathing space, she might come to me again.' He knew now that it wouldn't work.

'Slight problem with that,' observed Richard. 'You need to convince her that you want her. Difficult if you don't spend any time with her.'

He opened the door between their rooms very quietly. Verity sat before the dressing table, slender arms raised as she clasped the Blakehurst pearls around her throat. He felt his mouth dry at the memory of those arms twining around his neck, at the memory of the fluttering pulse in her throat just above where the pearls now sheened.

And the gown. Modest, demure in sky blue silk, with a pink sash and trim. It was the gown she had worn on his birthday at Blakeney. She looked…lovely. And all he could think of was how he had kissed her in the stillroom. How he had made love to her later.

He took a deep breath. And another. Just to make sure his voice didn't shake. 'There are earrings to match, Verity.'

Verity whipped around, her eyes wide. 'What…what are *you* doing here?'

'They should have been with the necklace.' He ignored her question and her sharp intake of breath as he approached.

The earrings lay on the dressing table.

'Permit me,' he said huskily as he picked them up.

'N…no. It's quite…I can—'

Her protests died as he carefully put on the first earring. Lilies of the valley wreathed through him in beckoning innocence. His breathing seized as her breath fractured when his fingers caressed the silken throat. Desire was an aching knot in his gut as he dealt with the second earring. Finished, he set his hands on her shoulders and drew her towards him.

'No…' A whisper, uncertain, vulnerable. But not afraid. He knew that as surely as he knew he wanted her. Whatever else she felt for him, she didn't fear him. For now, that was enough and more than he deserved.

'Yes,' he murmured and kissed her. Gently, tenderly, the fierce leap of passion savagely restrained. Her lips softened and he tasted her sweetness. And then he released her. Before she could struggle. Before he gave her a reason to do so.

Eyes wide, she backed away. 'I…no. Please—no more… Lady Arnsworth—she will be here any moment!'

Pain lanced deep. He inclined his head. 'As you wish, my dear. But I am your escort for this evening. We will see Almeria there.'

Her jaw dropped. 'You…you are escorting me? But—why?'

To spy on you? To protect you? 'For the pleasure of your company, my dear,' he lied. God help him, it would be more like torture.

Verity smiled and extended a hand automatically to her host and hostess. The brief carriage ride and the crush in the hall had not helped her confusion in the least. From Max's silence in the carriage she had the impression that he was bothered about something. He kept shifting restlessly and he avoided her gaze.

Still reeling with shock at his unexpected tenderness, she exchanged nods and bows, wondering who would cut her acquaintance this evening. To her frustration, on Max's arm, she was greeted by most with far more respect. By the ladies as well as the gentlemen. It was enough to make her spit. This was precisely what she needed—Max at the same ball, and everyone behaved as though she were a pattern card of respectability.

Except for the Duke of Calverston, who took advantage of Max greeting a friend to lift Verity's hand to his lips and simultaneously leer into her bodice. Her skin crawled at his touch even through the fine kid of her glove. Compared to the gowns some ladies were wearing, this one was positively chaste, but she found herself wishing she'd worn a fichu with it. Just in case Max noticed, she forced a smile for his Grace, ignoring a shaft of pain in her temples.

'How delightful to see you, Lady Blakehurst.' Calverston's smile left her feeling smirched. 'I believe you promised me a waltz this evening. I shall look out for you later.' He pressed her hand and she fought down the impulse to snatch it away. As he disappeared into the crush she surreptitiously rubbed her hand on her skirts.

'Really, niece,' hissed Lady Arnsworth from behind her. 'Must you encourage every man you meet to ogle you? People were shocked at your conduct last night! I felt myself obliged to inform Max!'

Verity forgot her role in a flare of rage as she swung

around. 'Good evening, ma'am. Yes, it was shocking, wasn't it?' she said equably. 'Just think, I merely stood there when I should have kicked him, or told him to get his snuff-stained nose out of my bodice and stop slobbering on my glove.'

'Niece!' snapped Lady Arnsworth. 'Remember where you are!'

'I did,' she said demurely. 'That's why I didn't kick him.'

A deep voice said, 'Good evening, Almeria. Your pardon, Verity. I was neglecting you.'

Verity felt every drop of blood drain from her face and her temples throbbed as she stared up at her husband. Had he heard her? His jaw looked as though it were about to crack under some sort of strain. Her mind whirled. Damn Almeria for her gossip No. Wait. She *wanted* Max to know. Oh! How could she think of anything after that kiss? Even knowing that he had only escorted her this evening in the hope of catching her in some compromising situation.

Seeing that Max had his arm crooked, ready to escort her again, she laid her gloved hand lightly on his sleeve. There. No tremors. No excitement. It was just an ordinary sleeve. With a perfectly ordinary arm in it. Anything else was pure imagination. Including the tenderness of that kiss.

Without warning his hand came across and anchored her fingers to his sleeve. Every nerve skittered wildly. It wasn't just imagination, his hand scorched her through the glove. She was trembling, especially since one long finger was gently caressing her wrist. She froze every muscle, every fibre of her body, to still the tremor of sensuous pleasure that washed through her at his touch. Just as it had when he kissed her.

He didn't look at her, but nodded to his aunt. 'Good evening, Almeria. Do excuse us.' He led her away. 'Verity, if Calverston or anyone else of that ilk approaches you—'

She baulked and pulled her hand away. 'So you *are* here to play watchdog! A spy!' she hissed. 'If you think for one minute—' Recalling her plan, she changed tack. Flapping her

eyelashes at him in what she hoped was a thoroughly vulgar
display, she cooed, 'Why, Blakehurst, are you come to make
sure that I am behaving myself? How charming!'

His brows snapped together. 'Are you referring to what I
said to you down at Blakeney?'

Ice formed in her stomach, a solid nauseating lump. 'At
Blakeney, my lord? You said a great deal at Blakeney, on
one subject or another.' She forcibly curved her lips into a
glittering smile. 'Oh. I have it now! Do you mean on the
terrace?'

His jaw appeared to have turned to granite. 'Precisely,' he
ground out. 'I wish to inform you—'

'No need, my lord,' she said. 'My memory is neither at
fault, nor am I in the least stupid. I recall your words perfectly. Ah, here is Lord Selkirk.' She repressed a shudder and
her headache stabbed spitefully. 'I believe I am promised to
dance with him now. Good evening, Lord Selkirk!'

Max was forced to stand back and watch Selkirk, whom
he had no hesitation in stigmatising an oily brute, making up
to his wife. His fists clenched. What the devil was Verity
playing at, encouraging Selkirk? If he bowed any lower in
the dance he'd be cross-eyed staring down her bodice. Damn
it all! Just look at her! Flirting behind her fan as she extended
her hand! That ghastly giggle, high, shrill. But why had she
objected to Calverston? Selkirk was just as bad.

A familiar voice spoke at his elbow. 'Congratulations. You
certainly know how to put a woman on her mettle.'

He turned and glared at Richard. 'Oh, shut up! What the
hell is she playing at?' He jerked his head towards Verity,
now prancing about in some vulgar country dance.

'You insulted her and now she's giving you exactly what
she thinks you expect?' suggested Richard blandly. He helped
himself to champagne from a tray borne by a passing footman
and handed a glass to Max. 'Here, try this. It might make
you less bubble headed.' He cast a considering glance at Max.
'Might even cool you off a trifle.'

Sipping his champagne, he watched his sister-in-law. 'Can't think why you suggested she should try her talents at Drury Lane, Max.' He shook his head. 'She's a terrible actress! Even I'm better at pretending to enjoy myself than that.'

The calm words floored Max. *Pretending?*

Richard continued. 'The trick is to think of something else at the same time. Something pleasant. Then your smile has an odds-on chance of looking genuine.'

Shaken, Max focused on Verity's face rather than his own jealousy. Her smile looked as though it had been painted clumsily. And that blank look in her eyes tore at him. He'd seen it before—when she was hiding something. Fear, or hurt.

What was she up to? Surely she wouldn't court this sort of risk to make him jealous? She didn't want anything to do with him. Another possibility raked him. Vengeance. He dismissed it. Verity didn't have a vindictive bone in her body.

*My memory is neither at fault, nor am I in the least stupid…*she knew precisely what she was doing. He only wished he did. But if she thought he'd permit just anyone to waltz with her, she was in for a crashing disappointment.

He waited until the last possible moment to claim her for the waltz, until her hand had been claimed and Calverston was about to take the floor with her. 'Excuse me, Calverston. My dance, I believe.'

His Grace opened his mouth to protest, saw who had cut in, and promptly shut it again.

Verity had no such qualms about protesting. 'I am already engaged for this dance, my lord.'

Max observed, with a twinge of amusement, her outraged expression as his Grace beat a hasty retreat to the swell of the violins.

His brows rose. 'Perhaps you haven't realised, my lady— as your husband, *my* rights take precedence.' Then he saw that frozen look flicker across her face, and could have kicked himself. And did she look paler than at the outset of the evening?

'Your rights, my lord?' The storm clouds had gathered in her dark eyes. 'I was under the impression that you had renounced your rights. Or would repudiated be the correct word?'

He possessed himself of her hand and bowed over it, turning it slightly to press a kiss on the bare skin of her inner wrist. Her slight shiver racked him. 'I'm sorry, Verity,' he said quietly. 'That was not how I meant it. Come. Dance with me. Believe me, waltzing with Calverston will be infinitely worse than Roger de Coverley with Selkirk. At least you can trust me to keep my hands where they ought to be during a dance.'

Her eyes closed briefly. 'Yes. Very well.'

He led her into the dance, savagely aware of the soft, sinuous waist under his hand, the gently rounded hip just below. The temptation to let his hand slip, caress her, draw her closer…if he did that, he was lost.

Conversation. One was meant to converse with one's dance partner. Light, social chit-chat that could help a man ignore the scent of roses and lilies twining through him and the need pounding in his blood. He wanted to speak to her of love, of how much he wanted to take her in his arms… He groaned inwardly. He'd done that. She was in his arms. And it was killing him. He wanted to remove her from the ballroom and…he wanted to kiss her. Make love to her. Make her believe, understand that she was his. That he had been a damned fool. And he couldn't say any of that, let alone *do* any of that, in a crowded ballroom.

She stumbled slightly as he whirled her through a turn. His arms tightened, drawing her close, supporting her until she regained her balance. Ruthlessly he ignored her efforts to pull back to a more decorous distance.

'Max—people are watching. Don't you think…?'

'Too much,' he growled. If people were watching, and he

saw no reason to doubt it, then a waltz like this would send a very clear warning. A hands-off-if-you-want-to-keep-them sort of warning. Exactly what he wanted.

'You're my wife. Remember? No one can whip up a scandal out of a husband dancing with his own wife.' Not unless the said husband forgot his surroundings and did precisely what he wanted to do. He rather thought that might cause the sort of scandal to set the ear trumpets a-quiver for decades. Every muscle rigid with restraint, he concentrated on dancing, ignoring the heady scent of roses and lilies and the sensuous curve of a supple waist sheathed in silk shifting beneath his hand.

Richard claimed Verity for a stroll straight after the dance and Max watched her go, frowning. She was safe enough with Richard, but what *was* she up to?

My memory is neither at fault, nor am I in the least stupid.

He smiled automatically at various acquaintances and returned vague replies to several. Damn it. Anyone would think she was *trying* to whip up a scan— His whirling thoughts hitched on that, focused and saw the truth. Hell! That was exactly what she was trying to do! He'd said he would cast her off if she created a public scandal. Cold sweat broke out on him as he realised how far she would go to regain her freedom. He'd forged the weapon and she intended to use it. Against herself.

Verity smiled and answered politely as she strolled with Richard and greeted this person and that. Her headache pulsed brutally. How long would it take to spring the trap on herself? Could she get it over and done with this evening?

A light, charming voice greeted her. 'Good evening, Lady Blakehurst. Hullo, Ricky. Playing watchdog this evening?'

Verity looked up into Lord Braybrook's smiling blue eyes.

He bowed over her hand and said, 'I believe we agreed on this dance, ma'am.'

'We…we did,' she said, forcing a smile, despite the beat behind her eyes.

'Max is here this evening, Julian,' remarked Richard.

Braybrook glanced at him. 'Yes. So I saw. About time. Shall we, my dear?'

With another wholly false smile, Verity gave him her hand and curtsied.

Her headache worsened as she danced, until she felt sick with it and the blaze of light hurt her eyes even as the screech of the violins shredded her and the roar of conversation pounded on her brain. If only she could escape to some dark, quiet corner…close her eyes…

Braybrook whirled her through a turn and she stumbled, dizzy and confused. Even when they had completed the turn the room kept spinning.

'My lord…please. Could we stop?'

He frowned down at her. 'I think we'd better.' He swung her out of the dance close to one of the doors leading on to the terrace. 'Hmm. Breathe in through your nose and out through your mouth. That should help if you feel sick.'

She shut her eyes and obeyed him. It worked. Opening her eyes, she smiled shakily. 'Thank you, sir,' she said. 'If you would excuse me, I think I might go out on to the terrace for a moment.'

He nodded. 'Of course. A little fresh air will help too.'

Relieved that he understood, Verity took one, and then another, careful step. Now that she was not spinning around, she felt less dizzy, but the blinding ache remained. She would have to go home, but right now she doubted that she would make it across the ballroom without fainting.

Gratefully she breathed the cool air of the terrace. After the over-scented heat of the ballroom it felt like paradise. A broad balustrade ran around the edge, wide enough to sit on safely. Light poured from the windows, but she could see a darker corner where she could rest her eyes.

To her surprise she found that Lord Braybrook had accompanied her across the flagstones. 'It's very kind of you, sir, but I shall be better directly. I just need to sit quietly for a moment, you know,' she told him.

'Not at all, ma'am,' he assured her. 'A pleasure. The ballroom was a trifle stuffy.'

He sat down beside her. And Verity suddenly realised what she had done. She was alone on the terrace with one of London's most notorious rakes.

Chapter Fourteen

Max saw them go and swore under his breath. Julian's brain must be addled taking her out there! Damned fool! The last thing he needed was to have to go out to Paddington and face Braybrook over pistols just to keep up appearances. He cast a worried glance around. Who else had seen?

On the far side of the ballroom, Almeria looked like a bird dog on point. Damn and double damn! What would she do about it? Somehow he didn't think he could count on Almeria's discretion. To his absolute horror, he saw her lean towards her companion, the feathers in her turban nodding wildly. His fists clenched. If he didn't do something...but what? Almeria was making sure that as many people as possible would be watching that door when Verity returned.

He'd have to make sure they didn't see what they were expecting to see.

'A lovely night, Lady Blakehurst,' Braybrook remarked.

'Y...yes. I suppose it is,' she faltered. What on earth should she do? If Max had seen them... Her headache gave a vicious surge as she remembered that this was very much what she had planned. Sort of. For Max to believe...to believe...except she had meant someone else to break the news to Max that she was having an affair. And she certainly hadn't meant to linger on a darkened terrace with a rake whose reputation was only rivalled by her husband's. She clutched her reticule in shaking hands.

'And the refreshments are of excellent quality,' he went on.

Even through the haze of confusion and headache, it occurred to Verity that this was a most peculiar line of conversation for a man bent on seduction. Not that she had much experience of men bent on seduction, but he hadn't even touched her.

Even as she wondered, his large hand closed over both hers, stilling the trembling. She jerked back with a gasp.

'You know, Lady Blakehurst, whatever tarradiddles Lady Arnsworth and Ricky Blakehurst may have told you, I'm quite harmless.'

Footsteps sounded, and a quiet voice. 'Good evening, Julian. Verity.'

Max stood on the steps leading up from the garden, his face unreadable. The world contracted. Now would come the explosion she had invited, had planned for. She braced herself for the torrent of bitter accusations.

Braybrook hailed Max cheerfully. 'Ah, there you are, Blakehurst. I wondered how long it would take you to find us. Here's your wife. You might like to take her home, old chap. I fancy she has the headache.'

What?

Her husband regarded her for a moment. Then his gaze flickered to Braybrook. 'Thank you, Julian, for looking after her. I'm very grateful. Could you do me another favour and disappear the way I came? You'll find the library window open. I believe it might be best if *I* took Verity back inside.'

Grateful?

'Seen, were we?' asked Braybrook. 'Curst tabbies! A fellow can't even behave with disinterested chivalry without them hoping the worst! What the devil did they think I'd do to her out here with you present? I'd need to have a death wish! Servant, Lady Blakehurst. I'll be off. Evening, Max.'

Verity's mind flailed around trying to understand what the pair of them were about. *Grateful?* Max was supposed to be furious, wasn't he? Threatening to divorce her for creating a scandal? Instead he'd thanked Lord Braybrook and now sat beside her on the balustrade, his arm around her shoulders and his free hand massaging her temple.

She gave up trying to think and rested her forehead against his chest, while he rubbed gently. She could feel the tension ebbing in waves, slowly receding from her body, leaving her strangely at peace. He hadn't believed it. He had trusted her. Did she dare to trust him again?

'Better?' His voice soothed her insensibly.

'Much. Thank you.'

'Good. I'll take you home soon.' The husky voice caressed her. The hand that had been easing her headache brushed over her cheek, long fingers sliding under her chin, tilting it until she was looking up into his shadowed face. Longing melted her, dissolving her defences. He was close, so close. She could feel the heat in him, see the pulse beating in his throat.

From a great distance the sounds of the ball echoed, but she heard it only dimly above the sudden pounding of her heart. Gentle hands held her, casting a tender, protective spell. Reason, caution warned her: *The spell will not survive the dawn.*

She didn't care. The tenderness in his smile, in his eyes, breached every barrier.

The spell exploded in shocked accents. 'Well! Really! My poor nephew! Have you no shame, you hussy?'

Max froze at Almeria's self-righteous voice.

'If you think that Blakehurst will countenance…'

His arms tightened protectively as he turned very slightly to face his aunt.

The triumph leached from her face. '*Blakehurst?* But what happened to…I…I mean…' Her hand clutched at her throat.

Max wished she would strangle herself and have done. He knew precisely what had happened. Braybrook was about his height, with dark hair. From the back, in the shadows, it must have looked as though all Almeria's cards had turned up trumps. Rage seared him as he saw how many avid scandal-mongers she had brought with her. They crowded at her back, gathered for the kill.

He fought to keep his voice indifferent. 'Do you know, Aunt, you are decidedly *de trop*. And I completely fail to see why I should be pitied. Being caught on a terrace with one's *own* wife is unusual, but hardly a crime. I'm certainly not going to call myself out over it. Perhaps you would be good enough to excuse us. My wife has the headache and I am about to escort her home.'

They spoke very little at first. Max settled her in the carriage, draped his coat around her shoulders, then her evening cloak and a rug he pulled from under the seat. Then, ignoring her feeble protest, he pulled her into his arms and held her.

She gave up and rested her head on his shoulder. Whatever his reasons, she couldn't fight his tenderness, his consideration.

The carriage had turned into Berkeley Square before Max spoke.

'I want one thing clear, Verity. No matter what sort of scandal you kick up, how appalling, how public, it won't induce me to release you. Do you understand me?' The harsh voice, so at odds with the gentle fingers massaging her temple, froze her.

Confused, she said, 'But…I thought you wanted to be rid of me, that you wanted your freedom?'

His arms hardened. 'You won't gain your freedom that—' He broke off. Shocked silence burned between them. 'Did you say *my* freedom?' Angry fingers gripped her shoulders, digging in as he swung her to face him. 'Damn it, Verity! Did you try to kick up a scandal to release *me*? *Did* you?'

Seeing the hard-edged anger in his face, she could only nod.

'*Hell's teeth!* What sort of brute do you take me for?'

The hurt fury in his voice choked her. 'You…you said…'

'You little idiot! I was angry! You *can't* have believed I meant…' His voice faded. 'Oh, my God. You did believe it, didn't you? That I'd leap at the chance to be rid of you?'

She nodded, wriggling her shoulders a little at his fierce grip. It slackened very slightly.

Lead formed in his gut. Then—had she thought he would simply kick her out with nothing? To starve? And she had gone ahead anyway?

He shut his eyes and gritted his teeth against the urge to shake her. First he had to protect her. Even from herself. Then he tightened his grip on her again and spoke urgently. 'Listen to me, Verity. Under no circumstances will I divorce you. And I will have your word that you will *never* try to free yourself, or me, in this way again.'

'But—'

'Your word!'

'I won't share your bed!' she flung at him. 'If you want that, buy another woman!'

Pain streaked through him. 'So be it,' he ground out. 'Your word, Verity.'

'Very well. You have my word.'

He let out a shaky breath. She was safe. He could trust her word.

To Verity's shock he insisted on coming upstairs with her. Her headache had returned tenfold and she could only be grateful for the strong hand under her elbow. The steps kept on shifting oddly. She stumbled and found herself swept up into his arms. Through the pain she protested. 'No! I said I wouldn't—'

He cut her off. 'Verity, I have no intention of dragging an unwilling woman to my bed. Let me help you. Please.'

She didn't understand how he managed to open her door without setting her down or dropping her, but he did it. He carried her to the bed and placed her on it. Dizzy, she sat with her face buried in her hands, listening to him move around the room. There came a slight rattle as he drew the bed hangings. She looked up to see that he had closed them on three sides and he was coming towards her, one of her night-gowns over his arm.

'Can you change or should I ring for your maid?' he asked, laying the night-gown beside her.

'I can manage, if…if you would unhook my gown.'

There was nothing he wanted more. Without a word he slid his arms around her, reaching for the back of her gown. For an instant he felt her stiffen. He stilled, waiting. And felt her soften, her brow resting on his shoulder, her body relaxed. After her innocence, it was the most precious gift he had ever been given. He didn't deserve this either.

First he undid the soft pink sash and then applied his shaking fingers to the hooks, battling the urge to trace the shadowy hollow of her spine beneath the chemise, lean forward and close his teeth lightly on the sensitive curve of neck and shoulder.

The dress hung open, his hands rested lightly on her shoulders. 'All done,' he said.

She remained in his arms. And his heart clenched. Grimly he reminded himself that she wasn't well, that he must not abuse her trust. He sat back, releasing her. 'I've left a lamp on your dressing table, out of sight,' he said gently. 'Does the light bother you?'

'No.'

'Good. Change while I'm gone. I need to fetch something for you.' He bent and dropped a kiss on her hair. 'I won't be long.'

To his immense surprise, upon entering his brother's bed-chamber he found Richard taking off his coat.

Richard looked up with a grin. 'Hullo. Looking for something? I left early. Braybrook fled too. Never seen Almeria in such a tweak.'

'Ricky, have you got any laudanum?'

Richard's fingers stilled on his cravat. 'Laudanum? For Verity?' His mouth tightened. 'That might not be such a good idea for her. Is her headache very bad?'

'How did you…?' Max smiled wryly. 'Julian.'

Richard shrugged. 'He walked back here on his way to White's. Listen, Max—laudanum's funny stuff. Gets a grip on you if you aren't damned careful. Myself, I'd prefer the headache. Mama kept giving it to me after my accident. Gave me nightmares. Eventually I used to pour it out and tell her I'd taken it.'

Max stared. 'You? Nightmares? You never told me.'

'While I was awake,' said Richard grimly. 'It was after you'd gone back to school.' He walked over to a tallboy and picked up a bottle. 'Here. I'll measure it for you. She shouldn't have much.' Under Max's startled gaze he measured two drops into a tumbler of water.

'Two drops?' queried Max.

Richard grimaced. 'Believe me—it's enough. I have to be desperate before I'll touch the stuff. Chap I knew at Oxford—' he grimaced '—he'd go nearly crazy with pain if he didn't get his dose. Frightening. Brilliant mind, but useless—no power to finish anything. The nightmares got to him too. He used to write them down. All snakes and cavernous ruins.'

Max stared into the tumbler Richard had handed to him, the brownish drops barely colouring the water. Verity's father had drunk laudanum. 'Ricky—could it drive a man to suicide?'

He shrugged. 'Probably. If he didn't get his dose. If he was heavily habituated.'

Max set the tumbler down very carefully. 'Thanks. Sorry I disturbed you. I'll leave it.'

* * *

He went back to Verity's room and found her nearly asleep. Softly he went over to the bed and gazed down at her. She looked so small and vulnerable, nearly lost in the shadows of the heavy brocaded bed hangings. Her lashes lay on her cheeks. He bent to tuck the covers more securely about her shoulders.

'Max?' The dark lashes flickered as she blinked up at him.

The sleepy murmur shook him. He sat down on the bed and stroked the tumbled curls. 'Yes. I'm back.'

'What did you go for?'

'Nothing. Is your headache still bad?'

'A little.'

He brushed his fingers over the satin curve of her cheek. 'Shall I rub your head again?'

A slight pause. 'Would you mind?'

'No. Not at all.' Carefully, he shifted to sit with his back to the headboard and lifted her into his arms, ignoring the sweetness of tender curves under the lawn nightgown. Settling her safely against his chest, he cradled her forehead in his hand and began—slow, circling motions with fingers and thumb. Her sigh of relief breathed against his wrist and he felt his body tighten. He jerked the reins taut on his self control.

'Max? Thank you for trusting me.' The sleepy whisper pierced him.

An hour later she lay sleeping soundly in his arms, her breathing regular and the little frown smoothed away.

He should put her down and leave, before he was tempted to slide into the bed beside her. His self-discipline hovered on the brink of bolting as it was. Something to do with the slender arms snuggled around his waist, no doubt. And the delicate scent of roses and lilies sinking into him.

Stifling a groan, he made to lay her down, only to feel the arms tighten and hear her protest as she half-woke. He froze. Damn. What was a man supposed to do in this situation?

Answer: behave in accordance with the precepts of chivalry. He couldn't lay her down without waking her. So he would have to hold her. At least until the choice was between waking her up by laying her down and waking her up in a far less chivalrous, if more satisfactory, way.

Somehow he needed to distract his mind from the temptation of soft breasts nestled against him, from the silken tangle of hair spilling over his chest. His gaze lit on a leather-bound book on her bedside table. He picked it up with his free hand. Anything would be better than lying here, thinking about seducing her.

Opening the book, he flushed and started to put it down. It was handwritten. Damn. He couldn't read her private journal. Then, despite himself, a name leapt out at him. Two names. His own and—*Slender Billy*? Why would Verity write about the Prince of Orange... unless—his breathing tore— unless it wasn't Verity's journal.

Slender Billy in a miff. That young idiot Max B. had the temerity to wonder, in his Highness's presence! when Old Hookey would make it back from Vienna.

Max choked back a laugh. Good God. He'd forgotten that. Slender Billy imagining that he could command the Allied army in the field against Napoleon in Wellington's absence! Of course everyone in Brussels had been terrified that Boney would cross the frontier while the Prince of Orange was in the saddle. Everyone except the Prince, that was.

He read on. He'd never realised that William Scott kept a private journal. His eyes widened. A very private journal, he hoped. How in Hades had Scott known about *that* affair? Heat stole along his cheekbones as he realised just how much his C.O. had known about him. He scanned the pages rapidly. Lord! Even his brief connection with Lady Gainfort had not escaped notice!

A sudden thought sent even more heat flooding his cheeks. Verity had read this? *And you had the hide to take exception to her deciding, in desperation, to become your mistress.*

He wondered that she hadn't stuffed the journal into his mouth and forced him to eat it. He read on, reliving the whole Waterloo campaign, the breathless gaiety of Brussels as they waited throughout that spring until the entry on the morning of the fifteenth of June. The main item on Scott's mind that morning had been the Duchess of Richmond's ball that evening. And his mixed regret that his pregnant wife had elected to remain in England.

As well that they aren't here. I cannot believe that Wellington will suffer defeat, but if, God forbid, the worst should happen, I could not bear to think of Mary and my little Verity caught up in the horrors of a flight.

Max looked down at the dusky curls spilling over his shoulder. *Little Verity.* Now lying in his arms. His wife. What would Scott think of his son-in-law?

He flipped the page. And found a different man. The first outburst of rage and despair didn't surprise him. Returning minus an arm to discover your wife and son dead and buried—Max shuddered. Scott's grief cried out in the bitter words. A page further on, he frowned. The writing sounded almost…insane? Rambling. Here and there what sounded like nightmares were jotted down.

He shifted restlessly. Perhaps he ought not to read this—another name leapt at him: *Verity.*

Snakes. Her eyes are full of them. hiss and slide Mocking. She won't stay in her grave…looks at me. I can't look at her. says she is Verity I can't look at her. The snakes haunt me. She won't go away. I scream at her to go she won't go.

Max closed the journal with a helpless shudder. Dear God. No wonder Verity didn't speak of her father. No wonder she had flinched when he remarked on her likeness to her mother. Thank God he hadn't given her the laudanum.

What had Richard said about his Oxford friend? *He'd go nearly crazy with pain if he didn't get his dose. Frightening. Brilliant mind, but useless—no power to finish anything. The nightmares got to him too. He used to write them down. All snakes and cavernous ruins.*

Pain splintered inside him as he understood what Verity had been through. No. He *couldn't* understand. No one could, who hadn't lived through something like this. But at least he knew now what had happened. After this, her father's suicide must have been the final catastrophe.

Only to be followed by the Faringdons. Who stole her name and her inheritance. Who had driven her to the point of becoming his mistress just to escape…or was that it? *I'd like…to belong. To be part of people's lives.*

The memory of her innocent wish raked him. She had wanted to *belong*. Everyone had refused her that, even her own father in his inexorable slide to self-destruction. Yet she had still loved him. She had still gone out to try and give his burial some honour.

Without disturbing the sleeping woman in his arms, he replaced the journal. It was still a very private journal. Perhaps he should not have read it, but he couldn't regret it. He had needed to know what was in it. But that didn't mean Verity need know he had read it. She had not chosen to share it with him. At least he could respect her desire for privacy.

Very gently he lay her down on the bed and eased away from her. She had expressed another desire this evening— namely not to share his bed again. Grimly he faced what he had done to her. He had taken her and promised protection, demanding her trust. She had given it. Completely. Then he had pushed her away. He had called her back. She had come. Hesitantly, but she had come and given her trust again. And he had broken faith again, shattering what he had been given so freely.

Tonight something had changed. She had begun to trust again. Perhaps there was hope after all. If he was careful not to ask too much, too soon.

Over the next week Verity found Max constantly at her side. He attended her to balls, routs, dinners and the theatre.

His mere presence quelled every malicious rumour and innuendo. He treated her with kindly consideration, a gentleness that left her defences in tatters.

She couldn't maintain her coldness. It melted in the tender warmth of his smile. She couldn't maintain her guard. It retreated since apparently it had nothing to do. *He won't hurt you. You know that.*

But he made no move to persuade her to his bed. She had woken alone the morning after the Torringtons' ball and he had not come to her since. He didn't want her, no matter how much her own heart clamoured that she wanted him. Perhaps all that had happened was that he had decided to accept the situation with a good grace. Make the best of it. He would not wish to know that his foolish wife still harboured her pathetic dream of love.

So she accepted his escort and quiet presence. And in the afternoons when he often went to his club, she slipped out to the Green Park with the dogs.

Max watched from the drawing-room windows as Verity appeared on the footpath below, closely chaperoned by Taffy and Gus. With the spaniels whirling around her in a mad tangle of leashes and flapping ears, she set off.

Feeling like a spy, he gave her time to reach her destination before he left his post. He knew where she was going. Or at least where she had told her maid she was going. This afternoon he would find out who she met in the Green Park.

She had only given her word not to cause a scandal. A shudder went through him. She had to be meeting someone. She came back from her solitary excursions flushed, with something of a sparkle in her eyes and a spring to her step. And it terrified him. Not that she looked as joyous as that week at Blakeney, merely less *un*happy.

And she always came in ravenous. It all added up to a raging affair. Except the dogs always came home exhausted enough to collapse in a heap in a corner of the library where they remained until the word 'dinner' penetrated their rabbit-infested dreams. And he simply didn't believe it of her anyway.

The idea of following her left a nasty taste, but he ignored it. He had to. If she *was* meeting someone in all innocence, he needed to know who. Thinking that she might find herself at the mercy of someone who would not hesitate to take advantage of her inexperience… He reached the front hall and flung on his coat.

She had a big enough start that he need not fear the dogs noticing him. The last thing he wanted was for Verity to think that he distrusted her. He had regained a fraction of her trust. He couldn't bear to lose it again.

He reached the Green Park and strolled through the gates. Time contracted, catapulting him back twenty or more years. Memories flooded him—playing cricket here in the holidays with Richard and Frederick. Other dogs that had preceded Gus and Taff. And further back, coming here as very small boys with Nanny. And being dragged home in disgrace on one memorable occasion after an indiscretion involving a cowpat. He wondered if Richard remembered.

He should be looking for Verity. Carefully, from the cover of a convenient tree, he quartered the park. Cows munched placidly by the lake. She shouldn't be hard to find…not in that very smart and very visible turkey-red pelisse. Two lads playing cricket brought a smile to his face. They might be Richard and his own younger selves… One was making runs hand over fist, while the other jumped up and down, shrieking at a toiling figure racing back with the ball, an older sister by the look of it…his searching gaze passed on. And then swung back sharply as Gus and Taff careered up to the boys, barking madly. Where the dogs were, surely…and then he recognised her, pelisse discarded, curls flying as she flung the ball with all her strength and commendable aim.

The gown was the last thing he would have expected under

that pelisse she had set off in. It must be one of her old ones. No London modiste had fashioned *that* abomination but, he had to admit, it was admirable for cricket.

Dazed, he watched. A very few minutes served to convince him that Verity was a prime favourite with the boys and that her popularity extended far beyond her obvious willingness to field for them. The younger one gave up his bat to her with great alacrity and corrected her grip with all the aplomb of a master.

And Max noted with approval that the ball sent down by the elder lad was nothing like the scorchers faced by his younger brother. Which, chivalry aside, might have been a serious error, he admitted, as his hoyden of a wife hooked it for what would have been a clean six at any public school in England.

He watched Verity race up and down the wicket, conscious of a queer ache in his heart, an ache that he scarcely dared acknowledge, because to do so would lift the lid on everything he had thought buried. His longing for Verity had been bad enough when he could pretend it was merely lust, a physical desire for a lovely woman. It had been worse when he realised he wanted all of her, the laughter he had destroyed, the unconscious pride and dignity he had trampled and the sweet, innocent passion he had shamed.

Now it ripped him apart to see her like this and to know that but for his own irresponsibility and its consequences, he could have been looking into the future. His future. And hers. But all he could taste were the ashes of the past.

He didn't realise how long he had been there until a halt was called to play and they all sat down under a tree to share a sizeable repast. His mouth practically watered at the sight of what he thought *might* be plum cake and biscuits, washed down with what was no doubt lemonade.

Champagne and lobster patties never tasted that good.

He should go. Verity could not possibly get into trouble in this company, always excepting the odd stray cricket ball, but somehow he remained. Watching, soaking up their pleasure like a thief. Knowing that it was just making the pain worse. Seeing what he had wanted. And could not have—unless he broke that damn vow. A vow he was fast coming to realise he should never have made. A vow that should never have been asked of him. But the fact remained that he had made it. If not willingly, at least in full knowledge of what he was doing…no, not full knowledge. He'd been—how old? Twenty-seven? He hadn't really understood the enormity, the responsibility of his unexpected accession to the title. He had been full of determination that Richard should never see himself as 'Max's spare'.

It hadn't occurred to him that he would ever want his own family. Not just an heir, but children, sons—and daughters— who would share the summers and cricket matches of childhood and munch plum cake in the Green Park as they fended off a couple of greedy spaniels.

For the first time it occurred to him that he had never really cared that Freddy was the heir. He just hadn't liked being seen as little more than a back up. He needed to talk to Richard. Explain his decision… His decision? Dazed he realised that he had already made his choice. That it had been made watching Verity and these boys. She was his. She had trusted him, loved him. And he loved her too much to ask her to be his wife—his lover—but never bear his child. He couldn't do that to her.

He blinked as he came around the corner within view of the house. Richard's curricle stood in the road and a footman was heaving luggage into the boot. Damn! Where the devil was he off to, just when he was needed?

He lengthened his stride and reached the bottom of the steps just as Richard limped out of the door, shrugging himself into his driving coat.

'Where the devil—'

Richard cut him off. 'Blakeney. I've had enough of London.' He nodded to the footman. 'Thanks, Charles. That's all.'

'Yessir.'

The groom holding the horses looked at Richard expectantly.

'Ah, Payne. Walk 'em, please.' He turned to Max.

'I need to talk to you,' said Max. On the street wouldn't have been his choice of venue, but needs must.

'Mmm. So I see,' said Richard. 'First things first. I'm going down to Blakeney because I think you and Verity need time *alone* to sort out your marriage. Sorry if I've gone beyond the line, old chap, but there it is.'

'Just…just what…' Max tugged at his cravat '…um, what do you think needs sorting out?'

Richard spluttered. 'Confound it, Max! Do you need it spelt out? I want to be an uncle! Does that help?'

Max felt his jaw drop. 'An uncle?'

Richard grinned sheepishly. 'Oh, very well. And a godfather. In fact, I'll damn well call you out if you ask anyone else!'

'Not…not an earl?' The moment the words left his lips Max knew his mistake.

'An earl? How the devil can I…?' Richard stared, his eyes narrowing in sudden suspicion. 'Damn it, Max! Is *that* what this has all been about? Did Mama…?' He swore violently. 'She did! You've been putting Verity and yourself through hell over my supposed expectations? You *idiot*! As if I minded being *your* spare!'

He barely paused for breath. 'Listen, Max—if Mama dragged some deathbed promise out of you, forget it. Utter fustian! She had no right! She said something of the sort to me, but she was rambling. I didn't take her seriously! I never expected you to stay single for *me*. I thought you *preferred* it.' He grinned slightly. 'After all, your mistresses were the prettiest in London.'

He ran his hands through his hair. 'The only good thing

about the whole business is that it stopped you marrying years ago out of some stupid sense of duty to the blasted title! At least it kept you free for Verity.'

Max shut his eyes, remembering his mother's words. He'd come to sit with her, to say goodbye, and try to make his peace with her. But all she'd been able to think about had been Richard's future. His brother's life—ruined, as she put it, by his reckless nature, because he'd dared Richard to ride that damn horse.

'Max…' Richard's voice was very quiet '…she was wrong. Wrong to blame you. Wrong to ask that of you. Good God, I could just as easily have been maimed or killed out in the Peninsula if I'd joined the army! I never did have your luck. I got on the blasted horse because I wanted to. *My* choice. *My* decision. All you owe me is a pack of brats in your image. Or, better still, Verity's. She's prettier.'

Max let out a great sigh. 'I came to that conclusion myself. That was what I needed to tell you.'

Richard's mouth twitched slightly. 'I see. Well, I didn't say it at the time, but I will now—congratulations on your marriage, brother. I'll be off.' The lingering irritation in his eyes dissolved into a raffish twinkle and he added, 'Enjoy your honeymoon.'

Watching Richard drive off, Max heard his cheerful prediction over and over: *Enjoy your honeymoon*. First he had to convince the bride. And before he did that he had to tell her about her inheritance. Her independence. To truly win her, he must first give her the means to fly.

Chapter Fifteen

'Why didn't you tell me?' Verity struggled to understand what Max had told her. Her grandmother had changed her will. Twice. She had been disinherited because of the Faringdons' lies. It all made sense now. No wonder they wouldn't let her leave and forced her to change her name. They had stolen everything.

With a sickening lurch of memory, she heard her uncle, offering to sell her to Max as his doxy. Perhaps he regretted not accepting the offer. A vile little voice suggested something else—*a man has no claim on his mistress's private fortune.*

'Why didn't you tell me sooner?' she asked again painfully. Not that it would make any difference.

He cleared his throat. 'The lawyers came to me at Blakeney. You didn't see them. It was after our—'

'I see,' she said. After all, he hadn't *needed* to tell her. She had no say in what happened to the money, no rights beyond what her husband granted her.

'No. You don't!' he said sharply. 'You were upset enough after what had happened between us. I had no idea what, if anything, could be done about the will and I decided to find out before telling you!' The taut, hard note in his voice lashed at her. No doubt he had not wanted more feminine tears to deal with.

Fighting tears, she nodded. 'And what have you discovered, my lord?' She thought he stiffened.

His voice hardened even further. 'I met with your uncle and cousin. I offered to settle for fifteen thousand pounds and the jewellery.'

With careful hands, she set her tea cup down on the table. 'Fif... fifteen thousand, sir?'

'And the jewellery. Anything you don't like, you may give to Miss Faringdon.'

'And the jewellery,' she repeated dutifully. Then, 'Why?'

'Why?' The topaz eyes narrowed.

'Yes. Why? Do you need the money, my lord? Does it compensate in some part for an unwanted marriage?' For a brief moment she thought that something inside him had nearly escaped its leash.

Then, in quiet controlled tones, 'No, Verity. I don't need the money. But you need it. I wanted you to have something that was unequivocally yours. Not mine.'

Not mine.

Heartsick, she focused mercilessly on that. Understandable that he should grasp the chance to provide for his unwanted wife without broaching his own fortune. In a queer way he was right. She would certainly feel better about it. It remained only to know when he envisaged her departure.

Better to know at once. Better the surgeon's knife than a long drawn out torture. 'Then, you will arrange with the lawyers for a—what is the term? A deed of private separation?'

A moment's chilled silence hung between them. The only thing to move was the relentless pendulum of the clock on the chimney piece, telling Max that it was all too late.

He inclined his head. 'That is the correct term, madam.'

'Thank you, sir. I am very grateful. When...when would you like me to leave, my lord?'

'No.'

'I...I beg your pardon?'

His voice expressionless, he said, 'I won't release you.'

'But—'

'No!' The protest burst from him. 'Dammit, Verity! You told me you loved me! Do you think I'll just let you leave?' He strode towards her, intent on taking her into his arms.

'A mistake,' she said quietly.

He stopped dead, fear choking him. 'A...a mistake?'

'Yes. I...I was mistaken.' *Mistaken. Mistaken to trust him with her heart.*

He had destroyed her love for him. Very carefully, he said, 'I see. That changes everything.' He had to think. Fast. He could force nothing from her, but he couldn't let her go. He couldn't!

'We shall discuss this again,' he continued. 'I have a...responsibility for you. It must be quite clear to me that you are sure of your own mind. If, in six months, you still desire it, I shall see the lawyers. Arrange to settle the lease of a house on you.'

She flinched. 'No...I would rather—'

'You will remain my wife,' he said harshly. 'As such you will live in one of my houses and remain at least nominally under my protection. And I will not agree to a separation in under six months. Those are my terms, madam. You may take them or leave them.'

Her eyes searched his face. 'Max—please—'

'Six months,' he insisted.

'Very well,' she whispered.

He bowed and walked out. Six months. He had gained six months in which to rekindle her love.

Verity hung on to her composure until the door shut behind him. Until she heard the front door slam and knew that he had gone. Then she wept. She wept until there were no more tears and even if there had been, she no longer had the strength to weep them.

* * *

The words on the page danced in a mockery of joy… *The chiefest sign of conception is, when there is at first a loathing of meat…or preternatural appetite and vomiting…desire strange and absurd things…*

In the three days since Max had told her about her grandmother's will and agreed to separate she had scarcely left the house, denying herself to all visitors. Max had retreated to his club, coming home in the early hours of the morning. When they met, he treated her with a gentleness that left her numb with pain, especially as an appalling knowledge crept upon her. There had been ample time for her to realise the truth—that her constant tiredness and nausea meant something.

Focusing with difficulty, she read on… *Signs of conception—Tops of the nipples look redder than normally… The breasts begin to swell and wax hard, not without pain and soreness. The veins of the breasts are more clearly seen than they were wont to be…*

Added to all this, she hadn't had her monthly courses since well before she left the Faringdons. Certainty shuddered through her. How could she have been so stupid as not to realise sooner? With shaking fingers she closed the copy of Culpeper's *Directory for Midwives* that she'd found in Max's library. She did not attempt to delude herself with the hope that she might be wrong.

She touched a careful hand to her tender breasts. No wonder she felt as though her chemise was too tight these days. And no wonder her courses were so late. Not that she had ever been regular, but this time apparently they weren't late. They weren't going to come at all.

The book was old, but she could remember her mother vomiting constantly in the early stages of her pregnancy. She could no longer ignore what her body was telling her.

Clipstone's voice recalled her to her senses. 'Lady Arnsworth, my lady.'

Horrified, Verity opened her mouth to deny herself—then

Lady Arnsworth swept in. She was only surprised that her ladyship had given poor Clipstone enough time to announce her.

'Good afternoon, ma'am,' she said politely, stuffing the book under a cushion.

Lady Arnsworth's gimlet eyes bored in. 'I'm sure it is no concern of mine if you choose to further pollute your mind with rubbishy novels. It is for Max to control you. I called merely to ask after your health.'

Verity gritted her teeth against the urge to tell her ladyship to go to the devil. 'Thank you.' She left it at that. Lady Arnsworth would know the truth soon enough.

'Are you breeding? Is that the reason for your indisposition?'

The unexpected question flooded Verity's cheeks with embarrassment. 'I...I...' *Dammit!* 'I fail to see how that may concern you, ma'am!' she snapped.

Lady Arnsworth seemed to swell. 'Not concern me? You presumptuous upstart! When I recall the agony my sister suffered after her eldest son died! Knowing that the earldom would pass to Max, that she had failed in her duty!'

'Pardon?' Verity stared at the mottled face.

'Max! He had never the least sense of responsibility!' said Lady Arnsworth bitterly. 'Thoughtless! Richard would never have ridden that horse had not Max dared him! And then it fell on him. My sister was devastated.'

'I beg your pardon?' None of this made sense. Max was the most responsible man she had ever met. He would not walk away from his duty. Not even an unwanted wife.

Lady Arnsworth's next words clarified everything. 'But Max *had* learnt his lesson, or so it appeared. He agreed to remain single, that Richard should inherit. No doubt he enjoyed the freedom to mount mistress after mistress. Until he married *you*!'

Black horror gaped before her. 'He promised their mother that Richard should inherit?'

'On her deathbed.' She went on with devastating candour. 'Now of course you will be able to indulge your *liaison* with Braybrook without fear of repercussions.'

Braybrook? Verity stared at her. 'I beg your pardon?'

'Oh, don't play the *ingénue* with me, girl! With his child safely in your belly, Max won't care if you play him false if you're careful. Assuming it *is* his child! A pregnant wife is the safest of all possible targets for a rake like Braybrook. Most husbands will turn a blind eye to a discreet *affaire*. No doubt Max only stepped in at the Torringtons' to save his own face.'

Verity heard very little after that. Vaguely she was aware that Lady Arnsworth had left. That she was alone again.

Grimly she faced the appalling reality of her situation. She was pregnant. With a child her husband most definitely didn't want. Her vision blurred. She had caused him to break a promise given to his mother in circumstances he must consider inviolable. He would see himself as forsworn. Dishonoured.

Max had agreed to a separation. And she was pregnant. Tonight. She must tell him tonight. Her hand clenched on the arm of her chair. Tonight of all nights. Her birthday was bad enough without this to tell him. Each year she had relived the nightmare of this night alone. The shot. The discovery of her father's body. And the guilt. There had never been anyone to hold her. To tell her that it hadn't been her fault.

The clock on her chimney piece chimed three times. Max had returned an hour ago, but he still hadn't come up. Shivering, she huddled in her chair, watching the clock, all her senses at the stretch. The half-open door gaped blackly at the edge of her vision, taunting her.

Never before had she needed so desperately to be held, to be reassured. Why now? Always she had made quite sure no one realised how this anniversary tormented her. She didn't *need* anyone. She had always managed alone.

A shudder ripped through her as she realised that she had survived this each year by remembering Max and his tender care of her at that dreadful grave. She had clung to that memory. But now she needed *him*. His arms, his deep voice. Just to hear the words spoken...*It wasn't your fault*.

She might never believe them, but it would be a comfort to think that someone else did. It was comfort she could not have. She had to tell him about her pregnancy and she could no longer hide behind the pretence that she was merely waiting for him to come up. Fear twisted into a tight knot. She was frightened to confess and see the horror and fury in his eyes.

Shivering, she pulled on her dressing gown, picked up a candle and slipped out into the dim, silent corridor. Clipstone had long since snuffed the wall sconces and gone to bed. Reaching the library, she set her candle down on a side table and opened the door very quietly to peep in.

Time rolled back, into a nightmare she had never fully escaped. The familiar silent figure sitting in his shirtsleeves in the flickering glow of the fire, a wine table at his elbow bearing a full glass and a nearly empty decanter. A broken cry escaped as the past leapt to hellish life. *Not Max. Not him too*.

At the ragged sound he turned and she bit back another cry as she saw his face. Angry, bitter, the usually bright eyes dulled. His cravat was askew and his waistcoat hung open.

'Max?' she whispered. He had never done this before, had he? Why now? Why *this* night of all nights?

He blinked owlishly. 'Verity?'

Her own pain doubled and redoubled in the space of a heartbeat as she saw his, heard it in the cracking of his voice. She remembered his affection for her father, his belief that he had been partially responsible. Without further thought she sped across the room and knelt beside him, wriggling into his arms. 'Oh, Max. I'm sorry. I never realised how badly you must feel it. Please. You mustn't blame yourself.' The reek of stale brandy shocked her as his arms closed around her, dragging her even closer. She could feel him pressing clumsy kisses on her hair, her brow, her temple, anywhere he could reach. Caring for nothing except the driving need to comfort him, she raised her face and gasped in shock as his mouth crashed down on hers, possessing it with savage urgency.

Desperately she returned his kiss, sensing his need and surrendering to her own. A need for comfort, a sense of belonging. His arms imprisoned her as he kissed her, ravishing her mouth until she could only cling, helpless in the furnace of their need. Dazed, she barely realised when he slid off the chair and took her down to the floor. Mouth locked to hers, his hands a fire at her breasts.

She could hardly breathe as he released her mouth, but she whispered, 'I used to think of you every year, how you helped me plant the bluebells… It wasn't your fault he shot himself. Please, Max. You must believe that. It was my fault…'

His kiss silenced her as he understood what she was saying, why she thought he was drunk. He shouldn't be doing this. Somewhere beyond the pain and the brandy Max knew that, and he didn't care. He didn't care that she had misunderstood his pain. She was his. And he had lost her. She had not come to tell him she had changed her mind. But he would have this, one last night. Her response seared him to the core. She wanted it as badly as he did. For this one night he would have her. Tomorrow would be time enough to hate himself for taking advantage of her vulnerability.

Need raked him. He should slow down, take her gently. But his fingers were tugging at the ribbon of her nightgown, pushing the robe off her shoulders. The bodice gaped open and tore as he pulled it down to expose her breasts. He bent his head, drawing the sweet flesh deep, suckling until he felt her body arch, heard her breath break on a cry of pleasure. It fuelled his own leaping desire, scorching at his control. He couldn't slow down. He wanted her. Now.

Verity felt the hot rhythm of his mouth at her breast, felt urgency spread, burning through her body as tension coiled tighter and tighter. She wanted him. All of him. But this time pleasure was not enough. It had never been enough. She wanted to give, to give herself without reservation.

She couldn't bear it. Not again. Even as she felt his hand pushing her nightgown up over her thighs, she cried out in protest. 'Max…' Her voice fractured as he scored her tender flesh with his teeth, raking her with fire. 'Please…no… stop…'

He froze. His mouth lifted from her breast and he stared down at her. 'Stop?' His voice was harsh, barely recognisable.

'Yes,' she whispered. 'Please…I can't…'

With a savage curse he lifted away and rolled off of her. He sat up and swore again. 'That shouldn't have happened,' he said tightly. 'Obviously I'm not as foxed as I thought. Or not enough anyway.'

Her throat closing, she asked, 'Drunk enough for what?'

'Drunk enough to look at you without giving in to the temptation to take you.' A grim laugh shook him at her shocked gasp. 'Yes. You see, this was about the only way I could think of to control myself—by getting drunk enough so that even if I did succumb, I wouldn't be able to do a damn thing about it. I thought I could control myself. But I can't. Every time I lay eyes on you I want you more, so… I'm sorry. I didn't mean to do that.' He reached for the brandy.

He hadn't wanted her. Or rather he hadn't wanted to want her. That was worse. He had been prepared to drink himself into oblivion to forget his desire.

He spoke harshly. 'You had better go. The longer I look at you, the more likely I will forget myself.'

She couldn't help it—as she looked at him, at the bitter line of his mouth—a single tear escaped her control and burnt its way down her cheek. Verity shuddered as the past swirled around her and she saw another man who had destroyed himself rather than look at her. Every beat of her heart was a merciless hammer blow as she faced the prospect of watching another man sink into ruin because of her. This time the man she loved. Her husband.

She watched in horror as he emptied his glass. Another tear fell. Max would destroy himself rather than ask her to leave immediately. Six months. She couldn't watch him do this to himself.

She had been far too young even to understand her father's despair. Now she did understand how it felt to lose everything you cared about. She understood what it was like to feel a knife twisting deep inside until the pain became part of you. And she was not prepared to inflict that pain on anyone. Ever again.

Her hands numb, she clutched her ruined nightgown around her and grabbed her robe, struggling to guide her arms into the sleeves. Somehow she got to her feet. Max didn't move as she stumbled to the door, her legs still uncertain in the aftermath of passion.

At the door she looked back, seeing him in a misty blur. He sat staring into the fire. Her blurred gaze took in everything: his broad back, the sleekly muscled shoulders, the dark, slightly curling hair. She remembered how the coarse silk had felt under her fingers, how his body had felt against, around, inside hers. 'Goodbye, Max,' she whispered.

'Left?' Max winced as Harding pulled back the bed hangings, and wished his head would stop aching. Why in Hades had he drunk so much brandy? 'And you let her go? Where has she gone?'

Harding's mouth set hard as he jerked back the curtains with a tooth-jarring rattle. 'Not exactly easy to stop her, sir. I did ask her to wait until you woke up, but…'

He flushed and turned his attention to opening drawers with what Max could only describe as malice aforethought.

'But, what?' demanded Max.

Harding hesitated, then squared his shoulders and said, 'Well, sir, I got the idea that leaving before you woke up was *why* she was leaving so early. Just gone five it was when the chaise was at the door.'

Horrified, Max looked at the clock. Past two. She could be anywhere by now! 'Harding, where did she...?'

'Blakeney, sir. I...I believe she left a note for you. In the library.'

Some slight relief made it possible for Max to breathe again as he strode to the library. Blakeney. That was something. She hadn't left him. Yet. After last night... He groaned mentally. He couldn't quite recall what he'd said—she'd come to him. And he'd nearly forced her into submission.

He found the note easily enough, propped up against a vase on the chimney piece. Taking it to the desk, he found his letter knife and broke the seal.

Dearest Max,

Please don't be angry with Harding for letting me go. He tried very hard to stop me.

I have gone to Blakeney because after last night I think it is better that we do not see each other again. Please believe that I did not come to you with the intention of teasing or tempting you. I know you do not want me as your wife. And I cannot bear to be the cause of further pain for you. Almeria explained to me yesterday afternoon the promise you had made to your mother. I quite understand, Max. If I had known I would never have permitted you to marry me.

If you do not wish to formally dissolve our marriage, could you please let me know upon which of your smaller properties you would wish me to reside. I have no desire to live in London, or anywhere that we may meet each other.

Verity

Shaking, he put the letter down on his desk and stared blindly out of the window. The letter stabbed deep. Her first concern had been to make sure no one else suffered for her actions—not even the servants. He had to go after her. Explain that it wasn't her fault...that it was his. If she would see him...

She thought he didn't want her. Last night had been one hurt, one insult too many, even if he hadn't meant it that way. The knowledge that she had left him hammered in his brain. All he could see was Verity's stricken eyes, the wound he had dealt her reflected in them, staring up at him, as a single tear spilt over in gut-wrenching silence. He now knew the pain of weeping silently, the dreadful cost of hiding every hurt deep within.

Verity's voice...*Max, I'm sorry...I never realised how badly you would feel it*...and something else...*I used to think of you every year, how you helped me plant the bluebells...*

The significance of the date took him like a bayonet thrust. He closed his eyes in pain as he understood why she had come to him. She had come to him for comfort, unable to bear her pain alone any longer. And he, arrogant fool that he was, had thought to take what he wanted, what he needed.

The knowledge of what he had done splintered inside him, jagged shards tearing him apart. All the time he had thought she didn't want him, she had believed that *he* didn't want *her*. Last night her need for comfort had finally brought her to him. And then, despite her own pain, she had offered him comfort. Only to be rejected. Again. One time too many.

There was room in his brain for only one coherent thought. He had to go after her. He had no idea what he was going to say to her, but he'd have to say it anyway. Whatever it took to stop her leaving him.

I cannot bear to be the cause of pain for you. Would she believe that losing her would be the deepest pain of all?

He'd have to go straight down… He rang the bell and waited, staring at the letter, every smudged word a cry of pain.

'My lord, Lady Arnsworth is—'

'Not now, Clipstone!'

Almeria stalked in, her face livid, and Clipstone, gauging the massed firepower with one horrified glance, beat a hasty retreat.

'Max! I must demand that you cease this ridiculous persecution of the Faringdons! Poor Caroline is distraught! No doubt that wretched girl has told you some farradiddle, and you—'

'Enough!' he snapped. 'Verity told me nothing. Her grandmother's lawyer approached me. Whatever the Faringdons may have told you is a pack of lies!'

Radiating outrage, Almeria announced, 'I shall see your wife myself and tell her exactly how society will view—'

'The devil you will,' said Max coldly, 'even if she were here. As it is she has gone to Blakeney for a few days and I am joining her there. If, when we return to town, I hear the least murmur against her, the Faringdons will rue the day they decided to cheat her. I will have no hesitation in making public exactly what they did and seeing Lord Faringdon in court for criminally defrauding and neglecting his ward.'

Almeria appeared to swell. 'Then, this afternoon's meeting with the lawyers—you are determined to press your ridiculous claim?'

'I will press my fully justified claim, yes,' he said, between clenched teeth. Meeting? Oh, *hell*! He glanced at his watch, strode over and hauled on the bell pull. 'Clipstone will show you out.'

Almeria didn't bother waiting. She stormed out, nearly flattening Clipstone in the hall.

'Clipstone!' bellowed Max.

'My lord?'

'A hackney. And when I return I want my curricle and the greys at the door within ten minutes. See to it.'

Every fibre, every nerve cried out to go after Verity now, but he couldn't. Thank God Almeria had reminded him about the meeting. He knew Wimbourne's ability. Verity's inheritance was safe. But still, a violent urge to see personally to the Faringdons rose up in him. And he had to make sure they understood the consequences of any gossip concerning Verity.

The sound of swift, halting boots on the flagged terrace jolted Verity out of the book and she swung around as Richard strolled into the library through the French windows.

'Hullo, Verity,' he said with a grin. 'Come to kick me out? Henny said you'd arrived. You must have left London very early. When's Max coming down?'

Verity closed her eyes in pain. 'He's not. Richard—'

'Not? What the devil do you mean?'

If not for the ache in her heart, Verity would have laughed at the indignation on his face.

A frown puckered his brow. 'Verity, are you feeling quite the thing?'

He came towards her and she forced a smile. 'I'm quite well, thank you.'

'Well, you don't look it,' he informed her. 'You look as though you haven't slept a wink.' Verity flushed and then paled.

'Richard—Max and I have agreed to…separate.'

'*What?*'

He came to a dead halt beside her. 'What the devil do you—?' He broke off, distracted, and stared at the book in her lap. 'Culpeper… *Directory for Midwives*?' His jaw dropped. 'Um, Verity, is there something you…are you…oh, hell!'

He swung away. 'I beg your pardon,' he said stiffly. 'I'd no right, I didn't mean...'

'It's all right, Richard,' she whispered. 'I'm sorry. I never meant this to happen. I didn't realise that you...that Max had...' Her voice failed her, as she thought of telling Max, imagined his response. She should have told Max. If not last night, then in the note she had left. But her eyes had flooded over as she searched for the words.

Stunned brown eyes bored into her. 'Didn't realise what?' His voice was deadly.

Her breath tearing, she said, 'That Max promised you the earldom, that he always intended you to inherit.'

'Didn't you?' His voice sounded odd. 'And you never meant to get...I mean, you never intended to...' His voice trailed off into ominous silence.

She bit her lip. 'I'm sorry, Richard. It...it might be a girl.' It might never come to be, but she couldn't voice that thought, to suggest that the tiny life within her was unwanted. She wanted the baby so desperately. Because this was the only child Max would ever give her.

For a moment, she thought Richard might explode. 'Tell me,' he said in the sort of tones that suggested he had a very tight rein on his temper, 'was my dear brother aware of this when you agreed to a separation?'

She shook her head. Oh, God. The cold anger in his eyes bit into her.

'He doesn't know. I meant to tell him last night, but... well...we...we didn't talk very much,' she whispered.

'I see,' he said, in a strangled voice. A moment later he said conversationally, 'I think I might just kill him. Excuse me, Verity. I had better return to town immediately.'

He *couldn't* be serious. Could he? 'Richard, please, it wasn't his fault! You mustn't—'

'What!' He cut her off, staring at her in disbelief. She swallowed and fell silent.

His voice cut into the silence. 'Believe me, Max will be

damned lucky if I leave enough of his hide for the scullery maid to use as a dish clout!' He swung around and stormed out the way he had come.

She was still crying when Mrs Henty came in ten minutes later. Mrs Henty didn't bother asking. She had her plump arms around Verity in a flash, patting her shoulder and wiping her eyes.

'Now, just you stop crying, dearie. His lordship will be down quite soon, I dare say. It's just the baby upsetting you. Funny how women get all teary when they're breeding. Never you mind. And that great looby Master Richard charging around like a mad bull! I'll be having a word with the pair of them, so I will!'

The truth dawned on Verity. She lifted her tearstained face from Mrs Henty's shoulder. 'You *knew*?'

Mrs Henty's smile broadened smugly. 'Well, of course, dearie—my lady, I *should* say. What with you being sick all the time. And knowing his lordship.' She coughed discreetly and changed the subject slightly. 'Don't know what he's thinking of, letting you gallivant around the countryside unescorted! Anyway, he'll be down soon enough.'

The note of absolute certainty nearly broke Verity's control. 'Of course, Henny. What did you want to tell me?'

Mrs Henty smiled. 'Only that it's time and more that Sarah went over to Martha's. I thought to send her over in the gig this afternoon.'

Verity drew in a breath and thought about that. Anything was better than telling Henny the truth. That Max would not be down, not while she remained here. So—if one of the grooms drove Sarah... No. Definitely not.

'No, Henny. I'll take her. Better to show the villagers that she hasn't been turned off in disgrace. Let them see she has our support. Send down to the stables for the gig to be brought around.'

Mrs Henty frowned. 'Well, I'm not denying it's a good

idea. But not today. Tomorrow, when you're rested. I'll send a message over to Martha to expect you then.'

'But…'

Mrs Henty fixed her with a steely eye. 'No buts, my lady. You'll do as you're bid and that's all there is to it.'

Verity managed a smile that threatened to turn upside down. 'Yes, ma'am.'

Chapter Sixteen

In the event Max didn't return from the meeting until after five o'clock. The Faringdons had signed without a mutter, the jewellery had been handed over and Max had transferred the money to a trust in Verity's name. Hers. Absolutely. Mr Wimbourne produced cognac in a way that precluded a hasty departure.

Max sipped his drink, responding automatically to Wimbourne's toast, concealing his impatience to be gone. And his fear that he might already be too late.

It was five-thirty before he finally stepped out on to the front steps, ready for the drive down to Blakeney. Just as he was about to swing up into the curricle after the dogs there was a rattle of hooves and another curricle came around the corner at a spanking trot.

Disbelief held him as Richard drew his lathered chestnuts to a halt, cold fear slithering down his spine. Richard never drove his horses hard.

Verity. Something had happened.

'What—'

'You bloody *idiot!*' The roar of fury had Max's greys snorting and throwing up their heads.

Max stared as Richard levered himself down from the curricle and limped towards him. He frowned. 'What's wrong with your leg?' Richard hadn't limped that badly in years. And he couldn't remember ever seeing Richard this angry.

Richard consigned his leg to oblivion in a few choice words. 'All that's wrong with it,' he continued, 'is driving up from Blakeney without a break to make damn sure I caught you! Do you have any idea of what you've done?'

Max stiffened. 'Yes. As a matter of fact I do,' he said. 'I made a complete mess of everything and I'm going down now. I only stayed to go to the meeting with the lawyers over Verity's inheritance.'

Richard's remarks about Verity's inheritance blistered the air. He went on without pause. 'What I *do* want to know is— what the devil went on last night? I went down to Blakeney to give you privacy for a honeymoon! Not for you to tell her to leave!'

Max flushed and glared. 'Damn it, Ricky! Verity is *my* wife! What went on last night is none of your business!' He dragged in a breath, forcing his fists to unclench. 'And I didn't tell her to leave, she—'

Richard silenced him in one pungent and graphic phrase. 'I don't give a damn about my expectations! I told you that!' he went on furiously. 'What I do give a damn about is that your *wife*—and thank God you've finally realised that!—is sitting down there in Kent, crying her eyes out because she's breeding—'

'What!' Max's stomach lurched violently and his heart stopped totally. Pregnant. Verity was pregnant and she hadn't told him?

'And you told her I was supposed to inherit the earldom!' Richard finished.

'*I* didn't tell her that! Almeria did!'

'What difference does that make?' snarled Richard. 'You obviously didn't give her any reason to disbelieve Almeria. For God's sake, get down there and tell her you love her. I did think of telling her for you, since apparently you haven't the wit to tell her yourself, but on reflection I thought it might come better from you!'

Max arrived at Blakeney to find the house in darkness and drove straight to the stables. A very startled, sleepy groom came out to take the horses, ineffectually smothering a yawn.

The dogs sprang down, barking, and raced out of the stable yard towards the house, plainly delighted to be home. Max followed slowly, whistling for them. He could force the catch on the library windows—it was something he kept meaning to have mended and forgetting about.

To his surprise a light appeared at the side door. He changed direction. Who on earth…?

'Henny!' he said as he came close enough to see who held the lamp. 'What are you about?'

A snort greeted this. 'What does it look like I'm about? Letting you in, of course. Pesky dogs. Barking fit to wake the dead. If so be as her ladyship is asleep, which is unlikely. Just as well you're here, my lord—something's eating at her or my name's not Maria Henty!'

'She's in her own rooms?'

'Aye. Sitting staring into the fire when last I looked. Wouldn't say a word about why she came home.'

He stared at the door leading from his bedchamber to Verity's. He opened it softly, without knocking. If she had fallen asleep, he didn't want to wake her. Shadows flickered and danced in the dimly lit room.

Mellow lamplight lit the small figure huddled in a chair by the fire, curled into it as though for protection. Verity. His wife. The mother of his child. She was awake. The tension in her body cried out to him. Gentle chimes rang out from the clock on the chimneypiece and he saw the jolt of shock that ran through her. She'd been miles away. Lost.

For a moment he hesitated. Should he go away? See her in the morning? The small figure eased back into the chair.

A stifled sob decided him. If Verity needed to cry, this time she was not going to do it silently, without anyone to hold her and comfort her. He tapped lightly on the doorframe.

'I'm quite all right, Henny. And I ate my supper, thank you. Please go to bed.' Her voice was soft, controlled. Too soft, too controlled.

His heart tearing, he kept his own voice gentle. 'I'm sure Henny will be pleased to hear that. May I come in?' He saw her freeze. Saw the way her head lifted sharply. She turned very slowly.

'Why are you here?'

'For you.'

'For me? Why?'

He nodded. 'Because…I was an idiot last night. When I realised what I'd done…why you came to me…and when Richard told me…' He went to her and knelt beside the chair reaching for her hands.

She pulled them away. 'No. It doesn't matter.' Then, warily, 'What did Richard tell you?'

He lifted one small hand to his lips and brushed a kiss over it. 'Amongst other things he told me that I am to be a father. Dearest, listen—'

'*No!* It's all right, Max. Please. Don't do this to yourself. I…I didn't understand with Papa. I thought if I just looked after him, helped him, told him I loved him it would be all right. He'd get better, stop taking the laudanum. It never occurred to me that just seeing me was a nightmare for him. That he literally couldn't bear the sight of me… that *I* was the problem…until it was too late.'

Ignoring her efforts to stop him, Max grabbed her hands and gripped hard. 'What the hell are you talking about?'

'Last night. I came to tell you—'

He broke in. 'I *know* why you came. It was this week that he died, that he was buried. If I'd realised then—'

She cut him off. 'That wasn't the reason, I came to tell you about the baby, but then I thought you were upset about

Papa. That *you* needed comfort as well. I never meant to tease you… I…I know *you* don't want me that way. Almeria explained it all. Why you wish Richard to inherit, but…' Her voice shook but she forced it on. 'It might be all right…the baby might be a girl. If you'll just tell me where to live.'

His grip on her hands tightened fiercely. 'Here,' he said. 'With me. With our child.'

She shook her head, tugging against his grip. 'No. I can't. Not if it means you sit there every night trying to forget me in a bottle of brandy.'

Pain shot through him. What woman wanted a sot for a husband?

Her next words put him right. 'I won't let you destroy yourself because of me. The…the way Papa did.'

'Verity.' His voice cracked. 'What are you saying?'

She looked straight at him, her eyes bleak. 'I loved him so much, Max. He was all I had, but he didn't want me. He couldn't even look at me without seeing her ghost…so, I won't…I *can't* do that again. Your vow…you'll hate me…'

Understanding pierced him. She blamed herself for her father's death. Believed she had destroyed him. And that, if she remained, *he* would drink himself to death because of his vow. He stared at Verity's slender hands, lost in his grasp. She had blamed her very existence all these years.

Somehow he must free her from the nightmare. 'Verity— it wasn't your fault. He was sick. He didn't know what he was saying.'

She met his gaze and whispered, 'I know. I understand that now. That's why…there's more, you see. The night he died—it was my birthday. My fifteenth birthday. He hadn't spoken to me all day. I'd tried so hard and he wouldn't even look at me. I…I was…'

'Hurt?' suggested Max quietly. 'Angry?'

She nodded, shivering. 'Yes. So angry I threw away all the laudanum. Every last drop.'

He shut his eyes briefly, remembering Richard's comments. *He'd go nearly crazy with pain if he didn't get his dose. Frightening.*

Could it drive a man to suicide?

Probably. If he didn't get his dose. If he was heavily habituated.

'Go on.' He knew now what was coming, but she needed to say it.

'He…he went quite mad. After a few hours he was frantic, screaming in agony. Begging me to find some.' She swallowed. 'But it was late. And I was so frightened, I locked myself in my room. I heard him crashing about downstairs, cursing me, hating me, screaming that he'd kill himself.' A sob tore from her throat. 'I didn't believe him… until—' Her hands clutched his as her voice failed.

'Until you heard the shot,' he finished savagely.

She turned her face away. 'Yes. So you see, it was my fault, my stupidity…'

'No! Who the hell told you that?' Suddenly furious, he remembered all the guilt he had felt over Richard's accident. Guilt his mother had rubbed in constantly every time she sighed over Richard's limp. Moaned over the stillbirth of Richard's expected military career at every opportunity. The ongoing need to expiate his stupid, youthful mistake.

And Verity had spent the last five years hating herself because of some fool. Who? Lady Faringdon?

'Who? Who told you that it was your fault?'

She stared. 'No one told me. I never told anyone what really happened.'

She had buried it within her heart for five years, bleeding, eating at her from the inside out. He didn't stop to think before he had his arms around Verity and had dragged her off the chair into his embrace. Ignoring her struggles, he held her tightly. He had to make her see, make her understand.

'Listen to me, Verity. It wasn't your fault. I read his journal after the Torringtons' ball. It wasn't you. The opium destroyed him. You were a child! How could you cope with something like that? You should have been *his* responsibility. Not the other way around. *It wasn't your fault!*'

He tucked her head into the curve of his shoulder and went on, tenderly stroking her hair. 'As for my stupidity last night—that was my fault. *My* responsibility. And it's over. You're mine. And I want you. Now.'

Every fibre in his body raged with longing for her. With the need to press her down beneath him and give what he had denied them both for so long. To feel her mouth under his, her body yielding and soft as he slid into her and claimed her. With a groan he lowered his mouth to hers in fierce possession.

Struggling she broke free and flung herself away from him, her breath coming in ragged gasps.

She didn't want him. The knowledge pounded into him with every beat of his heart. He had thought he knew what pain was. He'd been wrong. This was pain, this dreadful racking knowledge that he had finally driven her away completely. Last night had been too much. She had trusted him once too often.

'I won't be your whore again.'

The low words slammed into him.

She went on. 'You told me—you didn't want a wife. And even if you did want one—you wouldn't want a woman who would, who *did*, consent to be your mistress.'

Understanding twisted inside him. She believed that he thought of her as a...he couldn't even think the word now. That he had ever, in his hurt fury, used it, horrified him. He confronted what he had done to her—he had convinced her that he thought her a whore. Worse—he had made *her* believe it, all the more easily because of what she believed about herself.

She had come to him an innocent, trusting him in a way he could barely comprehend. In return he had stripped her of her innocence in every way possible. Words weren't going to be enough. Even if he could find them. If they weren't choked useless in his throat. She was his. His wife.

He reached for her again, pulled her into his arms.

'No,' she panted. 'I told you—'

He brought his mouth down on hers.

Verity gasped, stunned. His mouth on hers was devastating, his demands absolute. Her fainting reason shrieked a protest, even as her body melted against his, her mouth opening in helpless surrender. Instantly his lips gentled as he claimed all the sweetness she offered, taking her mouth in a surge of penetration.

She clung to him, giving back kiss for kiss with wild abandon, absorbing his taste, the hot textures of his mouth. In the morning she would hate herself, but right here, right now, all she could do was love him. In any way he would let her.

A sob of protest escaped her as he broke the kiss, lifting his head slightly.

'Not here.' The possessive growl shivered through her.

She stared. Her unspoken question hung between them.

He stood in one swift powerful move, taking her with him. An instant later he had swept her up into his arms and was heading for the door to *his* bedchamber.

Her throat closed. 'My…Max…what are you doing?'

His eyes blazed at her. 'Taking my *wife* to my bed. As is fitting.'

'But…'

'But nothing. You're mine. My wife. And it's about time we both remembered it.'

Hope seared her as he stalked through the door. His face was harsh, set in grim lines, yet his arms cradled her tenderly against his chest. Her breath broke on a gasp as he lowered her to the silken counterpane with a brief, hard kiss and stepped back.

'First things first,' he said huskily as he turned away. She lay watching him as he took a taper off a tallboy and lit the fire. He straightened, smiled at her and blew out the taper. And every other candle in the room.

His face was shadowed as he came back to her and sat down on the edge of the bed to remove his boots. His coat sailed into a corner, the waistcoat followed an instant later. Firelight slid over hard, muscled curves as he stood up and stripped out of his shirt and breeches and her mouth dried. She had never seen him fully.

The first time he'd already been in bed when she came to him, the bedclothes pulled to his waist. All the other nights, in her bed here, he'd come to her in the dark. As if he hadn't wanted to know who she was.

Shock and desire mingled as she gazed at the hard, powerful body, the broad chest with its light covering of curls. Taut flat stomach and... She breathed raggedly...he had been so deep inside her...it seemed impossible... A melting rush of heat took her breath away. She forced her gaze back to his face, met the scorching desire in his eyes.

She wanted him, but what was she supposed to do? What did he want? Eyes wide, she reached out to him. Then, uncertainly, she dropped her hand.

He came to her then. He captured her hand, and brought it to his lips, biting tenderly at her fingertips, and then drew it lower, over his chest, his stomach, as he feathered light kisses over her face. Lower he took her hand until she felt the fierce heat of desire. Gently he curled her fingers around his flesh and groaned.

Verity gasped. So hard, so silken. And so hot. She stroked, fascinated, feeling the leap of passion under her fingers.

All at once he pushed her hand away with a groan. She jerked back at once, thinking she had displeased him, that her curiosity shocked him.

Max felt her withdrawal and knew at once what he'd done. He caught her and drew her back, shuddering at the caress of soft breasts through the light lawn. 'Your touch is beautiful. Too beautiful. But I want all of you.' The uncertainty in her eyes, the unconcealed longing, burnt at his control.

'All of me?' Her shaken whisper scored him.

'All of you,' he confirmed, easing back from her to un-button the nightgown. He stripped it from her with swift, urgent hands and flung it away. He couldn't wait. She was his and he had denied it too long.

'You are mine. You are carrying my child. And there is nothing to hold us apart any longer.' Then, needing to show her, he slowly bent down to kiss her belly. Tenderly, rever-ently, as he caressed the gentle curve with shaking fingers.

His wife. Quickening with his seed. His. In every way possible.

Shuddering with the force of his need, he rose over her, pressing one knee between her silken thighs, opening her fully. This time there was no resistance. Eagerly she obeyed his unspoken command, yielding to him, clinging. His thigh rested over hers, pinning it to the mattress. Every muscle locked with restraint, his fingers sought her softness, caress-ing, stroking tenderly. Soft, wet heat bloomed under his touch in the sweetest surrender.

Taking her mouth gently, he settled in the cradle of her body. She tensed. Despite the pounding ache he forced him-self to stop. He released her mouth, kissed a hot trail down her throat and drew one hardened nipple deeply into his mouth. With a wild cry she arched into him. He suckled lightly, biting and laving the tender flesh until broken cries rippled from her and she twisted urgently against him, her uncertainty consumed in a blaze of yearning.

Releasing her breast, he kissed his way back to her mouth, distracting her with featherlight kisses as he fitted himself to her.

Her mouth clung to his as her hips tilted to accept him. He groaned and clamped one hand to her hip, holding her still. 'No,' he whispered against her trembling mouth. 'Not yet.'

'Yes. Now!' She twisted beneath him, the slick heat of her body caressing him, pleading for him.

He forced his body to restraint and pressed into her entrance. Just. He moved carefully, teasing her, feeling her breath break against his mouth, feeling her body arch frantically against his, the soft breasts pressing hotly.

'This is how I should have taken you the first time,' he whispered, sliding a little deeper, savouring the gasp of pleasure. 'If I'd known what you were giving me.' His tongue traced her lips, tasting her, loving her as trembling fingers grazed his jaw, buried themselves in his hair as her mouth opened against his. He smiled and evaded her, the sweet cry of frustration burning to his soul. 'I should have taken you slowly, very slowly, feeling every inch of your softness.' He rocked against her, lips and tongue tracing the curves of her ear, groaning as she arched beneath him, pleading mutely for his complete possession.

'More?' he murmured against her throat.

She lifted against him wildly, caressing him with the silken fire of her body. 'Yes! Oh, yes! Max…please—'

'How much more? This much?' He pressed deeper, still gripping her hip to hold her. Her frantic cries and the petal-soft touch of her body shredded his control. He fought the urge to sheathe himself completely.

His body on the verge of rebellion, he withdrew to her entrance. Releasing her hip, he reached between their bodies to stroke her tenderly, finding and caressing the taut, sweet bud of desire. Her body responded.

'Open your eyes,' he whispered. 'Come. Look at me.'

Slowly her eyelids lifted, revealing pupils dilated with urgency, leaving only a smoking rim. Her lips were parted, soft and moist, swollen from the fierce possession of his mouth.

Gently he stroked one rounded thigh, urged it back against her waist, then the other, tilting her, opening her completely. He felt her breath jerk in, saw her eyes widen even further as she realised her vulnerability. Burning on a knife edge of desire, he forced himself to wait, needing to be sure of her trust.

'Please, Max…love me…now.'

The aching whisper undid him. He lowered his mouth to hers again, deepening their kiss as he sank himself slowly, inexorably, into her welcoming heat until they were completely joined. Lifting his head, he gazed down at her, yielded beneath him. So sweet, so hot. And his. All his. Shaken to the depths of his soul, he whispered, 'I do love you, Verity. Now and always.'

Her mouth trembled. 'Max? No, you can't. I didn't mean…'

He kissed the corner of her mouth. 'Yes, my darling. You did. And so do I.' He rocked against her gently.

She cried out, shifting beneath him, caressing his aching, buried flesh, and his control splintered. With a groan he began to move, deeply, powerfully, claiming her for all time.

Verity gasped, her body burning as he took her repeatedly, all restraint gone. The tension coiled fiercely inside her, tearing free from her throat in desperate pleas. His mouth took her cries mercilessly as he possessed her, merging their bodies so completely that she no longer knew where she ended and he began.

Her world shattered, breaking apart as ecstasy poured through her in a cataract of fire, consuming her utterly as his body drove into hers again and again until his own release shuddered through him and he spent himself deep inside her.

Chapter Seventeen

Max awoke to find the day far advanced. He stared at the clock on the chimneypiece in disbelief. Past midday? How in Hades had he slept that long? And where was Verity? He looked with a grin at the tumbled bedding. Now he thought about it, he hadn't really slept that long.

He yawned and stretched. No doubt she had gone to get dressed. A note on the pillow caught his eye. Hmm. Better than nothing, but he would have preferred to find Verity there, all warm and soft and sleepy. Ready for his kisses. As she had been throughout the night. His heart pounded just thinking about it.

He unfolded the note, wondering what she was up to.

Max… He read and swore. A quick glance out the window confirmed his fear. A sea mist was coming in. Surely she hadn't gone out in that? They wouldn't have let her. Would they?

Twenty minutes later he was running for the stables.

'Took the gig? In this?' Max's stomach chilled as he stared at his head groom. The sea mist drifted around them in the stable yard. Beyond it the gardens and house were lost, as if they had never been. He'd watched it roll in and devour them.

Faster than he'd ever seen it. And Verity had left three hours ago.

'Damn it, Marley! She's not used to this part of the country…'

Marley nodded. 'Aye. Didn't think she'd be this long, or that the mist would come on this bad. But I made sure she had Bessie in the shafts. That little cob knows the way back from hell. And she's got the dogs with her.'

A cob and a couple of gun-shy spaniels?

He was being ridiculous. She'd gone to the village, to take Sarah to Martha Granger. The road was safe in daylight, even in a heavy mist. It went nowhere near the cliffs. But even so… 'Fig out a fresh one, Jem. I'll meet her.' He caught the man's guilty eye. 'Never mind. I dare say she's safe enough. But…' he left the sentence unfinished, all too aware of Marley's suspiciously straight face.

He *was* being ridiculous. The road from the village was excellent—she couldn't miss the turn. It was straight after the beech wood. Even if she did, Bessie wouldn't. But he wanted to see her. To be with her. He hadn't said everything that needed to be said. If only she'd waited, he'd have gone with her.

Verity clucked to the cob between the shafts and glanced around in disbelief. How could a mist roll in that fast? A sea mist? She could taste the salty tang. It hung in the still air, shrouding the road until she felt as if there were no reality beyond it. That the world had vanished into wreathing, clinging whiteness.

The old stableman's voice came to her… *Be a mist later, I shouldn't wonder. If'n ye're still out, don't worry. Give the mare her head. She'll get ye home.*

The dogs sat beside her, tongues out, panting happily. She shouldn't have come out, or if she had, she shouldn't have stayed at Martha Granger's so long. If only she had a watch with her. Time stood still in this white, lost world without landmarks. She had no idea how far she had come. Blakeney was only two miles from the village, but until she reached the beech wood she couldn't know where she was.

She kept the little mare to a walk, unsure of the road. The mist lay so thickly, blanketing everything. Why hadn't she waited for Max? He would have come with her. *You know why you left before he awoke. You never would have left the bed if he'd been awake and you promised to take Sarah over yourself.*

Her body still sang with the rhythm of their loving, deep and sweet. Max had claimed her repeatedly through the night, there in his bed. Their marriage bed, he had whispered. And safe within her, their future blossomed and grew.

The dogs heard something first, Gus standing up and wriggling around until he faced backwards. Then Verity heard it—a trotting horse. Her hands tightened on the ribbons, then relaxed. Obviously she wasn't the only one out. She cast a brief glance back over her shoulder. Nothing. Literally. She strained her eyes into the mist. The hoofbeats sounded clearer. A dark shape loomed up. The horse. A tall one. Gus barked loudly.

She swallowed. Of course, company would be nice, but who was it? She didn't know anyone down here yet. Her stomach tightened. No doubt the rider would come up with her. Flicking another glance back, she frowned. She could see the faint, dark shape of the horse more clearly. Whoever it was was holding their distance. Of course, the rider might well be cautious about coming up with an unknown. Not that dangerous criminals usually travelled about the countryside in gigs with a couple of spaniels. Taffy was staring back now, uttering short barks.

It might be another woman. Verity pulled Bessie up and waited. The dark shape halted too. It must be a woman. Verity relaxed. Probably whoever she was, she had exactly the same qualms about strangers.

'Hello,' called Verity. 'Do you wish to ride alongside?'

The horse came forward, materialising out of the wreathing gloom. It wasn't a woman. Even as she recognised the rider, he spoke.

'Well met, cousin. What a piece of luck to find you so easily. A pity I'll never be able to thank Lady Arnsworth for the service she did me when she assured Mama that Blakehurst had sent you down here.'

Her lungs seized with fright. What did Godfrey want with her?

The answer gleamed in a raised pistol as Godfrey halted, ten paces away.

Frantically Verity swung around, yelling, slapping the reins on Bessie's rump, knowing it was useless. Bessie couldn't outrun the other horse, let alone a pistol shot. The mare broke into a reluctant jog. Oh, God! Why hadn't she brought a whip? She slapped the reins again, and Bessie tossed her head, snorting indignantly.

A sharp crack and something hot whizzed past Verity's cheek, scorching it. Her cry of shocked pain was drowned out as Bessie screamed, plunged and bolted. The dogs went crazy, barking and whimpering in fright. Gripping the reins with one hand, Verity hung on to the side of the gig with the other, nearly flung out at the jouncing as the little mare thundered along the road. Desperately she hauled on the reins, but Bessie had the bit between her teeth and pounded on.

Wildly, Verity looked back. Godfrey was catching up. Easily. Terrified, she realised that he might not have to fire again. If he was lucky, Bessie's bolt would do his job for him. No one would think anything of it, save that she had lost control of the mare.

Sobbing, she fought to rein Bessie in. Ahead the beech woods loomed. The turn off was just past them. She had to slow Bessie enough to make that turn. She had to! Hauling on the reins, she prayed and pulled harder, until her hands throbbed with the effort. As they flashed under the trees, she realised—Bessie had slowed, was steadying, coming back to hand.

She looked back. Godfrey was twenty yards away. Too far for a pistol shot from horseback with a moving target. He couldn't have more than one more pistol. He wouldn't risk it.

She dragged on the reins again as the turn loomed up and felt the mare stagger but somehow keep her footing. Then Bessie was swinging into the turn, still at a gallop. Too fast. Verity knew it was too fast, even as they turned. The nearside wheel slid into the ditch and the world flipped upside down as she tumbled out of the gig.

She was alive. Unless the dogs had died too. They were barking as though possessed. Yes. She was definitely alive. Her cheek stung and breathing hurt too much for anything else. She felt bruised all over. A wet nose was shoved in her face.

Dazed, she opened her eyes. Gus. Then he backed slightly, snarling. She looked up. Godfrey sat his horse, a hopeful look fading from his face.

'Bloody inconvenient bitch!' he said savagely. 'Any normal woman would have broken her neck. But not you! Oh, no. You have to be shot, damn your eyes!'

Dragging in a breath, she struggled to understand, to sit up. The effort left her faint. She shut her eyes, dizzy, leaning on one elbow. On either side, the spaniels growled, hackles raised.

'Godfrey…why?'

'Did you and Blakehurst really think I'd let you steal my inheritance?' Her throat closed as his words penetrated. He was going to kill her.

Desperate, she tried reason. 'Godfrey, killing me won't give you the money. If I die, it's—'

'His!' he spat. 'Don't think I haven't realised. But he won't have you. And he said it himself—revenge. I'll have it every time I look at him. And there won't be a damn thing he can prove!'

He levelled the pistol. Point-blank range. He couldn't miss. She would never see Max again.

Then she heard it—the sound of another horse, ridden hard. Hope flared. 'Godfrey, don't be a fool. Someone's coming...' A rider, perhaps Max looking for her... She screamed his name.

Godfrey cursed violently and squinted down at her, sighting along the barrel. Terror dried her mouth, choking her. The rider would be too late.

She rolled wildly, scrabbling for purchase in the dusty road. She heard him swear, heard the horse edge nearer as the dogs' barking became frantic above the thunder of the other hoofbeats. Her numb fingers closed on something, heavy and rounded. Ice cold, silky. A flint. Her only chance. Ignoring the stabbing pain in her ribs, she flung it as hard as she could.

The mist was thickening. Having started out at a canter, Max eased his horse back to a trot. Probably by the time he reached the beech wood, he would meet Verity. That, or she would have stayed at Martha's cottage and he'd have to ride all the way into the village to bring her home. Either way, she was perfectly safe.

A shot echoed, blanketed by the fog and distance. His breath jerked in, then relaxed. A poacher, probably. Nothing to worry—then he heard the dogs, barking hysterically. And the sound of a runaway horse.

He put his gelding into a flat gallop within four strides. Never before had he wished for a whip and spurs to use on a horse. He leaned forward, urging every ounce of speed out of the animal, fear hammering in his blood. He could hear nothing above the hoofbeats and the creak of harness, save the pounding voice in his brain, *Too late...* Verity, oh,

God… She screamed his name. Ice-cold rage edged with despair ripped through him as he heard the screaming horse and the second shot.

The flint struck the already upset horse full on the muzzle. It reared up even as the dogs hurled themselves forward, barking insanely. Verity shrieked in terror as the horse came down, steel-shod hooves slashing at the dogs. She could hear Godfrey yelling as he tried to control the horse and force it forward, still aiming the pistol at her.

Gus charged in, snapping at the horse's fetlocks, closely followed by Taffy. The frightened beast reared again, striking out wildly as the pistol discharged. For a moment time hung suspended as the horse hovered and then collapsed on top of its shrieking rider, legs flailing feebly.

The mist and the woods spun in a whirling gold-and-silver blur around Verity as she became conscious of more pounding hoofbeats, a hoarse voice yelling her name over the barking and the dreadful, gurgling moans from beneath the fallen horse…and then nothing.

She was safe. She couldn't move, but she was safe. Someone was holding her. Powerful arms held her close, as though they would never release her and a breaking voice whispered her name over and over. 'Verity, oh, God. Verity, sweetheart, my love. For Christ's sake, say something!'

'Max?' It was all she could manage, through the dizziness and confusion that still swung about her. She burrowed a little closer, needing his warmth, his closeness. Clumsy hands trembled over her face, pushing back her tumbled curls.

'Are you hurt badly, dearest?' His voice shook too.

She tried a deep breath and winced. 'My ribs. I think one's cracked.'

He swore and eased his hold on her. Panic flooded in. She shrank against him. 'No! Please, hold me. Please! Where… where is he?'

His arms tightened. 'Shh. It's all right. You're safe. He can't hurt you.'

'Where is he?' She had to know.

She felt the tension, the fury that surged through him.

'Under his horse. Dead.'

Horror sliced through her.

'I…killed him too, then,' she whispered. 'Max…I never meant to…' Abruptly she found herself facing him.

His eyes blazed into her. 'No! Stop it, Verity! It wasn't your fault. He accidentally shot his horse, from what I could see. It fell right on top of him. You had nothing to do with it. Verity, listen to me—you didn't kill him.'

She felt sick, shaking. Seeing again the horse rearing as the flint struck it. Falling backwards. She opened her mouth, but he put his fingers over it, gently silencing her.

'No more, darling. You need to be at home.'

The doctor gave it as his considered opinion that Lady Blakehurst had a much tougher constitution than her husband credited her with. And that, despite the cracked rib, she would be perfectly well in a few days if she rested and were properly looked after.

Max cleared his throat slightly. 'One thing, doctor. I understand that my wife may be…that is, she is…!'

'Expecting a happy event in about seven months?' suggested the doctor with a grin. 'She mentioned it. As I said. Rest. No reason to think there'll be a problem. Whatever you do, don't suggest such a thing to her. Upset can do as much damage in these cases as the fall itself! I have pooh-poohed the idea, but insisted that she remain in bed for a few days because of the cracked rib.' He fixed Max with a fierce glare. 'However—she needs to put on a little more weight. See to it, my lord.'

Max went back to Verity's room and dismissed the maid and Henny. The latter had to be almost forcibly ejected.

Verity huddled against her pillows, her hands wrapped around a cup of tea.

For a moment Max just looked at her, unable to believe that she was alive. That somehow she had been spared.

She looked up at him. 'Max—will there be a trial?' Her eyes were huge, shadowed.

'No, dearest. He's dead. He'll have to face a higher court.'

'I…I meant…me.'

'You?'

She still believed that it was her fault. Three swift strides had him beside her on the bed. Grimly he removed the teacup from her icy hands and enveloped them in his, pulling her into the shelter of his shoulder. Gently he held her, feeling the tremors rack her body.

'Verity, listen to me. You have never killed anyone. Not Godfrey and not your father. They made their own decisions. You were never responsible for either of them. You were a child when your father died. And as for Godfrey—' He broke off, unable to speak for the aftershocks of terror shuddering through him as he carefully touched the mark on her cheek where the ball had grazed it. She had been *that* close to death.

'I threw a rock—a flint, I think. It hit the horse so that it reared. That was—'

He interrupted savagely, 'Why he ambushed you in a sea mist with two loaded pistols? Damn it, Verity! Listen to me! He brought it on himself, trying to kill you. You saved yourself!' Grimly, he continued, 'Even if you hadn't thrown that stone he'd still be dead, because *I* would have killed him! It wasn't your fault! Do you hear me?'

'You'd have *killed* him?'

His jaw dropped. She could even *ask*? He shut his eyes. 'Verity, Godfrey was a dead man from the moment he fired that first shot. I told you that I love you. I think I always loved you, but I was too damn blind to see it!' He covered her lips with his, kissing her until she clung to him, her body pliant and yielding. Then he released her mouth. He had to tell her, make her understand.

Pushing back a tousled lock, he said, 'Darling, I've made such a mess of things. When I asked "Selina" to be my mistress, I thought I could never marry. But I knew I didn't want the sort of liaison I'd had with other women.' He hesitated. Oh, God. How to say it? 'You were different. So very different. *I* felt different.' He smiled. 'I planned a very long affair. Believe me, sweetheart, no *other gentlemen* were going to *see* you, let alone further your apprenticeship! But you refused me. I thought that was that. You'd refused. I would forget you. But I couldn't. You wouldn't be my mistress, but I couldn't leave you unprotected. Do you understand? It wasn't just desire. I wanted to protect you. And one way or another I was going to do it.'

'You didn't want a wife, though,' she whispered.

'Not then,' he agreed, holding her closer. 'Do you know what would have happened if I'd known who you were?'

She shook her head.

'I was already planning to take "Selina" to Aunt Almeria as a companion,' he told her, brushing his mouth tenderly over hers. 'So I'd have seen you. Frequently. And fallen in love anyway. With Verity, *or* Selina. No matter when you told me the truth.'

'But…'

He kissed her again and then continued. 'But you came to me that night, and my conscience didn't stand a chance. I knew that I ought to suggest to you that you could go to Almeria. That I would see to your safety, but I *wanted* you. I needed you. Just *you*. Whoever you were. And even if "Selina" had been real and I'd taken her as my mistress, the moment I discovered she was bearing my child, I'd have been banging on the doors of Doctors' Commons for a special licence!'

'But…'

'But nothing,' he said. 'We would still have reached the

point where I realised that I wanted you as my wife. Not my mistress. Where I had to say to you—sweetheart, I love you. No matter who you are, no matter who your father was. I love you and you're mine. Always. In every way there is.' He bent down to her and kissed her gently. 'My love…my wife…the mother of my children.'

Each tender avowal was punctuated with a kiss, deepening each time until Verity clung to him, her tears salty on her cheeks.

'But Richard—'

'Would prefer to be an uncle and godfather rather than an earl. He told me so in as many words.' He kissed her again. At last he whispered, 'God knows why you love me again, but you do and I'll never let you go.'

She drew away a little and raised a trembling hand to his jaw. 'I never stopped loving you, Max. Never. I always loved you. That was why I came to you that first night, because—'

His fingers gripped her shoulders and amber burned into her. 'You loved me *then*? But why?'

She saw him through a mist. 'You need ask? After what you did for me when Papa died? I dreamed of you for years. Read about you in Papa's journal.' Love was an aching lump in her throat. 'And then I saw you again and you protected me without knowing who I was. You even protected me when you did know. Even though you were furious with me.'

'Even though I was a damn fool,' he muttered, holding her closer. She gave a contented little sigh and wriggled further into his embrace, settling her head on his shoulder.

He rested his cheek on her hair, breathing the fragrance deep, absorbing it. His future, his life, encapsulated in the woman in his arms and the tiny life blossoming within her. He had it all now. Everything he'd never known he wanted. He didn't know the words to express what he felt. They probably didn't exist. Fortunately Verity seemed to be quite content with the usual, inadequate words.

'Did I mention that I love you?' he asked softly.

2 FREE

BOOKS AND A SURPRISE GIFT!

We would like to take this opportunity to thank you for reading this Mills & Boon® book by offering you the chance to take TWO more specially selected titles from the Historical Romance™ series absolutely FREE! We're also making this offer to introduce you to the benefits of the Reader Service™—

- ★ **FREE home delivery**
- ★ **FREE gifts and competitions**
- ★ **FREE monthly Newsletter**
- ★ **Exclusive Reader Service offers**
- ★ **Books available before they're in the shops**

Accepting these FREE books and gift places you under no obligation to buy, you may cancel at any time, even after receiving your free shipment. Simply complete your details below and return the entire page to the address below. You don't even need a stamp!

YES! Please send me 2 free Historical Romance books and a surprise gift. I understand that unless you hear from me, I will receive 4 superb new titles every month for just £3.59 each, postage and packing free. I am under no obligation to purchase any books and may cancel my subscription at any time. The free books and gift will be mine to keep in any case.

H5ZED

Ms/Mrs/Miss/Mr ....Initials ....

BLOCK CAPITALS PLEASE

Surname ....

Address ....

....

....................................Postcode..........................

Send this whole page to:
UK: FREEPOST CN81, Croydon, CR9 3WZ

A Regency Invitation

to the House Party of the Season

*Nicola Cornick, Joanna Maitland,
Elizabeth Rolls*

On sale 3rd December 2004

*Available at most branches of WHSmith, Tesco, ASDA, Martins,
Borders, Eason, Sainsbury's and all good paperback bookshops.*

Published 17th December 2004

Susan Wiggs

THE CHARM SCHOOL

From wallflower to belle of the ball…

"…an irresistible blend of *The Ugly Duckling*
and *My Fair Lady*. Jump right in and
enjoy yourself."—*Catherine Coulter*

MIRA®

'Yes, but you can remind me, if you like.'

'Oh, I will. I promise you,' he said fervently. 'Always.' It was a vow made freely and openly. The most important one of his life.

* * * * *